THE Given

BOOK ONE OF THE GIVEN TRILOGY

MICKEY MARTIN

First published in Australia in 2019
by Making Magic Happen Academy

www.makingmagichappenacademy.com
www.karenmcdermott.com.au

This is a work of fiction. Names, characters, businesses, places, events and incidents are either the products of the author's imagination or used in a fictitious manner. Any resemblance to actual persons, living or dead, or actual events is purely coincidental.

National Library of Australia Cataloguing-in-Publication data:
The Given/Making Magic Happen Academy

ISBN: (sc) 978-0-6486984-3-2
ISBN: (e) 978-0-6486984-5-6

Acknowledgements

To every single person that read the original "THE GIVEN" and loved it despite its flaws.

My mother, Lynette Martin, was one such reader that absolutely adored "THE GIVEN", its darker plot and colourful characters. So this revised edition is for her, and every single one of you. Thank you for all your support, and faith in me as a story teller.

To all the survivors who have endured, fallen, gotten back up and continued on with strength and courage. So much respect.

To all the nurturers that walk amongst us, and go that extra mile and pay it forward. Thank you. We need more people like you, who generously give to help many.

To all the Dream Givers, that go beyond the limits of exhaustion, to help others dreams blossom to reality. Thank you for weaving your magic. Your power is incredible, and appreciated.

To all the gardeners who cherish mother earth, plant trees and care for the Bees. Thank you.

For all the carers, to both humans and our furry critters, that just keep on giving, caring and soothing those that have a harder time walking along the same path as others. You're actually Healer's and Hero's. I Thank you dearly.

And for all those that think they'll never make it, that they're not as good, special, talented or worthy. You most certainly are. In every way.

To my lover, children, family and friends in my world. I thank my lucky stars for each and every one of you, every single day. I love you all beyond.

Mickey xx

Do not pray for an easy life.
Pray for the strength to endure a difficult one

BRUCE LEE

CHAPTER 1

Present Day

The scent of the approaching storm soothed Lilliana as she opened the lofts window above the stables. Taking an appreciative breath, she sat on the window seat stretching out her tired limbs as she gazed out across at the property she called home these past nine years. She considered it a haven, a place to be educated in any available field within the establishment, with the ability to grow and become someone who could give back to a fallen society and help those in dire need. She knew some considered it a prison and for the unfortunate and deserving, it was. She let out a frustrated sigh, trying to block out one of those 'deserving' reasons she had felt the need for the two-hour horse ride in the first place. She had hoped it would relax her and put her in a better frame of mind, after she had sent an only-mildly-abusive email to the man in charge, whilst his older brother was away. She ran her hands over her face, trying to shake off what she could not change. It was time to go in and face the music; Cameron would have surely received her email by now and would no doubt be searching for her. As nice as the thought was, she could not hide up here forever.

Lilliana closed the window and headed down the lofts ladder. Black riding boots encased small feet, jodhpurs fit snugly to firm calves and shapely legs and a cream riding jacket hugged a curvy body. Her long, jet-black hair was held back in a braid, messy after her vigorous ride. She walked down the long aisle that held over 300 stalls and walked up to one that held her Palomino and kissed her noisily on the nose. "Hi sweet girl." She rubbed Beauty's neck before heading out.

"Are you off Lilliana?" Thomas, the leading veterinary-stable-manager called out as she walked by the stall he was leading a prized stallion into.

"Yes, unfortunately Thomas," She smiled. "have to get back to work."

"Ah, no rest for the wicked." He waved her off.

"Supposedly." She headed briskly along the blue stone path, lined with magnolia trees and vibrant coloured flowers, past the pool house and up the large steps that led into the main house. Glancing behind her, as someone called her name in greeting, she waved and stopped for a moment, appreciating the sight before her. She imagined what the outline stated in any Officials booklet describing this establishment that was hers, and hundreds of other Givens home. A refuge for those who had retaliated after they'd had horrendous crimes committed against them. A rehabilitation facility for the innocent. The world outside these walls was done-and-dusted with second chances and after hundreds of years, the jail system no longer existed, after being strained, fed up and chocked with repeat offenders who could not reform to a civilized, no-crime-tolerance world. The Official Law had two paths for the guilty: 1. You commit a crime, yet have skills that can benefit the world, you get sent to the 'Ruins establishment' in South Africa.

2.You do the crime, your punishment quite simply: Death.

For those that had been dealt a similar hand to Lilliana, The Given, with many locations in every country worldwide, was to become their new home.

The Louisiana's Given facility sat on 800 acres of land, comprising sustainable agriculture, and horticultural departments, with an expert team of horticulturalists, that had developed drought resistant crops and seeds for the outside world, as the lands had been raped for decades, depleted of rich growing soils. Alongside enthused Permacultureists that specialised in food forestry, the establishments diverse gardens thrived all year round, offering the Given an array of delicious fresh fruits, herbs and vegetables as well as making a tidy profit for the establishment.

Thick forests surrounding the property were encompassed by a sixteen-foot-high, military-designed electric fence, set to seriously fry one's brain if they tried to enter without authorization, or escape.

The main house was a thirteen-storey mansion that housed, educated and trained over 2000 Given, comprising an underground hospital, psych wards and offices for staff, and laundry facility. First level held several common rooms for gatherings such as study sessions and social time, an assembly hall, four large dining rooms, kitchen area and a two-level library. A large, open office was used by Damon Night, heir to the establishment and operated beside his brother, Cameron, along with expertly trained staff. Upper Levels held small, compact bedrooms, with Given students on the first five levels, staff and Team Leaders on six through to nine with the entire tenth level allocated to Health, Beauty and Rejuvenation: H.B.R. The eleventh floor was off limits to all, bar Cameron and Damon, with their own rooms being floors twelve and thirteen.

Secured, restricted passageways, that the Given were forbidden to access, linked the hospital, psych wards and the Black Op sector, where criminals of the most undesirable nature were kept and used to bring down Black Market, Dark Web and other illegal organisations, that the Officials could never seem to eliminate entirely.

Lilliana cringed a little, thinking back to a time where she had broken a house rule and entered a restricted passageway. That memory brought with it a sharp jolt of pain, as the handsome face of Damon Night flashed in her mind. She shook her head and turning back, jogged up the remaining stairs.

Not a moment before her foot landed inside, a hand grabbed her by the arm, and jerked her out of her thoughts.

"Hey." She laughed as soon as she saw who the culprit was.

Her dear friend, Josephine, seemed glad to have finally found her. "I should have thought to check the stables first, I've been looking for you for ages." Josephine motioned to Lilliana's riding outfit.

"Yeah, I needed a bit of soul-therapy."

Lilliana looked closely at her friend. Big, pretty, honest brown eyes bore into her sea green ones. She looked worried and not her usual, smiley self.

"What's wrong?" She immediately felt a ball of worry form in her stomach.

"Let's walk." Josephine linked her arm through Lilliana's and led her past a large, round water feature that trickled soothingly, as they quickly headed up the enormous staircase that led to the above rooms.

Greeting a few friendly faces as they hurried up the stairs, past many Given on their way to classes, work or recreation time. Josephine was stopped by a co-worker from the Horticultural Department to ask a quick question regarding the next despatch of vegetables. As Josephine chatted to Rupert, Lilliana glanced ahead as two figures approached. She tensed as Natalie, an individual whom she had forever been at odds with, sneered at her. Some things never change, Lilliana sighed inwardly and forced a smile for the tall, stunning red-haired woman beside Natalie; Fox. The Givens number one Model was adored world-wide for her feisty and generous nature, and ran the H.B.R. Her crime before entering the Givens gates; murdering her stepfather who had repeatedly abused both her and brother.

"Hello Fox."

"Lilliana, how are you?" Fox asked this question like she knew something untoward was up.

"Fine, you?"

"Good sugar. Come find me if you need a chat."

"Okay." Lilliana watched them walk off as Josephine was finishing up with Rupert.

"Finally." Josephine tugged Lilliana the remainder of the way towards Lilliana's room and after typing in her friend's code, pushed her through the door.

Lilliana tugged off her riding jacket and hung it in the closet, curious at her friend's impatience. She pulled the band out of her braid and combed her fingers through her hair, letting it fly around her like a black cloud till it fell in soft curls to her waist.

She walked across to her desk where a water jug sat and grabbing a glass turned to her friend holding it up.

Josephine shook her head no, so she filled herself a glass, drained it, poured another than sat at her desk facing her friend, who by this stage was anxiously pacing beside Lilliana's bed.

"Ok, Josephine. Get it off your chest."

"Just remember to keep breathing when I tell you." Josephine looked nervously at her friend. Never a good thing. "And know, I'm here for you, always. It's going to be alright."

Lilliana nodded, thinking, 'How bad could it be?' "I'll be fine, what is it Jose?"

"Damon is back." Josephine blurted out, and waited a beat, watching as Lilliana's face drained of blood.

'That bad.' Lilliana thought. Her hand shook as she placed the glass down on the tray, pressing her hand to her lips, she stood and walked towards the window, opening it to let in the fresh air. She tried to catch her breath, keep her balance. All her emotions felt as though they would choke her, she closed her eyes and the image of 'him' flooded her. Silky, black hair that framed a face chiselled like that of a devastatingly handsome angel. Steele blue eyes that could bore into your soul and delve into your darkest secrets. A mouth wide and firm, that lit her heart when he smiled in her direction. A body sculptured hard to perfection, and his soul pure and giving, generous and only dangerous when the need arose. Tears threatened and she swallowed them down.

It had been five years since she had last laid eyes on Damon Night.

CHAPTER 2

Nine years ago

She had been fifteen, when she first laid eyes on Damon Night. Frightened, depressed, angry and close to death, after weeks of abduction, imprisonment and terror.

She'd been flown into the Louisiana's Given, covered in blood, not all her own and other foul matter that should never have been inflicted on a soul, let alone a fifteen-year-old innocent.

She had not arrived alone, for there had been another young girl that night, in which the two had formed a friendship weeks prior to being abducted. They did break free, with help from the most unexpected kind, along with a price on their heads.

Three months before Lilliana's sixteenth birthday, her mother decided the family should take a vacation in New Orleans and revisit her childhood hometown and reconnect with their Cajun ancestors.

Lilliana loved meeting up with long lost cousins and enjoyed the vibrant gatherings that allowed her mother to totally let her hair down and be carefree. Being married to a high-level politician who worked for the Officials, was a serious, uptight lifestyle. Being under the publics' watchful eye, one had to set an example and could not step out of line without harsh recourse.

Her father, always with a stiff attitude, tolerated his wife's family for short periods of time, but spent most of his free time in the holiday house they had rented for the two months stay, making conference calls and kept business rolling with company he preferred.

In-between getting to know all her relatives, Lilliana took great joy in exploring the beautiful city, with its colourful characters, music and artwork. Purchasing a small postcard sized painting in the French Quarter one afternoon, she met the sister of the artist, and the two girl's became fast friends.

Jessica; blonde hair, sky blue eyes and an open, trusting smile.

She had some of her brother's skill as an artist and enjoyed taking Lilliana along with her to the atmospheric swamps and other diverting locations, where they sketched for hours, getting to know one another, marvelling at how opposite their lifestyles were. Jessica adored the beauty of New Orleans and cherished her life. She had so much freedom, where she only had her brother to please, after losing their parents when she was eleven, they were very close and supported each other in all things.

Where-as Lilliana felt pressured by her parents, to be the best at everything from school grades, team and individual sports, music, art and dance and volunteering her time at a local animal shelter. Alongside being a politician's daughter, there were days she wanted to hide under her covers and simply disappear. The more time she spent with Jessica and Stephan, the more she wanted to remain in their world of a cosy, loving peaceful sanctuary. Spending hours being immersed in nature, painting, or hanging out at Jessica's house listening to soulful Cajun music, whilst eating copious amounts of Stephan's mouth-watering, marinated pork spareribs and bowls of gumbo.

Jessica did volunteer work also and asked Lilliana if she would like to join her at one of the groups the following day. Lilliana was more than happy for the experience and see what her new friend did to help people in her local area. They delivered meals to the elderly, down

Catfish Lake way, care packages for the homeless, and helped hand out first aid kits at a medical clinic. It was there where they heard news of a sixteen-year-old girl, illegally giving birth without the Officials consent. They assisted the girl's family with baby supplies, and vitamin shots for the young mother, and with Lilliana's resourcefulness, she gently pried information from her father in the guise of a future school project, regarding how to get around the Officials with an illegal birth. The following week Lilliana and Jessica went back with all the appropriate forms and set the young mother and her son on a path of legal, documented identity.

With all their activities, the girls were unaware they were being monitored by some of the filth the Officials had been trying to eradicate for decades.

In a society that had been attempting to clean up all evil, there were always going to be individuals who were not happy with the clean slate the Officials had ordered, and the so-called mundane life that had been preordained for them. There were those who wanted what their dark souls sought; fresh flesh to pleasure themselves with or torture, to profit by illegal trade, organ thievery, human and drug trafficking, snuff films and slavery. The list was endless.

Simon Grey was one such individual that profited very well through torture, sex and snuff films, and after watching the girls for a good fortnight, had set a plan in action on how he would take them.

It was one afternoon that the girls took a bus to Jean La fitte reserve to have a picnic and do some sketches, with a group from Holy Cross, to help educate the youngsters about nature and the benefits of keeping the parks free from waste and desecration.

Simon blended well into the group, chatting in a friendly manner to a few parents that had come along on the trip. His seventeen-year-old son, Orlando, seemed unimpressed by the entire outing. Looking bored, with a scowl on his handsome face most of the time, except when his gaze fell on pretty Jessica.

He had caught her eye too, and she sketched him into one of her drawings, appreciating his black jeans and boots, bright purple singlet top with a skull smoking pot on the front. Thick blonde hair that fell sexily over his eyes.

She blushed when he caught her staring at him and whispered to Lilliana, he was the sweetest boy she'd ever seen in her life.

When Simon made Orlando share their cool drinks with them, she couldn't wipe the smile off her face. After thanking Orlando and his father for the refreshing drinks, the girls' went back to sketching under the shade of the trees, escaping the heat of the afternoon. Before they could comment to each other how tired they felt, life as they knew it, was over.

CHAPTER 3

A steady drip, drip, dripping sound filled Lilliana's head as she groggily came-to, almost wishing she hadn't as her head throbbed mercilessly. The floor beneath her, so hard and cold, bore through her body like frozen, bony fingers.

Panic pulsed inside her as she tried to focus on her surroundings in the dark space. She pushed herself into a sitting position, almost too frightened to move, as her current predicament dawned on her.

"Jessica," She whispered, shivering uncontrollably, the pain within her was close to unbearable. She presumed whatever drug Orlando and his father had put in the drink they had offered them, was the culprit for her current situation. "Jessica." She pleaded, hoping her friend was not with her, but safe elsewhere.

"Lilliana." Jessica moaned from across the room, she started crying softly, pushing herself up into a sitting position, then moaned in pain.

"Be still Jess, breathe slowly." Lilliana advised, doing the same. It seemed to help a little with the unrelenting pain.

"Where are we Lilly?" Jessica tried to stop the tears of terror, but it was no use, she began to sob hysterically. "What are they going to do to us."

Lilliana could feel her own terror surface and knew she had to comfort Jessica before they both lost it. She pushed herself up onto her hands and knees, and achingly crawled across the dark, cold floor towards Jessica's crying.

"I'm coming." She whispered, so as not to frighten her friend when she touched her.

"We certainly hope so." A perverted voice boomed around the room as harsh lights flashed on. Both girls' froze as they spotted each other. Black dog collars around their necks. Jeans and tee-shirts had been removed, replaced with a red slip of a dress.

Lilliana quickly made it across the floor and put her arms around Jessica, whose crying had frozen in her throat as soon as the lights had come on. Taking stock of their prison, they noticed three walls of solid black brick, the fourth wall, a mirror with a red light pulsating in the middle of it, like an angry eye, ever watchful.

Jessica's arms tightened around Lilliana, her breath quickened as she spotted a bucket near a filthy, stained mattress across the room and in the middle of the floor on a raised alter, was a man-sized iron cross, with manacles and chains attached either side of its arms.

"Welcome to your new home girls', we are going to make you famous. There's water in that bucket, you'll need it to flush out your systems. Do exactly what we say, and you'll make it back home to your families. If not, well, you won't."

It was Simon Grey's voiced that filled the room and after his statement, evil, joyous laughter followed, before the lights dimmed and silence followed.

Jessica's tears flowed silently as she dropped her face against Lilliana's shoulder, her body shaking. Lilliana reached up a hand and stroked Jessica's hair whispering, "It's going to be alright Jess. We're going to be alright; we'll make it out of here, I promise." Praying it was the truth.

She didn't know how long they sat there in the dark, cold, forbidding room, terrified of what was to come. The drugs seemed to be taking forever to exit their system, and Lilliana's mouth felt like it was full of cotton wool.

As revolting as the stained mattress had looked, Lilliana persuaded Jessica to move and sit on something that wasn't rock hard and freezing cold. They sat on the thread-bare mattress, that held an unbearable odour. Lilliana knelt as she felt for the bucket of water, gasping in yet more pain, as a sharp spring broke through the mattress, and cut into her knee. Cursing quietly, she scooped up a handful of water and brought it close to her nose, sniffing, before taking a tentative sip.

"Jessica, the waters fine, come drink."

Jessica moved forward and after a few moments, filled her belly with water. Sitting back, she thought of Orlando and wondered how a young person could live with himself, after what he had done, to help his father kidnap them. "Lilly, what do you think they are going to do with us?"

Lilliana rubbed her throbbing knee, worried a little at how much blood was seeping from the wound, hoping it wouldn't get infected. "Nothing good I fear."

"Stephan will be looking for me by now, we should have been back hours ago."

"We don't even know how long we were out of it Jess." Lilliana had been going to spend the night at Jessica's and thought of her mum having a good time with her family, unaware that her daughter was in hell.

"I'm so scared Lilly. I'm so scared of what they might do to us." Jessica began to cry again, desperate, terrified sobs that drowned out all Lilliana's fears as she tried to comfort her friend.

"I won't let them hurt you Jessica, I'll do what-ever it takes." Saying it at least made her feel like she had a choice. Like she had some sort of control over their desperate situation. She closed her eyes and allowed her tears to fall silently as she put her arms around her inconsolable friend. Both unaware, that the red light in the middle of the mirror, was an infrared camera that filmed day and night, 24/7, of what would be their horrific ordeal. Each 12-hour slot would be sold, as a series to those that bid the highest, to make Simon and his crew, an absolute fortune.

The first time the door opened, three men entered as the lights flashed on harsh and bright, waking the girls' from their uncomfortable slumber, frightened beyond anything they could imagine. As the men approached, the girls' jumped to their feet and ran to the furthest wall. Although there was no escape, they at least had to try to avert whatever was to come. Lilliana pushed Jessica behind her, and swallowing her fear, held up her small fists, ready. The men laughed, all too glad of the pretty little hellcat and lunged forward. Lilliana got one good punch in, before she got a large fist rammed hard in her belly, knocking the wind out of her. As she went down on her knee's, her hair was jerked back painfully making her eyes water. The man who held her hair leaned down in her face and whispered, "What are you gonna do now baby?"

Lilliana didn't even think about it, her hand automatically shot forward and her fingernails raked along the man's cheek, tearing flesh.

He howled in pain, then pulled back his hand and slapped her as hard as he could. Her face was on fire, but she didn't have a second to think about it, as she was grabbed and dragged to the filthy mattress. Hearing Jessica's screams had her fighting more, crying in despair when she couldn't shake the heavy body off her, as another held her wrists behind her head.

The men's stroking hands, and pure pleasure in her struggles and cries, had Lilliana stilling in moments. Her tears lay heavy on her lashes, she took a deep breath and screamed to Jessica, "Don't let them in Jess. *Don't let them in!*"

She closed her eyes, trying to block out the desperate screams of her friend, and let her mind disappear into a world of its own.

***

They were subject to these horrific attacks for days on end, each day rolling into the next in a long black seemingly endless pit of turmoil and despair. It wasn't always sexual. It was mental torture and blackmail of sorts. If either girl wanted no harm to come to the other, then she herself would have to step forward and perform whatever degrading task that was asked of her. A lot of the time the task was too foul, and neither girl could not protect the other, so they would both be punished. They were drugged some days, in the hope that that would mellow them out, and be easier to manipulate.

Almost four weeks in, Jessica sobbed to Lilliana one night that she just wanted to die.

"I hope they kill us soon Lilly. I hope they just kill us" She had whispered feverishly, before slipping into a drug induced sleep.

It terrified Lilliana to hear Jessica say such a thing. Although truthfully, in the middle of many humiliating tasks, she herself had silently wished for the same thing. But hearing her sweet friend say it out loud, woke her protective side more, and from the next day she stepped forward and volunteered as often as she could, to allow Jessica's mind to heal at least a little.

Orlando oversaw that the girls' were fed, hydrated and clean. He took them, one at a time to a small room that had a hose to clean them when they became too filthy with their own vomit, or other foul matter.

There was a moment when Jessica collapsed, sobbing as Orlando washed her with the cold water. He felt so bad for the beautiful girls' but had no way of giving them hope without giving himself away.

He bent down and gently wiped Jessica's hair out of her eyes. She looked up at him, startled by the gentle gesture after weeks of nothing but cruelty, her big blue eyes never-ending pools of tears.

"Please," She whispered, helplessness echoing each word. "won't you help us, please help us."

It killed him, hearing the desperation in her voice, and made him think of another. To this, he whispered, "I will help you, I just need the right time, stay strong and make sure your friend does the same."

He yanked her to her feet, knowing he was being watched, pulled her close and squeezed her firm breast, pretending to enjoy the pain he was inflicting.

She cried out in protest, as he dragged her back to the room. He pushed her inside, and before he closed the door she thought she heard him whisper. "I'm sorry."

After Orlando's cryptic message to Jessica, they were on tender hooks, waiting for his message of some-sort-of-hope, to make sense. Time became irrelevant, and they were simply doing everything they could not to lose their minds during all the horror.

The afternoon finally arrived when Orlando was instructed to clean the girls' up with glossy lips, shiny hair, perfume and innocent eyes.

As he dressed them in white leather outfits, he slid a knife into each girl's garter belts high up on their thighs. At their questioning looks, he said, "You need to be ready. It's kill or be killed. Tonight, you're being snuffed out. It's the end of your series."

Jessica and Lilliana exchanged a look of pure relief and nodded to one another. "We can do this." Lilliana said firmly.

Jessica's eyes filled with tears and she reached for Lilliana's hand, squeezing her fingers.

When they were presented to a room full of hungry, drunken eyes, the girls' were unsure of when to make a move on their retaliation.

They were placed back to back against the iron cross and Orlando made a good show of locking them in tight but leaving enough room for their slender wrists to slip out of the manacles when the need arose.

"Hurry up boy." Simon slurred greedily; he had not as yet had time with the girls' and tonight he was taking them both before helping end them.

Lilliana stared at the leering faces, feeling a rage build within her. One man approached Jessica, and she heard her friend curse. She hatefully eyeballed a man who stepped up to her and placed his hand around her throat. He was old enough to be her grandfather. She stared without blinking, into his glazed eyes as he squeezed the breath from her. She didn't give him the satisfaction of gasping. She didn't know how long she could handle any more torture, without pulling her hand out of the shackle and into her garter belt for the sharp little knife Orlando had placed there.

Orlando had been passing drinks around to the feral group of men, watching closely as the drink started to take effect. His father had the bulk of the drugs locked away, but he had found a small stash of rohypnol. He knew it wouldn't be enough to take down the twelve men in the room, but the amount he put in the alcohol should make them a little easier to take down and out.

He felt uneasy as he watched his father approach Jessica, and cup his hand between her legs, before reaching up to strangle her. Once she started to lose consciousness, he'd release her throat, torment her, and strangle her again.

Orlando was feeling his own rage build and pulling out the knife tucked in his belt, stepped forward and rammed it in the nearest man's neck, whilst screaming out to the girls'. "*NOW.*"

They did not need to be told twice, and pulled their hands out of the shackles, grabbed their knives and slashed at any man who was near. Having a bit of height being on the raised altar helped. The men, being taken unawares whilst being inebriated, gave the girls a slight advantage.

Simon still had his hands around Jessica's throat, and as much as she was trying to stick him with her knife, she was losing consciousness.

Orlando was strong and fast; running between two men, kicking one down hard, he fell on top of him and plunged the knife into his chest, pulling it out, he spun as the other man reached for him and plunged the knife into his face. Blood was spilling everywhere, and the men were screaming their rage. Lilliana closed her eyes briefly, before opening them as a rough hand squeezed her breast, she slammed the knife into the man's temple, screaming as blood gushed from his wound. She pulled the knife out, sickened by the sound it made, and was prepared to use it again quickly as another man lunged at her.

Orlando rushed up to his father and stabbed the knife into his father's neck, again and again, whilst shouting, "That's for Nadia, you deserve this!"

Jessica fell hard, along with Simon, slipping on the blood that was gushing everywhere. Orlando had no time to appreciate the fact that his father was dead and continued helping Lilliana cull the men that were still standing, as Jessica was in no state to help.

Lilliana sensed another moment of victory, when an overweight man lunged at her, reaching out as he stumbled, his foot catching on the ledge of the altar, slippery with blood. She dodged to the side and slashed the knife along his belly. He screamed in pain, clutching at his bleeding wound, she plunged the knife into his spine, twisting it. Another man came at her, but Orlando was fast and furious and took pleasure in taking him down, before he was slammed in the head from behind. Lilliana screamed as Orlando went down, and knew the last man standing was her responsibility.

"You stupid bitches," He snarled. "you are going to die." He stood still, gaging if she would run. He walked slowly towards her, hoping to frighten her with his slow, methodical pace.

Lilliana was breathing heavily, exhausted and scared and trying not to lose hold of her knife, slippery with blood. But her fury gave her the strength to stand still. "Not today," She shook her head slowly and repeated. "not today."

His lip curled and he reached for the knife in Orlando's limp grip. As he bent down, Lilliana seized the opportunity to pounce on him and stab him in the shoulder. As he reared up, screaming, she pulled her arm back, before thrusting with all her might and stabbing her blade into his chest. Stepping back away from him, she watched as he fell to his knees, before falling flat on his face, the knife being forced in deeper, ending him.

She could her Jessica screaming behind her and as she turned, saw her friend, sitting in a pool of blood stabbing two men repeatedly over and over again. They looked like they had not moved in many minutes.

Lilliana rubbed her hands over her wet face, not registering that it was blood, trembling, as she looked around her. It was a stinking blood bath.

She turned and walked over to Jessica and reached down to console her friend.

Jessica, still screaming and jabbing the dead bodies, spun around and stabbed the knife deeply into her friend's arm, unseeing.

Lilliana fell to her knee's, clutching as the blood flowed.

Jessica took a moment, blinking, then sunk down beside her friend, crying softly, "I'm sorry Lilly, I'm sorry"

Lilliana shook her head, wanting to tell Jessica it was alright. That everything was going to be okay now, but she had not an ounce of strength left in her.

Orlando came to, clutching his head, and saw the two girls sitting in filth, one crying softly, the other as pale as death.

He staggered to his feet and left the room. He was gone but three minutes, when the girls heard a very loud grating sound, and looking towards the mirrored wall they watched, as it opened up. Behind it, the large camera sitting on an tripod, its red eye blinking, sending live footage out into the underworld of crime.

Orlando stood, a phone to his ear, speaking quietly. He hung up and walked towards the girls, who were unsure what to say to him.

"Come on, we're getting out of here." He reached down to put an arm around each girl's waist to pull them up, but Lilliana was too weak. He scooped her up effortlessly; Jessica not letting go of her hand.

Looking at her pale friend in this boy's arms, she said with a voice full of raw emotion, "We're nearly there Lilly, hang on, we're nearly there."

CHAPTER 4

And so it came to be that night, Lilliana and Jessica became murderesses, whilst defending their young lives. Although defending themselves, it was still an action that resulted in the consequence of being sent to one of the worlds rehabilitation facilities.

Orlando had rung the Officials, who in turn contacted the correct authority, in this case, the closest establishment, The Louisiana's Given.

The footage that had been broadcast to the underworld of crime, had now been forwarded to the Givens head representatives. The girl's families had been contacted, and their heartache at what the girls had endured, was smoothed over only by knowing they were now safe and being sent to the best possible place for their recovery and for their souls rehabilitation.

Within an hour of the last man dropping dead at the girl's feet, these matters were set in motion and the Givens helicopter had been dispatched to collect them and bring them to their new home.

Lilliana was in and out of consciousness, as she was placed on a stretcher and carried inside the Givens main entrance and down the hospital's stairs, catching glimpses of a long, white corridor with strange portraits of individuals in black and white. Not pretty portraits, but portraits that depicted the most horrific, sad tales of what these individuals must have endured. She would learn later, that each person brought in, would be photographed; their story to be placed on the hospital walls, marking a new beginning of purpose and survival after tragedy.

She lost consciousness after passing a portrait of a beautiful fair girl, with eyes that reflected a world of endless pain.

"This girl needs stitching serum and a complete detox bath before her psych evaluation." A warm, soothing voice broke through her reprieve from reality, and she stirred, her eyes felt heavy and were difficult to open.

"I'll do the evaluation myself, once everything is settled." A deep, soothing rich voice responded.

The throbbing of her arm and the all over pain her body felt from weeks of torture, grew as her haze of unconsciousness dissolved. Her mind went into overdrive as images of the blood bath she'd helped create, flooded her senses.

Of Jessica's poor mind becoming so dejected throughout the weeks of their imprisonment. She covered her eyes and began crying softly, feeling her nerves ready to burst. Against her eyelids, her fingers felt stiff and leathery, pulling them away she forced her eyes open to look at them. Dark red and caked in dry blood, Lilliana lost it, and began screaming, brushing her hands together frantically, trying to rid them of the unwanted gore.

Nurse Rachael, stated firmly, "She needs sedation."

"On it." The other leading nurse in this section, Billy, grabbed the appropriate needle and passed it to Rachael.

Lilliana felt a firm hand on her shoulder pinning her in place. A large, male hand. "*NO.*" Lilliana protested and fought to get away from that hand, her green eyes so large, frightened; her heart beating anxiously as she struggled, her breath coming out in irregular pants.

Rachael grabbed the needle off Billy and leaning over the figure that was trying to keep Lilliana still, quickly jabbed it into the resisting girl's arm.

Lilliana cried out, before she sagged back against the pillow, feeling herself fade under a cloud of fog.

The last thing she saw, as her head tipped back, were beautiful blue eyes in a face like that of a furious angel.

***

The furious angel was the man himself. Damon Night, head of The Louisiana's Given establishment. Tall, dark hair, his face was beyond beautiful. The darkest, intense blue eyes that saw through all, and often held a serious look to them.

He did not take his responsibilities lightly, regarding the duties that had been passed to him and in matters like these, a sensitive heart not many knew he possessed.

He looked down at the young girl laying limply on the bed.

She was a mess. Her white leather outfit covered in blood and several foul matters. Her black hair spread out on the pillow drenched in blood also, her features although pale looked very pretty. She was in fact, stunning.

He ran his hand through his hair, disgusted with himself.

Thinking she was attractive was beneath him at such a time as this, considering what the poor young thing had been through. Still, there was something deeply beautiful about her, despite being covered in filth.

He had watched part of the CCTV footage that had been sent to him as the helicopter had been dispatched to collect the injured party.

Every week, he thought he'd seen it all, and he was always wrong. Every act inflicted on the innocent screamed at his heart strings and what these poor girls had endured increased his fury at a world where wrong just kept on going. He had five discs on his desk that he had to view before he could do this girl's psych evaluation, along with this establishment's leading mental healers; Dr. Richard and Dr. Hillary.

And he was dreading it. He frustratedly ran his fingers through his hair and let out a long, hard sigh.

Rachael looked up at him. "Is everything all right Mr. Night?" She asked, as she started cutting of Lilliana's clothing.

He turned away as a breast was revealed near the shiny, sharp scissors. "No," he replied. "everything is not alright." He strode angrily from the room, pulling his phone out of his back pocket, he punched in a number and waited impatiently for his brother to pick up.

"Where have you been Cameron?" His voice was like ice.

Cam immediately knew he was in trouble. "Hello brother." He answered simply, always safer when his sibling used his full name. He instantly remembered they had new Givens arriving, and he was supposed to have met Damon down at the hospital earlier. He almost felt guilty at his alternative distraction. Almost.

"Please give me a good excuse as to why you weren't with me half an hour ago." Damon truly hoped Cam could give him something to ease the stress he could feel slowly building inside him. When their father had passed away five years ago, Damon had been nineteen when he felt the weight of the world fall heavily on his shoulders. Not only with stepping up and filling his father's role that he had been trained for since his early teens, but being a parent to his fourteen-year-old brother.

At nineteen, Cam was very good at the duties allocated to him. Along with two highly trained Watchers, he ran some of the physical therapy groups, in which to assist new Givens in the general rehabilitation of their abused, damaged bodies. He worked with the horticultural crew, filling out orders, from the garden centre to the cargo plane, oversaw Fox's modelling assignments and sat in on any meeting that would aid in his learning with the running of the establishment. So occasionally, if he felt he was owed a bit of down time, which included sneaking off and releasing sexual frustration with a willing participant, he took it.

Cam contemplated a good excuse but knew it would be no good. "Just think of a good punishment brother, I won't waste your valuable time with bullshit."

Damon at least appreciated Cam's honesty, as he headed up the stairs leaving the hospital section. "If you need to have a session with Hillary or Richard, sort it out would you. I really need you on board when we have new arrivals Cameron." He entered the passageway that linked the hospital section to the Black Ops unit and headed up several flights of stairs towards the back entrance to his rooms on the thirteenth floor.

Cam shivered as Damon mentioned Richard's name, grateful his brother couldn't see him roll his eyes.

"I'm fine, I talked to Hillary yesterday. Look, I'm sorry, I won't let you down again." They both knew that was a blatant lie.

Damon held in the sigh that wanted to escape and punched in a code to his rooms. The door slid open and he strolled in, happy to have some quiet time.

"Finish up your next therapy session and come find me when you're done. I'll probably be in my home office."

"No probs brother." Cam was happy to hang up the phone. He hated letting Damon down, but sometimes he felt his brother took life way too seriously. Yeah, life as they knew it in a world full of mayhem sucked at times, no doubt, but more reason to make time to chill out and relax. He'd make it up to Damon by being full of enthusiasm with his next group of injured souls that needed his full attention.

**

Damon walked the length of his spacious domain, past a large stone fireplace, its mantel adorned with a few antique framed photographs and thick bold candelabras.

Oak stained floorboards gave the entirety of the space a warm feeling despite its vastness, with reading chairs, lounges, rugs, pillows and coffee tables placed strategically opposite a fireplace and near the floor to ceiling bookcase to suit any mood.

A stunning old mahogany desk faced the balcony, with French doors opening up to a breathtaking view of the property.

A scratching sound at the door had Damon heading towards it, as he flung the door open, he looked down at two wriggling dogs, ecstatic to see him, and a smiley faced girl with the largest, warm brown eyes.

"Hello Josephine," Damon smiled. "what are you up to? Shouldn't you be in class?"

"Um, well yes actually Mr. Night. Fact is, Angela, you know she's a new Given, anyway she slipped coming down the library stairs and landed on her wrist. Ms Bonnie told me to go fetch an ice bag and when I went into the kitchen, I found Rusty and Nails getting chastised by Cook, because they were trying to get into the chicken necks. I'm sure he was about to kick them until he saw me." She rushed on. "Anyway, I thought I would rescue them, so after I took Angela the ice bag, I brought these guys up to you, and as I passed Fox, she yelled at me, called me lazy and to get back to class." She let out a breath before continuing. "Seriously, you'd think she was in charge at times the way she bosses everyone about." She shook her head, as she folded her arms across her chest.

Damon held in his smile, loving her youthful vent at such an uncomplicated matter, compared to the one he was about to embark on. He had loved Josephine the moment he'd laid his nine-year-old eyes on her, and his mother had held her on her hip. She'd been two, and it had been back in the day when the establishment could take on infants and toddlers. The past ten years it was more suited for new Givens from the ages of fifteen to mid-thirties, as other establishments were designed to handle birth to early teens, and others mid-thirties to older.

He knew how wrong favouritism was, but with Josephine he could not help himself. He adored her and thought of her as his little sister. It was only formalities such as these were, until she was eighteen, had to address him as Mr. Night.

Her eyes looked troubled as she frowned. "I didn't mean to miss class Mr. Night, honest, I just didn't want the dogs to get kicked by Cook." She shrugged a shoulder.

Damon knelt and rubbed Rusty's smooth belly as the dog went into a divine floppy coma, Nails stepped over his brother for some affection.

"I certainly appreciate that you wanted the dogs safe from harm Josephine, so thanks for that." He smiled up at her as he thoroughly rubbed both the dog's bellies. Standing, he stepped back inside his doorway and pressed the intercom.

"Yes Mr. Night, what can I do for you this afternoon?" A stern, older voice responded.

"Cook, I'd appreciate it if you could get a couple of those chicken necks ready on a tray for the dogs and send them down to the stables, as a very kind Josephine is looking after them for me."

"Anything else I can do for you Mr. Night?"

"Yes Cook," He replied dryly, "stop kicking my dogs." He pressed the intercom off before he heard Cooks usual dry retort.

He looked down at Josephine and smiled. "Do you mind quickly taking these two down to the stables for me, and make sure Thomas gets them penned in for the night with their treats?"

"Sure thing Mr. Night." Josephine patted her thigh as she began heading towards the stairs, the dogs trotting behind her.

"Sweetheart." Damon called after her, waiting for her to turn and look at him.

"Yes Mr. Night?"

"Please don't miss class again."

She grinned, looking only slightly ashamed. "Yes Sir Mr. Night." As she disappeared out of sight.

Damon shook his head, a smile on his face as he closed the door. Pressing the intercom again, he said. "Cook, please send a meal up to my room tonight, I won't be coming down for dinner." He clicked off before a reply came, knowing it would be done.

He headed towards his bedroom, stripping off his clothes as he went. At twenty-four, a love for working out, horse riding, archery and running, revealed an extremely fit, attractive body. Dropping his clothes down the laundry chute, he walked into his large airy bathroom.

The occasional blue glass tile broke up the white of the bathroom, a large sunken tub under the window overlooking pastures so green. He stepped into the four headed shower and ran the water hot and hard on his shoulders, trying to relax the tension he could feel creeping into his muscles, as the thought of the task before him started to compute. Sighing, he dropped his fist to the wall, his forehead to his fist and closed his eyes to escape for just a moment.

A flash of the dark-haired Lilliana came to him; covered in blood, her eyes reflecting the sheer terror and pain she had clearly endured.

He slammed his fist against the tiles, once, twice the third time he spat out, "Fuck it." before reaching out and shutting off the water. He stepped out and walked under his body-drier, running his fingers through his thick, silky black hair and was dried in seconds. Heading into his spacious bedroom, he entered his walk-in closet and pulled out a pair of faded jeans and a black tee shirt. After pulling them on and shoving his feet into a pair of socks, he headed into his main living area.

It would be an understatement to say he was not looking forward to what the next few hours would entail. This was a part of the job he detested but was completely necessary. Researching, studying, trying to understand what his survivors had been through, in order to support them the best way possible.

Sitting in the well-worn, comfortable leather chair that had once belonged to his father, he clicked four glass computer screens on, each set up to play separate discs at the same time. Damon took out his tablet from the desk draw and turned it on, rolling onto his notes to get ready to jot down some thoughts on what he was about to review.

He wished he could state that he wasn't shocked at what he viewed, that this was nothing he hadn't seen before; and although it may have been, it still sickened him to his core, at what a grown man could do to an innocent.

Watching the girls wake to the reality of being drugged, abducted, and imprisoned. Watching their fear magnify to absolute misery at the first abuse, to the ongoing hours, days, weeks of sheer terror and torment.

Watching them suffer in agony at the hands of such filthy creatures made his stomach churn.

He was grateful when Rachael rang, five hours in, interrupting his purgatory.

"Hi Rachael, how are the girls going?" He took the opportunity to stretch his legs, and pushed the French doors open and stepped outside into the comforting darkness.

"I'm sorry to say Sir, Lilliana had an episode and we had to sedate her again.

Jessica is extremely upset she can't see her brother, but we were able to calm her enough to get her into a detox tank."

"Can you get Lilliana into detox whilst she's sedated? It may be less stressful for her, considering what she has been through." He waited a beat.

"I don't know, Sir, it may be upsetting for her if she comes to in the middle of the procedure." Nurse Rachael explained.

"Just do it please, and make sure she doesn't come to in the middle of it."

"Yes Sir. I'll get onto it immediately."

"Thanks Rachael, I'll be by tomorrow afternoon. Do whatever you can to make them comfortable. Goodnight." He clicked off the phone and went back inside.

He ate his meal that had gone cold hours earlier, and poured himself a water from his mini bar when Cam sauntered into the room.

"Hello big brother, having fun?" He gestured towards the computer screens.

Damon looked at him over the rim of his glass and drank till it emptied.

Frowning, he shook his head, leaning his hip against the desk, he placed the glass down, folding his arms. "The only fun occurring in here, is in my imagination of what I would have done to those men if they weren't already dead."

Cam glanced at the glass screens, paused on images from hell. "Bastards," he agreed. "sorry I wasn't around earlier." Seeing the stress on his brothers face always increased his guilt and made him want to keep apologising.

Although it frustrated Damon at times, when Cam let the team down, he understood his brothers' condition. He shrugged, tiredly. "Next time I need you to be on hand just be there, Okay?"

"Yeah. You want me to review a bit with you?" He nodded towards the screens.

"No, I have Hillary and Richard viewing them, so the evaluation team is in order. "How did your night group go? Any problems?"

"Nope."

"Is Fox's next shoot organised?"

"Yep, all set for next week, we are promoting the benefits of the H.B.R and introducing the meditation swing program. There's a company that want to add the swings to the disadvantaged kids' homes in seven countries, they just need the funding."

"We can certainly donate funds and set up a team to do the building."

Cam nodded. "We've also booked Tim and Pierre for a diamond shoot here and we'll have the swings featured, should be around two months' time. So, Fox will be busy enough".

"Excellent. Well, I have to get back to it." Damon pushed himself off the desk and went to pour a coffee.

"I'll see you in the morning." Cam saluted as he headed towards the door. "Night." He called over his shoulder.

"Good-night." Damon took a mouthful of the steaming, black liquid and went to sit down, resuming play on the screens as his brother left. It only took seconds for the feeling of dread to return to the pit of his stomach.

The knowledge that the girls were safe and secure from the filthy devils' hands, did not ease having to watch their journey through hell.

It was going to be a long night.

CHAPTER 5

Lilliana woke to a calming voice reading about botanical plants. She opened her eyes and saw a girl that looked about the same age as her, sitting in a comfortable chair, twirling a curly brown piece of hair around her fingers. It was clear she was thoroughly enjoying the chapter about cross pollination and how Bees are continuing to be a gardener's miracle, as her legs swung enthusiastically back and forth.

Lilliana glanced around the room, taking in her surroundings. She remembered vaguely being carried in from the helicopter to what she presumed was some sort of hospital, but she wasn't sure where. Her eyes focused on a canvas opposite her bed; a landscape of stunning green rolling cliffs, dropping down towards a calm, peaceful ocean. Lilliana was wondering if it was of Ireland, when a smiley, curious face with pretty, warm brown eyes blocked her view.

"Great, you're awake, how are you feeling?" Josephine turned away and putting her book down, reached for the water jug and filled a tall glass. "My name's Josephine by the way," She turned back, handing the glass to Lilliana. "I'll go get Nurse Rachael for you."

"Thank you." Lilliana replied softly, watching Josephine leave.

As she went to take a sip of water, the glass slipped from her fingers, shaking with nerves and fatigue, the cold water spilling across her chest and lap before the glass rolled off the bed, smashing into sharp shards against the hard marble floor. 'Great.' She thought, pushing the covers off and swinging her legs over the side of the bed. She pinched at the wet gown, pulling it away from her body as she placed her feet on the cold floor, glancing around the room to see if there were something, she could use to clean up her clumsy mishap.

She didn't often need her mother's help, being raised in an environment that called for independence, but right in this moment not knowing where she was, or how long she had been here, wondering if Jessica was okay, whilst trying to block out every unwanted image from the past weeks that continued to plague her, was too much. Staring at the broken glass, tears pooled in her eyes of their own accord as her assaulted mind tried to process what she should do, as the continuous feeling of dread consumed her.

Approaching footsteps had her whirling around; the sight of the man entering, had her breath catching in fear.

Damon noted the spilled liquid and smashed glass dangerously close to Lilliana's bare feet. Seeing the tears in her eyes, accompanied by fear, he slowly took a small step back, holding up his hands to let her know there was no need to fear him.

Lilliana's heartbeat continued to thump uncomfortably in her chest as she stood frozen, staring at the tall, dark haired man before her. It took her but a second to realise he wasn't that much older than her, and another to notice how gorgeously handsome he was. His eyes. She remembered those piercing blue eyes, in a dream.

She brushed away the tears that fell upon her cheeks and quietly took a deep, steadying breath as Josephine walked in, followed quickly by Nurse Rachael and a male nurse.

"How are you dear?" Rachael asked Lilliana, noting the glass and gestured to Billy, her second in charge, to clean it up as she gently took Lilliana's arm, steering her towards the chair.

Lilliana sat and whispered, "I'm okay, thank you." she glanced towards the doorway to where Damon and Josephine stood, then looked at Rachael. "Where am I?"

"You are safe Lilliana, you are in your new home. All your questions will be answered, but first, how does a nice hot shower sound? Then we'll get you into some comfortable, dry clothes." Rachael stroked Lilliana's hair, hoping to calm the uneasy girl. In the past couple of weeks whilst Lilliana had been in and out of consciousness, she had been very unsettled.

"I need to see Jessica?" Lilliana said quietly, worried about her friend.

"I'm sure after your shower, you and your friend can have your meal together, how does that sound?"

Rachael looked across at Damon as she asked this question, making sure it was alright by him.

Lilliana followed Rachael's gaze, watching as the handsome man placed his large hands upon Josephine's shoulders.

He nodded. "That shouldn't be a problem at all." He smiled at her, "Lilliana, I'm Damon Night and you have already met my friend Josephine."

Lilliana nodded, remembering his smooth, rich voice from when she had first arrived and forced her eyes to Josephine, who smiled brightly in her direction.

"Once you've freshened up, Josephine will take you to the hospital dining room and you can have some time with Jessica."

Lilliana nodded, twisting her fingers together.

Damon continued. "I can only imagine how you are feeling right now Lilliana, but you are in good hands with Nurse Rachael and her staff." He watched as she nodded her dark head in thanks to Rachael, as Billy turned around and offered her a small smile before leaving the room with a dustpan full of the broken glass, muttering about it being time to order the recycled plastic back.

"You and I will have a chat tomorrow, after you've rested up a bit, so for tonight, enjoy catching up with your friend and try to get a good night's sleep. I'll see you tomorrow."

Lilliana didn't know what to say to this extremely handsome man, who intimidated her in such a way that made her want to be in an entirely different room. She dropped her gaze to the floor and simply nodded instead of replying.

She knew he had gone as his crisp footsteps headed down the corridor.

"Alright Lilliana, let's get you freshened up. Josephine, can you come back in an hour to take Lilliana to dinner?"

"Sure, Nurse Rachael, I'll see you soon Lilliana."

"See you Josephine." Lilliana forced a small smile for the friendly girl and watched her bound out the door with energy she wished she had.

"Come with me Lilliana." Rachael waited for Lilliana to stand and gently taking her arm, guided her out of the room and down a long corridor. Walking past the nurse's station Lilliana caught a quick glimpse of men and women dressed in white uniforms, busily heading off into various directions attending those in need. A gleaming white, wide reception desk held a large vase of the most colourful blooms Lilliana had ever seen, the scent almost making her feel cheerful.

"Here we are Lilliana." Racheal said as they arrived at a large frosted door. Pushing it open, Rachael led Lilliana into a brightly, blue tiled bathroom; showers divided by long bamboo panels. Glistening taps adorned one long wall, with a large, single wash sink.

Lilliana froze when she faced the mirror above the sink area and spun away from it and her reflection, covering her face, trying to catch her breath.

"It's alright Lilliana." Rachael walked across to the mirror and hit a small button on the wall. The mirror went instantly blue, like the tiles around it.

"There are many people here that don't like their reflection, it will take time after all you've been through, to face yourself again." She said.

Lilliana let out a silent sigh. It wasn't just her reflection she was afraid of, but the possibility of what could be behind the mirror.

"Have a relaxing wash, when you're finished, these showers are installed with body driers, so once you've shut the water off, the air will dry you in seconds." She smiled and indicated to a door behind

Lilliana, that was concealed by the tiles. "In that room you will find clothes to fit you, and once you're ready, come on back to the nurse's station, I'll be waiting there for you. Will you be okay alone Lilliana?"

"Yes, thank you Nurse Rachael."

Rachael smiled and left the room.

Lilliana let out a sigh and walked into a shower stall, firmly shutting the heavy bamboo door behind her. Taking off her hospital gown, she flipped it over the top of the door and turning, hit the water jets on. The water was everything she needed in that moment. Hot and cleansing, she imagined it washing away every vile touch, every second of darkness right down the drain.

She knew she was clean. Nurse Rachael had described what the detox tank did for her, cleansing her of any infection and getting her to a high level of hygiene, restoring nutrients back into her body after weeks of neglect and abuse, but she somehow felt like she would never be truly clean again.

Little pumps jutted from the wall with a symbol above each: hair, a face, a body. Lilliana took a small squirt from the pump under the hair symbol and took a sniff at the green looking cream. It smelt divine and lathered beautifully as she attacked her scalp. The face cream looked like it had little particles of plants in it, as did the body wash. By the time she shut the water off and stepped out from the body drier she did indeed feel cleansed. Pushing open the door she grabbed her hospital gown and holding it against her chest, rushed over to the tiled door searching for a handle, she realised she only need to have touched it for it to swing open into a room lined with clothes. Shutting the door behind her she headed over to a rack with jeans and grabbed one in her size, then searched for a tee shirt and jumper. There were large, clear stacked draws, labelled: bra's, socks, underwear, and that's where Lilliana headed over to next, grateful to find black knickers and a bra in her size. Quickly putting those on, she pulled up her jeans, threw on her tee shirt and was grateful for the soft, green turtleneck jumper that made her feel safe. She couldn't see any shoes, so pulled out a pair of thick socks and shoved her feet in them.

On a table beside the draws sat brushes, hair clips and bands, lip gloss and eye shadow. She pushed those to one side. Quickly brushing her hair, her fingers darted in and out as she did a quick braid, her mind raced to Jessica and she wondered how she might be doing. If she was as confused and as raw as Lilliana felt herself? She forced the unwanted images out of her mind, that seemed to flood her unexpectedly and fought the sob back down her throat that almost escaped. She was safe and free, that's what mattered now.

Her stomach rumbled. It was time to move on, time to see Jessica. She took a deep breath and headed out the door and in the direction of the nurse's station.

Rachael was talking softly on the phone, whilst typing against a thin, glass chart that another nurse was holding, circled a section with her finger and nodded. The other nurse moved on. Rachael looked up and smiled at Lilliana, as she hung up the phone.

"Green suits you well with that gorgeous black hair." She smiled kindly at Lilliana.

"Ah here's Josephine now, to take you to dinner."

Josephine was bounding enthusiastically towards them. Her bright smile and curly hair bouncing, made Lilliana feel a little more light-hearted, even though it was just for a few seconds.

"Thank you Josephine, for your help this evening, could you bring the girls back here after dessert?" Rachael asked.

"Sure thing, not a problem. Come on Lilliana, you are going to love dinner tonight, it's not far, this way." She checked over her shoulder as she headed off, making sure Lilliana was following her.

They walked for a few minutes in silence, Lilliana was curiously looking at the portraits that lined the corridors walls. She remembered seeing some of them in a flash and blur the night she had been brought in.

Lilliana stopped in front of a portrait where a sweet toddler was crying her eyes out, arms outstretched, desperate to be held.

"That's me." Josephine said quietly beside her. "My mother went on a drinking binge after she found out my dad had been cheating on her. She left a note stating she was going to end the Devils line and drowned my twin after she shot my dad. She sliced her own throat open before she got to me, I guess with a bottle of tequila in her, she forgot that she had one more Devil child to get rid of. My lucky day I suppose." Josephine lifted a shoulder before gently tugging on Lilliana's braid, "Come on." She continued down the corridor.

Lilliana couldn't help but feel shocked for Josephine. Such tragedy at such a tender age. She didn't think she could feel any sadder as she followed Josephine into a beautifully lit room, full of mouth-watering aromas.

There were twenty long tables, covered in crisp white linen, occupied by hungry diners, busy chatter and constant clatter of cutlery against dinnerware.

Lilliana looked about the room until her eyes found what they sought the most in that moment. Jessica. Sitting at the end of a table halfway down the room dressed in a grey and pink track suit, her blonde hair hung in a long ponytail, her skin so pale.

Her chin resting in her hands, watching a lady gather bread sticks and butter. As the lady headed back towards her table, Jessica glanced around the room, her eyes falling on Lilliana.

They both froze; eyes unblinking, hearts stopping, the sight of each other and the reason why they were here, carried with it intense mental pain, guilt and unease.

Jessica stood slowly, hesitant for but a second, before running towards an already running Lilliana.

They collided halfway, knocking the wind from each other's body, arms reaching around the other, involuntary laughter soon turned to sobbing, as each girl turned her face into the others hair, hiding from the onlooking world of the dining room.

Minutes passed as the girls clung to each other, tears slowing, both feeling safe in each other's arms.

They stepped apart as they heard an 'Ahem,' beside them.

They turned to the lady that had collected breadsticks and butter for Jessica, drying their eyes on their sleeves as they did so.

"Hello Lilliana," The lady greeted. "I am Ms Bonnie and I am here to settle you into the hospitals dining area tonight and any other meal you will be having here with us." She had a crisp, shrill voice that reminded Lilliana of a pesky minor bird.

"Sit and chatter quietly amongst yourselves and your meal will arrive shortly." Lilliana nodded as Ms Bonnie turned away and sat at a table a little distance away, to keep her eyes on the newcomer.

"Come on," Josephine said, leading the girls back to the table where Jessica had been sitting. "I have to say, I am starving myself." Sitting down, Josephine reached for a chunky slice of bread. "How have you been since our scrabble match today Jessica?"

Jessica smiled. "Good thanks."

Josephine turned to Lilliana. "Did you know I lost to your friend today Lilliana, for the first time in years. Mr Night taught me how to play when I was six years old, he was thirteen and very patient." She chattered on, barely taking a breath as she reached for another chunk of bread and slathered it in butter, before stuffing a reasonable amount of the soft, fluffy bread into her mouth, chewing with enthusiasm preventing her to say another word for a moment or two.

"It was fun, it took my mind off, well, everything." Jessica trailed off as she reached for a piece of bread and slathered it in butter. Lilliana sat and watched the two girls, busying their hands and mouths.

Jessica passed an already buttered piece of bread to Lilliana, who smiled her thanks.

The three girls sat; one, stuffing her mouth enthusiastically, one nibbling and the other breaking the bread back into bread dust.

Lilliana watched as Jessica and Josephine were served a plate of steaming lasagne topped with cherry red tomatoes and for dessert, a sweet pastry topped with gelato.

Lilliana wondered if she could eat anything at all, when a server appeared, placing two small plates in front of her, almost causing her eyes to tear once more.

It was her most favourite meal of all time, especially when she was feeling blue.

A calzone stuffed with grilled vegetables, roast chicken, garlic, herbs and feta cheese, and for dessert, a piece of lemon cheesecake.

It looked like her mother's exact recipe. Lilliana looked at Josephine. "This looks like my mother's, how can that be?"

Josephine popped a roasted cherry tomato into her mouth, licked her finger before replying. "Mr. Night likes all our new family members to have their favourite meal, for their first meal. He can't do it all the time, but when possible, he contacts the family and gets the heads up."

Jessica nodded. "My first meal was Stephan's pork ribs. The marinade was just like the way he made it. I cried so much, I barely had more than a mouth full, which was a shame because it was so delicious."

"The food is always delicious, fresh and healthy as we use all our own produce. Cook, who has been with Mr. Night's family for decades, was one of the world's top-hat chefs." Josephine said proudly. "You'll love the meals in main house."

"Main house?" Lilliana asked, before taking another bite of her mouth-watering calzone.

Josephine pushed her empty plate away and looked over at Ms Bonnie, who was reading a sturdy looking book. As she seemed pretty engrossed in it, Josephine turned towards Lilliana in a conspirator's way, lowering her voice.

"We are in the hospital section, which is underground to the main house, which is absolutely ginormous. All newcomers arrive at the hospital, or psych ward, until they are deemed safe enough to enter main house."

"Safe enough?" Lilliana took a mouthful of water.

"Without wanting to cause injury to themselves, or harm to anyone else. Although in some cases, some are allowed entry into main house whilst healing but always accompanied by a Watcher."

Lilliana wasn't sure what a Watcher was and was feeling more confused about her whereabouts and would have questioned Josephine more when Ms Bonnie approached them.

"Finished girls? Ready to go?" She seemed to be counting all the cutlery as she addressed them.

"Yes Ms Bonnie, I'll take Jessica and Lilliana back to Nurse Rachael now."

"Very good Josephine. Goodnight then." She waited for the three girls to get up and leave the room.

Josephine led the girls back through the corridors, to the nurse's station where Nurse Rachael was waiting for them. "Thank you, Josephine." She smiled at all three of them. "Was your meal nice?"

They all nodded yes.

Josephine turned to Lilliana. "It was real nice meeting you today Lilliana. Best of luck with Mr. Night tomorrow, don't worry, you'll be fine."

Lilliana hoped that was true.

"Well, goodnight." She waved as she headed off.

"Goodnight." The girls called out together

"Now," Rachael turned, giving them her undivided attention. "I imagine you would like to sit and have a nice cup of hot chocolate and a chat before bed?"

Lilliana nodded, noticing for the first time how pretty Nurse Rachael was with her small face and lovely light blue eyes and dimples when she smiled. Her short, soft blonde curls peeked out from her white nurses cap.

"That would be nice." Jessica replied.

"Follow me." She walked down the corridor and around a small bend which led to a double door. Pushing it open they saw two couches facing each other, with a long coffee table in the middle scattered with magazines. A wall-length fish tank and a coffee, tea and chocolate dispenser, which sat beside a wall full of books and old black and white photographs of the property and its developments over the years.

Rachael pointed to the beverage machine and said. "All the hot chocolate or tea you'd like, and I'll be by in about forty-five minutes to take you to your rooms." She smiled and left the room.

Jessica walked over to the machine for a hot chocolate, holding up the green cup.

Lilliana raised her eyebrows as she pressed for a herbal tea. "What's the go with the green." She asked Jessica, who wandered over and sat down on one of the couches.

"I was told it is some sort of herbal, safe for the environment, invention that goes into the recycling for the animals." Jessica took an appreciate mouthful. "Doesn't change the flavour thank the stars, because I have to say this is the best hot chocolate I have ever had."

Lilliana sat on the ground opposite her friend, leaning back onto the couch, carefully sipping her hot tea.

They were silent for a few minutes, both having so much to say but not knowing where to start.

"I miss Stephan." Jessica began quietly. I've been told I won't see him again. Is that beyond crazy or what. Have you been told where we are?" She looked at her friend.

Lilliana shook her head. "I've only been solidly awake these past few hours. It only seems like yesterday that we left that evil place. I can't believe what's happened, I feel almost calm, yet underneath, I feel like I'm going to explode. My feelings don't feel as if they are my own." She finished quickly, the words rushing out. She put her tea on the table and pulled her legs up, wrapping her arms around them, dropping her chin on her raised knees.

"That's the drugs in your system, calming drugs. Be grateful for them. It's when they start to wear off, you'll feel like you actually will explode."

"Great." Lilliana whispered, unenthusiastically. Like it could get any worse.

Jessica drained her chocolate and jumped up to get another, before sitting on the floor beside Lilliana, sipping slowly.

"How's your arm?" Her head dropped as she asked the question, feeling guilty about slicing her friend's arm open.

"Oh Jessica, please don't feel bad about that, it was an accident. Honestly look," She pulled up her sleeve. "they used some sort of cream that knitted the skin together, it probably won't even leave a scar." She wanted to add they had worse scars to worry about, but didn't want to upset her friend further.

"How are we supposed to move on?" Jessica shook her head. "I have had two hours of therapy every day for the past two weeks and I still feel like I'm going insane. What we saw Lilliana, what they did to us." She cried, her hands shook, and she had to put her chocolate down on the table beside Lilliana's tea.

Burying her face in her hands, she wept quietly. "I haven't been sleeping well, my dreams are repetitive and full of those monsters. I wake up screaming. I have no escape from our nightmare, it's like there's nothing I can do to get away from all those men. I smell them I feel their hands on me." Her voice broke and she covered her face. "What we had to do Lilly, to each other." She trailed off, unable to say another word.

Lilliana quietened her own struggling demons, that she could feel rising, at Jessica's descriptive words, and put her arms around her sobbing friend, dropping her chin on top of Jessica's smooth head, internally pushing her tears away she said quietly. "We did what we had to do, to survive. It wasn't an option, a truth or dare. It was real. We would have suffered a fate worse than we did, if we hadn't done everything we were told. I don't blame you for anything that happened in that prison. Do you blame me in anyway? If you do, I honestly don't think I could handle that." Lilliana held her breath, waiting.

"No, no. Of course not." Jessica reached up and grasped Lilliana's hand, squeezing it in conformation.

They sat quietly again, the vibrating fish filter the only sound in the room, and reached for their cups again, silently drinking from them.

"It's so strange, being here, isn't it?" Lilliana said. "I mean, is it true, we are never going home again? I won't see my mum, my dad. You won't see Stephan? How can that be?"

Jessica shrugged a shoulder as she stood "I have to say, if it weren't for you being here with me, I'd definitely be losing it way more than what I have been."

Lilliana rubbed the back of her neck, watching as Jessica stood and moved to the wall length, ceiling high fish tank.

"I'm not supposed to tell you where we are Lilliana, apparently that's what Mr. Night is going to do tomorrow." Jessica turned to face Lilliana. "But I can't not tell you. Get ready for it."

Lilliana raised an eyebrow, waiting. How bad could it really be?

"We are at the Louisianans' Given facility."

That bad, Lilliana thought. "Oh, my Stars, for real? We are actually on The Givens lands?" Lilliana ran her hands over her face, pressing her fingers to her lips.

"My great, great granddaddy was one of the founding fathers who had a part in opening this establishment. It's full of the fallen, the lost, the desperate. Are we that now Jessica?" Lilliana got up and started pacing.

"My Dad won't leave me here," She shook her head. "my Mum won't let him, surely they are doing everything they can right this second to get me home again."

Her voice was rising, getting a little panicky even to her own ears.

"It doesn't work that way, honestly Lilliana according to our new friend Josephine, we are in the best place, possibly anywhere in the world. The way she describes it, it is a safe paradise."

"Well," Lilliana ventured cautiously. "I guess she has lived here basically her whole life, she would feel that way. She seems down to earth and honest. I hope for our sakes she has been, with describing this place to you."

"I'm sure she has Lilliana." Jessica assured her friend. "I'm being taken to my permanent room tomorrow in main house." She sat again, facing Lilliana. "That's why they let us have a tonight to talk, so I could reassure you everything is going to be alright."

"Tomorrow." Lilliana nodded, processing the information. She'd only just woken from one nightmare, been told they were stuck in another and now, her only link to the outside world was being removed. 'Toughen up', She whispered to herself.

"Right, well, do you feel okay about that Jessica, will you be alright? I mean, who's going to look out for you?"

Jessica smiled for a spilt second before it quickly vanished, as she recalled Lilliana putting herself in harm's way, to deflect it from her, when those vile men entered their prison time and time again.

"I'll be fine Lilliana, and hopefully, it won't be too long for you to be moved to the main house. The psych evaluation is tough, and they test you in ways that may force you to lose it, but try to keep it together. There's one doctor I know you'll be uneasy with, I was too, but if anyone can get through this, it's you Lilly." Jessica crossed the room and hugged her friend. "We are going to be alright, believe that."

"Thanks Jess." Lilliana squeezed her as a knock sounded before the door opened. Rachael, along with another nurse, smiled at them. "Ready for bed?"

Lilliana didn't realise until that moment, how extremely exhausted she was, and nodded in agreement.

Rachael led the way and they all headed off down the corridor towards Lilliana's room, Rachael opened the door for her, giving her a chance to say goodnight to Jessica before the other nurse led her off.

Jessica held up her hand in a farewell wave, before disappearing around the next turn of the corridor after a few moments.

Lilliana sighed inwardly and walked into her room, feeling empty once her friend was out of sight.

She sat on the side of the bed and fought her tears back whilst the friendly, smiley Nurse was in her room.

"There's fresh pyjamas on the bench for you Lilliana, and some magazines on the horses we breed here. Do you like horses?"

Lilliana nodded. "My elder cousin had two, he would never let me ride them though, but I helped out in the stables. I find horses relaxing to be around."

Rachael smiled. "Animals certainly hold their own therapeutic magic. Now, I'm going to give you a little sleeping pill that should give you a good solid deep sleep. But if not, just ring the buzzer. Dr. Ryan will be on call tonight. He will assist you with anything you may need." As she spoke, she poured a glass of water and handed it to Lilliana.

"The next week or so is going to be tiring, but we are going to do everything we can for you, to give you peace with your new life here after everything you have been through." She reached into her apron pocket, pulled out a small vile and popped two round silver tablets onto her palm.

"Swallow these for me please Lilliana." She handed them over.

Lilliana popped the pills into her mouth and swallowed them with a large mouthful of water.

Once Rachael was happy that Lilliana had swallowed the

medication, she made sure Lilliana had everything she needed, before she turned to leave. "Goodnight Lilliana, I'll see you tomorrow."

"Goodnight Nurse Rachael, thank you."

Rachael smiled as she left the room, shutting the door firmly behind her.

Lilliana quickly stripped her clothes off and pulled on the soft flannel pyjamas that smelt of lavender. Folding her clothes neatly she placed them on the chair and picked the magazines up off the table before hoping into bed and pulling the covers up. It felt warm and comforting, like one giant wheat bag. She nestled back against the pillows, glancing around the room as she held the magazines to her chest.

Her mind was full of the conversation she'd had with Jessica. She was so relieved that she had seen her friend, and although Jessica was as distraught as she herself felt, Jessica had obviously had time to process their new surroundings.

The more she thought about her meeting the following day with Mr. Night, the more stressed she felt. If she were honest with herself, she was closer to terrified than stressed. The unknown was something she couldn't deal with right at this moment. She wished she'd asked Jessica more about him when she had the chance.

His eyes. So intense, like they could see through your darkest secrets.

She shook her head to clear the image of his face when he'd approached her room this afternoon, watching her as if she were a frightened rabbit. "Enough." She said out loud and picked up a magazine with a glossy cover. A distraction is what she needed.

She appreciated the beautiful black stallion standing tall and graceful on the front cover, along with the headline, *'The Louisianans Given us the best: Beast'*. She flicked through the pages, reading a few small articles on the latest horse treatments, tack and gear and quality new foods grown on The Givens land that was being promoted and shared with horse associated organisations around the globe. Picture after picture of exemplary horses. Lilliana could feel herself relax, when flicking to the next page, her eyes fell on the man himself.

Mr. Damon Night, dressed in black, standing tall beside the majestic stallion: one foot raised on a bale of hay, a halter dangling down beside his long leg, and Beasts head over his broad, strong shoulder, his hand stroking the animals glistening black neck.

Lilliana bit her thumb nail as she looked over the article, then her eyes darted back to the extraordinarily attractive male, smiling into the camera, seemingly right at her. Her breath, she hadn't been aware of holding, rushed out.

She had to stop this thought flow, and immediately. She shouldn't be thinking of him as attractive. Shouldn't really be thinking of him as anything at all, except as the man that was going to question her tomorrow.

She closed the magazine and picking up the others, gathered them together before placing them on the small bedside table. She slipped down into the bed, pulling the covers up to her chin, imagining sleep wouldn't come easily now. Her mind jumped to the reason why she was here in the first place, and she quickly squeezed her eyes shut. That didn't help as images rushed towards her closed eyelids, men tormenting her, hurting her, destroying Jessica's sweet fragile soul. She sat bolt up, opening her eyes. How was she supposed to sleep when her mind wouldn't allow her a second's peace? Rubbing her hands over her face, she stared at the door, as screams echoed through, from an unhappy soul.

Lilliana fell back into her pillows and rolling on her stomach shoved her face deep into the pillow.

She couldn't remember falling asleep.

CHAPTER 6

Lilliana let out a bloody curdling scream as the hand around her throat tightened, trying to cut off her air. She clawed at it, trying to pry it from her as her screams turned to cries.

"Lilliana, Lilliana, you're having a dream, wake up."

Her eyes flew open and she slapped the hand away that was attempting to comfort her, her cries turned to distraught whimpers as she saw the man in the doctor's uniform, step back to give her space.

"I'm sorry." She whispered, glancing behind him at the open door as she sat up in the bed, pushing her long hair off her face. "I'm sorry."

"Lilliana, you don't have to apologise. I'm Dr. Ryan, did Nurse Rachael explain that I'd be seeing to you this morning? He asked mildly, watching her carefully. She looked exhausted and wary.

"Yes." She replied shortly, feeling like she hadn't slept in years. She couldn't remember ever feeling so tired.

"Why don't you freshen up while I fill out your report. I've been told Josephine is coming to collect you for your morning shower followed by breakfast."

Lilliana nodded.

"Just through that door Lilliana." He gestured to a door to the left of the room.

She slid out of bed and hurried into the small bathroom, and as she pulled the door shut, she quickly glanced at the doctor who was typing on his glass tablet. After using the toilet, she avoided the mirror as she washed her hands, splashing some cold water onto her face hoping it would wake her up a bit more, and wash away the fuzzy feeling.

Going back into the room, she stood near the bed, unsure whether to get back into it, or wait.

Dr. Ryan smiled at her as he clicked off his screen as a knock sounded at the door. "Come in." He called.

Josephine fell through the door, a smile plastered on her face.

"Morning Dr. Ryan. I've come to take Lilliana to freshen up and have breakfast," She said, "If you want me to that is." She waited, looking at Lilliana.

"Yes please." Lilliana was grateful the smiling, light-hearted girl was here. She didn't like being in a room alone with any man now. She wondered if that feeling would ever change.

"Excellent." Dr. Ryan nodded. "Once you're finished with breakfast Josephine, could you please take Lilliana to Mr. Nights hospital office?"

"Of course Sir, come on Lilliana, follow me." And off she went.

Dr. Ryan smiled at Lilliana and held his hand after Josephine. "Off you go Lilliana, I'll see you later."

She nodded and dashed from the room.

The shower was heaven, and Josephine's cheerful chatter was a pleasant distraction. Lilliana lathered and listened as Josephine went on about some boy called Rupert that had been brought in a few weeks ago, and was as cute as a button with the sweetest damn smile she thought she'd ever seen, with a head of glorious red hair.

After her shower, Lilliana went in the room next door, and she chose a black pair of jeans, felt black boots and a soft blue sweater.

She was about to pull her hair up, but decided to let it fall in soft, shiny waves around her face and down her back. At least she could hide behind it this way, if need be.

Breakfast smelt delicious and Lilliana realised she was very hungry, helping herself to pancakes topped with fruit, along with an orange and ginger smoothie.

Josephine piled her plate with bacon and eggs and grabbed a cup of tea, all under the watchful eye of Ms Bonnie.

Lilliana ate slowly, whilst Josephine chattered around mouthfuls of food. It was nice not to have to say anything, just nod in between, and try to put on a happy face whenever they made eye contact.

Lilliana's mind wondered to Jessica, concerned if she'd been moved already, hoping she wouldn't be too unnerved by her new surroundings.

Josephine must have sensed her distraction, and reached across the table, taking hold of her hand. "I know you don't know me from a jar of pickled horseradish, but I just believe you and I are going to be great friends. Everything will be alright, once you get past the next week or so. There's a lot of support here Lilliana, everything will fall into place, you'll see. And I will be here to help, okay?" She squeezed Lilliana's hand, waiting.

Lilliana didn't need to force the next smile she directed towards Josephine. The girl's genuine warmth and concern filled her battered soul with a sense of peace. "Thanks Josephine, you are a real sweetheart." She squeezed Josephine's hand back, before gently removing it and reached for her smoothie.

"I'm just trying to get my head around everything that's happened. It feels like one giant nightmare I can't wake up from." She stabbed the bottom of her glass with the long straw, before draining the frothy, orange liquid and pushed the glass into the middle of the table before folding her arms anxiously. "What's going to happen to me today," She asked Josephine. "how deep is it going to get?"

"How deep is the ocean my friend?" Josephine shrugged. "Shallow in parts, deeper in others, but don't fret, sooner or later there will be a life raft at the end. Mr. Night is good at what he does. You'll be okay, I promise."

Josephine stood and waved to Ms Bonnie who came across to do the cutlery count. After a nod from Ms Bonnie, Josephine turned to

Lilliana. "Come on, best get started."

Lilliana wished she'd piled her plate up more to prolong this dreaded session. She took a quiet, deep breath and followed Josephine out of the dining room and down the long corridor, past the ever-busy nurses station and into another set of corridors.

One of the portraits caught her attention. Two photos, black and white, offset each other in a macabre way. A stunning long-limbed girl sat perched on a high branch wrapped in a sheer, white gown, her arms outstretched, adorned with thin swamp snakes and Spanish moss.

The other photo was of the same girl, covered in blood and screaming furiously into the camera, her arms restrained by nursing staff. As angry as she looked, she was sublimely beautiful. The only colour in the photographs was her flaming red hair, flowing around her head like a halo of fire.

"That's Fox. She's trouble and troubled. She is our very own celebrity model."

"I think I've seen her before, on a billboard." Lilliana mused.

"No doubt, she is highly sought by companies large and small. The money she earns helps our establishment enormously and allows us to give generously to specific charities."

Josephine tugged Lilliana's arm to follow her and chattered away whilst they continued, occasionally greeting nursing staff as they walked past.

Josephine stopped suddenly at a large, black glass door causing Lilliana to bump into her back. They both laughed. One merrily, the other nervously, trying to catch her breath as Josephine raised her fist and rapped softly on the door.

As nervous as Lilliana felt and underprepared for what was about to take place, she was oddly curious enough about what was going to happen to her from here on out, not just this session, but life in general.

Josephine knocked quickly on the door again and smiled at Lilliana.

Lilliana put her hands behind her back, then crossed them and finally linked them together in front of her, clenching her fingers tightly.

The door slid silently open and there he stood tall, dark and handsome.

Lilliana was shocked at her own reaction to this man. Her cheeks flushed red and she quickly avoided looking into his eyes.

"Good morning, I hope you both slept well." He noticed immediately how tired Lilliana appeared and not surprisingly, anxious. "Come on in and find a seat where you will be comfortable Lilliana." He gestured around the room before turning to Josephine.

"Thank you for escorting Lilliana here, Josephine."

"No worries Sir." She smiled.

"You are welcome to come back later and join us for lunch break?"

"Absolutely Mr. Night, I'll see you later Lilliana." She gave her new friend a reassuring nod, before quickly leaving, hoping she would not be late for her first class.

Damon turned once the door closed and watched as Lilliana looked around the spacious office.

Similar to the room the night before where she and Jessica had had their alone time, this room had a wall-long, ceiling-high fish tank, which was soothing to the soul as the fish swam silently by, their iridescent colours shone like glass.

Three, two seater brown leather couches faced in and around the fish wall, in a semi-circle with a low glass coffee table in the centre; a jar of jelly beans and a water jug with drinking glasses sat perched on a silver tray.

To the back of the room, a large desk with six thin glass computer screens hung against the wall. Lilliana took stock of her surroundings, then glanced behind her to see Damon watching her intently.

She quickly looked away and walked to the couch closest to the fish wall and sat. Furthest away from him, he noticed, before he walked to the desk, grabbed his tablet before sitting opposite her. The table between them.

"How was breakfast?" He thought small talk may put her at ease before the session started.

"Delicious, thank you." She replied.

He leaned back into the soft leather and casually crossed an ankle over his knee, balancing the tablet on his calf muscle, using it as a table.

He looked extremely relaxed. The complete opposite to how Lilliana was feeling.

She crossed her legs, hands clenched together jammed between her knees, her eyes remaining on the fish.

"Relaxing, aren't they?" Damon stated, turning on his tablet, he began typing.

Whilst his head was down, concentrating on what he was doing, Lilliana risked a glance towards him, watching him under her long eyelashes, ready to look away as soon as his head turned.

She flushed red as his eyes flicked directly into hers, his head not shifting as he tapped once on the keyboard, staring quietly, unblinking.

Lilliana quickly averted her eyes and looked back towards the fish.

Damon felt for the nervous girl. After all she had endured, he wished there was some way he could skip this part of the induction before she entered main house. But that wasn't the way the system worked and this was a part of the process to help with the placement of new Givens.

"Lilliana, this evaluation will help us with your placement, to see if you're ready to enter main house or if you need more recovery time with us here at the hospital, or possibly the psych ward."

Lilliana's gaze dropped uneasily to her knees at the mention of the psych ward.

Damon continued. "I know this will be difficult after all you've endured, and I do not intend to hurt or upset you in any way, but I may have to ask you questions that you will find uncomfortable to answer. Please be as honest with me as you can."

Her eyes remained downcast as she nodded once.

He felt for all the young people when they first came to him, battling with emotions, struggling to hide how uncomfortable they were, just as Lilliana was this very moment.

She was holding her breath, sitting rigidly still.

"I'd like to reassure you, there is nothing to be afraid of, but then I'd be lying. These sessions can get intense and we will stop for short breaks when need be, but the faster we get through them, the faster we can get you on the path leading to main house."

Lilliana folded her arms, fisting her hands under her armpits and nodded again, slowly releasing her breath before taking another shallow one.

"You are at the Louisiana's Given. I understand your great great-grandfather had a hand with getting this place running in its early days?" He waited a beat to see if she would answer.

"Yes," She replied. "he did. It was something my Mother was very proud of."

Excellent, Damon thought. It was the most he'd heard her say in one breath.

"My great-granddaddy thought the same. He found this establishment and many like it, a necessity for the way our world has fallen. It is a haven for all those the Officials send our way. But with the gift of living here, we will expect a lot from you in return."

Lilliana met Damon's eyes briefly and nodded slowly, trying to take in every word he was saying, as a small buzzing sound began whispering in her ears.

"Once you enter the main house, you will be assigned a Team Leader, who will discuss with you all our rules, which are in place for your safety.

There are secured sections from the main house, along with a Black Ops division. These parts of the house are forbidden for one such as yourself to enter." He poured himself a glass of water and took a mouthful before continuing.

"We try not to segregate here, but we do have certain Given, that once released into main house, need to have constant surveillance and these individuals are assigned a Watcher."

'There's that word again.' Lilliana thought to herself. 'Watcher.'

"Watchers are assigned to keep these Given safe from harming themselves or others. In time, these Given can join in classes, house activities followed by employment with the rest of our family, but it is under my rule and ending decision what happens to them whilst under my roof, depending on their rehabilitation."

Watching her closely as he spoke, she seemed to be going paler with each piece of information he gave her. He placed his water back on the table.

"Once again, these issues will be discussed with you in detail once you have a Team Leader. Hopefully, with our support it won't be too long until you can join main house with your friend, Jessica."

"I hope so." She replied quietly.

He typed for a moment before continuing. "All Given under the age of eighteen, address me as Mr. Night. Once you enter main house, you will be involved in a compulsory, weekly group therapy, will take all mainstream classes for the first year, and following that I, along with senior staff will determine which classes you will take that will be most beneficial to your career path within this establishment. This is something we will discuss in due course."

Lilliana ran her hand down one pale cheek, realizing that this was it.

This is where she would spend the rest of her life, until, she didn't even know when.

Every festive holiday. All without her parents. Her mother.

Thinking of her mother had her almost doubling over in pain, filled with longing. That intense pain, accompanied with every unwanted image from the past weeks, slipping into her thoughts like an unwelcome visitor was too much for her tired mind.

The whispering buzzing in her ears seemed to grow louder and she struggled to catch her breath, to focus. Her hearing started to fade in and out, her vision clouded with black and white flecks.

'Oh no,' Lilliana pleaded with herself. 'No, no, no, no, no, this cannot be happening.' Yet it did, once again, out of her control, she passed-out as elegantly as any fifteen-year-old could. In a heap.

A few minutes later, she came to in the arms of Nurse Rachael, stroking her forehead with a cool face washer.

"You're okay." Rachael smiled warmly.

Lilliana sat up, to see a worried looking Damon pacing alongside the swimming fish. "I've never fainted in my life." She apologised uncomfortably.

"It's not surprising, dear," Rachael said kindly. "considering all you have been through the past few weeks; it is completely normal for your young body to react this way."

Rachael looked across at Damon. "Perhaps you can call it a session Mr. Night?"

Damon always respected Rachael's insight when it came to the new Givens journey to health, both physically and mentally, but shook his head at Rachael, before glancing down at Lilliana.

"No, I'm sorry, but we've barely even begun this session, stopping now is not an option"

"It's all right, I'm okay." Lilliana pushed at the dark cascade of hair from her face. "I just need a glass of water, I'll be fine." The last thing she wanted to be was a problem. She forced a smile of thanks as Rachael poured a glass of water and pushed it into her outstretched, shaky hand.

"Thanks Rachael, that will be all for the moment." Damon said, dismissing her.

Rachael rubbed Lilliana's back as she turned and gave Damon a look, that told him she had a few words for him, that she would share in private.

Damon held in a sigh, as he watched Rachael leave the room, before taking a seat opposite Lilliana. "Are you sure you're alright to continue?"

As much as Lilliana would have liked to say, 'Actually no, I think I'll head back to my room,' she replied instead. "Yes, I'm fine."

"Excellent." Scooping up his tablet, he scrolled down a list, reading. "From all the background information given to me by your parents and teachers. It seems you are a very well-rounded teenager. Born in Arizona lived in Denver, New York, Texas, Memphis. Trips to Italy, Ireland and you lived in Australia for a year."

He looked up, smiling. "I had a trip there myself when I was your age, a stunning country. My good friend Russell, runs one of the Given establishments over there."

She shifted a little in her seat as he continued looking at her.

He noted when he watched her for any period, she became very uncomfortable. He dropped his gaze back down to his notes and continued reading.

"Beyond exemplary grades, qualified for scholarships in compassion-arts and legal.

Team captain on the volleyball team for Ohio. Very impressive."

He reached for the water jug and topped up his glass, offering her more.

She held up her half full glass, shaking her head.

"So," He said, bringing the glass towards his parted lips. "it seems moving around and settling into new areas doesn't seem a problem for you." He tipped his head back, draining his glass before placing it down on the tray. "Hopefully this transition will go just as smoothly for you."

"I hope so." She replied, trying not to notice the fluent way he moved, and instead concentrated on watching the fish swim lazily around their gorgeous world.

"Lilliana, in this session, we need you to be open to discuss what happened to you those weeks you were taken. I know how terribly hard it's going to be, and it will be a long road to recovery, which is why we insist on the compulsory group therapy once you enter main house. Please take these opportunities to openly acknowledge the painful reality of how you have come to be with us. Speak freely and know that you have every right to be angry, resentful even, okay?" He nodded. "Only then will part of your healing begin."

Every word he said after 'discuss what happened to you those weeks you were taken,' were nothing but white noise in Lilliana's ears. She swallowed nervously and blurted out. "Am I really never going to see my mother again?" Wanting to completely change the subject and stall the coming conversation.

"No." He replied shortly.

"What if something happens to her and she is sent here?" She sounded a little desperate, even to her own ears.

"Lilliana, people over the age of thirty-five, get sent to many other

Given facilities around the world. South America, Europe, Asia, Africa, and Australia. Not here. Depending on the drawer. There is no telling what the future may bring. I know it's hard, but it's best to try to move on. Face the fact, that this is your life now."

He stood and walked across to his desk, leaning over, he pressed a button on a round intercom and waited.

"Dr. Richard here." A haughty voice spoke through the intercom.

"Richard, it's Damon. I need you and Hillary in my hospital office now if you wouldn't mind." He checked his watch and glanced over at Lilliana.

"Yes Mr. Night, right away." The intercom clicked off.

Damon walked over to the floating paradise and looked above his head where an enormous Angel fish of bright blue and yellow swam by. He was not looking forward to the next few hours.

It would either build his relationship with this girl, or break it.

He turned, looking at her as he sat. "We're going to be joined by a couple of colleagues of mine, that specialise in many areas, one of them helping heal the mind of the abused, after major trauma. Please remember Lilliana, you are not on trial here, you are not guilty of anything. We are here purely to help break the chains your abuse has you bound in, okay?" His eyes did not flicker from her face

Lilliana took a deep breath. "Okay." She could do this, hell after surviving the past few weeks she felt she could pretty much survive anything.

A few minutes later, Dr. Hillary and Dr. Richard walked in, dressed in pristine white jackets, neither looking particularly friendly or approachable in any way.

Lilliana placed her glass on the table, crossed her legs and folded her arms. And these were the people that were supposed to help her feel better?

Her hair that had fallen forward when putting her glass down, remained where it was, a curtain of her own to hide behind.

Damon nodded to the two doctors, and indicated towards Lilliana. "Dr. Hillary, Dr. Richard, this is Lilliana."

"Hello Lilliana, we hope you'll be happy here." Dr. Hillary smiled, as both the doctors sat.

Dr. Richard said nothing in way of greeting, just sat there looking over the top of his horn-rimmed spectacles at her, fingertips at the ready on his tablet.

He instantly gave Lilliana the creeps with his tall, thin frame, pale hair and void expression. This must have been the one that Jessica had unfavourably mentioned.

"We should explain to you Lilliana," Dr. Hillary began, "that all the footage recorded, of everything you endured, whilst you were taken has been viewed by us three in this room along with selected senior staff, in order to help us support you in every way we can with the knowledge of what you experienced."

Lilliana could not help the small gasp of embarrassment that escaped her throat. That these people, and more to the point, Mr. Night, had witness her degradation. It was almost too much to bear.

"Lilliana, please do not be embarrassed. Whatsoever." Damon stated firmly. His gut clenched for her, as the outlined questions he knew the doctors were about to assault her with, stared up at him from his screen.

Her eyes met his, cheeks flame red. She rubbed her hands over her face, before folding them around her body. Oh, the humiliation. She didn't have time to wallow in her thoughts for long, as the first question was hurled her way.

"When you first understood your predicament, with being taken, how did you feel?" Richard asked pointedly.

'Wow, straight into it.' Lilliana thought to herself. "I was terrified."

"How did you cope with the first invasive assault?"

"Not very well. I was scared, then furious and sickened by those men." She moved a fraction in her seat, wanting to run.

"How did you support your friend?"

Lilliana felt that was an odd question, and answered guardedly, "As best I could under the circumstances."

"How did you feel when your friend was being attacked?"

"Helpless."

"Did you feel resentment towards your friend when you stepped in to defend her, therefore being punished by your abductors further?"

"What, No! Shouldn't you already know all the answers, if you've seen all the footage?" Lilliana threw back at Richard.

Damon shifted in his seat, taking notes as Hillary interjected.

"We know this is difficult Lilliana, but please, answering what may seem like already answered questions really will help you with your healing. Placing guilt on your abductors and accepting you are blameless for everything that happened to both yourself and Jessica, will put you on a closer path to healing."

Lilliana could feel that uneasy, hot sick ball grow in the pit of her belly as her breath became shallow. She nodded at Dr. Hillary, indicating she understood.

"Did you give up hope at any stage during the weeks you were taken?"

Dr. Richard asked his questions in a bored tone, which was starting to infuriate Lilliana. "Of course. Who wouldn't in our situation?"

Dr. Richard looked at her in a cool manner, before typing with his long, pale fingers. The questions kept coming, most made sense and a lot were easy to answer. But they were all draining, and Lilliana didn't know how much more of this session she could take, as question after question continued being fired her way. It all felt so pointless. Her head was throbbing two hours in, and the sick feeling she had felt earlier was remaining her companion.

Leaning forward, she dropped her forehead against her hands, squeezing her throbbing temples. She peeked through her hair at Damon who sat entirely silent typing occasionally, his eyes ever watchful.

Dr. Richards next question had her seeing red and standing up she marched towards the door wanting an immediate exit, not knowing in these sessions, the door could only be opened by staff. She stood there, feeling like a trapped animal once again.

What was wrong with the man, to ask such a stupid question?

"Would you have preferred Orlando touching you instead of the older men?" Dr. Richard repeated in his arrogant, quiet voice.

"I'm not answering *that*." She practically yelled, hating the way he spoke to her. He seemed to be enjoying the fact that she was having a nervous breakdown.

'Seriously,' she thought, 'I think this weirdo needs this session more than I do'.

She pushed her hands against the door trying to budge it open, and getting nowhere dropped her forehead against the cold, frosted glass offering her small relief from the fever that was coming on rather quickly. Emotional exhaustion overwhelmed her and she forced another swallow, willing herself not to be sick, as fat tears threatened to choke her.

"Richard." Dr. Hillary spoke sternly. "That question was not on the list."

Damon stood; his voice vibrated with anger. "That's enough Richard. This session is over. Leave. Email me your reports this afternoon."

Hillary nodded towards Damon as she stood and walked towards the door and quietly asked the clearly shaken girl. "Are you alright Lilliana?"

Lilliana turned around facing Dr. Hillary as the lady placed a warm hand gently on her back. Her eyes met Dr. Hillary's, but she didn't have the energy to nod, let alone answer her.

"You're going to be alright. I'll see you soon." Hillary gave her shoulder a squeeze, before tapping a button on her tablet enabling the door to swing open.

Lilliana took five steps hurriedly away from the door as Dr. Richard approached her. Turning her back to him she completely ignored the cool nod he offered her. She felt relief as the door shut again, removing Dr. Richard from her sight.

Damon pinched the bridge of his nose, forcing back the tension that was building. He took a step towards Lilliana, wanting to rub her back but knowing she would freak out if he touched her. Instead he said quietly. "Lilliana, please, come sit. Have some water, lunch is coming."

"I'm not hungry." She replied, not quite sulkily.

"No, you may not be, but a small bite will help settle your stomach.

Please, sit."

She sighed as she turned around.

Damon stepped back, giving her plenty of space to walk by him and as she sat, he poured her a water.

She wouldn't meet his eyes, but nodded her thanks as he placed the glass in her not quite steady hands. She looked so small, fragile, wounded.

Very slowly, he placed his finger under her chin and tipped her head up ever so gently, so her eyes could meet his. His heart squeezed as her complete look of sadness. "You're going to be alright." He said softly.

'So, everyone keeps telling me' she thought to herself, not being able to move an inch under his intense gaze, his warm finger holding her in place. She didn't know if it was relief or sadness she felt when he dropped his finger and stepped back.

Turning away, he scooped up his tablet and walked across to his desk, placing it down he punched in a code and the door opened.

Ms Bonnie walked in carrying a rather large tray and two steps behind her a smiling Josephine, looking ready to burst with some news about such and such.

Ms Bonnie nodded to Damon. "It's a bit late to be calling it lunch." She said snippily setting the tray down and just as abruptly, turned and left the room.

Damon bit his tongue, thinking he'd have to have words with at least three of his staff members before the day was out.

Josephine walked towards Lilliana after seeing her dried tears and tired expression. Concern for her new friend filled her kind heart. She had seen many in the same position fall to pieces during this part of the process, before entering main house. It was never easy. "Lilliana, you look like you could sleep for a year. Are you..?" Josephine didn't get a chance to finish before Lilliana cut her off, saying quietly.

"Please don't ask me if I'm okay, or tell me that I'm going to be okay, please." She sounded exhausted even to her own ears.

Josephine nodded, before looking across at Damon. "I hope you are looking after her Mr. Night, Sir."

Damon smiled at Josephine. "I'm doing the best I can, thank you Josephine. Now what have they got for us today?" He walked over and removed the covering from the tray.

Lilliana looked on at the easy banter and comfort these two seemed to have with each other, as they peeked at the rows of assorted sandwiches, laughing together about Ms Bonnie having a 'no cutlery count' today.

Once they placed their selections onto napkins, Josephine sat right beside Damon, and filled them in on events during her recent class, around mouthfuls of food. "Jessica received her first award for being most creative at the art challenge and received a free pass from class with a horse-riding period."

Lilliana laughed quietly.

Damon looked at her, an eyebrow raised in question

"Jessica is allergic to horsehair, her eyes swell up."

"Well, maybe she can join in an archery period with me instead." Damon smiled.

"She'd like that." Lilliana said quietly.

"Come on Lilliana, eat a little something." Damon popped two cuts of sandwich on a napkin and pushed it across to her. "I know it's hard sweet-girl, but you have to eat, okay?"

She looked up at him, as he used the endearing pet name her mother called her every time she was in a dark place. Did he also ask parents for pet-names when he asked for their favourite meals?

Tears automatically fell from her eyes as she reached for a sandwich. Cucumber and tuna, chicken and cranberry jelly. Her favourite selection her mum used to make.

It was heaven and hell at the same time.

And that was how the next three weeks went.

CHAPTER 7

The pounding of hooves striking the earth was music to Damon's ears. The powerful movement of Beasts muscles stretching and bunching under him as the horse galloped, the wind rushing in his face making his eyes tear; it was everything he needed in that moment to chase away the demanding events the past few weeks had inflicted upon him.

The sun beat down as he allowed Beast to have his head, taking jumps over fallen logs, frolicking in shallow parts of the river and galloping over smooth acres flowing with carpets of lush grass. Many parts of the outside world were barren, drought stricken, but their lands had been blessed with underground springs, and thanks to hindsight and careful planning decades ago, their establishment had plenty of resources to maintain and recycle water so it was plentiful for all, both agriculture, horticulture and humans alike.

For just over an hour he'd been enjoying the energetic ride, the glorious, familiar pull of aching muscles had been exactly he was looking for to alleviate his stress. Turning Beast around, they headed back for a long, slow cooling down walk towards the stables.

"Good ride Mr. Night?" Thomas called out as he approached thirty minutes later.

"Just what the doctor ordered Thomas." He smiled as he dismounted, lovingly slapping his horse's wet neck in appreciation. Thomas saluted with enthusiasm before turning to a bunch of Given students and their teacher who were taking an afternoon ride.

Damon shook his head, a smile on his face as he led Beast towards his stall. He appreciated Thomas's enthusiasm, skill and manners. Well over twenty-five himself, he still believed in addressing Damon by 'Mr' and not his given name. No matter what decade, some people's good and decent manners were just bred into them.

Closing the stalls door behind him, he removed Beasts halter and saddle and began the pleasant task of rubbing down, then brushing his beloved animal, as Beast snorted into his chaff bowl, swishing his tail in pure happiness.

Damon was no more than fifty strokes in, when he heard the desperate calling of his name.

"Mr. Night, Mr. Night, Thomas have you seen Mr. Night?"

"He's in Beast's stall." Thomas called out.

A panting, sweaty fifteen-year-old Brad turned up, hands on his knees trying to catch his breath, whilst Damon continued to calmly brush his horse. He was not quite ready to relinquish his moment of relaxation, but from the look on Brad's face, that thought was about to slip through his fingers. "What is it lad?"

"I was sent to get you immediately Sir, as Nurse Rachael couldn't reach you on your cell. One of the new Givens went crazy on Dr. Richard, sliced his chest open with a surgical instrument." Brad straightened, wiping his sleeve across his damp forehead.

Damon stopped brushing Beast and he felt the last hours relaxation evaporate from his body. Dropping the brush in the tools bucket, he pushed the stall door open calling out to Thomas to finish off Beasts brush.

"No worries Mr. Night." Thomas nodded as the tall man on a mission walked briskly by him.

Damon slapped him on the back as he headed out. "Thanks Thomas." He called over his shoulder. Walking quickly out of the stables and down the blue stone path towards the house, he hurriedly wiped his hands on his pants as he wondered how

serious Richards injuries were, and which new Given had possibly taken joy in delivering the blow.

Damon noticed Brad's laboured breath, and the fact that the poor boy was struggling to keep up with him without jogging. "Thank you Brad, that will be all, you can head back to class."

"Yes Sir." Brad called out, slightly disappointed he didn't get to tag along and see what all the fuss was about, but headed off in the direction of his next class.

After a few interruptions from people needing Damon's attention as he entered the house, it took Damon another fifteen minutes to get down to the hospital and another five to find out where Richard was.

Spotting Billy further down the hall, coming out of a room, his arms loaded with bloody sheets, Damon headed towards him. "Hey Billy, do you know where Richard's at?"

"Sorry Sir, you'll have to check at the nurse's station, I'd only just come out of psych when I had to collect a messy situation in this room." He indicated to the bloody sheets.

Damon turned and continued to the nurse's station calling out "Thanks." over his shoulder.

He assumed the trouble with Richard would be caused by a new Given, Allie. A gusty young girl that had come to them two weeks prior to Lilliana and Jessica.

Her story like oh too many, was an unbelievable tale of greed and corruption, and considering all she had endured for many years, her mind and attitude was inconceivably strong.

Her parents had been in a car accident when she was six and had been raised by a doting Grandmother. Walking home from school one hot windy afternoon, not long after her ninth birthday, she had been kidnapped by a couple who stole young children and raised them in a fortress-like bunker beneath their house.

The stolen children slept on scattered mattresses on their prison floor and shared a tiny washroom that housed a toilet and wash sink. Each day, one of them was hauled above stairs to clean, cook and take part in running the household.

As soon as they became of age, they were forced to couple with each other and then separated once the girls became pregnant. The males were locked in jail-like cells until they were forced to serve their purpose once again.

Once the girls had given birth, their babies were taken away from them and sold on all Dark Web and Black-Market platforms.

When Allie realised, she was pregnant she begged her taken sisters to punch her over and over. She threw herself down the stairs more than once and almost killed herself drinking bleach. She would have done anything to send her babies to the angels above, and not the devils who sought such a destructive path to have a child of their own.

She felt loss and sadness with each miscarriage but celebrated with her stolen brothers and sisters over their small victory. She was beaten daily once the 'Parents' realised what she was up to.

It was six days after her last beating, that had left her with swollen eyes, a fractured skull and broken ribs, when a freakish accident above stairs consumed the house in flames. Their 'parents' burnt to death and with the house smouldering to ash above them, the metal door to their prison was revealed to the authorities and they were rescued and sent to the Givens protective doors.

Damon approached to the nurse's station. Several staff immediately straightened at the sight of him. "Where's the commotion?"

"Which one Sir, there's been several today." Adam, a young male nurse answered, a phone tucked under his chin.

"Dr. Richard's incident." Damon leant his arms along the top of the bench, willing the relaxed feeling to come back, that his hours ride had given him.

"Oh, yes, he is in with Rachael getting stitched up. The girl in question is in solitude."

"Which room?" Damon asked as he pushed away from the bench.

"Seventy-two." Adam called after him.

"Thanks." Damon waved a hand as he headed off. A few minutes later he strolled into the room to find Richard laying down, with Rachael standing over him, cleansing his wound before applying the stitching serum.

It was a nasty gash, bleeding and deep from his left collar bone to the right of his chest.

"Nice." Damon said in way of greeting. "What happened here, and why, and which girl is in solitude?" He folded his arms across his chest, waiting.

Rachael flushed, as Damon did not look happy. "I told Richard I didn't think it was the best decision without yours or Hillary's second say so, but we couldn't reach you."

"It was absolutely the correct decision, the girl attacked me, totally lost it. I'll tell you now, that girl is not ready for main house." Richard's pompous twang was grating on Damon's nerves.

"I'll make that decision thank you now, which girl are we talking about?" He asked as patiently as he could.

"It's Lilliana, she'd had a bad night, nightmares worse than usual and was very down this morning. She didn't want to cooperate with the physical and when Richard got a little too firm, she lost it." Rachael began applying the serum. "I'm sure her being uncooperative was due to the breakfast incident. She caught sight of the boy that arrived with them. I'm certain that's what set her off."

"Orlando? You're *kidding* me." Damon almost shouted. "I gave strict instructions that he was to be kept away from Lilliana's routine until she was ready for a meeting with him and myself. Of course, she probably lost it." He was furious.

"All that work we've done, the progress she has made, I wouldn't be surprised if we were back to square one with her." He pinched the bridge of his nose, trying to calm down as he could feel a tension headache creeping in. It was these setbacks he hated the most, the ones that should have easily been prevented.

Rachael felt for Damon. "I'll get her out as soon I've finished here Damon, I'll handle it." Hoping to help.

"Don't bother," He uncharacteristically snapped. "I'll get her myself." He stormed out of the room and headed towards the solitary division.

"Hold up Damon." He heard his brother call out.

Turning, he watched as Cam enthusiastically strolled towards him. "What is it Cam?"

"You okay? You look tense."

"Just the usual." He didn't have time to elaborate. "What is it Cam?" He repeated.

"An acre of the root crops is ready to harvest, I thought it would be a beneficial active group therapy for some of my guys to get out in the fresh air, do some good for the establishment?"

"That's actually a great idea, did you run it by H.D?" He used the horticultural departments abbreviated name.

"Yep, we will be accompanied by a few of their team, make sure all the food babies are collected with respect."

"Excellent. Follow protocol and behave yourself Cam."

"Of course, brother, don't you go worrying about me." Cam winked before he turned and hurried off.

Damon shook his head, almost smiling before he remembered where he had been heading before Cam came along. Turning in the opposite direction to his brother he headed off to the solitude cells.

Arriving a few minutes later he found Sam, the cell guard, in his usual position sitting at his desk, watching the twenty cell cameras over a cup of steaming coffee.

Damon nodded in greeting as he went to the computer screens to see what was going on in each cell.

"Busy day Sam?"

"Yep, sure has been Damon." Sam took a sip of his coffee.

Damon looked at the screens, seeing who occupied their cells today, briefly watching as one girl stood facing the camera, making rude gestures and screaming. Another, a boy around seventeen ripping his tee shirt, some pacing, another doing push ups, and Lilliana, sitting in the corner of the white cell, arms wrapped around drawn knees, forehead resting upon them.

Damon pointed towards her screen. "Buzz that one open for me will you please Sam."

"Sure thing Boss." Sam reached over and flicked a switch.

Damon walked over and opened the door. "Lilliana," He called quietly. "come on out of there."

Lilliana had been deep in thought, in a world full of misery when she heard Damon call her name. She had not been expecting to be let out of here for quite some time after what she had done and was surprised to see Damon.

She looked up at him and rested her head back against the soft wall, eyes staring sadly.

He hated seeing any of his young people struggle and Lilliana was no exception. He wasn't sure why it was worse with her.

He held out his hand and waved it towards himself, beckoning. "Come." He said quietly.

Lilliana stood slowly; dressed in black sneakers and jeans with a purple tee shirt, her hair pulled back in a thick, long glossy ponytail, she looked every bit the fifteen-year-old she was. She walked over and slowly followed him out of the cell.

"Thanks Sam." He called as he walked out the door.

"No problems Boss." Sam called out.

Together they walked down the corridor and after a few minutes arrived at Damon's office. Pushing the door open, he offered her to go in ahead of him.

Lilliana walked over and sat down on the couch, as always, close to the fish wall. Damon walked over to the urn and poured her a steaming cup of relaxing herbal tea. Placing it on the table in front of her, he pushed the bowl of jellybeans towards her. Sitting with a coffee, he crossed his legs, took an appreciative mouthful and watched her sip her tea.

He waited a few beats before asking "How are you feeling Lilliana?"

Lilliana, who had been staring into her tea cup, as if looking for a rescue remedy, finally met his eyes. She was feeling so embarrassed about what she had done and didn't think there was anything she could say to make Damon understand why she had done it. The more she thought about it, the more upset she became. Especially as Dr. Richard had threatened her with a long-term stay at the psych ward.

"I'm very sorry about what I did Mr. Night." What else could she say?

"Did you feel threatened Lilliana? Unsafe?" He watched her over the rim of his cup.

"Yes, I did. Why else would I cut the man? Nurse Rachael was going to do my physical, but she had to leave the room, for some emergency, so that doctor…"

"Dr. Richard to you Lilliana, please." He could clearly see she had no taste for the man, but she needed to understand their rules regarding respect for superiors.

She took a deep breath, knowing she had just gently been reprimanded. "Dr. Richard," She forced herself to say it without venom. "began by explaining why we need to be sterilized when we come to The Given, what he needed to do before he injected me and when I refused for him to continue with the physical, he told me my next stop would not be main house, but a long-term stay in the psych ward."

Damon sat quietly, listening as her voice began to rise with emotions that she should not have had to endure whilst going through her healing therapy. He took another mouthful of coffee, as she continued.

"He then put his hands on me and physically tried to place me in a chair with straps, insisting I allow him to complete my physical, so I would not waste Nurse Rachael's time. He wrestled me into the chair, and I'm sorry, but I totally had a flash back, grabbed the nearest weapon and *cut him*." She practically screamed out the last few words, and slammed her cup on the table, tea sloshing over the rim, before getting up and walking to the fish wall folding her arms angrily.

Damon glanced at the hot liquid, which made a reflective puddle on the shiny tabletop, before looking at Lilliana watching her closely as he took another mouthful of coffee before carefully asking, "You saw Orlando this morning. How did that make you feel?"

She glanced down at her feet, then back to watch a fish glide by.

"Scared," She whispered. "seeing him scared me. Suddenly, I was back in that room, that prison. I was so angry watching him sitting there eating, like he had done nothing wrong? Why is he here?" She gave him what was close to an accusing look.

"He is as much a victim as you." Damon felt for her, heard the raw emotion in her voice showing him exactly how vulnerable she was.

Lilliana looked angrily towards the fish, giving her head a firm shake, not believing that Orlando was anywhere near a victim.

Damon understood how she must be feeling. "I can't tell you Orlando's full story. You will hear that yourself in group therapy. But for right now, know that he watched his sister suffer as he watched you and Jessica suffer. He tried to save his sister. That didn't work. He discovered courage and deep strength to save you two girls. I think he deserves a place with us. He is with us. We all need to accept what is and move on. Is that understood Lilliana?" He waited, placing his coffee cup on the table.

"Yes Sir." Seriously, how else could she respond?

"Good. Now, about slicing Dr. Richard open. I understand why you were so frightened, and I will have a stern talk to our staff regarding your boundaries at this present time, but let's not try that again, okay?"

"I'll do my best."

"Excellent, that's all I can ask for. I was hoping to get you upstairs to main house for your sixteenth birthday. Do you think you'll be ready in two days' time?"

Her eyes brightened immediately with the thought of seeing Jessica and Josephine every day.

"Yes Mr. Night, I promise. I'll do whatever I need to do. You won't have to worry about me hurting anyone, I promise." Her hands twisted anxiously in front of her.

"Well, that's all we can hope for." Damon smiled, relieved to see the first look of genuine happiness on her face in weeks.

***

The last time Lilliana had felt a sense of complete happiness, was an afternoon, after she had left Jessica's house, and met her mother in the quarter where they had shared gelato, laughter and stories of what they had been up to that week.

Now here she stood, months later on her sixteenth birthday in the middle of her new bedroom. It was a small room with a king single bed in one corner, comfortably crowded with orange and white pillows and what seemed like a thick, fluffy doona cover. In the opposite corner stood a small writing desk with two empty picture frames sitting on top and, dividing bed and desk, a long, narrow window seat sitting prettily under the window with views of complete serenity of green lawns, vibrant blooms and horses frolicking in lush pastures.

After being in the hospital section for a little over a month, Lilliana could have spent another quiet hour happily staring out of her open window as the breeze tugged playfully with her long hair.

Sitting amongst the pillows on her window seat, she propped an arm on the ledge of the sill and dropped her chin onto her arm as her thoughts raced back to the morning, and how busy the day had been with getting acquainted with so many new faces and hearing about the house rules and expectations of the newly arrived.

It would have been overwhelming, but Lilliana was comforted by being in the presence of Josephine and Jessica for the whole days tour. From leaving the hospital, to going up stairs and exploring the dining and common rooms and falling in love with the grand feel the library exuded in every nook and cranny with its opulent old furnishings sitting here and there for studying or escaping with a book, an ornate fire place in which five men could stand, with lavish mantel crowded with decorative old frames telling a story of the establishments growth over the decades, with vases flowing with sweet scented flowers. Bookcases crammed with books in every genre ever written, with ladders built on railings to easily roll around the vast area, so every enthused reader could reach their desired book with ease. An iron, spiral stairway drifted up to the loft where the old board games and leisure activities were stacked amongst old photo albums, books and magazines. Lilliana knew the moment she stepped past the water feature filled with Koi, into the entrance of the library, it was going to be one of her favourite places to escape to. If she'd have the time that is. Sitting in assembly with all the other Given, after being introduced to some of her instructors, she found out how gruelling her schedule was going to be and what was expected from her now she was in main house.

Damon had stood at the front of the assembly room, on a large stage with a handful of staff sitting behind him.

Lilliana had focused on all the information as best she could, as Josephine gave her a running commentary on who so and so was, and who best to stay away from.

"Oh my god, he's so cute." Josephine whispered in an excited high pitch spotting a newcomer with dark hair.

Lilliana nodded absently, trying to follow the two conversations as Damon continued.

"I expect all of you, to make our new family members feel welcome and do all you can to help settle them in, as you were once settled in. Help them adjust to our rules and offer positive advice and guide them back onto the correct path if they seem lost."

Looking past Damon she saw Cam Night, studying her closely from his seat on the stage. One arm draped over the back of his chair; ankle lazily crossed over his knee.

Josephine bumped her shoulder against Lilliana's. "Cam Night, Damon's younger brother. He never pays any attention to us young ones. He is sleazy, but hot damn, how cute is he." She sighed dreamily, leaning back into her chair.

Lilliana was about to look away, when Cam winked at her. She blushed and ducked her head down. Attention from someone like him was not something she was wanting whatsoever.

After the assembly they had lunch and a tour of the grounds with Lilliana's Team Leaders, Marcus and Lisa, who were very informative and helpful making sure to give Lilliana as much information as possible, on pool and stable times and rules. Chatting about the program selections for tennis, archery, working in the H.D buildings and other workshops available throughout the year.

It took three hours just getting around the grounds closest to the house whilst being informed about so many activities and all the do's and don'ts.

She was exhausted as they arrived back in the main foyer.

Jessica accompanied them upstairs, as it was close to freshening up time before dinner would be served. They left Lilliana alone after a quick hug and told her they would meet her on the stairs in a half hour.

Lilliana, sitting at her window seat glanced around her room feeling overwhelmed and exhausted, needed to close her eyes for ten minutes.

She awoke with a start to the sound of singing, '*Happy Birthday to you.*' She sat up, brushing her hair off her face and smiled at the sight before her.

Nurse Rachael, holding a small, pretty chocolate cake with candles of horses prancing around the top, their manes ablaze in flame.

Josephine on one side, Jessica on the other and Damon standing behind, leaning against the doorway watching.

She jumped up to blow the candles out, and make a wish.

"Okay, how about a photo before we go down to dinner." Damon suggested.

Lilliana sat in the middle of the seat with Jessica and Josephine perched either side, arms around each other smiling into the camera.

"Enjoy the cake my friend." Josephine smiled. "Jessica and I made it fresh this morning before you came down to join us."

"It looks delicious, thanks so much." Lilliana hugged her gently.

Jessica jumped up. "Damon said we can go for a night swim for your birthday after supper, would you be up for that after the day you've had?"

"After weeks being underground in the hospital, I would love to." Lilliana said happily.

Two hours later after enjoying a succulent roast with fresh garden vegetables, the girls were delighted to have the entire pool to themselves. Lilliana felt so relaxed in the calming water, the breeze soft and warm, the pool area surrounded with urns abundant in red and peppermint geraniums, hanging baskets spilling their gorgeous colours and sending their perfumed scent in the air, giving the night a feel of the Mediterranean.

They took this opportunity of solidarity, to talk about matters close to the heart.

Jessica had tears in her voice as she mentioned Stephan. "I miss him so much. I hope he's happy and not worried about me"

"He will be fine Jessica. Missing you, but fine." Lilliana tried to reassure her friend, wondering similar thoughts about her mother.

"It's all a bit strange though, isn't it Jessica? To think we are here after hearing stories for years about the Given Establishments for the wicked, the broken, the victims." She shook her head. "After all we have been through and done, I am having trouble fathoming it. It's so surreal."

"I can't even imagine life on the outside." Josephine interjected. "It sounds horrid, all those evil people, doing revolting things to the innocent, and then getting away with it." She shrugged.

"Well, clearly they don't always get away with it." Jessica said.

"And so they shouldn't." Josephine said. "We have a division here for those criminals. I've never been near that section, but I've heard stories that they get what they deserve."

"I was told something disturbing yesterday," Jessica began hesitantly. "that there was a priest who had committed the vilest acts towards the children of his parish. That Cam had taken this Priest out to the forest, tied him to a dead tree and set him on fire, and toasted marshmallows on the flames?"

Josephine shrugged. "Could be true, nothing Cam does would surprise me. I have heard that story also, although I don't know whether it is indeed, fact."

"I think if it is true, he got what he deserved. I like Cam, he took me for my first tour when I left the hospital." Jessica wiped her fingers gently through the water. "He seems cool. I think we are lucky we don't have creeps running this place."

Lilliana shuddered at the thought of Dr. Richard.

Josephine nodded. "Damon is basically like a brother to me, and if you do the right thing, follow the rules, you'll be fine. It's only if someone is a complete ass that you will see him become a tower of fury. Which is intimidating, let me tell you." Josephine stepped out of the water and reached for her towel.

"I've never seen him so angry as the time Cam was caught sleeping with a minor. It's the first and only time I have seen him strike someone. It happened not long after their father had died." She began rubbing herself briskly before adding, "Apart from his anger issues, Cam's other problem is, he can't seem to stop himself sleeping with any pretty face he sets his eyes on."

Wrapping the towel around her body she sat on a lounge, facing the girls.

"It's a real treat being out here this late, we're not usually allowed to be here alone, unsupervised."

"Well," A voice startled them from a few feet away. "you were never really alone my sweet Josephine" Cam stepped forward from the shadows. He chuckled as he heard all three girls gasp.

"Don't worry petals, I was told to watch you all and escort you safely indoors." He bowed to Lilliana, his hand on his chest.

"Nice to finally meet you Lilliana, any friend of Jose's, is a friend of mine. Let's go." He returned Jessica's smile as the girls scrambled out of the water to get their towels around them, feet into thongs and head towards him as he clicked his fingers and pointed to the direction of main house. He waited for the two new girls to walk ahead of him, before reaching out to take hold of Josephine's wrist, tugging her to a stop.

He noticed Lilliana turn around with watchful eyes, waiting for Josephine.

"Carry on girls, we'll be right behind you." Cam smiled charmingly.

Josephine gave Cam a no-nonsense look. "What do you want Cam?"

"Now that list is endless, but for starters, how about you stop spooking the new kids on the block, with tales of my little issues. Damon would not be happy." He tapped his finger on her nose, then lightly grabbed her chin, tugging it down so her lips would part.

She simply raised an eyebrow, giving him no reaction, even though her heart was beating fast in her chest.

He smiled before gently shoving her away and headed after Lilliana and Jessica.

Josephine rolled her eyes and ran after the girls, catching up, they all went indoors.

Twenty minutes later after a warm shower, a goodnight to her friends, Lilliana was snuggled under soft linen.

Although the day had been overwhelming with all the information regarding what was expected of her, the time spent with her friends overruled her anxieties. It was those hours spent with Jessica and Josephine that was holding her together at the moment.

Staring up at the ceiling, hands holding the blanket under her chin, she tried to block out all that had happened, but it was in these quiet moments, her thoughts crept back to unwanted images. She squeezed her eyes shut, but that was worse and rolled over towards the comforting light of the desk lamp.

She noticed the two frames that had both been empty when she had arrived at her room. Now, one held the photograph Damon had taken earlier of her and her friends. Beside it stood a note, "Happy Birthday Lilliana, Damon."

She felt a glow of warmth and although felt safe, kept the desk lamp on, hoping for a deep sleep, that did not come.

CHAPTER 8

Lilliana woke to the sound of waves washing up against the shore, gulls calling and a sweet haunting flute playing something whimsical.

She sat up, rubbing her eyes wondering where the sound was coming from?

A gentle knock at the door had Lilliana sliding out of bed to go hit the opening switch.

Josephine stood in the doorway, a towel slung over her shoulder, pink nail polish on her toes, and her usual smile on her face.

"Rise and shine my friend, shower time, then a light breakfast followed by our morning run. Damon has told me that you are to stick with me your first month, settle you in. How does that sound?"

Lilliana was relieved. "That sounds wonderful, I was a bit nervous about being without you or Jessica." She whirled her finger in the air. "What's with the surround sound?"

"That's our positive, mindful way to start the day, supposedly puts your nervous system at ease. It starts at six thirty, stops at seven. Come on, grab your robe, let's go."

The two girls headed off towards the showers, a short distance away from Lilliana's room. There were people everywhere, walking briskly to one destination or another.

The bathroom was stunning, and set out like the hospital's bathroom with every tenth tile a frosted green lotus flower.

Lilliana would have liked nothing better than to sink into the sunken spa in the centre of the room, but it was packed with about twenty gossiping, giggling girls.

As she and Josephine were about to step into their private shower, a gorgeous, rich voice called out softly, "Get out now, please." Had them turning around.

And there she stood, a face to die for, long legs that went to heaven, pale creamy skin, gorgeous flowing red hair down her back, hands on hips, proud, full breasts. Fox. Naked and stunning.

"Well come on, what are you waiting for? *Out.*" She snapped.

All the girls that were in the spa, quickly jumped up, climbed up the stairs and scattered, reaching for robes or dashing under the body driers.

Fox walked into the water like a goddess and gracefully sank into the bubbles, oblivious to watchful eyes.

Lilliana looked at Josephine, eyebrow raised.

"That's Fox." Josephine shrugged before disappearing into a shower stall.

A half hour later, Lilliana was seated at the dining table, eating a breakfast of light, fluffy eggs, wheat toast and fruit. The dining hall was filled with light chatter and Lilliana tried to ignore the many eyes, often flicking her way, making her feel nervous.

Everyone was dressed in the same outfits. White Shorts, tee shirts and running shoes.

Making the figure that entered the room stand out all the more.

Black riding pants, boots and a tight black riding shirt.

Lilliana's mouth went dry looking at Damon.

He'd walked over to the self-serve buffet, and munched on a strawberry, raising his coffee cup to his lips, he turned around surveying the room, until his eyes fell on Lilliana.

Her heart raced and she quickly dropped her gaze, bringing her own cup of tea to her lips. She told herself to get a grip and wondered why the hell she was freaking out at the sight of him.

"Lilliana, did you hear me?" Josephine gently bumped her arm.

"Sorry, what was that?" Lilliana apologized to her friend.

"That guy over there, keeps staring at you." She pointed behind her toast, so Lilliana could see, but the boy could not.

Lilliana glanced over and her eyes connected with Orlando's. She paled; her heart beat quickened. Memories flooded her. None of them good. Standing up abruptly, she overturned her chair. Like a rabbit she turned and made to bolt out of the room, but instead, bumped straight into a solid wall of delicious smelling chest. Strong hands grabbed her upper arms to stop her from toppling, his coffee cup sloshed messily on the table as he had abruptly placed it down before grabbing her.

"It's all right Lilliana." Damon said quietly near her ear. "It's fine, sit, eat. I'll be right here." He'd watched as Orlando had entered and spotted Lilliana and knew she would react this way.

She tipped her head back and lost her breath. By the stars, he had the most gorgeous, deep blue eyes. So dark, his eyebrows so black, slightly frowning.

"Sorry, I'm okay." She said, a little shakily.

He let go her arms and bent to pick up her chair, opening his palm, offering her a seat.

She sat. Josephine rubbed her arm. "You alright?" She asked.

"Yes. Sorry, just freaked out for a second." Lilliana shook he head. She reached for her toast and sank her teeth in.

Damon picked up his cup and taking a mouthful, watched Orlando who had now dropped his own, handsome head, nibbling on a piece of bacon.

Damon inwardly sighed, feeling for both his new comers as he walked over to a staff member, dressed in running gear, spoke quietly to him then left the room.

Twenty minutes later, Marcus walked into the room with Lisa, who blew a shrill whistle. "Okay runners, out the front in formation now." She called.

Lilliana watched as everyone dropped their utensils, stood briskly, and started exiting the room.

Her arm was tugged up by Josephine. "Come on champ, let's go get 'em."

When they walked out of the room, past another dining area, there were many Given and staff dressed in either riding or archery gear, gardening clothes, suits, lab coats and other outfits for a typical busy day at the Given.

Once they walked down the steps out the front of the building, the sight was spectacular. The sun was up and shining, with a hint of a breeze.

And thank the stars for that as it was already warming up at seven fifty in the morning.

Rows of magnolia and oaks, dripping in Spanish moss, colourful rose bushes aligned the path to the pool house and beyond that, the stables where a row of horses stood, prancing excitedly for a morning run, their riders sitting atop.

Damon, on a giant black Beast. The horse, Lilliana recalled, from the article in the magazine at the hospital.

His sunglasses not letting anyone see where his eyes were resting, as his hand stroking his magnificent horse's neck.

All the runners were lined up in three rows, of twenty. The whistle blew and before Lilliana knew it, everyone was taking off in a very brisk walk.

"We walk for the first fifteen minutes," Josephine said to her, stretching her arms above her head. "then, we run. Don't sweat it though, if it's too much for you, Damon said I could pull you out and walk."

Lilliana balked at the idea of appearing weak to anyone, especially Damon.

It wouldn't matter if she was full of stitches, she was not going to stop for anything.

Everyone seemed to stay in their lines, not stepping out of place, as the terrain went from soft green grass, past beautiful gardens and ponds, to open fields of lawn, staggered trees and a creek up ahead, that they began to run parallel to.

"It is so beautiful here," Lilliana sighed. "how is it so stunning and green here, when outside this property, apart from the swamps in Louisiana, mostly everything is brown and dusty?"

"Well, that's the billions of litres of water that's been purified for decades underground here since before they built this place," Josephine puffed a little. "some natural spring or other. They built ginormous concrete tanks way back when, sank them into the ground and saved water over the years also."

"How big is this place, I can't even see the walls I've heard people talking about."

"It is huge." Josephine said, swatting away a fly.

As they set into a steady pace, they could see the riders up ahead, jumping over fallen logs and trotting off towards what looked to be an equestrian area.

"Gorgeous huh?" Josephine nodded towards the horses. "We have endurance riding also. Spectacular to watch aren't they?"

"Oh yeah, they sure are." Lilliana agreed, puffing and sweating.

"What class is Jessica in? I haven't seen her today."

"Oh, you'll see her after lunch in your first Group Therapy." Josephine said.

"Great." Lilliana wasn't sure if that was a good thing or a bad thing. They had been fine with each other. Not uncomfortable at all, but she didn't know if group therapy would help their situation or not.

After a half hour running in the warm southern air, covered in sweat, the Givens arrived at a lake. Gorgeous and blue, with Lilly pads scattered here and there, proud flowers glistening like jewels on the water's surface. There was a large section in the middle of the lake, that was completely clear of all plants, offering smooth water in which one could easily glide through.

Marcus blew his whistle. Everyone lined up, facing him, waiting.

"Time for a swim people," He called out. "halfway, then back again. Let's go."

And with that, he waded in until the water rose up to his stomach, then dove under, coming up a good distance away, with a strong stroke.

"Great, if I knew I was going to be splashing around with snakes and toads today, I wouldn't have bothered showering." Josephine and Lilliana turned to the voice behind them. And there stood a very pretty pixie like creature. Short, blue spiky hair, freckles scattered across a very pretty nose, lips smacking away at a piece of gum.

"Hey," She said when she noticed the two girls watching her. "I'm Allie."

"Hi, I'm Josephine and this here is my friend Lilliana." Josephine saluted, Lilliana held up a hand in greeting.

"Come on," Josephine nodded to the water. "better to get this over with, otherwise be the last ones out with everyone watching."

"Well, you go right ahead, I can't swim, so I'll sit this one out." And with that, Allie plonked on the grass.

Josephine dove in, Lilliana followed. The water was so glorious, Lilliana felt cooled immediately. Settling into a rhythm, her stroke, smooth and strong. She was exhausted after all the running, which she was not used to at all, but swimming, it relaxed her, left her mind peaceful.

After twenty minutes to the middle and back, she pulled herself out of the water, to plop beside Allie, panting. She lay on her back and put her arm across her eyes.

Five minutes later, Josephine joined them. "How fast are you?" She said to Lilliana.

Lilliana smiled at Josephine and raised herself up on her elbows. "I absolutely love to swim."

She looked at Allie. "Maybe they'll let me teach you?" She asked the other girl.

Allie shrugged. It was her second week out of the hospital herself. She hadn't really made friends with anyone. It was nice to chat easily to girls that looked half decent.

"That would be okay." She said to Lilliana, before pointing in the direction across the lake. "That's really what I'd love to be doing though."

The girls followed the direction of her finger, towards those magnificent horses and riders.

"Yes, me too." Lilliana said. "I've always wanted horses. My cousin had them, he'd never let me ride them though."

"Pig." Was Allie's reply. "My god but that there is a very, sexy man."

Lilliana watched Damon swing back up in his saddle, and gently kick his horse into a quick trot.

But Allie's eyes were on someone quite different.

Cam, squatting by the water, his horse drinking whilst he was chatting to a young woman sitting in the water, throwing her head back laughing at something amusing he said.

"Now ladies," Allie said. "that is a man worth knowing."

Josephine rolled her eyes, but said nothing to this.

Allie stood, her intention of walking over and saying hello to Mr. Yummy, when Lisa blew the whistle, loud and clear.

"Alright everyone," She called. "time to get back, shower and then get to your class with refreshments on the way." She blew her whistle and the run back to main house began.

CHAPTER 9

Lilliana nodded at her reflection, letting out a nervous breath. Comfortable ankle boots, jeans and a white shirt felt appropriate for her first compulsory group therapy. She was slightly terrified. She didn't need to use mascara, as her eye lashes were so thick and long, but she quickly wiped a little black eye liner on her upper lid, setting her big green eyes off beautifully. She left her hair down, to float around her shoulders and down her back in a silky wave. Her curtain of protection.

There was a knock at the door and once Lilliana hit the switch for it to slide open, it revealed a very pretty Jessica.

"Hi," Jessica smiled, giving Lilliana a warm hug before sitting on the edge of

the bed. "how nervous are you right now?"

"Probably as nervous as you are." Lilliana walked over and sat on her window seat. "Are you okay Jess?"

"I am Lilly. Well, as okay as can be expected."

Lilliana nodded. A silence fell between them.

"Have you seen that girl Fox today?" Jessica said excitedly, trying to lift the mood. "Oh my god, she is simply stunning. I wonder how hard it would be to get into her line of work. I was told next week a lucky few could watch her do a photo shoot."

"Mm." Was all Lilliana could say, glancing out the window, watching Josephine in the distance running to the stables with two dogs at her heels.

Jessica sighed. "Come on, let's get this over with before you go into a coma."

She jumped off the bed and grabbed Lilliana's arm and they headed off.

When the girls reached the bottom of the stairs, Marcus was waiting for them. "This way, please ladies."

They followed him past the library where a group of Given were sitting around, chatting quietly about their subjects.

As they approached a large fountain in the middle of the large entrance, Lilliana appreciated the beautiful Koi, swimming lazily, without a care in the world. Marcus led them to what seemed nothing more than a wall when a door slid open, revealing a hidden room.

'Brilliant.' Was all she could think.

Marcus stepped aside, and indicated with his hand that the girls were to enter.

And so they did, stepping into a beautiful room, that although was large and spacious, was made to feel cosy with its placement of carved chairs and settees in rich fabrics, sitting on plush rugs. A desk sat between two large windows facing the stables and a grand old fireplace stood on the opposite wall.

Dr. Hillary smiled at the two girls. Dr. Richard did not. They were seated among the group of Given in the circle, waiting patiently for the session to start.

"Welcome Lilliana, Jessica." Damon said from behind them, with Allie in tow.

"Please come in and take a seat, now that we are all here, we can begin."

Lilliana looked around the circle, fifteen people plus the two doctors. This didn't look like a cosy group. Her eyes fell on Orlando and she immediately felt Jessica freeze beside her. She put her arm behind her friend's back, rubbing it gently.

"Girls, come." Dr. Richard motioned to the three empty seats.

Allie strolled over and plonked into one, beside a tall thin boy dressed all in black, wearing more eye liner than Lilliana. Allie pulled one ankle on top of her knee and began tapping a blue nail polished finger on her thigh.

There were two empty seats remaining. One, beside a mean looking girl chewing her nails beyond the quick, the other, beside Orlando.

Lilliana knew what she had to do and walked over sitting beside the boy who helped take her and her friend. She paled, crossing one leg over the other and kept her eyes on Jessica, who in turn sat next to the girl.

A tall, pale good looking boy sat to the other side of Lilliana, who had a creepy way of cracking his knuckles and clearing his throat. His name was Eric. He stared with interest at Lilliana.

"Welcome everyone." Damon smiled. He stood in between the doctors seats.

Lilliana couldn't help but notice how handsome he looked. Blue jeans that fit snugly around his hips, with a pair of casual shoes, crisp white shirt tucked in, showing off a tight chest and lean waist. His shirt unbuttoned just below his neck, revealing a strong, gorgeous throat.

'Oh my God,' She thought inwardly. 'Stop it.'

"Welcome to what we hope, is a very productive session. We are here to help you talk about your experiences. To not be ashamed of anything you have done to be here. Or anything that was done against you. These sessions will run every day for our first month out of the hospital, to help you adjust to our main house. After that, you will attend group therapy once a week."

He glanced at each of them as he spoke.

"Any Questions?" He waited.

"Yeah," The girl beside Jessica moaned, "when can I fuck you, Mr High and Mighty Night?" She shifted forward in her seat, rotating her backside into the chair. "I can ride you real hard. You'd like it, I promise." She chuckled.

Damon sighed. "Natalie I think you and I have had this talk." He was not at all shocked by her complete lack of dignity.

Lilliana felt like her face was on fire, just at the girl's comments, let alone her action on the chair. She glanced across at Jessica and Allie.

Jessica was equally as flushed as Lilliana, Allie simply raised an eyebrow inspecting her nails, looking totally bored.

"Well," The tall thin boy in black beside Allie turned towards the girl who many named, Nasty Natalie. "now that you have educated us all on your cheap crush for Mr. Night and embarrassed yourself in the long run, perhaps we can be here for the others now?"

Nasty Natalie flipped the boy the bird.

"Thank you Christopher, for wanting to proceed. That will be enough from you Natalie. Is that clear?" Damon stared at her frowning.

Lilliana didn't think Natalie had much of a brain, she would never want Mr. Night glaring at her like that. Ever.

Natalie shrugged, not looking bothered by the rejection whatsoever.

"Alright then, doctors, if you please, let's get this session started."

With that, Damon walked over to the desk and sat in a large leather chair, quietly typing on his glass monitor. And so the two hour session began.

"Rupert, perhaps you would like to share your feelings with us today?" Dr. Richard asked.

A sweet looking boy on the other side of Orlando straightened in his seat.

He fidgeted with his glasses, his red hair falling into his eyes. "Um, no, sorry not really." He stammered.

"Well, 'not really' is not an option in this session Rupert. This is for your benefit." Dr. Richard said sternly.

The more that man flapped his pie hole, the less Lilliana liked him.

"I'll go now, if that's alright." Lilliana heard Orlando say.

Her eyes met Jessica's. It looked like she was holding her breath.

"That's fine Orlando," Dr. Hillary smiled. "go ahead, start wherever in your story you are most comfortable. Remember everyone, you have many sessions this week and in the coming months. It is important to talk as openly and as honestly as you can.

We understand some of you have met in the outside world, so it can become difficult. But here, in our home it is our duty to listen to and respect each other, to empower your lives and move forward in a positive way." She gave the group a small smile before she nodded to Orlando, giving him the go ahead.

Orlando ran his sweaty palms up and down his thighs in a nervous way.

"My sister, Nadia, was eight when my mother went missing. I suspected foul play by my father's organization. My mother was beautiful and my father would have made a fortune selling her on the black-market sector. My Nadia was just as beautiful. She was a kind, sweet kid who I could always have a laugh with. My mates' sisters' annoyed the crap out of them, and always thought I was lucky having such a cool sister." His voice sounded light and carefree as he mentioned his sister fondly.

"I knew what the disgusting crimes my father did with his members. I tried to protect Nadia. Keep her busy and out of our father's way when he was home. It was easy at the start, when she was so young but, she was a real beauty at ten and then, she disappeared." His voice fell flat and he was quiet for a few moments before continuing.

"I knew my father had her, or had sold her, I had to get close to him in order to get to her, if she wasn't already dead." His hand trembled as he ran it through his hair.

Lilliana sat rigid in her seat, her heart beating fast for the young Nadia.

Even for Orlando maybe, she wasn't sure yet.

"It was then that I started to tell my father I was old enough to be part of his group, that I'd do anything to prove to him that I was responsible enough. He made sure I did some deep things to prove myself." Orlando stopped talking. His eyes down cast as he swallowed the lump that was stuck in his throat.

"Do you want to continue today Orlando?" Dr. Hillary asked.

"Yeah," Orlando nodded, "I'd like some girls here to try to

understand me a little more." His eyes flicked to Lilliana, then coolly rested on Jessica's face.

"Continue then." Dr. Richard said briskly.

"I need some caffeine," Allie said. "this show is about to get deep."

"Thank you Allie," Damon said from across the room. "once Orlando is finished, we will break for a few minutes."

Lilliana glanced over at Damon, she had been aware of him sitting quietly at his desk, the only sound the occasional typing of his fingers.

She turned back in her seat as Orlando cleared his throat to continue.

"For three years I helped my father pick up women, young girls and boys. His empire was growing larger every year and he was the 'go-to' man for snuff films, torture flicks. All broadcasted to the underworld crime channel. My father had quite a few connections with the Officials and was never raided. He did have an associate that was raided in New York. He was taken, sent to the Ruins Facility in Africa. I've heard not many live long there."

"Yes, that's right Orlando. It's not a good place to be. But if you do the crime and you're over thirty-five. That's where you go." Dr. Hillary said.

Orlando shifted in his seat and glanced at Lilliana.

"Basically, for years, I did whatever my father told me to do, in order to try to get information on what happened to Nadia. Where she might be. I was getting close when my father took Lilliana and Jessica. When I took them.

My father and his group sexually tortured these girls, made them..."

"*STOP.*" Lilliana cried out, her nerves screaming. She was so not ready to hear her own story from this boy's lips, let alone the whole room hearing it.

He dropped his head looking down at his lap fidgeting with his sleeve.

His hair flopped across his eyes, he reached up to flick it back, meeting Jessica's eyes.

Damon stiffened, the raw pain in Lilliana's voice warned him an explosion could be close. It was.

Jessica leapt out of her seat and pointed an accusing finger at Orlando.

"What you did to us, how could you? Even to get your own sister back."

Her eyes were furious, hands now fists at her sides shaking with pure anger.

Orlando's eyes were sorrowful, but then came his anger.

He too leapt to his feet, causing Lilliana to jump up also and go quickly towards her friend standing slightly in front of her, protecting her.

"I tried to *protect* you girls!" He yelled, stepping forward. "I did everything I could to help lessen your fear, your pain."

"Oh yeah!" Jessica spat, "Your sister and mother would have been really proud. Lessen our pain, our fear. *Oh* my god are you *insane*?" Jessica practically screamed.

Lilliana reached out and grabbed Jessica's hand reassuringly, feeling her own anger brewing, but keeping it in check.

"Alright everyone, calm down and sit." Dr. Richard ordered.

Lilliana glared at the distasteful man, still not forgiving him for their last two run ins. "What's the point of therapy if we have to calm down?" She turned to face him, hands on hips, giving him an angry glare, her green eyes practically glowing. "Isn't this healthy, getting it out of our systems anyway we can?" Her voice was rising. "Isn't this what you want?" She held her arms up in question.

"Miss Lilliana, if I wanted theatrics, I'd start up a drama department." Dr. Richard eyed her steadily.

Orlando and Jessica eyed each other warily, their breathing irregular.

Lilliana felt a firm hand on her back.

"Lilliana, please, sit down." Damon gestured to her seat.

She looked up at him, her breathing not quite regular, her emotions raw and angry.

She glanced across to Jessica, who was slowly sitting back down. Orlando had already taken his seat. She nodded and Damon stepped back to allow her to pass.

As she sat, Eric leant towards her and simply said. "Nice."

Lilliana shrugged and glanced around the circle.

Dr. Hillary was typing fast on her tablet.

The other Givens were staring at herself, Jessica and Orlando. No doubt wanting to ask a million questions.

When her eyes landed on Allie, the girl gave her a small salute and a wink.

"Orlando, do you have anything further to add in this session?" Damon asked.

"No," He said quietly. "that's all for today."

"Alright everyone, how about some refreshments before the last half of our session today, before your free time." Damon ran his hand through his hair, then glanced at his watch.

"I'll give you a free session Mr.-Fuck-me-sideways-Night." Nasty Natalie was leaning forward, trying to expose her overlarge bosom to Damon.

A groan of more than one person arose from the group.

It felt like the session would never end.

CHAPTER 10

After weeks of settling into her new life, getting up early, running, classes, group therapy and a multitude of activities, Lilliana was beyond exhausted.

Her free time was the only thing keeping her sane, and she would spend it with anyone of her friends when their free time coincided with hers. Today, she got to spend some quality time with Allie, who was in the stall beside her, chatting away about Christopher from group therapy who'd been teaching her how to swim.

Lilliana listened contently as she ran the brush appreciatively over the pretty mare's neck.

"I just can't believe how patient Christopher is with me, considering I can get a bit lippy. He's the coolest guy I've ever met, then again, I haven't had that much experience with cool guys. But I'll tell you now Lilliana, the first time he had his hands under my back, keeping me afloat well, I don't know, I could have cried. I felt so safe." She sighed. "I think he's the one."

Lilliana's hand paused, before continuing. "The One?"

"Yeah, you know the one I want to kiss, by my choice. The one I feel I can trust.

I mean, you see the look on everyone's faces in therapy when I tell bits of my story. That first time when I said out loud, that I had murdered my own babies, he just got it. That I wasn't a monster, I was trying to protect them from the life I had. He didn't judge me."

"I think you're amazing Allie, to survive what you have survived. I went through nothing compared to what you did. All those terrible years you suffered." Lilliana shook her head.

"Oh God Lilly, don't you ever say that. Pain is pain." Allie walked over to the stall Lilliana was in. "What you and Jessica went through. I can't fathom it. I mean, I was a kid when I was taken from my Grandmother. I was in that hell-hole for years and as weird as it sounds, the other kids that were taken, became my family." She shook her head.

"But you two, I mean, you had a normal life, then BANG," She slapped her palms together, "Months of hell, than life as we know it here, changed forever." She looked Lilliana directly in the eye and said softly,

"Don't ever discredit that you have been through an awful amount in your young life. We are lucky to be alive, be here and to tell our tale." She returned to her task.

"That's the thing Allie, I don't want to tell my tale. I've skirted around it the last few weeks in our sessions. I absolutely cannot stand to say any more than I must, in front of Dr. Richard. I simply hate the man. I'm almost sick when I look at him."

"Why? What is it about him that freaks you out so much?" Allie asked. "Apart from his charming personality of course." She winked.

Lilliana chuckled. "Oh yeah, there is that. No, it's just that he reminds me of those men. Their coldness. His aloofness." She paused before quietly adding. "He scares me."

"Don't worry about him Lilliana, you are safe here." Allie reassured her.

"I know. It's just hard to shake the feeling of uneasiness sometimes." Lilliana shrugged, sliding the brush over the horses back.

"I know, I get it." Allie said. And she did. All too well. "Just remember, we are all here for you, we're in this together." She finished brushing her horse and dumped the brush into a hanging bucket on the stall wall. "Now my friend, I'm heading back, will you be okay?"

"I'll be fine, thanks Allie."

"Cool, I'll see you at dinner then?"

"Yeah sure, I'll see you later." Lilliana smiled, finishing up with the mare.

As Allie left, Lilliana wiped her hands on her jeans and walked down the corridor along the stalls, enjoying the comforting smell of the stables. There was nothing more relaxing than the quiet noises of the horses settling in for the afternoon. The stables were like a cathedral to her soul. Especially on the rare days when no one else was around. Thomas had gone out to supervise the hay baling, after he had given the girls some tasks to do with the horses, so she was completely alone and loving the solitude. She wandered along to the furthest stall at the end of the stables.

This stall was four times the size of any other and pacing restlessly around it was Beast.

"Hey Boy," She crooned softly, offering him her palm to smell. "how are you big fella, come on, come on over."

"No worries Baby, I'm coming, this big fella wants to be stroked by you." Eric, who'd been quietly watching from a distance, walked towards Lilliana.

She froze, startled for a second before turning to face Eric. 'Play cool,' She thought to herself.

"Eric, don't bother. You're wasting your time with me."

"Am I?" He stopped a few paces away and looked at her closely.

"You know, you are absolutely stunning. No," He held up his hands as she raised a perfect, dark eyebrow. "You. Are. Stunning."

Lilliana looked at Beast, hoping she looked bored enough for him to leave her alone, or just leave altogether.

"Lilliana." Eric whispered in her ear, his chest suddenly pressed against her back, pinning her against the stall door.

His hands grabbed her tightly around her slim waist, pulling her buttocks against his crotch, rubbing it against her. He inhaled deeply into her hair and groaned. "Fuck me but you are beautiful." His hand slid down, cupping against her sex, his fingers pushing her jeans into her.

"*Stop it.*" Lilliana cried, fear and anger creeping in. "Get off me, and I mean *now.*" She tried to buck him off, which only excited him further.

His hands ran up her flat stomach to her breasts.

As his hold changed, Lilliana spun around and with all the might she had, slammed her hands against his chest, pushing him back. As he stumbled she gave him a front kick as hard as she could to his knee cap.

Rubbing his knee, he smiled as he watched her take off at a run, before leaping forward and in three strides, caught her about the waist.

They both went down hard and Lilliana's head spun for a few seconds in disbelief that this was actually happening.

Eric shifted his weight to turn her over onto her back. She wiggled to get free, but he simply sat there, folded his arms over his chest, his weight keeping her in place. A sly grin spread across his face.

She was breathing heavily, forcing her tears not too come. How do I play this to get away from him? She thought, hating what popped into her mind, but knew fighting him was useless. He out-weighed her and she was in no position to have the upper hand. She needed him closer. "Okay," She forced a pretty, watery smile running her tongue over her lips. "I'll stop playing hard to get now."

"Now that's more like it baby." He said quietly, not believing his luck as he slowly moved down for a kiss.

As he drew closer, she took a deep breath and smashed her open palm into his surprised face, making him see stars, and his nose bleed. He fell off her, clutching at his streaming nose, cursing.

Lilliana leapt up and ran, feeling slightly victorious as she bolted out the stable door, glancing behind her to make sure Eric was still down, she collided into a solid wall of chest.

Damon. A little breathless himself.

As soon as his arms went to catch her, she flung herself against him surprising herself with the tears of relief that escaped her. Her fists curled up tightly into his sweater, her face pressed against her fists.

"Hey," He said, stroking her back. "it's alright, what's going on?"

"Eric," She said quietly. "Eric."

It was all he got out of her, before Eric caught up to them. His stride slowed once he spotted Damon.

"Eric, what has happened here?" Damon stared at the younger man, hair scattered in hay, rubbing his kneecap whilst his other hand held his bloody nose, his tee-shirt wearing a good amount of it too.

He pointed a finger at Lilliana. "She attacked me for no good reason Mr. Night."

"You liar." Lilliana spun around to face Eric, the warmth of Damon's back giving her courage to look her attacker in the eye.

Damon noticed that Lilliana had hay in her hair also. He frowned.

"I was helping Thomas out in my free time and Allie left a little while ago. I was talking to Beast when Eric came up, hit on me and when I rejected him, forced himself on me." Her breath hitched on a frustrated sob.

"Eric, don't lie to me, is what Lilliana saying the truth?" Damon asked. He already knew the truth but needed to hear it from the boy's lips.

Eric folded his arms and glared at Lilliana.

She folded hers and glared back at him. To think she thought he was good looking when she first saw him in group. Pig.

"Well Sir, in a round-about way, yes."

"It either is, or it isn't Eric, which is it?" Damon, hands on hips was running out of patience.

"Yes Mr. Night." Eric admitted.

"Well, apologize to Lilliana. Now." Damon placed his hands on Lilliana's shoulders, and squeezed gently.

Eric looked at Lilliana and bowed a little, giving her his gorgeous, even smile.

"I apologize Lilliana, for misreading your feelings for me. Please forgive me."

Lilliana stared at Eric. She could not believe he had the gall to stand there with his arrogant smirk and bullshit his way out of this. Before she thought twice about, or before Damon could stop her, she quickly stepped forward and slapped Eric as hard as she could across his face.

"Sure Eric," She smiled just as sweetly back. "I forgive you for being a total jerk." She quickly stepped back again as Eric took a step forward.

"That's enough." Damon snapped. "Both of you, enough. Eric, get on into the house and report to Lisa please. You'll have night detention for a week and no free time in between classes for a month. We do not tolerate this conduct here. Is that understood?"

"Yes Mr. Night." Eric walked on by, rubbing his slapped face. His eyes flicked to Lilliana before he sauntered off.

Lilliana slowly turned around to face Damon. Not wanting to look at him but having no choice, her eyes raised to his, waiting.

He looked frustrated, one hand on his hip, his other dragging his long, elegant fingers through his hair.

She'd seen him do that a lot when he was frustrated.

"Well Lilliana, are you alright?"

Yes Sir, I am now." She replied.

"Are you hurt? Do you want to see Nurse Rachael?"

"No." Lilliana ran her own fingers through her hair, shaking out some of the hay she'd collected, being rolled around on the ground. "I'm just tired." She said. "I did nothing to lead him on Sir, I swear it."

"It's alright Lilliana, I believe you. Don't worry. Eric will be punished for his behaviour." He couldn't tell her that there were video feeds throughout the entire establishment and he had seen Eric rush to Lilliana's back, whilst doing a review with the head of security, in his office. Knowing Thomas and stable staff were out, thought he'd better get to the stables pronto. He had enjoyed the fact that she was so at peace in the stables and hoped Eric hadn't destroyed the one place she seemed happy in.

"Eric will be banned from this area." He hoped that at least would be a comfort to her. "Come, let's get you to your afternoon class." He stepped aside and together they walked to the house.

***

A fortnight later, they were all seated in group therapy, quietly listening as Natalie was finishing talking, about her step brother and sister.

"The fact is, this world is fucked up, and no amount of rule change or punishment is going to change anything. If you're a fuck up, then you're a fuck up. End Of."

"Well as enlightening as that is Natalie, it's not quite helpful in these sessions, is it?" Dr. Richard said dryly, peering at her over his horn-rimmed glasses.

Natalie stared at him silently, before adding. "It was helpful to me, imagining your ass-hole clench at the thought of my step-sister going down on me."

Lilliana inwardly groaned, as the group echoed her thoughts aloud. It was the same thing every session. Natalie just kept right on being nasty.

"Alright everyone. Natalie. Enough." Damon called from across the room.

Allie looked at Lilliana shaking her head as Jessica's face turned bright red.

Dr. Hillary cleared her throat. "Orlando, would you like to continue from where you left off last week?"

"Yeah, sure." He fidgeted for a moment before folding his arms and stuffing his fists under his armpits. "The week before I helped Lilliana and Jessica escape, I found a recording. It was of Nadia. She had been sold to a Diplomat in New York. I couldn't believe it was my little sister, all done up and stunning, she looked like a super model, and drugged out of her mind, doing whatever they wanted her to do. I felt dead watching them. There were other girls recorded with her, and the last episode was a snuff film. I couldn't watch it. But it was after that recording that I made the decision to kill my father. Reporting him just didn't seem enough anymore. I wanted him to suffer. To simply not exist on this earth." Orlando sat silently for a few minutes. Jessica had a pained look on her face and raised her eyebrows at Lilliana.

Lilliana just nodded once, as if to say, 'It's okay, let him be.'

"And, well you know the rest. I killed my father, helped Lilliana and Jessica kill the others, called the Officials and they contacted this Given and here we are today." He raised his saddened eyes across to Dr. Hillary.

"Thank you Orlando. Even though it has taken you many, many weeks. You have been strong in talking about all your feelings and experiences so openly with us. Well done." Dr. Hillary clapped, nodding to the rest of the group. Everyone applauded.

Jessica felt an odd sensation rising in her stomach as she clapped, watching the boy who helped change her life forever. For the better or worse was yet to be determined.

***

Two weeks before Christmas, all new Given received a letter, asking them to write out a wish list and return it to their head representative. In Lilliana and Jessica's case, that was Marcus and Lisa.

All the girls wanted, was to see their family, but they'd already been told that requests to see or speak to family members was not possible. It's just the way it was.

Sitting around Allie's room, Jessica, Josephine and Lilliana were enjoying some quiet catch up time before bed, sharing their past weeks activities, enjoying the odd spread of food Allie had sourced. Fresh baked chocolate chip cookies, chilli tortilla chips and a jug of cinnamon milk.

"It is so cool that everything is made here. I love that about this place, the sustainability." Jessica groaned appreciatively as she bit into a soft, moist biscuit.

Josephine laughed. "You sound like a Team Leader giving a tour."

"How'd you get all this?" Josephine asked Allie. "I've been here for years and Cook still terrifies me."

"Ah my young friend, it's not what you know, it's who you know. And I know a very handsome lad who has started cooking in the kitchen recently."

"Christopher?" Lilliana poured some milk.

"The sexy one and only." Allie smiled nibbling on a chip.

Jessica took another biscuit. "You are such a legend Allie."

"Yeah, true story." Allie smiled, stretching out on the floor tossing back her short blue hair.

"Okay, Christmas lists. I don't understand how this works. Ask and we shall receive, right?" Allie looked at Josephine.

Josephine crunched down on a chip. "Basically, yeah."

"How does that work, I mean, Santa doesn't exist in this place. What, everybody just gets what they want, no matter what they've done?" Lilliana asked.

"Absolutely not." Josephine answered. "But Damon makes sure he gives all new Given a good first Christmas here. That's the way it's been for generations. His dad, and his dad before him did it, so he has kept up the tradition. The families of new Givens have the opportunity to give funds to the establishment, if they don't, Damon puts things right."

"I'd be happy with some art supplies." Jessica licked chocolate from her finger.

"Oh, I'd love to see some of your artwork Jessica." Josephine smiled. "Lilliana said you're very good."

Jessica beamed at Lilliana. "Well, Lilliana would say that, but yes, I have actually been blessed with my brother's talent." Her smile faded slightly.

Lilliana rubbed Jessica's shoulder as she passed her a cup of milk. "Your art will keep Stephan with you Jess, every time you paint or draw."

Jessica nodded. "Thanks Lilly."

"What about you Lilliana?" Allie nudged her.

"Oh, I'd be happy with anything to be honest. A riding lesson with Mr. Night would be great." She looked at friends, hoping they wouldn't detect the fact that her face flushed at the mere mention of his name.

"You wouldn't be the first to ask for a riding lessons this Christmas with Mr. Night." Allie said mischievously.

The girls all exchanged a look, before Allie yelled out, "Nasty Natalie." She jumped up and started riding the arm of the window seat, moaning, "I'll ride you fast Sir, Mr. Fucker-luscious, Sir."

The girls were all in a heap laughing, before Josephine sat up to wipe the tears from her eyes. "My god, you have to stop that, he's basically my brother."

Their laughter continued for a few minutes, before Allie said softly, "I only want one thing for Christmas, and that's to see my two sisters and brother that came here with me."

The room fell silent as they all looked at her. In the eight months they had all been getting to know one another, this was the first time they had heard any mention, that Allie had arrived here with others, and that those significant others were her taken brother and sisters.

Allie looked at each of her friends faces, before quietly continuing. "They didn't clear psych. They're still being treated and I've been informed I am too young to receive clearance to that section."

"Oh Allie, it's true. Only people who are qualified in the field of therapy or have a senior role, are allowed in the psych and Black Ops section. Unless your sisters and brother become well enough, you won't be able to see them." Josephine felt said for her friend.

Allie forced a smile. "I know. It's alright. I'm not giving up hope."

"No," Jessica smiled, "you shouldn't. If it's one thing I am learning here, there is always hope. On that note, Lilliana will you walk me to my room. I just want to talk to you about something."

"Of course." Lilliana stood with the girls and gave Allie and Josephine a kiss and hug. "Goodnight. See you tomorrow."

"Goodnight." The girls replied as Jessica took her arm, and they left the room.

Walking along the corridor, they heard screaming from the floors below.

The girls stopped walking, looked at each other as the screaming grew louder, and rushed towards the stairway, to peer below.

What they saw was a spectacular sight of a furious looking Fox, dressed in red leather high heeled boots, wearing a red, shiny leather G string and matching bikini top. On her head sat a pointy Christmas hat, her long, red tresses hanging to her waist.

It seemed Cam was the focus point of her anger, along with an unhappy looking photographer.

Damon came out of his office as another piece of Christmas crystal was flung at Cam, shattering on the wall behind him as he ducked.

"What, may I ask, is going on now Cameron." Damon directed his gaze towards his brother, ignoring the angry red head.

Cam pointed at Fox. "Princess Fox has decided she doesn't want to shoot the ad she signed up for." He turned on Fox stepping towards her, hands on his hips. "The commercial her contract states, she has to do."

"What? Where the hell did it say anything about me laying on that fat naked bastard in there, pretending to be Santa?" Fox screamed at Cam.

"Hardly naked." Cam muttered as Fox screamed over him, to Damon.

"Damon, seriously, why is your brother in charge of my shoots?" She glared at Damon.

"Fox, you know why, now get back in there, calm down and do what you signed up for. Or first thing tomorrow you are welcome to resign from your prestigious role and simply run H.B.R. Now, stop complaining, so the rest of us can get on with our work. Now!"

Lilliana had seen Damon frustrated before, but his voice was laced with anger.

Jessica sneezed, unfortunate timing and had Damon looking up to where the two girls stood. He frowned. "Shouldn't you both be in bed."

The girls leapt back out of sight and took off towards Jessica's room. Opening the door quickly they darted in the room, releasing a nervous giggle as the door shut behind them.

"Oh my Lord." Jessica shook her head. "I love a bit of drama, especially when it's nothing as serious as Franklin trying to slice Rupert open every morning."

"Yeah, was is it with that?" Lilliana sat on the edge of Jessica's bed. "Poor Rupert."

"I know. I'm surprised he hasn't been injured yet." They were referring to Franklin, a new Given who'd arrived in main house a week ago. Every morning, he had some sort of episode where he tried to stick Rupert with a bread knife. He was assigned a Watcher who was always with him, so things never got out of hand. It had provided some entertainment to a few of the Given when breakfasting.

"Okay." Jessica said nervously.

Lilliana watched as she went to her desk draw, pulled out a pile of letters and handed them to her. She flipped through the letters, not recognizing the handwriting, until she spotted a name down the bottom of one.

Lilliana looked up at Jessica, holding up the sheet. "Orlando?"

Jessica was sitting very still, holding her breath.

"It kind of just happened. It started after our third group, he kind of found me in the garden and asked if we could go for a walk. I thought, why not right? I'm here, he's here, we have other sessions and classes together. I was curious to what he had to say." She swallowed, unsure how Lilliana was taking the news so far, so hurriedly continued. "He'd told me he didn't sleep at night, his moods swinging from black to blacker. He's had to get extra therapy to help him stop self-harming. He has suffered Lilliana. Did you know, he was brought in the same night as us?"

Lilliana simply shook her head.

Jessica continued. "You were passed out in shock and I was hallucinating. The entire time he said he prayed that you and I would be alright. Prayed that we could survive the horror done to us. I couldn't talk to him at the start, could barely look at him, so for the first three months I started writing to him, about my life before he took us, to what I felt afterwards, about him and his father's group. It was the best form of communication, and he wrote back, as you can see."

"He sure did." Lilliana held up the stack of letters.

"Anyway, we've been spending a fair bit of time together and," She paused uncertain, before finishing in a rush. "I kind of have the hots for him. Does that make me a sicko?"

Lilliana could hear the uncertainty in her friend's voice and looking at her, standing there twisting her hands together nervously, waiting to see how she would react, broke her heart for Jessica.

"I wasn't sure if you'd understand," Jessica continued. "but I hated keeping it a secret from you, and so well. Now you know." She looked at Lilliana, waiting for the questions or accusations.

There were none. She should have known.

Lilliana stood, walked over to Jessica and handed her the pile of letters.

Jessica took them, put them on the desk and turned to face her friend, relieved when

Lilliana stepped forward and put her arms around her.

"If you're happy Jess, that's all that matters. After everything, you deserve to be happy."

Jessica hugged Lilliana. "Thanks Lilly." She sighed, content that her secret was out, and that Lilliana didn't seem hurt by her choice.

Lilliana squeezed Jessica before stepping back, looking her in the eyes. "I guess I'll have to forgive him too now?"

"Only if you find it in your heart to Lilliana. If you don't, I'll understand."

"No, I'll give it a shot, for you. Maybe in our next group I'll surprise us all." They shared a smile.

"I'd better get back to my room, curfews way over."

"Okay Lilly, thank you. See you in the morning." Jessica waved as the door closed.

Lilliana turned, startled as a voice surprised her in the darkening hallway.

"A bit late out, aren't we?" Cam stood against the wall, arms folded.

"Yes, I'm sorry, but it was not intentionally done." Lilliana turned to walk to her room.

Cam kept pace. "You do know about the punishment we have for breaking curfew, don't you?"

Lilliana stopped, and turned to face Cam. "Yes Sir, I am sorry."

He waved his hand and gave a charming smile. "Listen, I was coming to look for you anyway. I was wondering what you thought about doing some modelling. I think you'd be great at it; you have a stunning face."

Lilliana raised an eyebrow, thinking of the scene below twenty minutes ago. "Me? I don't think so, but thank you anyway." With that she turned and headed towards her room.

"Listen, wait up." A persistent Cam caught up to her as she reached her door.

"Let's just do a small shoot tomorrow, I promise it will take an hour of your time. I've checked, you've got a free after breakfast. Its good way to make some of your own credit."

"Credit?"

"Yes, we all have a role to lead within our walls. And some of those roles benefit our facility in a big way. Modelling is one of those ways that extend past our establishment, and reap big rewards, allowing us to help more of society. Which earns you credit within. So, a modelling shoot that pulls in some chunky cash to do good, allows you to have some freedom. Pay it forward, to a cause of your choosing, help a friend, that sort of thing."

It almost sounded too good to be true, but it got her thinking. Christmas was coming, and if she couldn't gift her family, maybe she could gift her new friends? And Nurse Rachael did so much for everyone. Maybe she'd even get brave enough to gift Damon with something?

"Okay." She nodded "But I'm not taking any clothes off."

"Sweet Lilliana, with your face you won't need to. I'll find you in the morning after breakfast. Goodnight." With that, he sauntered off looking very pleased with himself.

She wondered what tomorrow would bring, as she got into bed, snuggling under the soft, heavy covers. Not knowing that the photo shoot the following day, would change her life, and others forever.

She took a deep, relaxing breath and closed her eyes, hoping for a peaceful night sleep. But her sleep was not that kind, and she once again fell into a dark pit of never ending nightmares.

CHAPTER 11

The following morning, Lilliana was impressed that she could force a smile on her face. The usual images and unwanted thoughts haunted her after waking, showering, dressing and heading into breakfast.

She pushed them away as far as she could to make the most of this new day. But they were never too far away, poking into her mind every now and then, like bony fingers, reminding her why she was actually here in the first place.

She sat down to enjoy a delicious bowl of fresh fruit and yoghurt, listening to Allie flirt across the table with Christopher. She could understand the appeal. His polite, quiet personality shone through the dark, mysterious look he created through wearing Goth makeup.

Lilliana thought he and Allie made a very cute couple. She glanced further down the table, spotting Orlando and Jessica just looking at each other, not talking at all.

Now that Jessica had told Lilliana about her feelings for Orlando, she wasn't hiding in public with him.

Josephine was slurping on a fruit smoothly and turned to Lilliana. "I'm permitted to come help you with your shoot this morning, Cam found me before shower time, cool huh?"

"Oh, that is fantastic, I won't be so nervous now." Lilliana finished her fruit.

"I heard the helicopter land earlier; I can't wait to see what sort of set they will be creating for you." Josephine rubbed her hands together.

Lilliana looked at Josephine. "It makes me nervous you just saying those words, how am I supposed to relax and do this?"

"You'll be fine. Come on, let's go have a peek." Josephine jumped up, pulling Lilliana with her. They waved to Allie and Jessica as they left the room and bumped into Rupert, who stood in front of Josephine.

Pushing his glasses up on his handsome nose, his serious eyes meeting hers. "Hello Josephine. Mr. Night said you'd take me to the H.D later today and show me what you do there. I myself, am interested in a future in grafted plants."

Lilliana did not hear him pause for one breath.

"Oh my how exciting, you know," Josephine said, becoming animated, "not only do we produce the highest quality fruits and vegetables here for our family, we also make millions of dollars feeding the outside world. Many vegetables and fruits can no longer be grown in the soils outside, but here, we do so much for all." Lilliana could feel Josephine's passion build with each word.

"I mean, it is phenomenal what we do in H.D. I'm sure we will benefit from your insight in the future Rupert." She smiled at him, taking Lilliana's arm, leaving a happy Rupert behind.

The girls continued heading outside. Josephine couldn't wipe the smile off her face, which wasn't unusual as she always seemed to be smiling.

Fox was waiting at the bottom of the steps, looking as stunning as always in a fresh green, silk sundress and strappy green sandals, her gorgeous red hair floating around her like a halo of fire. She looked as if she had just walked along a beach in Phuket. "Hello. You're joining me in this photo shoot and I expect you to listen up and do exactly what you are told." She smiled tightly. "Is that clear, Lilliana?"

Lilliana looked hesitantly at Josephine, then back at Fox. "Well, I'll certainly try my best."

"Relax Fox, sheesh." Josephine linked her arm through Lilliana's. "She'll smash it."

"Great." Fox pulled out a phone and pressed a button with a long elegant frosted green nail. "Bring the jeep up, we're ready."

Within two minutes the jeep arrived and after pulling up, a driver got out and opened a door for Fox, who climbed in, followed by the girls.

They drove silently for several minutes, in a direction Lilliana had not been before.

The gravel road taking them through thick trees and tufts of high grasses scattered with wildflowers. Lilliana felt exhilarated seeing a different landscape. Not that every other part of the property she had seen wasn't picture perfect and gorgeous, but being in a vehicle for the first time in months, felt like she was actually going somewhere else.

They passed an open field, outlined by tress, where a small tower stood alongside a tarmac and opposite the tarmac, a helipad and perched upon it, a black, sleek helicopter with bright red lettering on the side reading: 'Given.'

Lilliana shivered, wondering if it was the helicopter that had bought her, Orlando and Jessica in the night they'd arrived.

After twenty minutes the jeep pulled up near a large canvas tent, that had coffee, lemonade, baked goods and a fruit platter, along with a photographers gear and prop people.

Cam turned as the girls got out of the jeep and walked over to the organised group. "Excellent, here are my girls now." He smiled, holding out his hand towards the three approaching figures.

A photographer, Tim, smiled as he reached out towards Fox, and pulled her in for a gentle kiss on the check. "Hello Gorgeous."

"Tim," She crooned. "how's my favourite photographer?" She smiled ever so sweetly at the handsome man.

"Very good, thank-you dear heart," He turned towards Lilliana. "and you, you very pretty little thing, must be Lilliana?" He extended his hand out.

Lilliana stepped forward to shake it. "Yes Sir." She nodded.

His laughter was loud and infectious. "No, no, no Sir's today, unless you are addressing Cameron here, of course. You just call me Tim." He smiled gently.

"Okay Tim, thank you." Lilliana smiled back.

"You remember our special friend, Josephine?" Cam said, gently pulling Josephine forward.

"Hi." She said simply.

"Of course, Josephine. How are you?" Tim smiled, as he thanked an assistant who handed him a cup of coffee.

"Alright, let's get to it." Cam said, rubbing his palms together. "Josephine, if you wouldn't mind just waiting over here, grab a coffee or lemonade. Help yourself to the snacks. Fox, you know what to do. Lilliana, if you could step into wardrobe and make up, it won't take long till we can get started." He pointed to a small tent behind the larger one.

Lilliana nodded and headed over to the entrance of the tent. Stepping in, she wondered if she was in a tent at all. Cool and elegant, the ceiling appeared to be nothing but a clear blue sky, the walls appeared to have water flowing down the sides, and the floor, a colourful sea of daisies. She turned and opened the flap to look outside again. Sunshine, trees everywhere. Dropping the flap, she went to run her hand along the dripping tent wall, only to feel soft sheets of canvas.

"It's a way to create something pretty and peaceful, as many parts of our world are so forlorn to look at."

Lilliana jumped at the soft, unexpected voice behind her. A very tall, thin mousey haired lady, with a kind face and clear blue eyes stepped closer. "We all need a mirage at times." She smiled and reached out her hand towards Lilliana. "My name is Valerie and I will be doing your makeup." She quietly watched as the young woman took in her surroundings.

Lilliana shook her hand, as she glanced around the room taking in the dressing table full of makeup, skin care and perfumes. Hanging on a rack, pearl white, feather-soft angel wings, with layers upon layers of shiny white silk. It was stunning.

"Are you ready to get started Lilliana?" Valerie asked gently.

"Yes," Lilliana smiled at Valerie. "thank you."

"Just over here." Valerie pointed to a highchair sitting in front of large, lit mirrors.

As Lilliana sat, Valerie skilfully and efficiently began a deep cleanse, followed by a quick face and neck massage, before magically transforming Lilliana from stunning sixteen-year-old girl, to an older, very sensual, erotic looking female.

Lilliana couldn't take her eyes off her reflection in the mirror. "Um, where am I?"

Valerie chuckled. "You are right there Lilliana. That's why I chose my career as a makeup artist. It's another way to create a mirage of sorts. Although, don't get me wrong, you are a very pretty girl, but look out, you will be stunning when you reach full maturity." She stepped back after applying the last layer of deep red to Lilliana's lips. "Is modelling something you'd consider for your future?"

"I'm not really sure, there are so many options. It's all a bit overwhelming now."

"Yes, the first twelve months are the hardest, but it will get easier, I promise." Valerie smiled kindly, before calling out, "Nigel, we are ready for you now."

Within seconds, the tent flap parted and a very short, interesting looking man strode in, his eyes appeared cat-like and his eyebrows were as long and thin as a cats whiskers. His silver hair tied back in a ponytail at the nape of his neck and hung low, brushing his back side as he walked. He wore a charming smile and when he spoke, his voice was soft and velvety as he nattered to himself as he approached Lilliana.

"Yes, right, here we go, oh yes, make up perfect. Very pretty. Right now. Costume. Oh, you will look gorgeous, dashing, sublime. Right here we go, step this way."

And so he nattered on for the next fifteen minutes whilst he had her strip and step into the strapless layers of silk. They seemed to magically stay up, settling on her breasts, and flowing down in a white cascade waterfall.

He attached the large wings to a clip on the back of the silken layers, then pulled a stool in front of Lilliana, climbed up to perch on it, pulled out a comb and started styling her hair. It took him minutes. "So perfect, not much to do here at all really, just a silken pile of waves itself."

Lilliana glanced at Valerie who stayed and watched the entire time, making sure Lilliana was comfortable.

When the three stepped out of the tent and joined the group, there was total silence.

Cam's mouth was slightly hanging open, as Tim nodded his approval.

Fox had both eyebrows raised as she coolly sipped on her latte.

Josephine had the largest smile on her face Lilliana had ever seen.

"Excellent," Tim said. "let's get started." He nodded to a second photographer, Pier who smiled and said. "This way."

The small group followed and not twenty steps into the thicker part of the trees, Lilliana's breath was taken away by the design of the set and props before her.

Hanging between two very large thick peppercorn tree's, adorned with Spanish moss, was a swing with ropes camouflaged in vibrant and sweetly scented purple wisteria, which was also placed abundantly behind the swing, where a waterfall was flowing blissfully, spraying cool jets of water as it hit the pristine waters below. Lilliana knew the waterfall wasn't real as they were in the middle of the forest, but the way it was set and the ingenious minds that put these props together had her almost believing it was.

Cam turned to Lilliana and Fox. "Right, I want you," He pointed to Lilliana. "to feel completely at ease. Pretend we are not here. Josephine." He snapped his fingers.

Josephine strolled over to Cam, giving Lilliana a wink. "Yes Sir." She said, not quite sarcastically, flipping her brown curls over one shoulder in an exaggerated movement, causing the strap of her singlet top to fall, revealing too much cleavage.

Cam sucked in his breath and looked at Fox, as he impatiently stepped towards Josephine and sharply tugged her strap back up, whilst addressing Fox.

"I want Lilliana to appear sexy, seductive and innocent. Can you guide her through?"

"Easy." Fox nodded.

"Good." He looked at Josephine. "Your job, is to stand in Lilliana's peripheral vision, help her relax. Can you manage that?" He asked.

"Well, I don't know Mr. Night but I sure will try my hardest Sir."

Lilliana hid her smile as she detected Josephine's sarcasm, watching as one of the assistants stood a four foot ladder under the swing, motioning for her to climb up.

She was grateful for Fox's help, as she adjusted the layers of silk around her so she wouldn't get tangled.

"Just relax, have fun." Fox said, as she placed her hands near Lilliana's breasts, and pushed them higher.

Lilliana tried not to feel too uncomfortable with another person's hands adjusting her body, and felt herself flush under Cam's watchful eyes, as he handed Fox a very high, sexy white pair heels.

"I'm not expected to walk in these am I?" Lilliana knew she would fall flat on her face if she had to.

"Not walk. Just stand after the swing shoot. Relax." Fox had them on Lilliana's feet in no time before stepping back off the ladder.

Cam took two steps on the ladder and met Lilliana's eyes.

Her breath held, feeling slightly uncomfortable being so close to him. Having the photography crew around eased her racing heart.

He said quietly. "You are absolutely breathtaking. I cannot wait for Damon to see you."

"Thank you." She said quietly, not quite meeting his eyes.

He reached around her throat and as she froze, he whispered, "Hey, it's okay, this is a commercial for diamonds."

She heard the click of the clasp behind her and felt the heaviness of the cold jewels around her throat.

He was handed a pair of earrings, intricate and stunning in design, he held them up for Lilliana to see, before adjusting them onto Lilliana's ears.

She appreciated the sparkle of tiny diamonds forming the shape of butterfly wings.

If she'd known they were worth a quarter of a million dollars, she may not have been so happy to wear them.

"Everyone ready?" Tim called out, keen to get this shoot going.

Lilliana felt her nerves rush to the surface as Cam jumped off the ladder and an assistant took it away. He looked up at her and smiled, clapping his hands once. "Let's do this." He called, then and added for her ears only. "Just breathe Lilliana and have fun."

She nodded and wondered what she had been thinking committing to this, as everyone around her got into position. Tim began guiding her through some easy, fun snaps and in no time, she began to relax and it all began to feel natural. She was pleasantly surprised that Fox was so good at making it fun, and grateful that Josephine was directly in her line of sight at every turn.

There were close ups of Lilliana's beautiful bright green eyes looking directly into the camera, diamonds sparkling around her throat and ears. Shots capturing the wings in the background, giving her that absolute angelic look of a fallen, dark angel.

The swing, when in full motion had her long, black hair floating gloriously around the white wings, layers upon layers of white silk flowing around creating stunning shots with the waterfall in the background.

Once she was assisted off the swing, there were shots leaning against the trees, in different positions. Eyes open, dreamy, smiling, frowning, angry. Whatever instructions she was given, she carried them out effortlessly.

Tim was impressed. It had been a while since they'd had any promise of new potential at this Given, and he knew they were onto something special with this girl.

Cam called for a five-minute break and told Fox to get ready. As she left for hair and makeup, Lilliana smiled as Josephine handed her a tall glass of water.

"Thanks. I thought this was supposed to take one hour."

"Yeah, but I don't think they can get enough of you." Josephine gestured around them. "You look amazing Lilliana." She seemed genuinely impressed.

Lilliana smiled at her friend's enthusiasm. "I think with the experts they have; anyone would look this amazing. I must admit, I am having fun. Fox is pretty nice, she's being so helpful."

"Mm, what's her play I wonder." Josephine, ever the wise and having known Fox for years wasn't as easily impressed as Lilliana.

Cam walked over after chatting to Tim and Pier to make sure Lilliana was doing okay. "How are you? Can you handle another twenty minutes or so?"

"Of course." She drained her cup as Valerie walked over to do a quick freshen up of makeup.

"Oh, my stars." Josephine exclaimed.

Lilliana turned to see what Josephine was referring to and was as equally stunned as her friend.

Fox stood in an outfit identical to Lilliana's, but in pure black. Her red hair standing out even more, curled in long thick waves. Her jewellery bold, red rubies.

"By the Stars," Lilliana whispered. "you are so beautiful."

"Yes. Now, wipe your drool, girls. Lilliana, it's time for our shoot." She turned and walked towards Tim.

Josephine looked at Lilliana. "Can you handle that?"

"I can try."

Within minutes they were at it. Fox was a pro, and completely in her element, but she was impressed working with Lilliana. And it usually took a lot to impress her.

From a variety of positions; standing back to back, both with a cupid bow and arrow aimed at the camera, looking sexy and dangerous. Nose to nose, staring into the others' eyes, lips not quite touching, the jewels always standing out.

Lilliana had to stand on a stepladder for a few shots so that the girls would be the same height. Fox, standing in front of a blazing red fire, her rubies glistening.

Lilliana, in front of the waterfall, bursting with diamonds around her and along her angel wings. Eyes closed and in the praying position, her white silken gown flying around her. When Lilliana finally heard, "That's a wrap." she was ecstatic.

What a day. She shook hands with the photographers, thanked Valerie and Nigel for their guidance once she was back in her clothes, thanked Cam for the opportunity.

"That was so much fun." Josephine smiled as they headed towards the jeep. "Now back to reality."

As they climbed into the jeep, Fox who was sitting in the front turned to Lilliana. "You were pretty amazing out there. I think you should consider a career in this sector."

"As fun as it was, I'd rather do something that can really benefit people that need help."

Fox looked Lilliana straight in the eye. "Modelling helps the establishment more than you can know. I mean, feel free to work in the lab, be a nurse, work with the horses, work with the vegetables, or for them."

"Jesus Fox." Josephine exclaimed in horror.

Fox ignored Josephine and continued, "If you want a better life, where you can help others let me just say, this is one of the easier options."

With that, Fox turned to the front of the jeep as it took off towards main house.

The girls silently exchanged a look and Josephine tapped a finger to her temple before pointing it at Fox. Lilliana smiled and looked out the window as the scenery rushed by, not quite ready to think about having to make a serious decision about her future.

CHAPTER 12

Jessica and Lilliana headed in for breakfast as chaotic yelling burst from someone's lungs. Stepping into the dining room, the girls were shocked to see a sprawling match between a new Given, Leon, recently arrived at main house, and Franklin, whose Watcher had mysteriously disappeared.

The breakfast crowd was diving out of the way, as the boys threw each other against the table, knocking over chairs, smashing glasses and plates before Leon smashed a winning blow into Franklin's jaw, knocking him to the ground and pinning Franklin face down onto his stomach, grunting as he jammed a knee into his back.

Lilliana looked across the room to see Josephine sitting on the ground with Rupert, laying in front of her, obviously he hadn't escaped Franklins intentions before Leon saved the day, as blood seeped through a white serviette that Josephine was pressing to Rupert's arm.

Finally, Franklin's Watcher burst into the room, pushed past the excited crowd and grabbed Franklin by the wrists, dragging him up once Leon moved off his back. "Solitaire for you, mate." He sounded far from happy, and as he turned to march Franklin from the room, it was clear why. Blood was dripping slowly from a patch on his skull, where Franklin had thumped him in the head with some object.

"Thanks for the scar Franklin," Rupert called after him, going paler by the minute. "people dig scars." He chuckled weakly.

Lilliana, rushed over to Josephine's side, as the room settled down and people started putting things back in order.

"Lilliana, can you help me get him down to Nurse Rachael?" Josephine asked worriedly.

"Of course." Lilliana helped Rupert up, and the two girls, one under each arm, helped him out of the room, a few snide chuckles following them out.

Rupert grunted in pain, holding the serviette tightly against his arm as they approached the entrance to the hospital stairs.

"What's happened here? Rupert, are you alright?" Cam walked quickly towards the trio, placing a hand on Rupert's head.

"Yeah, I'm alright, I was just too slow this morning, so Franklin and I provided the breakfast entertainment." Rupert said sheepishly.

Cam shook his head. "Righto, are you girls taking him down to see Nurse Rachael?" He looked at Lilliana, then his eyes rested on Josephine.

"We sure are Sir." Josephine felt puzzled with the way Cam was watching her.

"Off you go then, quickly." Cam nodded, heading in the direction of the dining area as the girls and Rupert took the stairs.

Lilliana felt an unwelcoming sensation of Déjà Vu as they walked down the steep stairwell and along the wide corridor, walking past staff that were heading off in various directions. The lavender essential oils that were diffusing at the nurses station, failed to mask the strong scent of blood, antiseptic and disinfectant, all forming a repugnant combination that assaulted Lilliana's nostrils.

Billy was filling out some information on a tablet as they approached, and looking up, his intention was to offer them a smile until he saw Rupert's arm.

"Rupert, let's get you into a room." He placed the tablet down and walked around thanking the girls for their help.

"Can I come, please Billy? I have a free this morning anyway."

Josephine quickly kept pace as Billy efficiently steered Rupert to an empty room.

"Sure Jose." Billy smiled. "Lilliana, would you like to come?" He threw over his shoulder.

"Oh, no thank you, I have Group. Good luck Rupert. See you later Jose."

"Thanks Lilliana." Rupert called out weakly.

"Bye Lilly." Josephine waved as she followed Rupert and Billy into a room.

Lilliana stood for a second, hoping Rupert would be okay, before turning and walking back in the direction they'd come. She stopped short outside a room, as pained, desperate moans reached her ears, before the moans turned to heartbreaking sobs.

Looking down the corridor, Lilliana wondered if there was a staff member in the room. She knocked once on the door, waited a beat, then slowly pushed it open and stepped quietly inside. What she saw shocked her to her core.

A girl not much older than herself, was laying on the bed, totally naked. That's not what shocked her.

There were cult-like symbols burnt into her flesh, a thick, clear soothing gel smeared all over her. Lilliana felt her insides cringe on their own accord, as she looked over the wounds. Red raw and painful looking. The girls desolate cries no doubt had as much to do with her physical injuries, as her emotional scars.

Her cries slowed as her wary eyes rested on Lilliana's face.

"I'm Lilliana," She said quietly. "can I do something for you? Would you like me to get a nurse?"

The girl's cries stopped, moaning quietly now, not taking her eyes off Lilliana, she sat up on the bed, swinging her legs over the side.

Lilliana knew she should not have entered the room, but couldn't help herself. She didn't know how long the girl had been in the hospital, but she clearly remembered how she had felt when she had first woken and how uncertain of everything she had been.

This poor, sad girl must have suffered so very much and Lilliana had no idea how she could help her. She just knew that she wanted to.

"It's okay, would you like some water?" Walking to the plastic water pitcher, she filled the cup and slowly offered it to the girl.

The girl hesitantly reached for the cup, and taking it, gulped the contents down.

"Lilliana," A firm voice snapped behind her. "what are you doing in here?"

Lilliana turned, facing Dr. Ryan, a wave of guilt washed over her. She knew the rules, and right now she was breaking one of them.

"I'm sorry Dr. Ryan, I just heard her cries and wanted to make sure she was okay. I wasn't thinking."

"Well, that's a dangerous thing to do around here Lilliana, that's why we have the rules we do." He walked closer to the bed, a scowl on his face.

Lilliana was about to apologise again, when the girl began to scream hysterically.

"*No. No. No*" She threw the cup as hard as she could at the doctor's face, before grabbing at her hair, pulling it frantically.

"Lilliana, leave." Dr. Ryan said calmly, as he pulled a needle from his white jacket, taking off the lid he squirted a small amount of the liquid out, as he stepped towards the terrified girl.

The girl, scrambled off the bed had backed herself into the corner, screaming all the more as the doctor advanced towards her. The terrified look in the girl's eyes, reminded Lilliana of Jessica's when they were being abused. It made the hairs on her neck stand on end.

"*Stop.*" Lilliana screamed at him. "You're scaring her. *Stop.*"

The closer the doctor got to the girl, the more out of control she became, pulling strands of hair from her scalp, running her fingers nails over her face, drawing blood.

Lilliana felt like she was close to a panic attack herself, with all the emotions flowing throughout the small room and knew she had to decide. Either leave or help the poor soul who looked as if she had already endured more than anyone on this earth should have.

She quickly raced in front of the advancing doctor and placed herself protectively in front of the girl, who had started throwing out kicks and punches to keep the doctor at bay.

Lilliana held up her hands to Dr. Ryan, trying to reassure him that she could control the situation. And she would have done, if the door hadn't opened, with a male nurse walking in setting the girl off further, kicking and screaming.

Lilliana felt pain shoot through her lower back as she received a hard blow from behind. She flew forward as Dr. Ryan moved in with the outstretched needle, his aim hit the wrong target and in an instant, Lilliana's world went quiet and tipped on its side.

The last thing she saw was the girl's concerned face, leaning down to her, still hysterically screaming. The scene was almost comical, and Lilliana felt a small giggle escape her, before her world went black.

**

Lilliana slowly opened her eyes, to the sight of Angel fish swimming about their peaceful world. She could hear someone typing and realized it must have been Damon, as she was on his couch in his hospital office. Her head, feeling fuzzy and heavy, was on a soft cushion and there was a warm throw rug on her legs. Rubbing her eyes, she sat up and regretted it immediately as the room began to spin.

She reached out to the coffee table to support herself from falling, but large hands gripped her shoulders, gently easing her back down.

"Relax Lilliana, you have just had the human equivalent to a horse tranquilizer. Just lie back. Thirsty?" Damon sat on the table looking down at her.

Lilliana looked up at him, his dark eyes unblinking as he watched her. She swallowed, grateful to be leaning back into the cushion. She looked away towards the water jug, relieved her eyes had somewhere else to go, rather than his warmly, intimidating gaze. She nodded. "I am."

Damon reached over and poured Lilliana a glass of water.

She could hear ice cubes hitting the bottom of the glass.

He put the glass on the table before standing and reaching down around her shoulders, gently pulled her up into a sitting position and propped the cushion behind her back.

Her face was so close to his throat, and he smelt divine. She could see him swallow and wondered how soft his skin was just there. She felt herself flush as he sat back down, handing her the glass.

He smiled a little. "It looks like you'd do anything to skip group Lilliana."

She flushed, feeling slightly guilty. She had missed group last week because Cam had set up the photo shoot that went well over her free period and into her group therapy session. And now, today. She sipped her water, looking at him over the rim. "I know it must seem that way, but honestly, that wasn't my intention. I am not trying to skip group. I'm not that creative."

Damon nodded. "I'm only kidding Lilliana. How's your head feeling now?"

"Like I could sleep forever." She crunched down on a piece of ice.

"Well, I can't arrange that, but how does the afternoon sound? We will get you to your room shortly. As much as you will just want to sleep, we will have you woken for a meal, your body will appreciate it."

Lilliana nodded, before quietly asking. "That girl. Will she be okay?"

He sighed, shaking his head "It's always hard to say at the beginning when a new Given arrives. She has suffered terribly. It never seems to end." He said quietly, almost to himself, before looking her in the eyes. "That's the first time you've broken a house rule Lilliana. Entering someone's hospital room without staff's permission is a no-no."

Lilliana froze, embarrassed to not only have let him down but also because she prided herself on doing the right thing. But she also felt her intentions were right in wanting to help another Given. She was saved from a response, and the sharp look in his eyes, as his phone rang.

He sighed before getting up and going to answer the call.

Lilliana took the opportunity to have a good look at him as he stood, one hand on his hip, head tilted listening to the voice on the other end. So serious. So handsome. Seeming to help so many. He looked across at her, catching her gaze as he dropped the phone down after clicking off.

"I have to go assist my brother with a situation. Will you be okay waiting for Nurse Rachael to get you to your room?"

"Yes Mr. Night. Thank you for your help, sorry for being such a nuisance." She glanced down at her glass of water, not feeling brave enough to apologise for breaking a house rule.

"Never a nuisance Lilliana." He said seriously before turning to leave.

Ten minutes later, Rachael came to take her to her room.

She helped her get into cosy pink pyjamas and tucked her into the soft bedding.

"I'll get one of your friend's to come up with lunch, and Damon or I will check on you throughout the afternoon." She stroked her hand along Lilliana's hair.

"I heard what you did today," She smiled kindly "what was your intention with that girl Lilliana?"

Lilliana squeezed the sheets in her hands, feeling exhausted. "I just wanted to help her," She whispered. "she seemed to be in so much pain. I wanted to ease her pain, wanted her to know she wasn't alone." She closed her eyes and was asleep in a second.

***

It was Christmas week and the atmosphere around the entire establishment was festive. Even Franklin, who had done time in solitaire for his violence towards Rupert, had stopped trying to attack him at breakfast. Franklin's Watcher was feeling quietly relieved.

It was a quiet afternoon and Lilliana was helping Josephine pull weeds in the H.D building A gorgeous, solid three storey glass house, with laboratories underground where the expert team experimented with sustainability crops and gardens for the depleted soils in the outside world.

Sitting on the lower level with the glass roof opened three levels above, it didn't allow the air to cool the girls whatsoever and in no time the steamy atmosphere had their hair plastered to their necks and tee shirts clinging wetly to their bodies.

Josephine blew out a breath. "You know I've never seen snow, but I'd sure love some right now, this heat."

Lilliana was about to respond when a short girl, with red hair yelled out abruptly. "*Josephine* where do these pumpkin seedlings go?"

She stood there, hands on her hips, hair getting frizzier by the minute.

"Oh yes right, um just leave them by the door Sammy, I'll fix them up later."

"Right." Sammy grunted and left.

Lilliana looked at Josephine as she pulled a nasty weed that was choking a baby Mulberry. "There are just so many charming people around here."

"True story." Josephine grinned. "We should be called 'Charmed' not 'Given.'"

"Well, if that applies to anybody around her Jose, it would certainly be you."

Lilliana smiled at her friend. "You are as cool as the breeze I wish were in here."

"Oh Lilly, I feel the same way." Josephine grabbed up their pile of weeds and carried them to the composting bin, before saying thoughtfully. "You know, before you came here, I was pretty lonely. Yeah sure, I'd talk to anyone, get along with most people but then, not everyone wants to talk to me. Except Damon of course." She smiled fondly, as she always did when talking about Damon. "But you and I, we connected so suddenly and I'm very grateful for that." She dumped the weeds into the bin and headed back to her tray.

"At my old school I was too busy to have any friends. Lots of acquaintances due to my father's roll and connections with the Officials, but not real friends. That's why I had so much fun meeting such a decent, kind girl as Jessica and then you and Allie." She shrugged. "I got so lucky in the end, after everything that happened." Her voice grew quiet as those dark images started to rise to the surface of her thoughts.

"Lilliana." Josephine said brightly, knowing her friend could fall into a quiet void if left to her thoughts.

Lilliana met Josephine's eyes, and saw a cheeky grin on her face.

"I'll race you to the top, first one up gets the coldest water spray."

Lilliana took the offered piece of relief from both her dark thoughts and the humidity, and raced after Josephine, who was squealing all the way up the narrow stairway that reached the top of the open hot house. Josephine slammed her hand against a green button, and in seconds they were both drenched with a gentle mist that fell from the network of hundreds of pipes flowing in all directions to wet the levels below and the hundreds of colourful hanging baskets that made all the levels look like a never ending rainbow.

The girls were laughing their heads off, faces raised to the sky and enjoyed the gift of peace the moment offered them.

***

Thirty minutes later and still drenched, the girls entered the foyer which was crowded beyond anything Lilliana had seen since arriving. The enormous Christmas tree had been decorated in the most beautiful glass ornaments and rose in the middle of the staircase, almost reaching the second level. It had been put up at the beginning of the week and the scent of the pine needles filled the air, giving it that joyful Christmas aroma.

The sight that had her mouth almost hitting the floor was the enormous canvas poster of herself, blown up to the height of the first level staircase.

"Oh My God Lilliana." Josephine was stunned. "You are bloody breathtaking."

Lilliana didn't know how to respond without appearing vain, but she had to silently agree with her friend. She stared at herself, not quite believing it was her, blown up to such an enormous size for basically, her entire world here to see.

There she was, looking like an actual Angel. Standing proud, hands in the prayer position, eyes so green, staring intently back at herself, luscious red lips, slightly parted, a soft smile played across her stunning features. Her glossy black hair, flowing around her like a silken cloud, mixing with the white layers of silk floating about her,

the Angel wings, fluttering behind her. The waterfall looked as if diamonds were pouring gently from it, the diamonds on her body, glistening, shining like a million stars. She hoped the clients that had paid for this shoot were satisfied.

"Hey Lilliana," Simon, a boy from her group smiled. "you look brilliant, well done."

She smiled at him, a little embarrassed. "There's a lot of photo-shop in that." She lied.

"Well photo-shop or not, you both look awesome." He nodded across to the other side of the Christmas tree, and Lilliana didn't know how she missed it.

Equally impressed with the poster on the other side, Lilliana marvelled at the sheer beauty of Fox. She looked every bit of the top model that she was. Face to die for, scowling into the camera like a sex goddess.

Strong black wings, hair as red as fire, as were the stunning red jewels adorning her glistening body. 'Not sex goddess,' Lilliana thought, after a quick assessment. 'She-Devil. Speaking of,' Lilliana thought as Fox approached her, walking with ease as the crowd parted for her to get through.

"Nice Lilliana, very nice. Let me know what you decide about your career. I'm sure once you receive your credit for the shoot, you may rethink." She flipped her hair before turning on her high heel, and left.

"Lilly," Josephine said near her ear. "Let's hit the showers before class."

Lilliana took one more peek at her poster, before running after Josephine.

CHAPTER 13

Lilliana was sitting on her bed, catching up on some reading before group, when a knock sounded at her door. She jumped up and hit the button for the door to slide open, revealing Marcus standing there, a bag in hand a big smile on his face.

"Wow, it's all arrived then?" Lilliana said excitedly.

"Yes, the helicopter delivered early this morning and all us little elves collected packages for our newbies." He walked over and placed the bag on her desk.

Turning, he said to her. "You are very generous with your gifts Lilliana." He handed her an envelope. "Cam asked me to bring that up to you. It's the remaining credit left over, after you purchased these gifts. He's hoping you'll stick to a career as a model." Marcus grinned, "After what I saw downstairs, I'm inclined to agree with him."

Lilliana smiled, shrugging a shoulder. "I'm leaning more towards one of the healing therapy positions. I think helping someone on a deeper level is a bit more important than having a bit of fun in front of a camera." She fingered the envelope. "But, who knows, right, maybe I could do both?"

"Maybe," He said. "you'll need to take that down to Mr. Night for safe keeping."

"Okay." Lilliana smiled at him. "Thanks Marcus, you've been such a help."

"Well, that's my role Lilliana, I'll catch you round." He smiled before walking out, the door sliding shut behind him.

Lilliana tossed the envelope onto the desk and grabbed the bag, excitedly tipping the contents onto her bed. Brown paper bags, ribbon, labels and a pen.

She smiled happily at the gifts she had chosen for her friends. For Allie, Jessica and Josephine, a sweet bracelet, with an intricate pattern of the infinity symbol. Each bracelet had a different healing stone placed in the cross section of the infinity symbol. Celestite for Josephine, Citrine for Allie and Aventurine for Jessica.

For Nurse Rachael Lilliana had asked for a necklace with a Rose Quartz shaped into a tear drop. She reached for a small satin box and lifting the lid, revealed a black replica of Beast, carved from black Tourmaline. It was stunning and more beautiful than Lilliana could have imagined. She ran her fingers along the shiny, black coat of the stallion's tiny twin. Placing the lid back on the box, she began wrapping all her gifts, enjoying the feeling of doing something normal, that other people around the world would be doing this time of year. Sadness gripped her heart as she thought of her mother, spending her first Christmas without her daughter in sixteen years. "I miss you, Mama." She whispered, looking out her window, up at the fluffy white clouds scattered across the bluest sky. Wishing her Mother could feel her love for her, wherever she was. She shook her head, trying to snap out of the melancholy feeling that was creeping in to stay. She couldn't go to group feeling like this; vulnerable and unable to protect herself or Jessica if Dr. Richard decided to be his typical jerk-wad self.

She gathered her wrapped gifts and placed them back into the bag that they had arrived in. Snatching up the envelope with the credit, she went downstairs. Placing her gifts under the Christmas tree, she felt her spirits lift as a few other Given arrived, laughing joyfully, placing a homemade or brought gift under the tree too.

She walked over to Damon's office door and knocked on the panel.

It slid silently open, Damon was on the phone, but waved her in.

She walked forward, the door sliding shut behind her. It felt strange just standing there, listening to Damon talk on the phone. Strange, but oddly comforting. The room almost had a relaxed feel to it. Almost. She wandered over to a chair beside the bookcase and ran her fingers along the spines, reading the titles.

Damon glanced at her, as he listened to an Official talk about a new case they were being sent for Black Ops. Trying to focus on the conversation, not the attractive girl in his office was a little difficult. Her class reports had always exceeded the staff's expectations. Her mind was sharp and she was dedicated to learning everything necessary in the required fields of humanistic psychology, psychiatry, therapy healing. The list went on, as was expected from this establishment.

The acts of kindness she bestowed on any Given, especially the new that entered their home, although expected, was to be commended.

He appreciated how much she had grown the past several months. Always holding herself in such a serious manner for her age. He'd seen it many times, the wounded protecting themselves by shutting down. Those rare moments he saw her laugh with her friends, completely let go, allowing her guard to fall, lightened his soul. Her beauty shone through tenfold in those moments.

Group therapy was another story. She had some work to do, and he was worried that Richard was going to apply more pressure in this session. At least he would be there to buffer the situation. Hopefully.

He hung up the phone after typing down some information and smiled across at Lilliana.

"Hello Lilliana, how was your morning?"

"Good, thank you Sir." She turned to face him

He sat back in his chair, crossing an ankle over his knee, linking his hands across his waist. His dark hair fell over his forehead.

She would have loved to brush it back. She shook that thought out of her mind and walked over to his desk and handed him her envelope. "Marcus told me that you would take care of my credit."

Taking the envelope, he pressed his thumb print to a pad, on the bottom draw of his desk and once it clicked open, popped the envelope into a filed compartment.

"Did you enjoy the shoot Lilliana?" He pointed to the chair opposite his so she could sit if she wished.

She sat and nodded. "I didn't think it would be so much fun. Everybody was very friendly and helpful, Fox was amazing."

"Yes, Cam told me how obliging she was. Your photographs are breathtaking. Have you seen all the shots yet?"

"No, just the one outside." She said referring to the one beside the Christmas tree.

"Well, after group today, I'll make sure to send you the album." He referred to the box that was sitting upstairs on his rooms. He remembered every picture clearly in his mind. Of how elegant and innocent she looked in every shot. Desirable and sexy. How extremely beautiful she was.

Indeed, looking at her now, how much he himself would love a taste of those lips. To hold her close, breathe in her scent. 'Get a solid grip Man.' He hissed to himself.

She couldn't take her eyes from his. Dark, piercing, so intense.

It was almost as if she could read his mind. Her face became a very pretty pink.

The silence in the room was thunderous, with both their thoughts on the other.

He quickly rose from his chair, as did she.

She stepped back, and as if on cue the door slid open and in marched Dr. Hillary and Dr. Richard.

Lilliana groaned inwardly, as Damon greeted the doctors.

She walked over to the book case and pretended to be interested in a book about historical haunted homes in Ireland.

Thankfully after the doctors entered, the room began to fill up with the usual suspects. Jessica smiled at Lilliana and Allie gave her a hug as she walked past to sit in a chair beside Christopher. Lilliana sat, ignoring the look Eric was trying to give her, and held in a sigh as Natalie popped a bubble of gum in her face, before laughing and throwing herself onto a seat, thankfully on the opposite side to Lilliana.

As everybody took their seats and quietened down, Dr. Hillary opened the session.

"Good afternoon everyone. Let's have a productive group today, as it will be the last until the New Year. Rupert, how about you start." Dr. Hillary smiled at the nervous boy.

Rupert rubbed his hands together and seemed to have a light sheen on his forehead.

"I don't have much more to say really. Life's going well. I'm happy most days, except when Franklin tries to stab me every morning." He chuckled. "I've decided to take a career that can benefit many through sustainable plants."

"Your career with the horticultural department?" She queried.

"Yes, H.D." He replied, referring it to its most used title.

"Rupert has actually put a theory in motion, the beginnings of a rare species of drought tolerant vegetables." Damon said proudly. "Although it's a year or two in the making, it is the beginning of something exceptionally special."

Rupert grinned. "Thanks Sir."

"It's all very well and good that things are smooth for you here Rupert," Dr. Richard began. "but what is equally important, is you talking about what happened to you before you came here." He looked sternly over his horn-rimmed glasses at Rupert.

Lilliana was sure she wasn't the only one that cringed at his look.

Eric cracked his knuckles, breaking the silence that fell across the room.

Natalie chomped loudly on her piece of gum, looking like she had just walked off a video clip, wearing a very short pair of denim shorts over white stockings, high heeled boots, and a top that had her cleavage looking like the Bermuda triangle.

If anything fell in there, it would be lost forever.

Lilliana looked over to see both Jessica and Orlando holding hands, and Allie and Christopher holding hands. They looked so content, happy. It was nice to see.

She imagined if Josephine were here also, although she and Rupert may not be holding hands, they would be comfortable sitting close to each other, chatting about some plant species or irrigation. She smiled at the thought.

"Do you think it amusing Miss Lilliana." Dr Richard's dry, irritating voice took her away from her pleasant thoughts.

"Not at all, I was thinking of something else. Sorry." She addressed her apology to Rupert.

Rupert shrugged, indicating that is was alright with him.

"Rupert, begin by telling us what happened the day you found out, that your neighbour had been taking the neighbourhood pets." Dr Richard said drily.

Rupert cleared his throat, "Well, my friend Neville and I had been watching this guy, Derek his name was, for over six months, when Neville saw him creep over his fence one night, and grab his kid sister's rabbit.

We called him Demented Derek after that.

Derek was a bit of a hermit, we never saw him have any visitors in all the years we'd lived next door to him. He was beyond creepy, always talking to himself." Rupert chuckled, thinking about a memory. "There was this day when we thought he finally had a visitor. My Dad heard him have this huge argument, screaming out things like, 'Why do you do this to me or, 'What have I done to deserve this, I don't understand why you keep doing these things." Rupert shook his head. "What Dad didn't know was, Derek was talking to his cat. Anyway, one day my dog. Max wasn't in the yard when I got home from school. He was a Sheppard and a real softy. I was pretty upset, even cried in front of Neville." Rupert pushed his hands between his legs, looking uncomfortable with the memory.

"Go on Rupert." Dr. Hillary pushed gently.

"I knew Demented Derek had him. As soon as Dad got home from work, I was on his case to get over next door and see if my dog was there.

Dad told Neville and me to stay home and he went next door.

But no way in Hell were we gonna' stay behind. I couldn't just stay and do nothing, so we snuck near Derek's front door and hid behind a large bush. When Derek answered the door he looked totally weird.

Weirder than usual." His voice quietened, uncomfortable with the memory. "It was the first time I wish I'd listened to Dad.

I could hear Max whimpering and Dad could obviously see him from where he was standing. He started going berserk, screaming what a sick twisted fuck Derek was, and he was going to call the Officials immediately.

Then, my Dad punched Derek in the nose that hard, that Neville and I heard the bone break." Rupert cleared his throat.

"When Derek went down, my Dad stepped into the house, Neville and I were right behind him. I sure wish I'd stayed outside, the smell was unbearable."

Rupert went silent, pushing up his glasses, his Adams apple bobbed as he had a large swallow.

Allie got up and walked over to him, rubbing his shoulders. "It's okay Rupert, you can say anything in here."

She looked over at Lilliana and mouthed, 'Water.'

Lilliana quickly got up and walked over to where Damon was already pouring water from the pitcher into a glass. He placed it into her outstretched hand. His fingers brushing hers as he moved on, not meeting her eyes.

She walked over and placed the glass in Rupert's hands, cupping his fingers around the glass till he registered and held on.

She returned to her seat, as Rupert took a mouthful of the water, smiled at Allie, then at her.

"Rupert, are you alright to continue?" Dr. Hillary asked.

"Yes Ma'am." He said politely, placing his glass on the floor near his feet.

He wiped his hands on his pants, then folded his arms across his chest.

Lilliana felt sick for him, believing what was to come must have been horrific for this sweet, gentle boy.

"Right. Well anyway, what my Dad, Neville and I saw kind of pushed me over the edge. My Max was chained to this pipe in the wall, he had barbed wire around his neck and was bleeding, whimpering. His eyes well, he just looked beyond sad. His anus was red, swollen and bleeding.

He stared at Dr. Richard and said loudly, "That's all I'm saying on that part."

Dr. Richard simply raised a pale eyebrow.

"It's all right Rupert, go on." Dr. Hillary nodded.

"Well, my Dad used his bare hands to untangle the barbed wire off Max. His hands were bleeding bad. Max was whimpering and Neville kept saying, what a sick prick Demented Derek was.

Neville was not scared being in that house, he walked into a few of the rooms. It was disgusting, so many dead animals in jars and barrels made him sick. It was a nightmare." Rupert ran the back of his hand across his mouth.

"A week after, Max died of an infection from the wounds on his neck. Dad spent a fortune at the Vets, trying to heal him." Rupert wiped a tear from his eye, his throat catching.

Lilliana had tears in her eyes also, along with Allie, Jessica and a quiet girl named Reline.

Christopher wiped his nose quickly with the back of his sleeve, hoping no one noticed.

Everybody pretty much liked Rupert. He was an all-round, likeable guy. To imagine what he went through, they all felt for him.

Even Natalie was quiet throughout his story, without her usual indecent interrupting.

"So," He said, "why am I here? What did I do? Well, it's simple really, I killed Demented Derek. I made a chocolate cake, with three blocks of chocolate to make, it super-duper rich, and I put a shit load of poison in it.

I guess considering his lifestyle, he couldn't smell the poison and as I made it into the shape of a cat, I guess he couldn't resist." Rupert shrugged.

"I would have gotten away with it to, but the nosey neighbour across the road reported me. My poor Dad was devastated. Do I regret what I did? No way in hell. Yes I'm here but like I said, life's pretty good here and thanks to my Dads generosity and the Officials deeming my case, non-reoffending, plus my age and the situation, I have a better chance of a successful career here, than I would in the outside world."

"Thank you for finally releasing your story Rupert." Dr. Hillary said. "It has almost been a year, but well done. I'm sure you feel much better sharing with the group."

Rupert shrugged. "Maybe. Not really." He looked apologetically at Damon.

Damon gave the boy a slight smile and said. "Well done Rupert." He clapped and everyone joined in.

"As you have all heard today," Dr. Hillary began. "we each go through different levels of pain, grief and trauma which cause us to react in certain ways. The disgraceful way in which Rupert's dog Max, came to his death may not seem as evil and horrendous as say, Allie's abduction and abuse for many years, which resulted in her terminating each of her babies lives, yet the fact remains, as humans we all react to, and deal with tragedy one way or the other. Reline and Lilliana, it is time for both of you to tell our group your story." She hoped by her asking and not Richard, Lilliana would feel inclined to share.

Lilliana held up her hand.

"Brilliant Lilliana, well done." Dr. Hillary looked proudly at her.

"I'm sorry, but I really don't want to speak about why I'm here." She looked at both the doctors, unable to look at Damon.

"You know why I'm here, I talked about my whole ordeal for over a solid month. I didn't feel cleansed, I felt dirty. Furious. Disgraced. Depressed and there is no way I'm going to talk about it again. I don't see the point. It does nothing to take my pain away or change anything that happened. So, if there is a punishment for that, for not sharing in group, then give it to me, I'd rather be whipped than live through the whole stinking ordeal I dream about every other night." She sat back in her chair, folding her arms uncharacteristically.

The room fell silent. The doctors looked over at Damon, who had ran a hand over his strong, handsome jaw.

Reline stood up and screamed, "I'm not talking either, and you can't make us."

Everyone in the room was shocked at her outburst, as the girl had barely spoken a word in months.

"Well I don't really think that's fair." Eric said, leaning forward in his chair. "You've both sat there and listened to us share our stories. Why should you escape embarrassment?"

"Relax Eric." Damon said walking over to the group. "And these sessions are not to embarrass anyone." He looked pointedly at Lilliana.

"These sessions have been in place for many decades and we have improved our ways of helping any Given that have been through similar situations like yours.

Talking openly about our journey, can be not only be helpful for you, but your family here, to understand and be supportive." He looked at Reline. "Relax in this session Reline, as it is Lilliana's turn to share."

Lilliana's eyes darted to Damon's face, and by the way he was looking so intently at her, she realised she had to do this; Speak, openly yet again, about a world of pain, she was trying to conquer in her own way. Her breath caught in her throat as she quickly looked away from Damon, towards Jessica, who had dropped Orlando's hand and moved her body away from his slightly.

A look of hurt flashed across his face but also, understanding.

"Right Lilliana, as we know from Jessica and Orlando, how you were taken, we want to know in this session, what you went through and how you dealt with it." Dr. Richard stared stonily at her, his fingers taping on his folded arms.

Damon felt tense and a little guilty, wishing Hillary had started the opening for Lilliana. He watched as she took a deep breath, avoiding looking at him.

She pulled her long braid over one shoulder and played with the ends, pulling silky strands through nervous fingers keeping her eyes down, she started quietly.

"We first met Orlando and his father at a picnic." She didn't think it would be a good idea to mention, that Jessica couldn't keep her eyes off Orlando from the first moment she saw him. "They offered Jessica and me a cold drink, which is how we were drugged."

"How dumb can you be? Drinking something from a stranger?" Natalie interrupted, stretching her gum out into a long string between her teeth and fingers.

"Natalie, *enough*" Damon snapped.

"Jesus Natalie, shut the *hell up!*" Allie wanted to punch Natalie in her meaty thigh but knew better.

Damon held up his hands to the group, his voice tinged with anger. "Everyone *stop*, you know the rules in group, when someone is sharing, Silence. Or expect night detention. Sorry Lilliana, continue." He ended in a quiet tone.

Lilliana preferred the interruption, as awkward as it was. Looking back down into her lap, she continued. "When I first regained consciousness, at first, I didn't know if Jessica was with me. I was terrified and felt sick. My heart was beating so fast, like it knew what was going on before my brain registered to it all. I was so cold, freezing." She whispered the last word, her mind drifting off. She squeezed her eyes shut as an image slammed against her eyelids. Her heart, pounding like it had that day. She could feel a trickle of cold sweat slide its way uncomfortably down her back. She couldn't do this. Hadn't she been through enough already? She didn't realise she was frowning angrily as she looked across at Damon, imploring him to make this all stop.

Damon stood still, aching for her, knowing how uncomfortable she was and not really being able to do anything to help her.

She fell silent, watching him as he, unblinkingly watched her back. "Continue Lilliana."

He said it so softly, she wasn't sure he'd said it at all. She was going to give them her edited version, or nothing at all, and quickly said. "We were abducted, abused, tortured in that Hell-hole for weeks and then we escaped taking our kidnappers lives with the help of Orlando. And here we are." She folded her arms, feeling sick, hoping that would be the end of it.

It wasn't according to Dr. Richard. "Keep going Lilliana, I would like to hear more specific feelings if you will please."

Lilliana stared at him. If she had something sharp, she'd probably try slicing him open again. "No."

"I beg your pardon Miss." He raised an eyebrow, a sneer to his lip.

"I said. *No.*" She repeated, louder.

Allie jumped up. "We all know what happened to these girls, what, you want a hard on hearing Lilliana say it again? What the Hell is wrong with you?" Allie was beyond furious. She did not want to see Lilliana go through her nightmare. She'd heard her some nights, screaming in her sleep. Even the brilliant walls at the Given weren't thick enough for those nights.

"Allie please, sit down." Damon said calmly, yet firmly.

Jessica had gone very pale and Lilliana was a matching shade as she dropped her clenched fists into her lap.

Allie sat and said pointedly to Damon. "I'm just saying."

Damon checked his watch. "Alright everyone, I'm going to call it a session. We won't be back for two weeks, so enjoy Christmas week. I'll see you all at Christmas breakfast. Jessica and Lilliana, please stay."

The girls' eyes met. Lilliana shrugged and folded her arms again.

Jessica smiled up at Orlando as he ran his hand over her ponytail, he leant down and whispered if she'd be alright. She nodded her eyes resting on Lilliana as everyone left the room.

Damon sat in the chair beside Lilliana, with Jessica opposite.

"Right," He sighed. "let's try to work around this one shall we."

He ran his hand through his hair and looked at Lilliana. She kept her eyes on Jessica.

"Lilliana, I am giving you a pass on what Dr. Richard wants from you." His eyes remained watchful, waiting.

She raised her eyes to his, hope flickered in them. "Really?"

"Do you really thinks that's fair Damon?" Richard snorted, before jabbing a finger in Lilliana's direction. "Why should this girl not have to purge herself like the rest of the group? It's the way it is, it's the way it has been for decades. *It works.*"

Damon ignored Richard and spoke directly to Jessica. "I'm interested in your thoughts Jessica, what do you think? You and Lilliana share a story, do you feel Lilliana should tell her part as you had to? Be honest."

Jessica didn't have to think twice about her answer and shook her head. "No, absolutely no. Lilliana went through so much. She put herself in harms way to protect me in that place, when I couldn't take it for another second."

"Which is why she needs to purge more so." Richard began.

Daman held up his hand, stopping Richard, before nodding to Jessica to continue.

"She protected me time and time again. It was beyond brutal. I had no idea someone as young as Lilliana could be so brave." She ended quietly, looking at Lilliana with respect.

Lilliana met Jessica's eyes. She could feel tears threaten with the depth and unease of the conversation.

Jessica continued, addressing her elders. "After every single, painful moment and memory we now carry with us, I at least, have found someone that is helping me heal. Orlando and I can't believe we have each other, considering his part in it all." She glanced over at Lilliana and smiled. "I will do everything in my power, to protect Lilliana now." She looked directly at Dr. Richard. "I think she has been through quite enough already and you should just leave her alone."

"Well then, it's lucky we don't leave important decision-making to you Given then, isn't it?" Richard snarled.

"Richard, that's enough, thank you Hillary, you may go." He smiled at Hillary as she nodded getting up to leave the room, smiling at the girls as she did.

Damon kept his eyes on Jessica, extremely proud of the young girl, feeling very happy that Josephine had found herself some good friends at long last.

As soon as both of the doctors left, the door sliding shut behind them, Lilliana got out of her seat and walked to the fireplace, placing her hands on the mantel. Squeezing her eyes shut, she forced the mental images that sliced through her brain, away. Why? Why did it need to be spoken about? She just wanted to forget about it all and move forward.

Jessica looked at Damon, before walking over to her friend.

Damon stood quietly, watching.

"Are you alright?" She placed a hand gently on her shoulder.

Lilliana turned and wrapped her arms around Jessica's solid

warmth, burying her nose against her neck and wept quietly. Images of men's leering faces, the memory of feeling terrified, helpless and furious, had her breathing fast to an uncomfortable speed. Her tears stopped, but she felt close to a panic attack and even more so, due to feeling embarrassed about being so vulnerable in front of Damon. She just wanted to get out, go for a walk in the fresh air and forget.

Damon paced near the bookcase feeling useless.

How he longed to wrap his arms around her and have her cry on his shoulder. But that wasn't to be. Not legally anyway, and he was not one of those monsters that defiled young girls.

Lilliana peeked over Jessica's shoulder to see Damon watching her, a slight worried frown on his handsome face, one hand resting on his hip the other rubbing his neck.

She took a quiet, deep breath and squeezed her friend, before releasing her.

"Thanks Jess," She whispered. "for everything."

"No Lilly, no thanks required." Jessica smiled at her, then looked across to Damon.

"Is there anything else Sir?"

"That is all Jessica. I do thank you for your input, I'm sure that wasn't easy, speaking your mind to Dr. Richard that way." He smiled.

She flushed, just a tiny bit embarrassed. Shrugging her shoulder.

"Could you possibly round up Josephine for me and ask her if she would take Lilliana for a walk with the dogs?" He asked politely.

"Absolutely Mr. Night." She rubbed Lilliana's arm before leaving the room.

Lilliana turned to look at Damon wiping away any tears that clung to her lashes. "I do understand about the importance of sharing in group. The benefits to all the therapies that are here for us Given. I do. Truly, and I'm sorry if I've disappointed you by not going that step further in group."

He'd folded his arms, sitting back against his desk watching intently, as she expressed herself. He desperately wanted her to feel safe and comfortable with him. He chased the image from his mind of walking towards her, wrapping his arms about her and holding her to him. These feelings, towards a younger Given, had never once hit him like this. Ever. He took a deep breath, grateful for the furniture in between them.

Lilliana stared back at Damon, wondering why he was so silent, still. Watching her so closely. She was grateful when he broke the silence with his soothing, calm voice.

"Lilliana. You have not disappointed me whatsoever. Perhaps we can stop those nightmares of yours in hypnotherapy, if you're so uncomfortable speaking in group?"

"I'm not sure if anything would help." She said quietly. "I hate thinking about it."

"Yet, you do Lilliana. It all remains with you. Purging in group can really help get

rid of the demons." He was desperate to ease her painful memories.

Lillian shrugged. "I don't wish to seem ungrateful Sir, but I just feel like I know the best way to deal with this. For me. I just want to move on and put it behind me." Her eyes seemed to be begging him to understand, to stop all this pressure.

He was about to respond when the door slid open and in bounced three more of Lilliana's favourite things in this place. Josephine, Rusty and Nails.

She knelt to receive the dogs' love, in the form of licks and wiggling tails hitting her arms as she stroked their shiny coats. She smiled up at Josephine. "Hey Jose."

Josephine smiled at Lilliana and then noticed her tear stained eyes. Jessica had mentioned briefly what had happened.

"Hey Lilly, who made you cry? I am going to find them and break their arms off."

"Relax my warrior," Damon sighed, still at his desk, "It's all been sorted."

Josephine smiled at Damon. "Alright Sir, that's all I needed to hear."

Lilliana stood, turning to Damon. "Thank you again, Mr. Night."

"Lilliana, it is my pleasure. Now, you two ladies go and enjoy a relaxing stroll, maybe some volunteer time in the stables for the afternoon." He thought a few hours physical work would certainly help lift Lilliana's spirits.

"What, no afternoon class?" Josephine asked.

"No, you can both have the afternoon off, now skedaddle, some of us have work to do." He smiled at the girls, which faded the moment they left the room.

CHAPTER 14

Lilliana smiled as she woke to a sweet Christmas carol playing over the sound system. She sighed happily, amazed she had slept without one single bad dream and felt refreshed for it. A complete wave of happiness washed over her and she threw the covers back energetically before grabbing her robe and dashing off to the showers.

Happy laughter and carefree spirits seemed to be the theme for the day, as Lilliana entered the bathroom. She decided to plunge into the deep cranberry scented bath, and pumped some green scalp cleanser into her palm and lathered away at her hair, watching the unusual chaos of girls primping and getting ready for the special day.

"Hey you." Josephine may has well have bombed her, as she launched into the deep tub, causing a small tsunami. "Merry Christmas."

Lilliana went under, and came up laughing, hugging Josephine. "Merry Christmas."

"What a day this shall be my friend." Josephine had the biggest grin on her face, as she began the task of conditioning her mass of brown curls. Soon they were joined by a crowd of excited girls.

Lilliana got out to have a quick rinse from soapy bubbles, then stood under the body drier, before wrapping her robe about her. She called to Josephine. "See you in mine when you're ready Jose." All her friends had decided to get ready in Lilliana's room this morning.

Josephine waved, before plunging under the water.

Lilliana set off to her room, enjoying the music they had playing throughout the building this morning. It truly did feel like Christmas. Walking into her room, she stopped short, noticing a prettily wrapped box on her bed, tied with a huge green ribbon. Looking for a note and finding none, she undid the ribbon and popped open the lid. Inside was a gorgeous riding habit with a pair of boots. Pulling the boots out, an envelope fell onto the bed. She picked it up and opening it, read, -This gift to you, and riding lessons. Merry Christmas. Damon. -

Her heart sang. Riding lessons, with Damon? Did he pick this outfit for her himself? She certainly wasn't expecting anything like this.

A knock at her door, combined with excited laughter had her dropping the card in the box and rushing to let her friends in, who tumbled inside the room in a heap with their enthusiasm to get ready for the day.

"*Merry Christmas.*" They yelled together, arms filled with clothes, shoes and a makeup bag, supplied from H.B.R.

Once Christmas kisses were exchanged, Allie was the first to mention the box on her bed. "Where did this come from? It's gorgeous." She ran her fingers appreciatively over the soft, plush fabric of the black vest.

Lilliana passed her the note. Allie read it aloud with a "Ooh La-La, don't let Nasty Natalie see that."

Jessica laughed, squeezing Lilliana's arm. "That is so cool, how much will you love that?"

"Too much." Lilliana smiled. "I've been wanting to ride since I got here."

Josephine had a secret smile and quickly turned and started to get dressed.

Lilliana slid the lid back on the box, popping it under the bed to make room for the girls to throw their clothes and shoes on. It took them a solid hour, between sharing the full-length mirror, hair and makeup whilst sharing past Christmas stories. Once they were finished, they stood back and appreciated their handy work.

Jessica had her straight blonde hair, curled into ringlets and wore a pink baby-doll dress, knee length, soft brown boots.

"Orlando is going to eat you alive." Lilliana smiled as she adjusted the top of her white, strapless dress. It had the softest material, floating just above her knees, which looked lovely with white, low heels and silk ribbon straps, that criss-crossed up to her calves.

Allie and Jessica had done all the girl's hair and makeup and Lilliana had not felt this pretty in a very long time.

Her glossy, black hair was a mass of silky, thick waves, with tiny white flowers placed throughout. Josephine had thoughtfully picked them from the garden earlier.

"So pretty," Allie nodded. "good job Jessica."

"Team effort." Jessica smiled, packing up the makeup bag.

Lilliana's eyes glowed with the girl's handy work. Shimmering white eye lids, just a tiny smudge of eyeliner, framing her huge, green eyes beautifully and a dash of pink lipstick.

"Thanks girls, perhaps you should think about a makeup artist position? It wouldn't be so bad, travelling around to different locations like Valerie." Lilliana helped Josephine bundle their robes and popped them at the end of the bed.

"No thanks," Allie said. "I'm aiming for a career caring for the abused or the horses. Although, it's so hard to pick just one, there's a lot of good to be done in so many areas."

"Yeah," Jessica agreed. "there are so many options, I just hope we get a shot at something we feel passionate about."

"Righto people, enough of this talk, we have another six months before we seriously have to start thinking about this, and it's Christmas day, so no more career talk." Josephine said, turning around, looking gorgeous.

Her usual curls had been straightened and hung low down her back. Her makeup fresh and young and her dress, bright red with a big green sash around her waist. Very Christmas-like and very Josephine.

Allie's bright blue hair was not styled in her usual spikes but sat very elf-like and soft around her petite face. She wore a stunning one-piece jump suit, with high heels, looking like an explosive little package.

"Let's see if Christopher can keep his hands off me?" She smiled brightly turning away from the mirror. "Come on girls, let's go and enjoy this day."

Ten minutes later, they were trying to keep up with all the Christmas greetings that were being thrown around. There was a definite buzz in the air, as they made their way into breakfast, Allie was grabbed around the waist and thrown up and caught by Christopher. When she slid down his body, their lips connected in one long, deep kiss. When he released her, her face was flushed and she turned to her friends, eyebrows raised and smirked. "That's what I thought."

Christopher had a hard time taking his eyes off the vibrant girl but made the effort to greet the rest of the girls. "You all look simply beautiful." He smiled charmingly.

The girls thanked him as they walked into breakfast.

Overnight, the staff had made up the assembly hall up with all dining tables and chairs, so that the two thousand plus Given and staff could share their meals together. Lilliana stopped to take it all in, her first Christmas as a Given. She looked about, totally in awe of how beautifully the staff had transformed the assembly hall into a real Christmas wonderland. Tinsel and crystal-like domes hung from every inch of the ceiling at different levels. White, silver and ruby red, it looked like a dream. All the tables were adorned with candles, pinecones and stunning glassware filled with Christmas morsels. Cinnamon spiced milk scented the air with so many other aromas that had Lilliana's mouth-watering.

Damon stood with a line of staff, watching Lilliana's reaction, trying to focus on each person that walked past offering a Christmas greeting. An elbow in the ribs from Cam, had him clearing his throat and apologising to Jessica who had asked him how he was. He focused on the pretty girl, smiled and responded appropriately.

Cam wanted to chuckle as he took Josephine's hand and raised it to his lips, but looking at Josephine, his mouth went dry. Her hair, her perfume. He'd never seen her look so delicious. "Merry Christmas, Josephine." He said quietly.

Josephine smiled and curtsied. "Merry Christmas Mr. Night." Before moving on to Damon.

As Cam took Lilliana's hand, his eyes were still soaking Josephine in.

"Merry Christmas Mr. Night." Lilliana said politely, not wanting to disturb his view.

He kissed her hand and regrettably took his eyes off Josephine and smiled at Lilliana. "Merry Christmas my petal. May I say how stunning you ladies look today."

She smiled and thanked him, moving on to Damon.

He took her small hand in his large one, and ran his thumb over her knuckles. His eyes took all of her in, from her stunning face, beautiful green eyes, to the way her dress made her look like a dream.

"Merry Christmas, Lilliana." He said softly.

She smiled up at him. "Merry Christmas Mr. Night, and thank you so much for my gift. I don't know whether I deserve all that."

"Nonsense, of course you do." He raised her hand to his lips and kissed it.

She thrilled as his lips gently brushed her skin and prayed as she moved on to Nurse Rachael, she wasn't bright red. She hugged the Nurse and was introduced to a tall man beside her. "Lilliana, this is the head of our Black Ops unit and our security division. Johnson, this is Lilliana."

Lilliana shook the tall man's hand, immediately feeling drawn to his warm, kind eyes.

"Nice to meet you, Sir."

"It's a pleasure to meet you Lilliana. I've heard a lot of good things about you."

"Thank you." She smiled before moving on down the staff line and finally, went to join her friends.

Lilliana sat beside Josephine as Allie and Jessica sat opposite them with Orlando and Christopher.

Damon, who was seated at the head of their table, stood and gently tapped a spoon against a glass, drawing everyone's attention. It took a little while for voices to filter down to a level where he could be heard. He waited for total silence.

"Merry Christmas to each and every one of you. Let's have a wonderful day, a day to truly celebrate the year we have had. It's been a successful year for our establishment, and it will continue being successful with all of our hard work and dedication." He glanced around the room, feeling a sense of pride as he looked on at his staff. Protection, as his eyes fell across so many Given, that had endured what they never should have.

"The H.B.R has been set up for relaxation and pampering and Fox has organised some fun games that should benefit all those that participate. There are massages and facials being offered by our junior trainees." This statement caused a few of the nursing staff to 'ooh and ahh'.

"This is your day, to enjoy all the activities we have set up for you. An archery course has been set up, and I will be awarding prizes to the top twelve scores." This caused some excitement amongst Marcus and his mates. "Enjoy the day, it is yours to do as you like. Merry Christmas." He raised his glass to his lips, as everybody stood, raising their own.

'*Merry Christmas.*' Echoed around the room. And then, they all dove into breakfast.

Piles of ham and pineapple, waffles and ice cream, cream and fruits, sweet biscuits and cakes.

Coffee, tea and fruit drinks from sorbet to smoothies, frappes to punches. Lilliana had seen some excellent spreads for breakfast the past eleven months, but this was amazing and she appreciated every single mouthful.

With her mouth stuffed full with a delicious morsel, Lilliana nearly choked as Fox walked up to her, kissed her on the cheek and dropped a small box into her lap.

"Merry Christmas, Lilliana." She drawled in that sassy southern accent of hers.

Lilliana flushed at the fact that Fox had thought to get her a gift at all. Grabbing at her cinnamon milk, she forced the mouthful of food down her throat before clearing it. "Thank you, Fox, this is really sweet of you." She said, looking up at the tall stunner.

"Well honey, open it."

Lilliana looked at Josephine who was all eyes, before pulling the tiny lid off and gasped when she saw the contents. The beautiful butterfly earrings she had worn for the angel photo shoot, lay like two shiny stars. How had she got them?

Fox leant down and whispered in Lilliana's ear. "Hard work in any field you chose, pays off. Think about what you want to do, and who it could help." She turned on her heel and walked off without giving Lilliana the chance to thank her.

She looked down the table at Damon and saw him watching her over his coffee cup.

She looked away quickly as Josephine exclaimed. "*Holy Cow.*"

"I'd say." Allie was leaning as far across the table as she could without putting herself in the punch bowl.

"I thought they were stunning in your photograph but up close, simply gorgeous." Jessica smiled.

"You can borrow them anytime Jess." Lilliana popped the lid back on the box, slightly in awe of such a gift, wondering when she'd have the chance to wear them.

Once breakfast was over and people began heading out towards activities, Lilliana went out to the Christmas tree, and hunted around for her small parcels. Grabbing her friends' gifts, she bundled them together, so she could give them to the girls after the activities and spotted the one for Damon. Reaching for it, she heard him behind her. "Lilliana, would you like to put those earrings in my office?"

She turned around, smiling. "That would be good thank you Sir, I was going to run them up to my room."

"Well I think the best option is my safe box." He turned, walking towards his office.

She followed him, watching his casual stride.

As the door shut behind them, he stopped abruptly and her chest slammed into his back.

"Whoops, sorry." She laughed, embarrassed.

He turned and smiled at her, taking Fox's gift out of her hand.

"Not a problem." Walking to his desk, he pressed his thumb print to the same pad he had, when securing her credit.

"Breakfast was delicious."

"Yes, it was." He replied, putting his hands into his pockets, watching her.

She felt a tingling sensation clench in her stomach as she watched him, standing there, so tall, handsome and simply staring back at her. "It's so lovely, everyone being in such good spirits. Happy."

"Yes, it is." He continued watching her.

His intense gaze had her entire system on fire. 'Quick,' she thought, 'say something.' "I have a gift for you." Stepping closer to Damon, she placed the small box in front of him on to his desk.

He looked surprised. "Why Lilliana, thank you. That's very thoughtful."

"You can open it later on your own if you like." She suddenly felt shy, not wanting to be there when he opened it.

"I'd love to open it now, if you don't mind?" He smiled as he picked up the small box.

"Of course not." She lied, watching his expression with interest as he lifted the lid.

His eyes widened as he looked at the tiny replica of his beautiful Beast, amazed at her thoughtfulness. He authorized every single gift that came to this facility. Marcus must have worked with Cam on the quiet to organise this.

"Lilliana," He said quietly, humbled. "thank you. Aren't you the clever one?" His dark eyes smiled at her, before walking over to the mantel and placed it in between two thick candle holders.

It looked lovely and Lilliana was very pleased with his reaction.

He turned around and faced her. "Thank you, sweet girl." He said quietly.

Tears rushed to her eyes. She remembered the first time he'd called her that. And on this day, the first in sixteen years, she was celebrating Christmas without her mother.

"Hey, hey." He walked over to her, gently grasping her upper arms and stroked the soft flesh under her arm with his strong fingers. "I didn't mean to upset you."

Her head tipped back to look into his glorious deep blue eyes.

A tear fell, but she shook her head. "It's okay, I'm alright. Just high emotions today, I'm actually feeling happy." She smiled up at him, through her tears.

His thumb rose slowly, and caught the tear that slid down her cheek, resting near her pretty pink lips. 'Get your hands off her.' His mind screamed at him, but his body did not comply. "It is a day for being happy Lilliana."

"Yes Sir." She whispered, mesmerised by his dark eyes, his scent, the warmth of his hand on her arm.

He squeezed her arm gently, before stepping back, thankfully, breaking the spell. "Would you like to come for a quick walk with me for a moment, Lilliana."

"Of course, Sir." She wondered what this was about.

"Excellent." He smiled, taking her arm and linking it through his, led her from the office, past the Christmas tree and outside into the glorious sunshine where happy Christmas celebrators were making the most of the festive day.

He caught Josephine's eye, who was standing a few feet away, laughing with Jessica,

Allie and a few boys and held five fingers up to her.

She nodded, smiling, and gave him the 'Okay' sign.

Lilliana took a deep breath of the fresh air, enjoying the sounds of laughter as she walked with Damon, feeling his strong leg bump against hers through the thin material of her dress, his firm arm cradling hers. She told herself to breathe, to help settle the nervous butterflies flying around her stomach; she did not want to pass out today.

As they approached the stables, Lilliana was amazed to see how beautifully decorated they were. Edible wreaths for the horses hung everywhere and lined the paddocks fences. "So gorgeous." Lilliana murmured.

Damon smiled, as Thomas met them at the main door. "Morning Sir, Miss Lilliana."

Lilliana smiled at him as Damon asked. "Thomas, did you have a good breakfast Lad?"

"Yes Sir, gorged myself till I was nearly sick Sir, it has to be the best meal Cook puts together all year."

"Yes, he sure does out-do himself. As do you Thomas," Damon gestured to the decorations around the stables and paddocks. "everything looks great."

"Thanks Mr. Night, we have a bit of fun decorating this time of year. Can I help you with anything Sir?"

"No thanks Thomas. And you're not supposed to be helping anyone today. What activities have you lined up for yourself?"

"Oh, that's easy Sir, I'm doing archery with Marcus a bit later, and I have booked in for a deep-tissue massage. Cannot wait." He beamed and headed off with a wave as a friend called his name enthusiastically from the front of the stables.

Damon patted the top of Lilliana's hand, still linked through his arm and guided her to the end of the stables, past Beasts empty stall. Walking out the back-door Lilliana spotted the black stallion immediately, prancing about his paddock looking magnificent, frolicking about in the sunshine.

Lilliana's eyes were drawn to the beautiful white palomino, trotting prettily up and down the fence line. She knew every horse here like the back of her hand and had never sighted her before.

"She is beautiful." Lilliana exclaimed quietly and pulling her arm gently from Damon's, stepped up on the first rail of the fence for a better look. "When did you get her?" She glanced down at Damon as he stepped up to the fence.

"Yesterday, the cargo plane delivered her, along with some goats and alpacas." He heard a noise behind them and spied Josephine before she quickly ducked back into the stables.

"She truly is beautiful, what's her name?" She looked back out at the pretty horse, which was difficult, because looking at Damon whilst their eyes were level, made her stomach clench in the most pleasant way.

"Well," He said, feeling like an excited little kid himself. "I thought as she's yours, I'd leave that up to you."

"What? What?" In her utter bewilderment, Lilliana lost her balance and fell off the fence. Luckily, Damon caught her in his arms and gently set her back on her feet, on solid ground.

"She's yours, Merry Christmas." He said softly against her ear, before stepping away.

"*Surprise.*" Her friends yelled, laughing as they stumbled over each other to reach her.

She looked out at the gorgeous horse, which was now apparently hers. She couldn't help the bubble of laughter that burst from her. She covered her mouth with her hands and laughed so hard, fat tears of happiness rolled down her checks.

"No way." She exclaimed, shaking her head. "this is way too much."

Before Damon knew it, she launched herself into his arms, knocking him back a step. His arms came up around her to stop them both from taking a tumble.

Her arms about his neck, her face, against his throat.

He could feel her tears run warmly over his skin. Felt her chest smashed up against his. He dropped his face a fraction, to place his nose against her hair ever so briefly. She smelt like sunshine. He smiled over her head at her friends, letting them know everything was fine, but his heart was thudding and he knew he was enjoying the moment far too much.

She squeezed Damon quickly, before stepping back, wiping the tears off her face as she apologized. "I'm so sorry, I'm just so surprised and so grateful, I cannot believe that she's mine." She beamed up at him.

'This beautiful girl.' He thought to himself. 'will be the death of me.'

"Well she certainly is yours to enjoy Lilliana. Merry Christmas." He smiled down at her. "Your first lesson will be tomorrow morning if you'd like." He watched her face glow in happiness.

"That would be wonderful Mr. Night. Thank you."

He smiled, before turning to Josephine. "Now, Miss Josephine, before you all get on with the day, I do believe I have one small gift for you." Damon snagged her into the crook of his arm, and they headed back into the stables.

"Honestly Sir, I love the gardening tools you made and the sunflower kit. I think that's enough." She grinned up at him, as they both knew she loved receiving anything from him.

"Well, consider this a gift to share." They walked into a small stall and there in the corner on lovely soft clean hay, were three sleeping puppies.

"Oh Damon," Josephine said quietly, forgetting formalities. "they're adorable."

She hugged him hard. "Thank you."

"You are so welcome Missy." He kissed the top of her head. "I know you will give them the very best care and Rusty and Nails approved them, so one big happy family."

"Now, time for me to go, I hope to see you at some of the activities." He gave them all a smile before turning to Allie. "Would you come with me Allie?"

"Of course, Sir." She smiled at the other girls as she followed the tall man out of the stables.

Josephine grabbed Lilliana's arm excitedly. "Well Lilliana, what do you think about that?" She gestured to the direction they'd come, before seeing the puppies.

Lilliana shook her head slowly, eyes twinkling. "Josephine, I can't believe it."

"To think, in your free time you can ride anytime you like." Jessica sneezed three times in a row.

"Time to go my friend." Lilliana linked her arm through both her friend's arms, and they strolled down the long isle out of the stables.

***

Damon and Allie had walked down through the back section of the hospital, chatting casually along the way about how she had been doing in her classes. Reaching a large door which only opened after scanning Damon's eye retinal, they stepped into a world full of damaged souls that needed plenty of care. The psychiatric unit.

Allie's heartbeat quickened, immediately knowing Damon was taking her to see her sisters and brother.

She looked up at him in awe, so grateful in that moment, tears threatened to spill.

He looked down and smiled kindly. "Are you ready Allie?"

She nodded, silent, afraid to speak in case she cried in front of him.

He led her down a maze of corridors, greeting staff member's that dutifully dashed here or there. Stopping at a door, Damon punched in the code and pushing the door open invited Allie to walk in ahead of him.

She stepped into a room that reminded her of paradise. Gentle music drifted softly from unseen speakers. The ceiling had been painted to reflect the bluest sky with fluffy white clouds. She couldn't tell what colour the walls were, because every inch was covered in the most spectacular vines with bright bursts of flowers, scenting the room in a floral heaven. Padded bench seating framed the entire room and in the centre on a large table, sat wooden bowls and plates filled with a Christmas feast.

And sitting around the table, with paper Christmas crowns sitting lopsidedly atop their heads, were three people she longed to see. The sob that erupted from her chest shocked even her. Damon put a strong hand on her back, as the three heads turned in their direction, and happy chaos erupted. The three leaped from their seats, screaming, laughing and crying, all at once as they stormed towards Allie, who was halfway across the room to meet them. Hugs, kisses and four voices mingled excitedly, all talking at once, which had Damon grinning from ear to ear. He folded his arms across his chest, giving them a few minutes before he spoke. "Allie, Adam, Emile and Katy."

They all stopped and turned towards Damon.

He smiled. "You have three hours together; I hope that will suffice?"

Allie beamed. "It absolutely will, thank you so much Mr. Night." Her brother and sisters echoed her thanks.

"If there are any problems, please hit the emergency button," He indicated to the red button near the door. "Dr. Hillary will come to escort you out Allie, may you all enjoy your visit." He turned and left behind four very happy individuals that sat, ate and shared their stories of the past several months, without a second of silence in their three-hour visit.

***

Many hours later, into the early evening, Damon was enjoying a quiet drink in his rooms, thinking over the day. He had made sure every single Given and staff member had had something to look forward to, making the celebration of the day that extra bit special.

Sitting back, stretching out his long legs he enjoyed his Irish whiskey as a loud knock sounded at the door and seconds later, Cam strolled in. Of course, both brothers had the code to each other's room.

"Hello Brother." Cam saluted as he walked over and sat on the opposite lounge, sighing loudly. "What a day, hey?"

Damon got up, walked over to the small bar and poured Cam a drink, handing it to him, he sat back down and stretched out his legs.

"Salute." They raised their glasses to each other, before taking an appreciative swallow.

"Another successful Christmas." Damon smiled.

"It's been bloody brilliant." Cam agreed. "Fox is causing a bit of a ruckus downstairs, catwalk competitions."

"It's loud, I could hear the music from the passageway when I popped into Black Ops." Damon shook his head. "I hope she's behaving herself."

"Doubtful." Cam said wisely. "She has about forty girls up on the stage and I think the younger ones have dabbled in the adult beverages."

Damon shook his head. "I certainly hope not."

"Ah, come on brother, that's the fun of Christmas day. Don't you remember, sneaking cups from the adult punch bowl when no one was looking?" Cam threw back his drink, placing his glass on the table, watching Damon refill it.

"I hear there's a new Doc coming to work with our Black Ops team? About time we had some more manpower in that section. Man, we've been sent some real loons so far." Cam took a grateful swallow of the smooth whiskey, before continuing.

"I thought with Dad's contract, they'd send the worst to the ruins in Africa, even China. Did you hear about the guy that kept heads in his freezer? Shit, I mean, come on Damon, you have the power to get rid of these wack-ado's." He could see he was tainting the Christmas vibe, by the dark look that fell across Damon's eyes, but quickly, guiltily went on. "I say, let me help you out, give me some of them for the day. Give me and Marcus some real targets to aim for." He held up his arms, pretending to hold a bow and arrow. "If you know what I mean." He nodded his head, hoping to persuade his brother.

Damon raised an eyebrow. "Don't think I haven't thought about it Cam, I have.

Some of those bastards have committed crimes against our Givens' before they came here." He shook his head. "Let's not talk about that today, we have a meeting with all head of staff in two days' time, let's leave it till then." He rose and strode towards the door, opening it. "But for now, let's have a peek at Fox's show shall we, and try to enjoy what's left of this day."

"Hell yes." Cam, not needing to be told twice, followed Damon out and downstairs to where the party of the night was going with a bang.

***

The girls were having a fabulous time, dancing together, with a heap of their Given friends.

Damon joined Rachael, Johnston and Billy, and they chatted above the loud music as Cam went to join Fox on the dance floor. They moved well together, dancing to a vibrant beat.

Rupert joined their group and it was evident, due to his stumbling and hilarious comments, he had helped himself to the adult punch. He started to really get into the mood, enthusiastically jumping up and down, throwing his head from side to side to the beat of the music. It wasn't long before his red face, changed to a shade of green, and Josephine grabbed his arm and led him from the room, towards the library toilets. Just in time.

Lilliana went to follow them, but a strong hand grabbed her upper arm, pulling her against a solid body. Cam, sweaty and happy. "So, Lilliana, how do you like Christmas here?" He asked against her ear, moving her to the beat.

"I like it." She smiled up at him, enjoying the dance. It was always something she felt happy doing. Music was therapy and dancing, letting go, connecting to the beat was pure magic to her soul. "I like it more than I thought I was going to. Missing my Mother is hard though."

"I know Angel." He wanted to chase the sadness that flickered in her beautiful eyes. "I hear you have a horse-riding lesson with Damon in the morning." His eyes twinkled down into hers. "Have fun." He smiled, before spinning her into the arms of Christopher and Allie.

"Let's get out of here, I'm beat." Allie yelled above the blaring music.

Christopher nodded in agreement. "Yep, I've got an early start."

They waved to Jessica and Orlando, and the group filed out of the room in search of Josephine and Rupert.

Damon watched Lilliana leave with her friends, and silently wished her, Merry Christmas dreams.

CHAPTER 15

Lilliana's seventeenth birthday passed quietly, and the months that followed were a blur of intense classes that left minds, almost numb with gruelling information and an overloaded schedule that only seemed to get busier with every passing week.

Due to both Lilliana's schedule and the responsibilities thrown daily towards Damon, her riding lessons from Christmas, had been scattered widely throughout the months that followed.

Finally, a day had arrived where they both had two hours free, that coincided.

Damon looked as if he were born in the saddle, sitting with such ease on Beast, trotting around the pasture, giving Lilliana some fresh tips on seating, posture and rein grip, breathing and feeling the connection to her horse.

It was Lilliana's fifth lesson and the first day that they were going to take the horses out of the riding arena. Lilliana was very excited and happily gave Beauty's neck a loving stroke.

Her posture was very good Damon noted, she was an absolute natural.

Her hair hung in one long braid down her back, her riding habit shaped her curves beautifully to the hungry eye. And Damon's eyes weren't just hungry when he looked at her; they were starving.

She was trotting around, getting comfortable in her seat as Damon watched, telling himself to stop being such a bloody pervert.

He was reflecting back on Marcus's latest reports, included not only how impressed he was with Lilliana's natural gift of care towards their damaged Given, but also with the extra time she spent studying, how skilfully she completed extra exam tasks, and all the time she seemed to enjoy, volunteering in the hospital. She was completely dedicated to all things that led to the path of healing and nurturing the broken mind and assist in the healing after abuse and torment. Every report, well most he thought, dismissing Richard from his mind, was filled with praise and pride.

Rachael had been in his office earlier that morning and had mentioned that, of all the younger Given, Lilliana absorbed information in a way she'd never seen. Always asking a barrage of questions regarding the running of the hospital, and what more they could do to make the system thrive for the new or injured Givens She had also put in a request to apply for part time, nightshift work in the psych ward. Damon had to consider this carefully, considering her age and experience, although felt she would handle any situation that presented itself.

Like Josephine, Lilliana read to some of the newer Given that arrived and hadn't regained consciousness. Always keeping busy, with Allie right beside her. He could see them making a great team. His thought flow was interrupted by Cam, yelling out his name.

"*Damon.*" Cam repeated, running towards him.

He wasn't wearing his usual carefree smirk, which alerted Damon immediately, that something was very wrong. He leaped off Beast, and walked towards his brother.

"Cameron, what is it?" He felt tension creep into his belly.

"We have a body in the secured passageway." He stepped closer to his brother, looking over his shoulder at Lilliana, who had stopped riding and was watching them.

Damon held up his hand, silencing Cam as he was about to

continue. "Wait," He looked over his shoulder to see Lilliana, sitting prettily, watching him. "not here."

He held up his hand and waved her over. "Lilliana, come here please."

She gently nudged Beauty into a walk and reaching the brothers, dismounted.

"Sorry Lilliana, we will have to do this another time. Come." He reached for her horses lead, and the three quickly walked back to the stables, handing the horses to Thomas and stable hand, Edward to care for.

As they headed towards the house, Lilliana kept up with the fast pace both brothers seemed determined to keep. She sensed something was very wrong.

Cam looked down at her. "Are you enjoying riding Lilliana?"

"Very much so, thank you Mr. Night." She replied as they walked up the stairs into the house.

Before reaching the top step, Damon stopped her, gently taking her upper arm. She looked down to where his strong fingers circled round her bicep, before looking up at him.

"Lilliana, this hasn't happened since you have been here, but I am about to put the house on lockdown. Do you remember the rules about lockdown?" He slowly uncurled his fingers from her arm.

She nodded, meeting his dead-serious eyes.

"Find Josephine and do not leave her side, no matter what. Understood?"

"Yes Sir." She could feel the tension roll off him.

He nodded once, before quickly walking towards his office with Cam, the door sliding shut behind them. Damon was very grateful at this time, that Lilliana had no idea where the secret passageways were.

But someone else did, someone who shouldn't have been there.

He activated a switch and he and Cam entered the passageway through his office, to the crime scene above.

***

As Lilliana headed towards the library, a shrilling alarm sounded. Uncomfortably loud, eerie and unsettling.

People began walking quickly and with purpose. Lilliana spotted Orlando up ahead, and called his name, Jessica was right behind him.

"What's going on?" He pushed thick, blonde hair out of his frowning eyes, as Jessica reached for his hand.

"Mr. Night told me to look for Josephine."

"She was with us." Jessica looked behind her, through the moving crowd and spotting Josephine, called her name waving her hand in the air.

Josephine waved back quickly making her way towards them, a worried look on her face.

"Lockdown," She shook her head, looking worried. "usually occurs when something not so good is up. Pair up." She nodded to Orlando and Jessica.

Lilliana looked about them as people were rushing off in several directions, staying in groups. The eerie alarm, penetrated her ear drums like an angry swarm of bees, making her feel unsettled with every second that passed.

"I hope Allie and Christopher are together." Lilliana looked at her friends.

Josephine spotted the troubled look that was filling Lilliana's eyes and reached out, grabbing her arm. "They will be fine." She said confidently, hoping it were true. "Let's grab a board game and keep ourselves occupied till they call the assembly. Come on." She tugged Lilliana into the library, before releasing her arm and running to the board game section, selected something that would hopefully take their minds off whatever was going on.

The alarm was grating on Lilliana, as she perched on the edge of the fishpond in the centre of the library's entrance. She took a steadying breath as she watched a large orange and black Koi glide past, oblivious to her nerves.

Josephine returned and plonked down in a large comfortable armchair and began setting up a game of Rummy. "I wonder what's happened?"

"I can't imagine." Lilliana walked over and sat opposite her friend, selecting her Rummy tiles. "I hope it's nothing too serious."

"I was five when I experienced my first lockdown. I was terrified. There was this one guy, Kevin who went totally nutso, took a girl down to the back part of the property, and before anyone knew they weren't where they were supposed to be, he hog-tied her…" She trailed off, watching Lilliana's face drain of colour.

"Um the girl didn't come home. One of the Team Leader's found her body. Nobody could find Kevin, so, the house was put in lockdown. It was a tad scary." She finished quickly, lining up her first three tiles.

"What ever happened to Kevin?" Lilliana had to pick up.

"Cam, happened to Kevin. He found him trying to escape the border fence, shot him down with his bow."

"Oh." Was all Lilliana could think to say, trying to imagine the younger Night being so violent. She couldn't, he had been nothing but kind and charming to her, and she had never witnessed him being anything but that. She placed down her three tiles.

Josephine added to Lilliana's tiles, before reaching across and squeezed her friend's hand. "It's going to be alright Lilly, we simply stick together and nothing can harm us. Mr. Night will be on top of whatever has happened, okay?"

Lilliana nodded, forcing a smile for Josephine and they both sighed in relief when the insistent alarm finally ceased its nerve fraying screams, continuing their game in peace.

***

When Damon and Cam arrived at the scene of the crime, Johnson stood waiting, a disgusted look on his face.

"It's not pretty." Was his greeting to Damon. "Thanks for being so quick Cam," He nodded to the younger Night. "poor girl is starting to stink up the place, time to move her to the morgue."

He stepped back to allow Damon a view of the situation behind him.

The passageway was a bit of a squeeze for three big men and the body.

"Oh, *Jesus Christ.*" Damon breathed through his teeth, not wanting to believe the scene before him.

Twenty-two-year-old Sarah, a nurse only newly recruited from the Given academy six weeks ago. Her long black hair had been cut closely at her scalp and tied so tightly around her throat it was cutting into her flesh.

Her disfigured body was bad enough, but Damon looked across at Cam, his face had gone white. He had seen a lot in his time, but the fact that this had taken place in the supposed safety of their walls, infuriated him. He pointed towards her body and asked his brother. "Can you fathom this?" His eyes glanced over to Johnson. "Have you seen anything like this?"

Sadly, they both had.

Deep gashes covered her torso, arms and thighs, her hands had been cut off, and placed over her eyes, faeces had been shoved in her open mouth and nose, the stench was beyond repugnant. Blood and bruising around her pubic area indicated rape.

Damon turned away from the macabre scene, looking at Johnson. "Can we do an autopsy? I'm hoping she died, before he inflicted all of this." He waved a hand at the devastation, caused by someone he wanted to see suffer severely for their crime.

"We've got someone freely walking amongst our Given, right this moment thinking they've got away with this." Cam shook his head angrily. "Johnson, we need surveillance in these passageways. We need to get prints off her body, we need to check…"

"Cameron." Johnson calmly placed his hand on Cam's shoulder. "I've got this, it will be sorted. The scene has been recorded and we will take all prints in the morgue. My team's coming now." He nodded to Damon.

"Cameron, my office in five, we need to start interviewing immediately. Johnson, we'll need you there for that too, once you've got this under control, join us."

Johnson nodded as heavy footsteps approached them from the above stairwell. The clean-up crew and Johnson's team. "It's not good Damon." He said, turning to give his men orders.

"No," Damon replied grimly as he turned to leave. "no, it's not."

CHAPTER 16

Assembly had been called two hours after the discovery of Sarah's body.

The packed assembly hall was filled with weeping, fury, sadness and disbelief.

Damon, Cam, Johnson and senior staff stood silently at the front of the assembly, watching the crowd before them. A large hologram of the crime scene behind them, showing everyone what had been done to the happy, smiley girl that once was.

Johnson stepped forward, looking tall and menacing as he glared at the hundreds of faces before him, before letting everyone know what had happened to Sarah and what would happen to the person responsible.

As Johnson was going through his list of requirements and expectations, Damon searched the crowd for anyone looking suspicious.

Cam too was watchful, feeling a fire of fury ignite in his belly. An incident like this, had not occurred in years and he couldn't wait to get his hands on the culprit.

Marcus, Lisa, and all Team Leaders, were standing alongside the aisles, as Johnston spoke, typing furiously on their tablets, selecting names of anyone they may suspect due to strange behaviour or change in attitude the past week. All information gathered would be processed by the board.

Lilliana's head was spinning at the image before her. What that poor girl must have endured. Hopefully she died quickly before that individual had done all those savage, vile things to her.

She would never know, that Sarah's spine had been severed, preventing her mobility. Her hands, sawed from her wrists, the culprit relishing her screams. Then, those deep gashes inflicted cruelly whilst she had sobbed and pleaded for her life. She would never know that Sarah suffered brutally for hours, before death came to take her mercifully away.

She wiped her tears, looking over at Jessica who had her head between her legs, Orlando rubbing her back.

Allie was sitting, staring stonily at the image, arms folded across her chest, foot tapping quickly on the ground. Christopher had his head in his hands.

Rupert was vomiting in a corner. He was not alone.

No one was to leave this room; the cleaning crew would not be thankful.

Her eyes met Josephine's; her friend had a stream of tears flowing down her pale cheeks. She put her arm around her and whispered. "I know."

"I think I'm going to be sick." Josephine stated as she lurched forward and vomited, setting off a few others around them.

Lilliana glanced over at the stage to see Damon looking as angry as she had ever seen him; arms folded across his chest, surveying the room like he wanted to strangle somebody.

Johnson finished off by stating from now on, everybody was to stay in pairs. Eating, class, therapy, activities. Every minute.

"Once you've been paired, stay within your group allocated and check with Mr. Night if you have any problems. Until this matter is sorted, I want each one of you to be careful. The passageways are forbidden, and if anyone enters them that does not have access, you will be punished." He jabbed his finger at the crowd and snapped. "*Severely.*"

Lilliana was rubbing Josephine's back, wondering who in her group she'd be paired with. No doubt Jessica and Orlando would be paired off, as would Allie and Christopher, hopefully she'd be paired with Rupert. God not Natalie or Eric, please no.

Damon stepped forward, waving his hand and thankfully, the hologram disappeared.

"I know that this is hard on all of us. We need to work together to make the next few days roll smoothly. Everyone is to report to their Team Leader on time every morning after showers, breakfast, each class and every meal. I cannot state the importance of this. No tardiness. You will all be on time. It's for your own safety. Every room will be locked after nine pm." He looked out over the faces of his Given and staff, wondering who the hell could be sitting amongst them so calmly. He said quietly, with steel in his voice. "We will find you, and you'll wish you'd never been born."

Rachael quickly stepped forward, clearing her throat. "If everyone can just stay seated here till the pairing is done, which will begin immediately." She nodded across to the

Team Leaders, who began assigning pairs.

Rachael turned to Damon, placing a hand on his arm and suggested something quietly. He nodded and left the room through a side door with Cam.

It took half an hour for Marcus and Lisa to approach Lilliana's group. She'd been anxiously watching the other Team Leaders pair their groups. Josephine had already left, with one of her classmates, Shelley, whom Josephine got along well with. Shelley had been here for almost as many years as Josephine.

Marcus approached Lilliana, as she watched Orlando and Jessica leave together, Jessica gave her a wave from the other side of the aisle. Allie and Christopher had left five minutes beforehand.

"Lilliana, are you alright love?" Marcus was watching her, hoping she wouldn't be too upset with her partner. Natalie was standing just behind him, a frown on her face, hands on her hips.

Lilliana inwardly cringed, only slightly relieved it wasn't Eric. This would be interesting. "Yeah, I'm okay, hi Natalie."

"Yep, hi." Natalie was clearly as unimpressed with her choice of partner.

"Okay," Marcus could see this pairing would be a handful. "Mr. Night said pairs can freshen up before lunch."

Lilliana was grateful to hear that, as her feet had received quite a splash from Josephine's vomit.

"Lunch will be served in twenty minutes sharp, so don't be late girls." He said as he walked them out of the emptying assembly hall.

Lilliana looked at Natalie. "Do you need the bathroom?"

"Does it matter if I don't? I'll just wait in my room, knock when you're done."

Lilliana was about to protest, as Natalie turned on her heel and headed upstairs. Lilliana had no choice but to follow her and as Natalie shut her door in Lilliana's face, Lilliana quickly ran to the showers, happy to see only a handful of Given taking up a few stalls.

Stepping into the shower, she quickly removed her clothes and let the hot spray wash over her, feeling guilty that within the hour of being lectured about pairing protocol, thanks to Natalie, she was already breaking that rule. She closed her eyes, not being able to get the image of Sarah out of her head and quickly opened her eyes again.

Who could have done such a thing? She shook her head, trying to clear the image and quickly shut the water off. The burst of hot air had her dried quickly, and she grabbed her clothes and walking out of the shower stall dumped them down the laundry chute. Going over to the shelves where fresh robes were folded she took one and slipped it on, glancing briefly in the mirror. Her eyes were sparkling green in a very pale face. Even her usually red lips looked pale. She turned away and jogged towards her room.

Walking in, she longed to crawl into her bed and pull the covers over her head and forget about everything she had seen. The first act of violence she had seen since she had left her prison almost two years before. She slapped her hands over her face, pushing unwanted images away, before taking a deep breath and looked at her bed again.

She didn't know how long she had stood there, staring at her bed in a haze of disbelief, before a rude banging persisted at her door, until she opened it.

Natalie looked at her and snapped. "Would you hurry the bloody *Hell UP.*"

Lilliana sighed and slapped her hand against her button, shutting the door in Natalie's face, before snatching up her brush and dragging it through her hair, quickly looking inside her wardrobe.

If she couldn't put her nighty on, she'd settle for the next best thing, and pulled out a soft knitted, jumper dress of deep olive green that sat just above her knees. Shoving her feet into warm brown boots, she pushed her hair over her shoulders to hang gently down her back. Opening her door, she stepped out.

"Finally." Natalie spat as she strutted off, walking straight into Fox.

"Watch where you are walking." Fox hissed through her teeth. Beside her was her partner, Zack.

"Whatever." Natalie threw her hair over her shoulder as she stomped off.

Fox glared after her, then looked at Lilliana. "How are you?"

Lilliana shrugged, following Natalie down the stairs, towards lunch. "I'm alright, just shocked is all."

"Yes," Fox nodded, "it's not a good thing, that's for sure. Be careful Lilliana."

She strolled down the stairs, ahead of Natalie.

Screaming and yelling reached their ears before they reached the dining room. Walking in, they saw a group of boys in a stand-off, angrily accusing each other for Sarah's death. One of the boy's fists flew out and slammed into another's stomach.

Then it was on; fists flying, feet kicking, the onlookers surged forward, whilst some of the younger, newer Given began chanting, "*Fight, fight, fight.*"

"Oh, yummy, I love a good fight." Natalie walked as close to the fight as she could, squeezing past the onlookers. When one of the fighting boys got knocked into the crowd and stumbled to the ground, Natalie leapt on top of him and started slapping and punching him, before shocking Lilliana, started fondling his balls.

Strong hands pulled her off the boy, and spinning her around, slapped her face. Hard.

Damon looked furious. "*Enough.*" He shouted. "Get in Order. Now."

The fighting stopped immediately, the nervous fighters shuffled to their feet.

Cam had joined Damon in the centre of the room waving a few security over, pointing to the ones that were involved.

All the fighters were taken out of the room except Natalie, who was holding a hand to her check looking stunned, watching Damon, waiting.

Lilliana couldn't take her eyes off Damon, one hand on his hip, the other running through his hair in frustration.

"Alright everyone, lunch now, quietly if you please." He dropped his head and gave Natalie an angry look. "Enough from you Natalie, is that clear?"

Natalie nodded, and those that were in her group were surprised she didn't follow through with anything ridiculous.

Lilliana sat and was joined by a bewildered looking Natalie. Lilliana wondered how long that would last. Jessica sat on her other side, with Orlando.

They ate quietly, speaking about their thoughts on what had happened to Sarah.

"I have no words." Jessica whispered; her face still red from weeping. "I just do not understand."

"I want to know how the hell it happened here. Someone's obviously gone off the deep end." Orlando savagely stabbed his rissole, smearing chutney over it.

"I'm sure they will find out who has done this, and we will all be safe," Lilliana assured them. "if we just stick together, stay in our pairs and..." She trailed off, not knowing how to finish the sentence. The smells of the meat, the hologram image, it all flooded her senses. She placed her fork down, and grabbed her glass of water, gulping it all down quickly.

She glanced down the other end of the table, where Cam and Damon were in deep conversation with a few staff members.

She willed herself not to be sick and concentrated on taking slow, deep breaths as she sat still, looking away from Damon, her eyes met Eric's across the table.

He'd picked up a pork sausage and watching her, slowly slid it into his mouth, then pulling it out again, before slowly sliding it back in.

Lilliana flew out of her chair and bolted from the room, her stomach heaving. She made it into the library bathroom just in time, to vomit in the sink.

She heaved up everything that had been in her stomach, then dry retched for another minute. She felt shaky, and held onto the sink for dear life, collapsing onto the ground after she splashed cold water onto her face and rinsed out her mouth.

She rested her forehead onto her knees, and willed the room to stop spinning.

Jessica rushed into the bathroom, Allie on her heels.

Jessica knelt beside her friend. "Lilliana are you alright?"

Allie stroked Lilliana's hair, shaking her head. "That Eric is such a dick. A cute dick, but a dick nevertheless."

Lilliana smiled at Allie. "So very true. I'm alright, it's just been awful, seeing what happened to poor Sarah."

"Yeah," Allie said quietly, standing, "it's awful for all of us Lilly, but at least we can stick together hey. That will not happen to any of us." She said determinedly.

The door slid open and Josephine popped her head around the corner. "My friends, it's been a hell of a day, but we really do have to stick to our paired partner.

Mr. Night's waiting outside for you all." She stepped in and pulled Lilliana to her feet, before hugging her.

Lilliana gratefully returned her hug.

Allie linked her arm through Jessica's and they all walked out to face the music.

Damon was standing near the pond, watching the Koi fish swirl amongst the Lilies. He turned to face the girls as they approached him, his eyes straying to Lilliana.

"Thank you Josephine, you may go and find Shelley." The smile he directed towards her, did not reach his eyes.

She threw a sympathetic look at them all as she departed.

Lilliana nervously gripped her fingers together in front of her looking at Damon, waiting.

He stood in front of them, silently watching them each for a moment. Hands behind his back, looking taller and more serious than Lilliana had ever seen him.

Was it only this morning, that he was smiling proudly at her as she rode Beauty?

He didn't look so proud right now, slightly furious would be a good word to describe him.

"Allie, Jessica and Lilliana, would you all agree, that you are above intelligent ladies?"

"Yes Mr. Night." They chorused.

"And you are all aware of the pairing protocol. Correct?"

"Yes Mr. Night." They repeated.

"Then I ask that you please respect and obey it. That shouldn't be too difficult, should it?" He waited a beat.

"No, Mr. Night."

"The pairing protocol is in place for a specific reason; your protection."

"I had to leave Sir, I couldn't very well throw up in the middle of lunch now, could I?" Lilliana hoped she didn't sound defiant.

"And Jessica and I came together, Sir, so technically we were in a pair." Allie began.

Damon held up a hand for silence. "Please, from now until this matter is resolved, stay with your partner. Allie, Jessica, back to the dining room." He dismissed them, keeping his eyes on Lilliana as they left.

She didn't blink but kept her eyes on his face, feeling a mixed bag of emotions. One being concern for him. "Are you alright Sir? This must be an extremely difficult time for you."

He was impressed that she even considered his feelings at a time like this. He forced a small smile. "I'm fine Lilliana. How are you?"

She ran her hands over her face, then dropped them again and shrugged. "I can't honestly say right now."

He walked towards her, and gently placed his hand on her shoulder. "It's going to be alright. We will find whoever did this, but in the meantime, you must stay with Natalie." He'd had Marcus pair her with Natalie, because he knew she would fight anyone that came to give them trouble.

"Can you do that for me Lilliana?" He dropped his hand from her shoulder, as the urge to fist his hand in the end of her silken waves took hold of him.

"Yes Sir." She sighed.

"Alright then, back to lunch before class." He walked back to the dining room, with Lilliana one step behind him.

"Drama Queen." Natalie smirked as Lilliana sat back down beside her.

Lilliana poured some tea, ignoring both Natalie and Eric, who was staring at her from across the table.

How long was this going to last? She wondered, and would she survive Natalie?

Better still, would Natalie survive her?

***

The old white iron fence wrapped its arms lovingly around the cemetery. Tall ghost gums and magnolia trees were its companions. Statues of Angels looked over the headstones protectively, and clumps of coloured wildflowers burst from the ground.

The service was simple and touching and under the heat of the day, Sarah's friends had a chance to say something fondly about their time with her, and what she was like as a person. A chance to say goodbye.

CHAPTER 17

Six weeks later, and frustratingly still in pairing protocol, Lilliana was helping Thomas muck out the stalls. The day was muggy and she was covered in sweat and dirt. She couldn't have been happier if she was told she could do this every hour of the day. It was hard, physical work and she loved it.

Josephine's adorable trio barked around her ankles as she worked, whilst Rusty and Nails were laying out on the fresh hay, sound asleep.

The rhythmic sound of the shovel sliding through hay and horse dung, the sheer effort straining her muscles was the exact thing Lilliana needed to block out the emotional strain of the past weeks with Natalie.

She grabbed the wheelbarrow handles, and lifted her heavy load heading out towards the dung pile that Rupert and Josephine's crew were moving towards the compost heaps behind H.D. They at least, had the help of a fandangle little bobcat.

"Haven't you finished yet?" Natalie complained, sitting on a hay bale. "I am so bored."

"No Natalie, I have at least another hour to go." She pushed the wheelbarrow into another stall and picked up the shovel. "You know, if you gave me a hand, you'd feel better and the time would go faster."

Natalie inspected her nails. "I don't think so."

For the past six weeks, they had practically been joined at the hip.

Thank the stars for their own room, that they were locked into at night, otherwise...she didn't even want to think about it. That would have been a pure nightmare.

Classes were fine as they had others to interact with. Group was as normal.

But activities were a trial, as they both had to put up with the others interests.

Natalie hated the stables and any volunteer work Lilliana did. Lilliana hated listening to Natalie moan about everything, and then put up with her tasteless comments on every male she laid her eyes on.

Natalie's one activity Lilliana did enjoy was archery, only she wasn't very good at it.

Surprisingly, Natalie was excellent and bragged about being one of Damon's favourite students. I just bet she is, Lilliana had thought at the time.

Lilliana continued shovelling, her thoughts interrupted by Natalie, and she nearly died.

"I would just love to have that size dick in me." Natalie was ogling one of the stallions getting frisky with a mare.

Thomas shook his head and looked at Lilliana. "Is she always this gross?" "Unfortunately." She sighed.

"Alrighty then." He went back to mucking out his stall.

Twenty minutes later they heard Natalie call out. "Hello Mr. Night."

Lilliana was waiting for something crude to follow. She was almost disappointed when it didn't.

"Natalie, making yourself useful I see," Cam's dry tone almost made Lilliana laugh. "where's Lilliana?"

Natalie must have pointed in her direction, as a few seconds later, he was leaning against her stall, watching her shovel.

"Having fun?" He smiled.

She straightened her back and wiped her forehead with her hand, streaking dirt along it. "Always." She looked blissfully happy.

"Damon's coming with Pier. How does a quick photo shoot sound?" HHhhhhh

"What, like this?" She held out her arms, covered in muck.

He grinned at her. "Yep, exactly like that, for now."

Lilliana shrugged "Okay then." She would love to earn some credit that could go towards getting Allie a horse of her own. She'd been talking about it with Christopher and together, they were going to make an offer to Damon to purchase a horse for Allie's eighteenth birthday.

"That was easy." Cam turned as Pier and Damon strolled into the stables.

"What's the photo's for?" Lilliana asked Cam.

"One will be shot for the Unity of the Given. That's you looking like a hardworking, yet happy, stable young lady." Cam winked at her. "The other is for the finest horse breeders around, wanting the number one horse in the worlds, seed. They pay a fortune for his offspring. So, I thought, a picture of Damon looking his dashing, serious self, and you looking like a gorgeous princess on his naked back, will get the punters hungry."

"Oh my god, can I be on his naked back?" Natalie squealed.

"The horse, Natalie not Damon." Cam rolled his eyes.

Lilliana kept shovelling until her barrow was full and leaving the stall, rolled it past Cam and towards Pier and Damon.

"Thomas, can you take this off Lilliana please." Damon called out.

"Sure thing Sir." Thomas winked at Lilliana as she stepped aside for him to wheel it outside.

"You look hot Lilliana, we've got a cool drink for you." Damon handed her a bottle of ice-cold water.

Lilliana's eyes drank him in; dressed in black jeans and black shirt, unbuttoned, revealing a tight, firm chest. She forced her eyes on the water bottle.

"Thank you." She smiled at him, gratefully popping the lid and guzzling the cold liquid. In her haste to quench her thirst, some of it escaped her lips and trickled down her chin, falling onto her chest, leaving a clean line amongst the dirt.

Even covered in muck she was stunning. Damon's eyes followed that line, before quickly averting his eyes.

Not before Cam saw. He shook his head at Damon but smiled as he clapped his hands together.

"Pier, you remember our lovely Lilliana?" Cam placed his arm loosely over her shoulder.

"But of course, the beautiful Dark Angel. How are you dear?"

Lilliana flushed, not feeling beautiful under all the dirt and grime. "Very well, thank you."

"Excellent dear now, come this way, we are about to have a lot of fun." He continued walking through the stables, towards the back entrance where Beast was tethered to the fence, being brushed by one of Thomas's stable hands. Beast's magnificent coat glistened in the sunlight.

Lilliana could hear Damon behind her, asking Natalie if she would also like to participate in this photo shoot. Natalie's excited response confirmed her answer.

Hay bales had been set against the stables door, a wheel barrow and pick were there also, with horse blankets across the fence.

Pier began directing the girls, sitting Natalie on a hay bale, handing her a tablet and told her in this photograph, she would be presenting as if studying horse breeding and veterinary science. He asked Lilliana to hold the pick and stand beside the wheelbarrow full of hay and shuffle it about.

It was a quick shoot, that had Lilliana throwing hay in the air and at Natalie whilst Natalie had to look like she was having fun with it. Two carefree girls, working outdoors, helping the establishment whilst gaining a meaningful career.

Fox strolled up as they were finishing. "Your poor pores." She said in way of greeting Lilliana. She ran her finger down the younger girl's cheek. "This will take way more than ten minutes." She turned to Cam.

"You've got ten, hurry it up." He waved Fox off, as she took Lilliana's hand and they disappeared into the stables.

"Thomas," Fox called out. "we're using your shower, do not come in."

"As if." Thomas yelled, highly offended.

Thomas's shower area was not as modern as the main buildings, but it had a comfortable feel about it and Lilliana liked the rustic vibe.

Fox got the shower on as high as it would go and once Lilliana was undressed, handed her a loafer and body wash. "Scrub that grime away until you are sparkling, dear." She left the stall and waited in the next room.

Once Lilliana was washed and dried, hair brushed free of hay and laying down her back in a silken black wave, Fox quickly got to work on Lilliana's face, then slipped a slim black slip over her head. It had one thin shoulder strap with the other side of the slip, sitting just above her breast. Two long slits up both sides of her legs.

She looked stunning. "Your age is not to be depicted in this shoot Lilliana. So feel say, around twenty-four." Fox smirked, not unkindly. "That's what your hands will be doing anyway. Come."

They walked outside. Beast had been taken to a tree further down the pasture, where an old cartwheel was propped. Pier was adjusting his camera as he waited, Cam was looking at the tablet Natalie had before and Natalie was sitting near Cam's feet, crunching on one of the apples meant for the horses.

Then there was Damon, stroking his beloved horse, whispering to him looking every bit the alpha male.

"Brilliant Fox." Cam admired Lilliana's appearance, always beautiful, but Fox had transformed her into a sultry vixen. "You never disappoint,… actually…." He trailed off.

"Yes," Fox drawled, "it's best for you, not to finish that sentence." She tossed her hair over her shoulder and folded her arms. Nodding her head to Lilliana to go over to where Damon stood.

Damon couldn't take his eyes off her as she walked towards him.

Pier was snapping away as she walked, getting her from behind, capturing Damon in the back ground, one hand on the stallion's black neck, the other hand casually in his pocket as he hungrily watched the woman walk towards him.

She stopped in front of Beast.

Damon smiled. "Just beautiful." He said quietly.

Lilliana blushed, and reached her hand under Beasts chin to tickle him gently.

"Lilliana. These shots well, you and I will have our hands on each other, but I promise you, nothing indecent okay?"

"That's fine Mr. Night, I know photography and modelling is all about acting. That's kind of why I love it. Like a fantasy world you can escape into for an hour or so. It's fun." She shrugged and smiled up at him. "I know you'd never do anything to hurt me."

His breath caught as he inwardly punished himself. He did want to hurt her; not cruelly, but just crush her beneath him and lay his lips down on hers, hard. He smiled. "Excellent."

"Ready Damon." Pier called out. He'd moved closer and had set up on a different angle.

"We'll start off slowly Lilliana just so you can feel your way into this one." With that said, Damon gently reached for her shoulders and pulled her towards him, then turning her, pushed her back gently against Beasts side.

He smiled at her, hoping to relax her as he heard her breath hitch when he pressed his body closer to hers.

"Damon, no smiling please." Pier called out. "You're supposed to be dangerous looking, like your animal there."

"Beast, dangerous?" Lilliana whispered. "he doesn't know him very well, does he?"

"No, he's just a giant pussy cat that's misunderstood."

Cam had jogged over to the chatting pair.

"Right, this is what we need. Lilliana, your face will be half covered with your hair, or parts of Damon in these shots. We don't want perverts out there thinking we're playing around with our girls in here. So, we are depicting you as the woman we see you to be. Sexy, mature, sophisticated. In love," He winked at her. "how does that sound, can you pull it off?"

"If it gets me closer to enough credits to purchase Allie a horse, I can do mostly anything you want me to do." Lilliana nodded, concentrating. The closeness of Damon, the scent of his cologne was overpowering her senses in all the right ways.

Cam smiled. "Seems to be working." He muttered to himself, he clapped Damon on the shoulder, before turning and heading across to Pier.

"Okay Damon, ready when you are." Cam called out.

Damon ran his fingers through Lilliana's soft hair, pulling it forward so it fell over one of her wide green eyes, leaving her mouth exposed to the camera angle.

He placed one hand on Beast's side, beside her head then, slowly with his other hand, he slid it down Lilliana's side, down her leg cupping behind her knee and gently placed it on his hip.

Lilliana's eyes widened, her breathing getting faster.

"Lilliana." Damon breathed her name softly.

Her eyes looked up, straight into the depths of his, so dark, intense. She was so close; she could see the beautiful fleck of colour in his eyes. So close.

"It's okay." Leaving her leg wrapped around his hip, his other hand came up and gently stroked her cheek. "We'll have to look through our catalogues later to find Allie's horse, won't we?"

"Really? That would be wonderful." She whispered, struggling to form the correct words. His hands on her, his breath fanning her face, his lips mere inches from hers. His forehead dipped lower, till it came to rest on hers; he was enjoying this moment way too much.

"Fantastic." Pier called, as he was constantly walking around them, snapping at different angles. "Lilliana be a sweetheart would you and put your hands on the man of the hour."

Lilliana nodded, and placed one hand around Damon's neck, her other hand slid up his chest. Her heart was beating pleasurably, and she prayed she wasn't going bright red. She couldn't meet his eyes for fear she would explode, so she focused on his throat.

His chest was more than she imagined it to be. Rock hard and sculptured, and oh so warm through his soft, black shirt.

Her fingers took advantage of their position on his neck as if they had a mind of their own and were playing with the dark ends that brushed against his collar. So silky and soft.

He was being driven insane. "Close your eyes Lilliana," He whispered. "don't open them until I say."

She nodded, closing her eyes.

He didn't want to make her uncomfortable so, with her eyes closed, he placed her leg gently back on the ground, and took her wrists, placing her arms about his waist.

He placed both his hands around her face, feeling her soft skin.

He pushed his knee between her legs, opening them so the slits revealed long, strong thighs and bending his head, placed his lips very close to hers, as if to kiss her.

"Fabulous." Pier called.

Lilliana opened her eyes to Piers calling out, and both she and Damon stiffened at their extreme proximity to each other.

If she moved her head, just a fraction, her lips would meet his. Oh, she wanted to. Badly.

"One more shot, and we are done." Cam called out. He was curious as to how much pain Damon was in right at this moment.

As Damon straightened, his lips brushed her forehead then he released her and she suddenly felt all alone in the world.

"Lilliana, Lilliana?" Cam must have been trying to get her attention, as he looked a bit worried her not answering him.

Damon brushed his fingers along her arm. "Lilliana?"

"Oh sorry, yes all good. It's the heat." She smiled, shaking her head. "Sorry, what is it you want me to do next."

"I need both you and Damon up on Beast, it's kind of a cheeky shot. You're in front." He held up his hands. "Nothing indecent, we just want you peeking over his shoulder into the camera."

"That sounds easy."

Damon leapt on Beast's bar back with grace and ease.

He reached a hand down to Lilliana and smiled. "This will be quick, I promise."

She reached up for his hand, with Cam's hands on her waist, the two effortlessly had Lilliana up in front of Damon, facing him.

Her knees knocked into his and she gave a small, embarrassed laugh. "Sorry."

"Stop apologizing Lilliana, you are doing a brilliant job." Damon said. "Here, just let me help you." He placed his hands under each knee, and pulled them across his thighs, placed her feet behind his back, pulling her close to his groin.

She didn't know if she heard him groan out loud, as Pier was calling for her attention. But she was pretty sure it sounded like the sound she'd made in her head.

"Lilliana, one arm around him please. Looking this way. No, no, no, she's not high enough. Damon be a man would you and lift Lilliana so her head will sit above your shoulder for this shot."

Damon looked at Lilliana. She, right back at him.

"Seriously Pier, can't we just get the shot from a different angle?"

"Not for what I'm after," The photographer said. "trust me."

"It's okay." Lilliana said.

"Here," Fox strolled over, and had folded a horse cloth in half, and half again.

"not so touchy this way."

With Damon grabbing Lilliana by the hips, he pulled her up so Fox could slip the horse cloth under Lilliana's bottom, then Damon placed one hand under one side whilst supporting her, then his other hand under her.

"Oh my God, I'm too heavy for you to be doing that." Lilliana moaned, a little embarrassed.

Damon chuckled inwardly.

The fact that she was embarrassed, not by his hands being extremely close to her core, but that she was too heavy, or a burden. If only she knew.

Pier and Cam got the look they were after.

Beast's large rear end, with Damon's broad shoulders, long back and firm buttocks, with slim legs wrapped around his hips; and the beautiful face of a vixen, one bright green eye peering over his shoulder, a finger held to shiny red lips, shushing the world about the best kept secret. Fox had ruffled Lilliana's long black tresses, so they fell over one shoulder.

"That's it." Pier called after a few minutes. "That's a wrap."

Damon lowered her back down and rubbed her back in a friendly manner, as Cam reached up to help her down.

"Nice job brother." He said to Damon. "Lilliana," He smiled, placing her on the ground. "well done."

Lilliana thanked him and looked up at Damon.

He smiled at her as he dismounted. "Come to my office after dinner with Christopher, Lilliana. Please tell Allie and Natalie to pair up in the library when you do."

"Yes Sir." She smiled as Natalie walked up to them.

"Until then." He took Beast's halter and led him towards the stable, with Cam and Fox, talking to Pier.

Natalie just stood there staring at Lilliana.

"What?" Lilliana asked her when she kept looking at her but not moving.

Natalie turned her back on Lilliana and started towards the house.

Lilliana sighed, trying not to let Natalie's weirdness affect her mood. She couldn't wait to find Josephine and prayed they'd have five minutes alone so she could to tell her all about the photo shoot with her beloved 'Brother.'

CHAPTER 18

Forty-six-year-old, Johnson Fletcher was the most dedicated hard-working man Damon had ever known. His background; Ex-Official leading crime scene investigator, twenty-five years hauling in the most despicable the world had ever seen.

He believed in scientific facts, forensic evidence and chasing the hounds till they were exhausted. It was with all this combined with practically no sleep, along with five of his team, all with brilliant minds, that they had finally found the killer of Sarah, nine weeks after her murder.

A very clever twenty-five-year-old, Robert Wendell, another of Sarah's work colleagues in the hospital section. Using someone else's login to steal a glance at the Givens files, he re-enacted some of the evil crimes, and used them on Sarah.

Stealing drugs from the locked cabinet and an attempted assault on a new Given, had Robert busted.

When Johnson and Damon had gone through Robert's room, they found a panel behind his wardrobe with a list of people and the punishing and vile acts he wanted to perform on each of them.

There were fifty names on that list, and Rachael, Fox, Dr. Hillary,

Leon, Billy, Lilliana and Marcus's names were amongst them.

Johnson and Cam were in Damon's office, discussing his punishment.

"Look, it's quite simple really," Cam said to the other men. "let's take him out the back property and have a hunting party with him."

"This isn't the Hunger Games, Cameron." Damon said seriously.

"I kind of agree with Cam on this one Damon." Johnson said, leaning back into the chair. "What he did to that girl, what he planned to do with others, he does not deserve any more chances."

"He will not be getting them." Damon tapped his finger against his lips, thinking. "I just feel that it's time to make a public display to our Given, that this sort of thing offers no second chances once they enter our gates. It will not be tolerated. An arrow is too quick, I want him to suffer."

"What do you suggest Damon, an open assembly where it's free for all?" Cam got up and poured himself a coffee.

"Not quite," Damon said. "but yes, an open assembly. What do you think Johnson?"

"It sounds a good way to make a point, but also to give everyone piece of mind that justice is being done."

"Alright then," Damon stood and walked towards to door. "I'll go talk to Sam; we'll do it tomorrow. Cam, organize the assembly, let the Team Leaders know what is going on, I want the entire establishment there, that can be."

"Sure thing brother." Cam placed his cup down and followed Damon out the door, with Johnson behind.

***

Jessica, Allie and Lilliana were sitting in Josephine's room, as she was retelling her embarrassing story, of finally telling Rupert she had a little crush on him.

"I mean, honestly, you'd thought I'd told him I had sex with you three and a snake the way he swooned."

Allie laughed out loud. "Interesting."

"He's just shy is all Jose," Lilliana said. "it can't have been that bad."

"It was worse, he couldn't get away from me fast enough, he was so keen to leave, he knocked over a stack of precious experiments as he bolted for the door." Josephine chuckled. "Poor Rupert. I don't know who was more embarrassed."

"What happened when he came up to see you after dinner last night?" Jessica asked, nibbling on a celery stick, smothered in peanut butter.

Josephine let her breath out in one long huff. "He told me I was the best friend he has had since Neville. That I am the most wonderful girl he's ever met, and if I was his type, he'd go for me for sure."

"So, he bats for the other team." Allie dipped a carrot stick into thick beetroot dip.

"Yes." Josephine answered.

"Yeah, Christopher thought so." Allie nodded.

"Stephan does." Jessica said quietly.

Josephine rubbed Jessica's arm. "You must miss him."

"Stephan had such a busy social life. I know he probably misses me every day that I miss him, but I know he has his friends, his art."

"So, Rupert's all good now?" Allie asked.

Josephine waved her hand. "Totally fine, I mean, it wasn't a full-blown crush, like I wanted to rip his clothes off or anything like that." She laughed. "I mean, that would have been pretty awkward for me." She shrugged. "I just adore him as a friend, I guess. A friend crush."

"That a girl." Allie gave her a hug.

"So, assembly in ten minutes." Lilliana stood. "I'm going to head down to the hospital and grab my roster for next week."

"Can you ask Billy if he can give you mine?" Allie asked. "I've got to run down to the stables before assembly."

"Of course." Lilliana waved as she headed out downstairs, past the library and towards the hospital stairs.

A few minutes later as Lilliana got closer to the nurse's station, she could hear raised voices. Angry voices.

"I don't see the point Damon, why should I be there to see him die. I want him gone yes, but I don't need to see him suffer to know the rest of us will be safe. It's pointless."

"I need you there Rachael, as head of your unit, you need to stand by my side."

"I am on your side Damon, but truthfully, as much as Robert deserves your punishment, I cannot handle seeing a life be taken this way, so no, I'm sorry I will not be there."

There was silence. Lilliana stood frozen in the corridor, not wanting to step out in the middle of this uncomfortable argument. Curiosity had her peeking around the corner.

Rachael stood rigid, blonde hair peeking out from under her cap, arms folded across her petite chest, cheeks flushed and angry and a slight frown masked her pretty features.

Damon took a step towards her, he looked completely frustrated. Tired. He pointed a finger right under her nose and said in the quietest voice. "Johnson needs you there. The nursing staff needs you there. You will be there. *Billy.*" He snapped loudly.

Billy walked out of the back room, carefully, as if Damon were an unstable patient.

"Yes, Mr. Night?"

"Billy, can you hold down the fort for an hour whilst Rachael attends assembly upstairs?"

Billy nodded, not meeting Rachel's eyes. "Of course, Sir."

"Good. Rachael, please." He held out his arm, offering her to go ahead of him.

She sighed angrily and walked in front of him, colliding into. "Lilliana." Rachael grabbed her shoulders to steady her.

"Um, I've just come to get my roster for next week." She said, not able to look Rachael or Damon in the eyes.

"Make is quick please, Lilliana," Damon said in a voice he hadn't used on her before. "Assembly is in a few minutes."

"Yes Sir." She waited until he walked past, before walking over to Billy.

Billy pulled out her roster and handed it to her.

"Can I also have Allie's, please Billy?"

He smiled. "No worries Lilliana, are you alright? You look a little pale."

"I was kind of eaves dropping, I heard there's going to be an execution. Marcus told us that we all had to be in assembly, but I didn't realize it was for that."

"Yes well, this place is for second chances Lilliana, not thirds." Billy handed her Allie's roster.

She nodded. "I agree, it just seems a bit harsh is all. Why not just shoot him?"

Billy smiled. "We don't have guns here Lilliana and if you don't want to be late, I suggest you get going. See you next week."

"Bye Billy." Lilliana turned on her heel, making her way upstairs to stash the rosters in her room before making her way back downstairs to find her friends.

When Lilliana stepped into the assembly hall, she stood shocked still at the entrance door.

The feeling in the room was oppressive.

Robert Wendell was in the centre of the stage, ankles and wrists were strapped firmly to a frame in front of him. He was wearing nothing but a small cloth across his groin, nappy like in appearance. A very large, thick plastic drop sheet underneath him.

It made Lilliana instantly nervous, and reminded her of the cross Jessica and herself had been made to stand back to back to.

Behind him, for all to see as a reminder was the hologram of the horrific scene, of Sarah's mutilated body.

Damon was standing to the side of the frame along with Johnson, Cam and Rachael. Every single staff member that was not needed urgently elsewhere, were seated in the front row.

Lilliana felt sick and dizzy. She looked around the large room, trying to find a friendly face amongst the hundreds gathered. She could make out Fox's red hair, sitting up tall near the front of stage.

"Can everyone who is not seated, sit immediately." Damon was looking directly at her.

She flushed, meeting his eyes and looking to her left, saw an empty seat and quickly sat beside Leon. He smiled anxiously. She couldn't return it.

Damon waited for the hall to fall silent before beginning. "This assembly has been called for one purpose today. Robert Wendell has soiled our establishment with his sadistic acts and his punishment will be capital according to our establishment rules: Death." Damon looked around the room as he spoke, seeing a variety of emotions from anger, disgust, joy, relief. He worried how some of them would handle what they were about to see. Lilliana, looked small and pale as she slid lower in her seat, trying to block the stage from her view.

Perhaps if she knew what Robert had planned to do to her, she wouldn't look so ill at what was happening here.

He felt ill himself thinking about it. He looked at Johnson and nodded.

Johnson stepped forward. "Robert Wendell, I hereby sentence you to twenty lashes, followed by hot needles in which you will be bled to death."

There were gasps amongst the Given, but also claps and cheers.

Damon gave them a few moments, before calling out. "*Enough.*" The room fell silent again.

Johnson stepped forward. "We will not be giving Robert a chance for final words." He nodded to Cam. "Let's begin."

Robert snarled evilly. "Fuck all you little bitches and…"

He didn't finish as Cam had stepped forward and slapped him hard across the side of his face, silencing his rambles. Damon, Johnson and Rachael walked off the stage to sit with the other staff members.

Cam walked over to a side table, where the whip was sitting in a large bowl of alcohol. Picking it up, he walked back to his position behind Robert.

Josephine was watching Cam closely. All in black, with his hair falling across his eyes, legs spread, holding the whip, waiting. So serious.

She'd known him basically all her life. Most of the time, he just annoyed her with his cockiness. He was always teasing her and then flirting with anything good looking enough to tempt him. She knew he slept with the staff. Sleaze ball.

But boy he was just so cute. Oh my, I am going nuts, she thought to herself.

He is about to flog someone and here I am, thinking how hot he is?

She looked behind her in the crowd, trying to see Lilliana. She spotted Allie, soothing Sammy a few rows back as the other girl looked like she was about to have a meltdown.

Josephine held up a hand to say hi to Allie, then turned her attention back to Cam.

He was waiting for Johnson to give him the go ahead.

His cool blue eyes met Josephine's beautiful big brown ones. He forced himself not to smirk at her.

Johnson gave the nod, and Cam pulled his strong arm back, then threw it forward with relish, laying the whip down hard on Robert's back.

The scream was almost animal like, the alcohol making the wound sting that much more.

Lilliana held her breath for what felt like the twenty lashes. It was ghastly.

His screams had not lessened. Leon bent near Lilliana's ear and said kindly, "He deserves this Lilly, don't fret for the bastard."

Lilliana nodded. There was nothing to say.

Once the twenty lashes were over, Cam walked over to the table and dropped the whip, dripping in blood. He wiped his hands on a towel as he looked down at Damon and Johnson. He had volunteered to do the punishment, knowing Johnson didn't want to. Cam felt that had something to do with Rachael.

Damon did so much for the entire staff and Given, he thought he would take this extra task off him. It was a small thing plus, in a twisted way, he enjoyed it, punishing those that truly deserved it.

In a bowl of boiling water, ten steel metal skewers were sitting, heated to burning hot.

Slipping on a glove, Cam held one up, it looked like a giant silver knitting needle.

Instantly, Lilliana could feel a panic attack, which she had not had in almost a year, flutter to the surface.

Damon could not see her, nor any other staff that she could see, and Cam was busy pouring alcohol on the skewer. She got ready to get out of her seat and whispered to Leon. "I just have to get out of here."

He nodded, completely understanding.

Hunching over, she walked backwards, making herself small, hoping to slip away unnoticed. Six steps and she could feel relief building, before she backed into someone. Spinning around, she paled as she looked that 'someone' square in the eyes.

Dr. Richard pointed to her empty seat and said in a clipped tone. "Sit."

She couldn't believe her luck and frowned at him before unhappily turning around and marched back to her seat. Damn him.

Lilliana watched as Cam slid the first sharp, boiling-hot needle into Robert's side, as easily as a toothpick sliding into butter.

The man's screams were justifiable as far as Cam was concerned and the screaming continued as he strategically placed the other nine needles into the man's flesh, that would incur the most pain, hitting major organs resulting in death.

Once Cam had finished the task, he stood back as Robert's screams became mummified cries as he dribbled and moaned. Justice was a disgusting sight.

The entire room sighed, as the section of flooring that the dying man stood, lowered, returning to a section in the hospital.

Damon and Johnson returned to the stage beside Cam. To utter silence.

"Sarah's killer has now faced our justice; may she rest in peace. Let us resume our day. I know for many of you, it will be difficult to simply get on with things, so if you require council, please ask for it."

Damon turned and left the stage quickly, followed by Cam.

Lilliana stayed seated, not wanting to be caught in the rush as people started filing out of the hall. She was feeling a little unwell and was happy to see Josephine, who plonked down in Leon's vacated seat.

Josephine bumped her arm against Lilliana's. "Pretty deep huh."

Lilliana looked into her friend's eyes. "Just a little. Do we seriously just go to class after that?"

"You cross the line; you face the fine my friend." Josephine sighed.

"Oh, he deserved it alright," Lilliana nodded. "I just wish it was something I could un-see."

"What class do you have now?" Josephine stood, pulling Lilliana up with her.

"I have theory and practical with Dr. Hillary down in psych. I don't know how well my brain is going to work."

"I hear you there." The girls followed the crowd, stopping off to grab a herbal tea on the way.

"You be the fabulous student you are and after class, I'll meet you at the pool and we'll totally chill out. Okay?" Josephine finished her tea and gave her friend a hug.

"Okay then, I'll just go off and pretend all is well in the world." Lilliana forced a smile.

"That is exactly the way to do it." Josephine winked before heading off to the library.

"Excellent." Lilliana whispered to herself and headed to the hospitals entrance, then down to psych, for two hours with Dr. Hillary.

The classroom for psychology was a completely white sterile looking room, although not cheerless. Bench seats faced in a half circle towards a sunken front of the room where the teaching podium stood and behind that a one-way mirror, that often held a patient that the students would study, determine the disorder and discuss the best treatment.

By the time Lilliana took her seat beside Shelley, the classroom was full. She glanced over her shoulder and smiled at Allie, who was in the row behind her.

Dr. Hillary walked in, excusing her tardiness and perched her backside on her desk, clasping her hands in front of her. "Today I would like us to discuss Robert Wendell."

There was a groan throughout the classroom.

Dr. Hillary held up her hand. "In times like these, we need to focus on how we may have missed seeing Robert for what he was."

"Yeah," An eighteen-year-old from the back row called out. "a Psycho."

"Thank you Ralph. If you have no interest in the depths of the troubled mind, you may no longer take my class. For that comment, you may leave immediately. And anyone else who has nothing intelligent to contribute, you may leave also."

Ralph stood, apologized and left the room.

"Now. Who can tell me about Borderline Personality Disorder? Lilliana, please." She folded her arms and waited.

Lilliana cleared her throat and sat straighter in her chair, her brain trying to click into drive about the subject she'd studied last week.

"Border Personality Disorder, is a chronic condition that may include mood instability, high rates of self-injury and suicidal behaviour and difficulty with interpersonal relationships." Lilliana rubbed the back of her neck.

"Can you suggest treatments for BDP?"

"Group and individual psychotherapy, medication, mentalization based therapy, psychodynamic psychotherapy and cognitive behaviour therapy to name a few."

"Very good Lilliana, now Jaycee, what can you tell us about Antipsychotic medication and how it works?"

Lilliana let out a small sigh and allowed her mind drift somewhere else. Normally she was very interested in everything that happened in this classroom. But not today, she couldn't wait for the class to end. She was having trouble focusing on anything, other than Mr. Damon Night lately. He seemed unable to escape her thoughts. Awake, asleep, she could not banish him and if she was honest with herself, she didn't want to. The warm feeling she felt spread within her, with even the slightest glance at him, had her senses on fire.

After the first hour the class was split in two, and Dr. Richard came and took half the class off to do treatments for clinical depression.

Dr. Hillary took her group, including Allie and Lilliana, to the wards with the padded cells. She stopped in front of the double thick tinted glass window, allowing her students to look over her shoulder at the patient within.

Inside, a young woman was pacing bare foot, back and forth in her room, wearing a white singlet and loose track pants. The room had a mattress on a bed that was built into the wall, as was a small desk with two books placed on it. A toilet in the corner and a small sink. It was a very bare room.

Dr. Hillary faced the class. "I want you all to watch this woman carefully. I need you to study her behaviour, and in private you shall share with Mr. Night and I, your impression of her disorder through brief visual examination. No speaking, you have one hour. Come to my office when you are ready." She turned on her heel, leaving her class.

Both Lilliana and Allie knew not to utter boo.

Months ago when they were told to study a patient and be silent, a boy named Gary thought he'd share his opinions with the class once the doctor was out of sight.

Within five minutes, Damon had come to take him for a walk. He was no longer in that class but attended night shift rounds at the hospital.

It did pay to do as you were told.

After watching the woman for a few minutes, Lilliana realized there was something familiar about her.

As the woman paced she was screaming about the devil as she frantically ran her hands repeatedly over her shaved head.

"I know you see me. *Filthy scum.*" She rubbed her hands along her arms. Arms that had strange white scars all over them. The fifteen students watching, were not so shocked when she pulled her singlet off and flung it towards the window, where she would only see her own reflection.

Lilliana gasped as she realized who this woman was. Well over a year ago, when she and Josephine had taken Rupert to get his arm stitched after Franklin attacked him with the knife.

The girl that had been in so much pain, with cruel, deep carvings cut into her flesh.

She had now run up to the window and smashed her breasts against the glass screaming, *"Eat me. Go on. Eat Me!"*

She ran backwards and threw herself on the bed and started slapping the air with her hands and kicking with her feet, as if she were fighting someone off her. Screaming with so much pain in her voice. *"Get off me, get off me you evil scum!"*

Lilliana turned away and walked to the other side of the wall.

Resting her head back, she closed her eyes. She'd seen enough for one day. She headed off to Dr. Hillary's office. Once she arrived, she knocked and the door slid open, revealing the doctor in deep conversation with Damon.

"Come in Lilliana." Damon was not surprised she was the first student to arrive.

She entered, walking past the stacked bookcase that was full of old text books on every single topic regarding the mind.

Two couches faced each other and a desk sat at the end of the room.

Damon was seated on one couch, ankle crossed over his knee, tablet on his lap.

He pointed for Lilliana to sit opposite him. She did.

Hillary sat beside Damon, looking stiff and her usual formal self.

"Right Lilliana," Dr. Hillary began, "can you share with us your thoughts of our patients diagnosis?"

"Well," Lilliana started, "I feel it is a mental disorder characterized by symptoms such as delusion or hallucination that indicate impaired contact with reality." She rubbed the back of her neck.

Damon noted that she did that often, when deep in thought or plain nervous.

"Can you name the disorder Lilliana?" Damon asked.

Lilliana looked at him and realized how very tired he looked. Rugged. Handsome.

"Psychosis?" She attempted. "I mean, it is a severe form of a mental disorder, I could

guess schizophrenia or paranoia?"

"Could you please explain paranoia to me Lilliana, as detailed as you can?" Damon was taping away at his tablet.

"Yes Sir." She couldn't believe that this very serious man, was the very same one that had her body pressed up against his all those weeks ago in that photo shoot.

"Paranoia," She started. "a Mental Disorder characterized by systematized delusions and the projection of personnel conflicts, which are ascribed to the supposed hostility of others, sometimes progressing to disturbances of consciousness and aggressive acts believed to be performed in self-defence or as a mission."

"And do you believe that the young woman you have just seen has these mental afflictions?" Damon asked.

"It's hard to say as I only viewed her for a short while, but yes, I believe so." she sounded confident.

There was a knock on the door. Lilliana was relieved. She was desperate to plunge herself into the pool and swim many laps.

"Thank you Lilliana, that will be all for now. Enjoy the rest of your afternoon."

Damon smiled at her. She smiled back, thanked them both, and as the door slid open, Allie entered, and she left.

CHAPTER 19

After forty laps Lilliana dragged herself out of the pool and happily exhausted, plonked down on her towel in the shade with her friends. It was such a joy after the day she'd had, to sit and listen to the comfortable chatter around her.

Allie was telling them all about her first outing with Damon, her sisters' and brother that had taken place recently.

He'd taken Allie and her siblings to the cabin that was tucked away in the forest. It was a peaceful place for therapy, healing, bonding and building relationships. A large, airy, rustic building with wide windows allowing every inch of the forest to greet and sooth, with a wrap-around porch.

Lilliana loved hearing Allie's thoughts on how kind, caring and generous Damon was. She lay back and flung an arm over her eyes as she listened to Allie's detailed narrative that was filled with happiness and gratitude, with the extra time she'd had with her taken siblings.

"Was it just you five?" Josephine asked.

"No, they were assigned a Watcher, who drove the jeep. Poor Emile can explode with anger, without any apparent trigger. I mean, I guess we are all still pretty angry about what happened to us." Allie shrugged.

"Not surprisingly." Jessica chimed in.

"I'm hoping I can introduce you all to them and maybe Christopher too, Mr. Night said it's best to give them more time." Allie smiled, getting up, shaking out her towel, "I just feel so damn lucky to have had that extra afternoon with them. It was the best birthday present I've had in, well, years really."

Josephine jumped up, grabbing her towel too, slinging her arm around Allie's shoulder. "Well, your birthday presents are just starting girl, be prepared to be spoilt. We'll see you at dinner girls." She waved as they headed off.

Jessica smiled as she looked at Lilliana. "Do you think she has any idea about what you and Christopher are doing?"

Lilliana rolled on her stomach, watching the girls walk off in the distance and replied. "Absolutely none, we've been as silent as the night."

"She is going to die with excitement."

Lilliana grinned. "Well, I hope things don't go that far, but I sure am excited to see her reaction." Thanks to Damon, they had chosen a beautiful black colt. Allie had a particular fondness for the two year old horse, and cared for it along with the others when she volunteered in the stables.

The fact that Damon could have got an extremely high dollar for him, said how much he appreciated what Allie had been through and how he could see her future potential in benefiting their establishment.

Jessica watched as Cam and a Watcher, George, led a new group of Given into the pool. The two boys looked to be around their twenties, along with three girls, around Jessica and Lilliana's age.

One of the boys stood, glaring at the water's edge, arms tightly folded, an angry scowl on his face.

George was helping one of the girls into the water. Her left leg severely scarred, which appeared the reason for her limp.

"Poor thing." Jessica whispered.

Lilliana sat up and looked over to where Jessica nodded.

The girl was a pretty little thing, in a green one-piece swimsuit, her short blonde curls gently tossing in the breeze, her hand clinging tightly to George's.

"I wonder what she's been through?" Lilliana sighed.

"I can't imagine, it makes me sick to my stomach. I hope whoever has hurt her has been punished."

"Mm." Lilliana watched as Cam encouraged the other two girls to step into the warm water. One of them, tall with dark hair, began crying. Lilliana's heart jumped in her chest for the girl and she got up off her towel and headed over to the group.

"Excuse me Mr. Night, perhaps I can help?"

Cam looked at Lilliana, dropping his hands to his hips. "You're a strong swimmer Lilliana, that would be good." He looked at the Watcher. "That shouldn't be a problem, George, what do you think?"

George shrugged. "It'll be fine Mr. Night."

Lilliana stepped towards the girl slowly and held out her hand. "Hi, I'm Lilliana."

The girl looked at Lilliana shyly, arms folded, glancing down at the outstretched hand. "I'm Haley." She held her hand out to Lilliana, a quick shake before crossing her arms once more

Cam watched as Lilliana encouraged Haley into the water and after a few minutes, a slow, gentle breast stroke down the length of the pool, beside Lilliana.

George assisted the girl with the limp, Miranda, into the water to begin her muscle building exercises. He then turned his attention to the other girl, Naomi. Short, jet black hair. Mean, beady eyes as she stood, sussing out one of the boys. She looked like trouble, and reminded Lilliana of Natalie.

"Blake, Trevor," Cam said calmly. "time for a swim fellas. It will do you good after the last twelve weeks being shut in. Come on."

"I already told you dick head." Trevor snarled. "I bloody well don't want to swim."

Cam walked over to Trevor, almost placing his nose to the boys. "I'm sorry mate, but you don't have an option, it's part of your recovery and it's Sir to you, not dick head."

Trevor frowned. "Well *Sir-Dickhead*, I'm not swimming, and you can't make me."

George kept his eyes on the situation, as he was holding onto Miranda's hands, as she continued doing her exercises.

Naomi was at least in the water now, if only sitting on the steps.

Lilliana could see that Haley was tiring and suggested that they finish this lap, then go to the shallow end. Haley agreed and they continued down the pool.

Blake couldn't take his eyes off Lilliana.

For the past twelve weeks he had been subjected to detox and the evaluation routine with Damon Night and his team.

His story was like Orlando's. His father and elder brother subjected him to a life of crime and brutality, which led him on a path of substance abuse. It was the only thing that had helped him cope with the day to day gore, sadness and brutality. It was a lonely life and when he had felt an attraction, for one of their captives, thought he was in love and had helped her escape, after she promised to run away and be with him forever. Her dark hair and peach complexion ate at his core. So, he did release her. What he did not know, was that she was an Official's sister, and once she made her getaway, reported the location of their crime house.

Before they were raided, Blake's brother made the discovery that Blake had set her free, and went to town on him, beating him severely and knocking him unconscious.

The authorities had turned up and Blake's brother had made a run for it.

His father shot in the cross fire, and Blake delivered to the Given.

Cam was still going nose to nose with Trevor, and George had his hands full with Naomi and Miranda, it only took a split second for all hell to break loose.

As Blake watched Lilliana help Haley out of the pool, his anger increased. He could not believe how much she looked like his traitor: the same dark hair and creamy skin. He wanted to punish her for betraying him. He watched as Lilliana took Haley to the spa, and making sure the other men were busy, made his move.

Lilliana smiled as Haley exclaimed how delicious the spa was, when a roar exploded behind her. She spun around and was startled when she saw the large boy loom towards her. Turning on her heel she made a run for it, but not fast enough.

He tackled her hard to the ground, turning her over to face him, slamming her head against the hard pavers.

She saw a million stars thump painfully behind her eye's, in an angry red haze, his hands closing around her throat, squeezing tightly. Her fingers uselessly attempted to claw his away from her throat and the screaming she could hear, started to fade away. She blacked out, not seeing Cam grab Blake off her, yelling out to Jessica to get Damon and another Watcher.

Jessica set out as fast as she could and was knocking on Damon's door within a handful of minutes.

As the door slid open, revealing a panting Jessica in nothing but a bathing suit, Damon hung up the phone on whomever he was talking to, and rose quickly, heading over to the girl.

"What is it Jessica?"

"Mr. Night needs you at the pool immediately Sir, and another Watcher also. Lilliana's been attacked by a new Given."

Damon strode out of the building, Jessica heard him curse, and tried not to panic at his furious tone. She would never want to be in his bad books.

As they headed towards the pool, he snapped out his phone and barked out an order to a Watcher. As they neared the pool, two other Watcher's had arrived, with a small group of Given.

Cam had Lilliana in his arms and was walking towards Damon. "She's out."

Damon looked at her body in his brother's arms, basically naked, clad only in her skimpy purple bikini. Her pale face against Cam's chest, appearing asleep, hair still dripping and hanging down, tangled in Cam's arms.

"Give her to me Cameron." He said, opening his arms to take her.

Cam nodded, stepping forward he placed her in Damon's arms.

Damon turned and walked off, with Cam close on his heels.

As they headed inside the house and down to the hospital, Cam filled Damon in on what had happened. Billy was at the station when they arrived and quickly turned to direct Damon into an empty room.

Once she was placed on the bed, Damon pulled a sheet up to cover her body and give her a little warmth, then stood at the end of the bed arms folded across his chest.

Billy ran his hands gently down her throat and around her neck.

"She's going to be sore for a couple of days." He grabbed his flick pen, and lifted a lid, flashing the light into her eyes quickly. He got the response he was after and sighed with relief.

"She'll be fine, she should come back soon. I'll be back with Rachael in a few minutes, Mr. Night." Billy left the room quickly.

"Thanks Billy." Damon called after him as he looked at Cam.

"What the hell was she doing in your group with Blake, even Trevor? They have only just been released, for *Fucks Sake.*"

Cam rarely heard Damon swear and knew this wasn't good. He held up his hands. "I know. Look, George was with me, seriously I'm sorry Damon but we thought it was all okay. Lilliana just wanted to help with Haley, and she was doing a great job before Blake went AWOL." Cam put his hands on his hips, shaking his head. "I'm bloody sorry Damon, she's just so good with the newbies."

"I know she is, but at least when she's working with them in the hospital, it is in a controlled, supervised environment, *Damn it.*" He ran his hands through his hair and glanced back at Lilliana. She was staring at him, with half closed eyes.

"Lilliana." He breathed, walking over to her, he picked up her small hand. "Are you alright?" He bent down to look into her sea green eyes.

Cam walked on the other side of the bed. "Sorry Lilliana how are you feeling?"

Lilliana raised her free hand to her head, closing her eyes she whispered. "My head is pounding."

Right on Que, Rachael and Billy entered the room. "Oh Lilliana," Rachael inspected her bruised throat. "that looks painful, let's get some pain relief please Billy."

"On it." Billy left the room, returning quickly to hand Lilliana a cup of water with two silver tablets.

"Thank you." Lilliana washed the tablets down before handing Billy the cup back.

"I'll do a quick scan on your head, but you should be back in your own bed by tonight." Rachael smiled down at Lilliana.

Lilliana nodded. "Is Haley alright?" She directed the question to Cam.

"She is fine Lilliana you just rest up, okay." He looked across at Damon. "I best get back and sort it all out."

"Bring Blake to my office in half an hour please Cameron and appoint a Watcher for him, twenty-four- seven."

"Of course."

Damon watched his brother leave the room, before turning his attention back to the girl on the bed, that was constantly on his mind. It was not a good thing. Eight years his junior. His responsibility. You may as well call her my ward, he thought.

His great, great granddaddy had married one of his Given in his time.

"Damon." Rachael snapped him out of his thoughts.

He blinked, taking his eyes off Lilliana. 'Sorry, what?"

"I need to do Lilliana's scan now." Rachael was waiting for him to move.

"Yes, of course, just buzz me in my office to let me know how it went." He looked down at Lilliana. "Take care Lilliana, we'll speak soon."

She smiled at him before he turned to leave, hoping Cam wouldn't get into too much trouble for letting her help out.

Rachael took out a thin long metal tube and pressed a button on the end of it, a small screen lit up, as she held it over Lilliana's head.

She could see Lilliana looking up at her through the screen, and clearly her skull, and all that was held within it. All look well and normal, apart from a large bump that would go down within time.

She chatted to Lilliana about Haley. They both agreed she was a sweet girl, that needed a lot of T.L.C. As was Miranda.

"Once you graduate Lilliana, imagine the position you will be in, to help all those just like Haley and Miranda."

Lilliana nodded, wincing in pain with the movement, and said quietly. "It will be so rewarding, and Allie and I have talked about working together as we share similar ideas for healing and therapy. We would love to have a joint office, make it really cosy and comforting to hold our groups there." Lilliana shrugged. "Although I'm not sure how to go about getting our own office space."

"It may be doable Lilliana, this place has come a long way over the many decades it has been established, through people's fresh ideas." Rachael smiled. "And you have a couple of years yet, to build up your ideas before putting them forward."

"That's true."

"Hello Lilliana." Dr. Ryan entered the room. "I hear you had a mishap whilst trying to help out a new Given."

Lilliana shrugged sheepishly.

"Good job, sometimes getting hurt is part of the territory in places like this. It's people like you who really help make a difference at the end of the day, because you truly care." He smiled kindly, looking over Rachael's shoulder noting the scan was clear of anything untoward. "Look's good, clear."

"Right Lilliana, lets get you out of your damp suit, showered, a spot of soup and into a warm bed for the afternoon. Sound good?"

Lilliana felt drained and couldn't wait to curl up in her bed and sleep. She nodded tiredly and was grateful for Nurse Rachael's efficiency with how quickly she made that list of requirements, happen.

***

Once a month, the establishment celebrated its Givens' birthdays and there were several birthdays this day, that were to be celebrated, and Jessica Lilliana and Allie's eighteenth, were amongst them. After classes, work and rounds, one of the common rooms would be set up for two-hour party with cake, music and dancing for all those that wanted to attend. Lilliana had not attended last year for her seventeenth, but she thought turning eighteen, she had best celebrate for her beloved Mother's sake.

The kitchen staff always prepared one cake, large enough to share once numbers had been confirmed, and Christopher had designed a stunning white mud cake for the seventy odd guests.

The day had rolled along as it normally did for Lilliana, starting with her morning run, classes and a quick catch up with her friends at lunchtime, before another six hours of classes, combined with a lecture in the library and an hour in the hospital, and one hour down in psych.

It was after eight, when Lilliana had finally showered, dressed and finished her makeup and hair. She had chosen a stunning off the shoulder, black handkerchief hemmed dress that floated around her knees feeling soft and fluttery.

She'd piled her wavy locks on top of her head, with tendrils falling here and there on their own accord. She gave herself smoky eyes and popped on a little eye liner. The knock at the door revealed Jessica, almost identical, as they had planned, but her dress and shoes were electric blue in colour.

"Gorgeous Jessica."

"Likewise." Jessica sighed, sitting on Lilliana's bed. "It only feels like yesterday we met and now, here we are eighteen. It went so fast."

"It did, and it didn't." Lilliana took her friend's hand, noting the sad look in her eyes. "So much has happened from then, till now Jess, a lot of it really good."

Jessica squeezed Lilliana's hand smiling, chasing her sadness away. "You are right, as usual, a lot of good has happened and I will focus on that tonight. Let's go."

They headed off downstairs and entered the common room set up for the party and were not surprised with how fabulous it looked.

Cam was the D.J. and Rachael and Johnson were supervising.

Lilliana and Jessica wished the others a Happy Birthday and mingled with the guests. Marcus and Lisa kissed the girls and wished them a good night, as Fox sashayed over with a digital deluxe camera hanging around her neck. "Smile girls." She called, snapping them as they turned in her direction. "Lovely." Josephine and Allie quickly jumped into frame to be snapped with their friends.

Josephine whispered to Lilliana, "When are we doing Allie's horse?"

"He's not ready till next week."

"Oh my, it will be so worth the wait."

Lilliana smiled and raised her voice as Cam was pumping up the music. "She is going to love it."

"Right," Allie joined them, grabbing one of their arms and dragging them into the centre of the dancing crowd. "let's dance." And they did, for an hour non-stop, with all their friends. Lilliana felt totally exhausted after such a big day, and went to sit along the wall, watching her favourite people attempt the limbo that Marcus and Cam had set up.

Josephine plonked down beside her, handing her a cup of punch. "How are you?"

"Exhausted, but happy." She finished her drink and wrapped her arms around Josephine. "What would I do without any of you?" She asked wistfully.

"What would any of us do." Josephine hugged back tightly.

They sat back and smiled at each other.

"So," Josephine asked. "what do you do, about having the hot's for someone that is, firstly, wrong for you, and secondly, never going to happen?" Her eyes were watching Cam, as he threw his head back laughing at something Leon said.

Lilliana felt herself flush, understanding those feelings all too well. "Maybe we'll grow out of it." She said quietly.

"Mm, I don't know, I've spent most my life thinking he's a jerk and all of a sudden I'm noting him more and more, and half the time, he doesn't seem like such the jerk I thought he was." Josephine sighed. "And god damn it, he's so bloody *hot*."

Lilliana chuckled, loving the fact that her friend appeared head over heels for Mr. Night. Something she knew all too well. She inwardly sighed. She couldn't even look at anyone her age, without comparing him to Damon. Even Leon, at nineteen, who gave Lilliana all his good intentions, still couldn't compete with her thoughts of Damon. She was a lost cause.

"Okay everyone," Cam called into the microphone, last song of the night. Grab your guy or gal and make it a good one."

Cam jumped off the stage and strolled over, bowing to Josephine. "Will you do me the honour Miss Josephine, after all, someone's turning nineteen in a blink of an eye's time." He smiled devilishly.

"Why not." Josephine tried to sound carefree, but Lilliana could hear a slight nervousness to her tone.

Josephine kissed the top of Lilliana's head, before taking Cam's hand as he whisked her onto the dance floor.

Lilliana felt him before she saw him. Damon, two feet away, dressed in black jeans and a steel blue shirt.

Dark eyes staring into hers. Her breath caught as he stepped over to her and held out his hand. "Can't have the birthday girl missing out on the last song."

She smiled, taking his large, warm hand, as he led her onto the dance floor, pulling her close, but not indecently, as he expertly moved her amongst the dancers.

Lilliana breathed him in, and enjoyed the feeling of her hand being held in his.

The warmth of his other hand, pressing lightly against her back, occasionally stroking her soft flesh made her shiver.

He looked down at her, but she kept her eyes on the other dancers, smiling, watching as Cam dipped and spun Josephine around.

Orlando had his arms wrapped around Jessica, and they looked deeply into each other's eyes.

Allie and Christopher were in a lip lock battle, in a corner, camouflaged by the seventy odd dancers.

"Have you had a good day Lilliana?" Damon asked against her ear.

She nodded and turned her head up to answer him, her lips hitting his solidly.

He stiffened, and he heard her breath catch, as her lips parted.

He moved his head back a fraction, to look down into her green, liquid pools. He could lose himself in those eyes. "Careful." He hadn't realized he'd whispered the word out loud, but the look on Lilliana's face told him he had.

"Sorry." She flushed.

"No, Birthday girls don't need to apologize." The song ended. Damon stepped back, and raising her hand to his lips, he brushed a soft kiss over her knuckles.

"Happy Birthday sweet girl."

She smiled at him. "Thank you, Mr. Night."

Before she could say another word, she was grabbed from behind and swung away from Damon, by strong, firm arms. Leon.

"Happy Birthday."

She laughed. "Thank you."

Damon left the room, feeling, as always where Lilliana was concerned, uncomfortably frustrated.

CHAPTER 20

The day was fresh; thick clouds hung heavily in a greying sky. It did nothing to remove the cheer that surrounded the excitement of gifting Allie with her birthday horse. Christopher held his hands over Allie's eyes, her back pressed snugly into his chest. He had carried her to the stables, like a bride over a threshold, placing her gently on the ground, with her friends already standing around her new horse's stall.

"Surprise darling." He whispered against her ear, removing his hands.

Allie squealed, very unlike her, but proved just how excited she was.

"*No way.*" She cried. "This is beyond awesome." She wrapped her arms around Christopher, and gave him a deep, wet kiss.

"Okay love birds, break it up." Josephine said happily.

"He is just beautiful, Lilliana, did you do this?" Allie asked, giving her a friend a hug.

"We all did this," Lilliana said. "and Mr. Night of course."

"Ah, Mr. Night." Allie mused. "You know, we are permitted to call him Damon, being eighteen and all."

"True," Christopher smiled. "although I still find myself calling him Mr. Night when he steps into the kitchen."

"I just can't, it doesn't feel right." Lilliana agreed.

"My god," Allie jumped excitedly. "I simply have to go for a ride, right now."

Orlando and Jessica were standing just near the entrance door, Jessica already sneezing.

"Well, you'll have to count us out," Orlando smiled as he slipped an arm gently around Jessica's shoulders. "we have our first Team Leader practical with four new Given."

"That is brilliant." Lilliana smiled at them. "With Marcus or Lisa?"

"Neither, do you know Kim and Neo?"

"Yes, Leon's good friend's with Neo, I haven't met Kim though." Lilliana bent to pick up one of Josephine's rascals that started chewing on her boot.

Josephine scooped up one of his brothers.

"You'd think they would have grown out of chewing on everything wouldn't you? You silly dog you." She said, kissing the one in Lilliana's arms.

"Well," Christopher called to Orlando and Jessica. "good luck, you will both be brilliant."

"We can only hope so." Jessica smiled as Orlando turned her about and they left for their Team Leader roles.

"What do you say Lilliana, are you going riding?" Josephine asked.

Christopher had to get back to the kitchen for his shift to start.

And Josephine and Rupert were helping Cam organize a dispatch of vegetables going out to South East Asia. Josephine was very excited, as this is what she loved doing. Creating sustainable, ongoing crops to, not only supply huge amounts for this establishment, her home, but for the people out in the world where vegetables and fruits were not always in supply.

"I'm supposed to be in class with Dr. Richard." Lilliana said apologetically.

"How much trouble do you think you'd get into if you skipped it? We've got group tomorrow; we'll just say you were ill?" Allie was hopeful.

Lilliana looked at her friend, and smirked. "Why not? Maybe I won't be missed?"

Christopher kissed Allie goodbye, then hugged Lilliana appreciatively before heading off to the kitchen.

The two friends quickly saddled and prepared their pride and joys, for a ride.

They were heading out of the stables in less than ten minutes, taking off at a canter, before blissfully allowing their horses to gallop freely over the terrain. Once they hit the thicker trees, they slowed down, catching up on all the gossip, laughing hysterically in no time, about one of their classmates who had back-chatted Dr. Hillary the day before.

The air smelt divine with the coming rain and both girls were relaxed and relished this free time as they reflected on the work they had done, in order to set a solid path for their future, as carers of the mind and soul.

"I am so ready to do my part, you know, really pour myself into the work, be a part of the system." Allie was referring to how close to the end of their exams they were.

"Yes, I know what you mean. I can't wait to really get into it all, get my hands dirty and truly help someone." Lilliana agreed.

"That Blake has got some serious issues." Allie commented. "It's a good thing he has a Watcher twenty-four-seven."

Lilliana reached forward and ran her hand along Beauty's neck, appreciating her beautiful creature, not really wanting to talk about Blake. He constantly watched her and frankly, freaked her out. He was big and fast.

Allie noticed Lilliana close off and quickly changed the subject. "I think I'll call him Raven." She stroked the sleek neck of her horse.

"That's a perfect choice Allie." Lilliana smiled at her.

"I can't believe I have him." Allie sounded dreamy. "It is all so very surreal."

"You deserve it Allie." The rain hit them hard and the loud crack of thunder had them both laughing. They were drenched in seconds.

Allie yelled over another crack of thunder. "I'll race you back." She turned Raven, laughing and galloped off.

Lilliana lost sight of her quickly, as the rain fell in heavy sheets. The thunder had Beauty prancing about nervously, throwing her head, pulling at the bit.

"It's okay girl, it's okay." She soothed her nervous animal, stroking her neck. She allowed Beauty to set her pace, not wanting her to rush over the slippery ground.

She was not bothered by the cold rain drops that slid inside her collar, dripping down her back, she was enjoying being truly alone, with not one soul in sight.

She shuddered at a memory from a few days ago; stepping out of the bathroom and straight into Blake. It wasn't the first time he had put himself directly in her path. His Watcher always with him and, it seemed innocent enough. There were always people flowing to classes, work or activities. It was just that look in his eyes when he bumped into her, like he'd won something.

She pushed the unwanted thought of him away, and let her mind wander to the day before, to something more pleasant. Josephine's nineteenth birthday. Damon had had her room freshly painted with a soft green featured wall, and warm, earth colours on the remaining walls, with white leaves stencilled throughout. Fresh pots of flowers filled every spare space she had, and Josephine had been one very happy girl.

Lilliana and her friends had dedicated a garden patch of their own to her, with the help of Rupert, each having an aisle where they planted something, that represented Josephine to them. Lilliana had planted sunflowers. Allie had planted a row of tomatoes and Jessica had planted poppies.

Cam had made a metal sign, that read. 'Josephine's Joy.' Josephine had loved every minute of her day.

The barking of dogs pulled her out of her happy memory, and she stilled the scream in her throat, her heart momentarily froze in her chest, as Beast reared up, suddenly in front of her, snorting what looked like steam, from his nostrils. Beauty shuffled nervously.

"What the hell are you doing out here Lilliana?" Damon yelled at her.

She was in total shock. He had never yelled at her, surely Allie had told him they had gone for a ride? She must have gotten back ahead of her.

"I was out riding with Allie, I thought she'd be back by now?" She felt very unsure.

"She was back over an *HOUR AGO!*" He fumed. "And *YOU* are supposed to be in *CLASS.*" His stormy blue eyes glared into her startled green ones.

She watched as the rain dripped over his handsome face. "I'm sorry Mr. Night, Allie wanted to go for a ride, and I didn't want to leave her alone." She didn't know what else to say, to this furious looking man.

He half shook his head in anger, before snapping out. "Come." Spinning Beast around, they left in a canter.

She gently kicked Beauty after him, wondering how an hour could have gone so quickly. Once they reached the stables, Thomas took Beast off Damon, and Lilliana slid off Beauty and lead her to her stall, trying to wring out her long, wet ponytail at the same time.

"Edward," Damon called, "take Lilliana's horse please. Lilliana, follow me."

Lilliana handed the reins to Edward, and gave him a small, apologetic smile, before she followed Damon out of the stables. Very unsure as to why he was so furious.

They arrived inside the house within ten minutes, both sopping wet, and Lilliana shivering.

He walked into his office, Lilliana five steps behind. The door sliding silently shut behind her. He tugged off his jacket and walking to the chute in the wall, opened it, and threw his jacket down.

Turning to face her, he walked to the fireplace, hands on his hips, the flames dancing behind him. His clothes moulding to every chiselled muscle, hair dripping in his eyes. He looked like a fallen angel; his handsome face held a shadow of fury.

Lilliana nervously stood before him, arms folded, shivering. Black tendrils of hair, hanging everywhere, sticking to her pale cheeks. Her green eyes sparkling and standing out even more, with her long-wet lashes.

He imagined her stepping out of the shower. Hot and steamy.

He turned his back to her quickly, wanting to walk over to her, and crush her cold, wet lips to his, and warm them up.

Running a hand through his hair, he rested his hands on the mantelpiece, staring into the flames. The statue of Beast sat between the candle holders.

"Mr. Night, I really am sorry," She started quietly. "it wasn't my intention to worry anyone, and to be honest, I've never missed class in the years I've been here. I…" she trailed off, unsure. "I thought I'd get away with it just this once." She finished lamely.

She kept her eyes on his strong back, watching his fingers tighten on the mantel.

"Do you think you should be able to get away with things Lilliana?" He asked.

"No Sir, of course not." Lilliana was almost horrified. "I'm not a brat Sir."

Damon sighed, and turned to face her. "No. No of course you're not a brat Lilliana. That wasn't what I was implying." He watched her closely.

She stared back at him, her arms tightened across her shivering chest.

"Look Lilliana, as soon as Dr. Richard saw you weren't in his class, he notified me. When a student isn't where they are supposed to be, I worry." Especially when it's you, he thought. "I found Christopher, who told me what you and Allie were up to. When she returned without you, I was concerned. I worry about you Lilliana." He said her name quietly. "I shouldn't worry about you more than anybody else. But I do." He stayed where he was, holding himself still. He knew if he took one step towards her, he would not be able to stop himself from scooping her up in his arms and having his wicked way with her.

Lilliana swallowed, her heart hammering away in her chest. She could not take her eyes from his.

"Please go Lilliana. Shower, and get to your next class. I'm sorry to tell you, but you'll have to have night detention with Dr. Richard after dinner, in the library."

"Okay." She said quietly. "Thank you, Mr. Night." She didn't know why she was thanking him for night detention but didn't know what else to say.

He nodded once, watching as she quickly turned, and left the room.

She dashed up the stairs, and into the showers, before facing a gruelling two-hour class on hypnotherapy, hoping she would be able to concentrate with the multitude of feelings tumbling around in her head.

She only hoped her friend had not gotten into any trouble on this special day of receiving her horse.

***

The girls caught up over dinner, and Allie apologized for racing off on Raven the way she had.

"Don't be," Lilliana assured her. "if it wasn't for the rain, I would have been right there with you."

"Mr. Night was furious when you weren't with me," Allie said, spooning up a mouthful of sweet corn chowder. "I thought he was going to strangle me. Christopher's correct, I couldn't help but call him 'Mr. Night'. He terrified me."

Josephine chuckled. She couldn't believe anyone would actually fear Damon, even when he was furious.

Lilliana swallowed a mouthful of sweet potato and pushed her peas around on her plate. Damon must have been furious for someone as gutsy as Allie to be frightened of him.

Orlando leaned across Jessica and said to Lilliana. "I hear you're not alone in detention tonight, there's a few that have been out of order today. We had one of the newer girls, Naomi, slap one of her classmates. I think it was Miranda."

"And it looks like Nasty Natalie will be joining you. She and Fox had an altercation in the design room, and Natalie tried to cut off Fox's hair." Jessica shook her head.

"Oh no," Lilliana groaned. "that will be the icing on the cake."

She slumped back in her seat, dropping down her cutlery, no longer hungry.

"Hey Baby." A voice whispered close to her ear.

She whipped her head around, and was face to face with Eric, who was leaning down near her.

"Eric, charming as usual." Lilliana turned away from him.

"Eric, sit." Cam called from the end of the table. They all looked down, where he had been talking to Claire, a new counsellor in the Black Ops division.

He was staring stonily at Eric. Eric stared back.

Cam stood and with his finger, pointed to Eric, then towards Eric's empty chair.

Eric slowly walked to his chair, then sat, staring down the table at Lilliana.

"I thought he'd gotten over you?" Josephine sipped on her tea. "He hasn't bugged you for ages."

"Yes, it's been peaceful." Lilliana said, still watching Eric. She looked away after he winked at her.

Christopher walked into the room, and up to Allie. He was dressed in his kitchen uniform. He bent down, and quietly whispered in her ear. She smiled up at him and nodded. He kissed her quickly, then left the room.

Allie had a pretty, flushed look on her face. She beamed at her friends. "Birthday rendezvous." She said quietly. They continued chatting whilst they ate.

"Well, I'm off for ten minutes before I have to be in detention." Lilliana pushed her chair out and smiled at her friend. She bent down, and kissed Allie's cheek. "Happy gift day darling girl."

Allie squeezed her hand. "Thanks for the ride today my friend. Sorry it got you detention." She smiled apologetically again.

"Don't worry about it. I need extra time to frazzle my brain with a complicated, Higher-Order questioning night." She waved and left the room, heading upstairs to her room, to freshen up.

She stripped off, and popped on fresh deodorant, then pulled out a long sleeved, snug fitting black dress, that was comfortable and soft.

Her equivalent to a nighty.

It fell just above her knees, and she pulled on some leggings and soft boots.

Pulling her hair out of its band, she brushed it till it shone, then did a quick plait over one shoulder. She plonked on her bed, falling back and closed her eyes briefly.

Banging on her door had her jolting awake with a fright. She swore quietly as she quickly got up and flicked the switch for it to slide open.

Damon. Looking a lot more relaxed than he had earlier that afternoon when he was scolding her.

Hands in his faded jeans pockets, a black tee shirt fitting snugly across his chest.

His stunning blue eyes taking in her sleepy green ones.

"You are late." Was his way of greeting.

"Oh no," She groaned, embarrassed to be, once again, in the wrong. "I'm sorry."

He stepped back and opened his palm for her to go ahead of him.

She stepped out of the room and together they walked down the stairs.

A few of the younger Given, with their Team Leaders, were heading up the stairs to their rooms.

"Goodnight Mr. Night." They chorused.

He nodded and smiled at them, bidding them good night also. As they approached the bottom of the stairs, shouting could be heard in one of the common rooms.

She heard Damon sigh, and risked a glance up at his face.

His fingers pinched the bridge of his nose, his eyes closed for a second.

Before she knew what she was doing, her hand reached out, and placed it around his, squeezing gently.

He stopped walking, and looked down at her very feminine, small hand around his large one. He looked down at her.

She smiled quickly, then pulled her hand free, and went into the library, to hear Dr. Richard say, "Well, well, if it isn't Lilliana. Ten minutes late. It looks like you will be staying back after everybody else goes to bed. Sit." He pointed to an empty chair, right next to Blake's.

"Seriously?" She asked him. Did he not know that Blake was a danger to her?

Dr. Richard pointed to a man in the corner, playing on a tablet. Blake's Watcher.

He then pointed back to the chair.

Lilliana walked over, her boots tapping softly on the floor.

She didn't quite realize what a delicious sight she made, in her snug, black outfit that hugged her curves. With her hair pulled back off her face, it showcased her cheekbones and neck beautifully.

She plonked elegantly into her chair, crossing her legs, she took the tablet that Reline handed her, and smiled thank you, wanting to know what the softly spoken Reline had done to end up here this night.

There were six of them in total. Lilliana, Reline, Blake, Naomi, Natalie and Luke.

Luke was the only one, that Lilliana had not yet met. He was a bit younger than Lilliana and he looked shy, keeping his head down, concentrating on filling out questions the doctor had set down for him.

As Lilliana turned on her tablet, she glanced at Natalie, who, looking at her, flipped her the bird. Lilliana made a quiet noise, as if to say, 'Whatever'.

As her tablet turned on, she tapped to the section she was tasked to complete in detention. Glancing through the impossible list, she looked across at Dr. Richard, not believing how much she had to complete. "Excuse me, Sir."

He peered over his horn-rimmed glasses at her.

As he just stared at her without asking what she wanted, she held up the tablet to show him the extent of the work that needed completing.

"Am I expected to do all of this, in this detention, or do I have a day to finish it?"

"You have this detention, Miss Lilliana, so I would suggest you get on with it."

Lilliana stared hatefully at the doctor. He stared as equally hatefully back.

She looked down, furious at him, wanting to say something else, but thought better of it. She took a deep, steadying breath, not taking her eyes from the screen as she started counting to thirty, trying to calm her anger down. She could hear the others typing away, sometimes getting up to get a book for research.

She sighed inwardly and attacked the first question.

After forty minutes, she finished one short essay. Glancing at the clock, it read 8:15pm.

"Mental disturbance Lilliana." Dr. Richard barked out, jarring her out of her thoughts on how she was going to approach the next question.

'You're mentally disturbed', she whispered in her head, but responded instead, "What about it Sir?" She looked at him, wondering where he was going with this.

"Tell me about Neurosis." He demanded.

Lilliana was about to reach for the back of her neck and give it a rub, but she knew he would know she was nervous, so she gripped the edge of the tablet and squeezed.

"Also called Psychoneurosis. It is a functional disorder in which feelings of anxiety, obsessional thoughts, compulsive acts and physical complaints without objective evidence and patterns dominate the personality."

Dr. Richard stared at her. She glanced down at her boots, not wanting to look at him for longer than she had to.

"Do you believe it to be a serious illness?"

"It is considered to be a relatively mild personality disorder. It's typified by excessive anxiety or indecision, and a degree of social or interpersonal maladjustment. I believe if you are living with any mental illness, I'd consider it pretty serious." She said.

He nodded, and continued typing, leaving her to get onto her next question.

"I need to pee." Natalie stated loudly. She was sitting, legs spread, hands on knees.

"Well then go, Natalie." Dr. Richard snapped.

Natalie got up and winked at Luke as she sauntered past.

The library toilet was just off to the side, near the koi pond.

The trickling of the fountain was soft and comforting to Lilliana.

Within two minutes, moaning was coming from the toilet that Natalie had entered.

Reline and Lilliana looked at each other, holding in their groans.

Natalie decided that masturbating in the loo, was a bit more exciting than detention.

Her moans increased in volume, and as Dr. Richard got up to go and knock on the door, she screamed out as she orgasmed.

"What the hell?" Blake exclaimed.

"Nothing but bloody nut-jobs around here." Naomi muttered.

Luke had gone bright red and kept his eyes on his work as Dr. Richard sat back down, not looking uncomfortable in the least, which was disturbing to Lilliana in itself.

Blake leaned across and whispered loudly to Lilliana. "You want to come like that sugar, you come to me."

Lilliana gave him her stoniest stare. "Gee, thanks. I'll pass." She looked across at Reline. "Can you believe this?"

Reline shrugged as Natalie strolled past Dr. Richard then, walking past Luke, ran her fingers under his nose.

The poor kid didn't know what hit him. He flung himself back in his chair and cried out. "*No.*"

"Natalie, *get a grip.*" Lilliana shouted at her.

Natalie stopped in her tracks, and slowly walked over to Lilliana, standing over her.

"What did you say princess? Grip a tit." With that, she lunged down and squeezed Lillian's breast as hard as she could.

Lilliana yelled in pain, trying to slap the other girl off whilst Blake was laughing, yelling out, "Bitch fight, yeah!" before his Watcher stood beside him, pushing him back into is chair.

Dr. Richard grabbed Natalie from behind and yanked her off Lilliana. For a thin, frail looking man, he was very strong.

"Sit yourself down Natalie, or you will find yourself receiving some shock treatment." He said without blinking.

Lilliana believed him.

Natalie shrugged and smirked. Sitting down and picking up her work, she looked very proud of herself.

Lilliana stared angrily at the smirking girl, wanting to rub her sore breast, but did not want to give Natalie the satisfaction. She wanted to flick Natalie the bird so hard, her hand was shaking. She shook her head and got back to the next question. Bloody hell, she thought, looking at the clock, it was only 8:45pm. This was going to be a long night.

Two hours later, Christopher wheeled in a trolley.

"What's this?" Dr. Richard asked.

"Well Sir, Mr. Night asked me to bring in refreshments and call a ten-minute break for those doing detention."

"Fine." Dr. Richard waved his hand.

Christopher winked at Lilliana, as she got up to grab a cup of tea, he whispered to her, "How's it going?"

"You really do not want to know the answer to that," She smiled at him. "but tell Allie to get ready for a giggle tomorrow." She rolled her eyes in Natalie's direction.

"Righto," He whispered, pouring another cup of tea for Luke. "say no more." He grinned.

Lilliana wandered over to watch the Koi with her cup of tea, watching the fish lazily swim around in their night mode.

She finally had a few minutes for her brain to wander over to her Damon section.

Flashes of him flicking through her mind. Serious in group, laughing with Josephine.

Angry with certain situations that arose with his duty to this place every day. Drop dead gorgeous in the photo shoot. Drop dead gorgeous all the time really.

"Penny for your thoughts?" A voice said behind her. She turned and looked at Naomi.

"They're not even worth a penny." Lilliana said, not quite sure where this conversation was headed. The only other time Naomi had spoken to her, was to tell her, to go fuck herself, sideways.

Interestingly enough, is was only after Lilliana had asked her if she knew where her next class was, as she appeared lost on her second day in main house.

"So, Dr. Spock over there, what's his story and why does he hate your guts?"

Lilliana took a mouthful of her tea, calmly looking at the other girl over the rim.

"He doesn't hate me, that's just the way he is."

"Oh, sure." Naomi walked off.

Lilliana shook her head and whispered, 'weird' into her cup. Wondering who the hell Dr. Spock was, and could this night get any worse?

She walked back over to the cart and popped her empty cup down and grabbed a couple of sandwiches. Siting back down in her chair, she munched away, getting onto her next essay. As she ate, she realized they were her favourite sandwiches. Her Mothers. She felt warm to her toes, realizing that Damon must have asked Christopher to make these especially. She enjoyed them even more.

Once teatime was over, the room settled back into some serious work.

Lilliana went hard, typing away, answering questions. She felt so tired, and glancing at the tablet time, it read, 2:22am.

"Excuse me Sir, when does detention end?"

"When you have completed all your tasks." He answered without looking up, sounding bored.

Luke stood and walked over to the doctor, handing him his tablet.

"I've finished Sir." He said quietly.

"Thank you Luke." Dr. Richard took the tablet off him, settling it down on the table beside him.

"Finn," Dr. Richard asked the Watcher. "Could you please walk Luke to his room, it's on the fifth floor."

"No Worries Sir." Finn stood, and left the room with Luke.

He returned ten minutes later, as Reline and Naomi finished their work also. He then took them to their rooms.

Lilliana's head felt fuzzy, sleep would easily come, if she could just shut her eyes for one second. She glanced over at Dr. Richard.

His beady eyes were on her.

She got stuck into her work. Not having to get up to research anything, as she retained an incredible amount of knowledge. One of the things Dr. Hillary and Nurse Rachael appreciated about her.

After another hour, Dr. Richard got up to use the toilet.

She sighed, and thankfully dropped her head back and closed her eyes.

Just as she slid into that deep sleep, a sharp slap on her wrist startled her awake.

"Really?" She asked the doctor, rubbing her wrist. "You just slapped me."

"If you recall in your rules when you first came here, Miss Lilliana, I can slap you, shock you or whip you as I see fit." He stated, staring at her.

"Yes, but that's only if I step over the line of obedience." She snapped back.

"Well, you sleeping, when you should be working, is laziness, and that in my book, is disobedience in detention. And let's question why you are in detention in the first place? Think on that." He sat down and got back to his reading.

Lilliana was fuming. She considered walking out, but knew that would be punishment in itself, and she didn't want that to get back to Damon.

He didn't need the extra stress.

Natalie was smirking at her, and as the doctor was focused on his reading, she lifted two fingers up to her lips, in a 'v' sign, and flicked her tongue in and out.

Lilliana could not stop herself, and the tiredness was not helping. "You know *Natalie*, Intelligent character, some people have it, some people do not." She dropped her voice to a sharp hiss. "*You. Do. Not. Have. It.*" She spoke each word slowly, hoping it would sink in.

"Fuck you Princess." Natalie snarled.

"That's enough, both of you." Richard snapped out.

Lilliana put her head down and typed furiously at her keypad.

What a nightmare.

Blake and Natalie finally finished, the clock reading 4.57am.

As Finn took them to their rooms, Lilliana continued her next set of questions. She was quite proud that her brain was still functioning, moving onto the next set of tasks.

The morning waves of the ocean, filtered through the sound system indicating that it was 6.30am.

Lilliana looked at Dr. Richard. She could not believe he had kept her here all night. But then again. "Sir, I am not going to get this finished by breakfast."

"No, you won't. So, continue." He said, without looking up.

Lilliana stared at the hateful man but continued with the questions.

She could hear all the Given and staff coming down for breakfast.

She was too tired to even think about food.

Cam walked in a half hour later. She had one more question to complete.

"Hard night Lilliana?" He asked, smiling gently.

"No, not at all." She tried to keep the sarcasm out of her voice.

He looked over her shoulder, then, took the tablet off her and handed it to Dr. Richard. "Thanks Richard, I'll take it from here."

Lilliana cheered inside. Take that. She thought.

"Lilliana," Cam said, guiding her out of the room and up the stairs to the showers. "five minutes, then I need you downstairs for a running session. I want to put you in with a couple of our new, sensitive girls, can you do that for me?"

"Running," She asked, bewildered. "now?"

He smiled. "If anyone can do it, Lilliana you can, pretend you are on your first twenty-four-hour shift."

Lilliana nodded. "Okay, I may as well get used to that. Quick cold shower first to wake up."

He nodded. "Go for it."

She sighed, walking into the vacant bathroom. Most of the Given would be in class or activities. She stripped off, dumping her clothes into the chute then stepped into a beating hot shower, and after two minutes, ran it ice cold to wake herself.

She stepped under the drier, enjoying the soft warmth and felt sleepy under its gentle air. She quickly shut it off, and grabbing a robe, raced into her room, dressed in her running gear, pulled her hair back in one long, high pony tail and headed downstairs.

Marcus, and another Team Leader, Tina were standing in front of the running assembly, Orlando was also at the front with them.

Lilliana felt proud of him. He was pretty good at looking after people, and if he and Jessica became Team Leaders together, well, they would be together for a long time.

Orlando spotted her, and a look of concern flickered across his face. He said something to Marcus and jogged over to Lilliana.

"You look exhausted, what time did you get to bed?"

"Um, I didn't." She said.

"Are you telling me he kept you in all night?" Orlando did not look happy.

"Don't worry about it Orlando, really, I'll be fine. It's good practise for when I start my full-time training, plus Cam needs my help with a couple of girls." She forced a smile, trying to reassure him.

"Okay, but Marcus and I will be watching you." He rubbed her arm, and headed back to the front line, where Tina blew her whistle. Cam arrived and introduced Lilliana to Annabelle and Fee.

Lilliana smiled at the girls, said hello, then they were off, doing the warm-up walk before the hour run. The girls did quite well, keeping up with the group, as easily as Lilliana did. As the weather was still grey, the swim in the lake was cancelled, and they ran an extra twenty minutes. Another group was running in the distance, and Lilliana saw a group of horse riders in the opposite direction. She wondered if Damon were among them. Annabelle was a chatty little thing, once they did the warm down walk, she told Lilliana about her home in Canada, her pets, and how she missed her sister. Fee was as silent as the night, just jogged and walked, but said nothing.

Fair enough, Lilliana thought. As they reached the house, Tina blew her whistle, then shouted, "Showers everyone, twenty minutes, then straight to your classes."

Cam approached Lilliana as she walked inside. "How'd they go?"

"Good," She nodded. "Annabelle opened up; Fee was very quiet." She swayed, totally exhausted and very hungry.

Cam grabbed her arm to steady her. "Are you alright Lilliana?"

"Sure, I'm fine, I just need some food."

"Come with me." He took her hand and led her off, past the library, dining rooms and a common room, down a maze of corridors she had not entered, and finally into the most amazing kitchen she had ever seen.

Huge stainless-steel cook tops, with spotless pots and pans of all sizes, hanging from hooks above. Giant fridges and freezers, lined one wall, and the most glossy marble island bench in the middle of the kitchen, that could house fifty cooks comfortably.

By the stove top, stirring lunch, was Cook himself, glaring over his shoulder at Cam.

A short, serious looking man, that looked to be in his fifties.

"Why are you in my kitchen Mr. Night?" He'd known Cam and Damon since before they were on their mother's breast.

Cam strolled over to the fridge, opening it, looking completely at home. "Never mind Cook, just stir whatever you have over there." He pulled out some fresh milk, a banana and a handful of strawberries, and pushed the fridge shut with his knee. Dropping the goodies onto the bench, he pulled out a bar stool where he had sat often as a child, and patted it looking at Lilliana. "Sit."

Lilliana walked over and popped herself up on the high bar stool.

"Mr. Night, I'm happy to just eat the banana on my way to the shower. If I'm late for class again, I'd hate to think what will happen."

"Nonsense, you have my permission." He whipped up the milk, banana and strawberries in a blitz machine and seconds later, handed her a delicious, thick creamy smoothie.

She'd have to report this act of kindness to Josephine. She could see how her friend was falling for this extremely handsome, charming Night. She smiled and had a huge mouthful. "Oh yum it's delicious, thank you." She drank the rest down quickly.

"Not a problem." He smiled, enjoying looking after her.

She got up and walked over to the sink to rinse her glass. Looking for a tea towel to dry it, and not seeing one, she placed it on the dish rack.

She turned around to thank him again, and there, leaning against the doorway, in his riding gear, tapping his crop against his boot, watching her, was his brother.

"Hello Brother," Cam said. "How was your ride?"

'Very good, thank you Cameron. Good morning Lilliana." He said, looking at the tired, sweaty, attractive young lady.

"Good morning Sir," She forced her eyes away from his handsome-self, and looked at Cam. "Thank you again Mr. Night, I really needed that."

"Thank you for your help Lilliana. Enjoy your shower." Cam smiled.

Lilliana smiled back, and walked towards the door, looking up at Damon's face as she went to walk by him.

He gently took hold of her arm, stopping her. "What time did you get to bed Lilliana?" He couldn't remember seeing her so tired.

"She didn't." Cam answered for her.

"What?" Damon looked at his brother, then down at Lilliana.

"It's really all right Sir, the others were pretty much there all night also. I'm fine."

His finger stroked the soft flesh under her arm, before letting her go.

She resisted the urge to shiver, and still felt his touch, even as her skin cooled.

He nodded, not looking happy. "Enjoy your shower Lilliana."

As she headed out through the maze, she heard Cam and Damon's voices behind her, not too happy with her situation. She hoped Dr. Richard would get an earful for abusing younger peoples sleep patterns.

CHAPTER 21

Cam followed Damon through the passageways to enter Damon's rooms.

"What's going on between you and our dark angel Damon?"

Damon stripped off his shirt, whilst kicking off his riding boots. He unzipped his jeans, but left them to sit on his hips as he poured a coffee from the jug.

He took a mouthful, staring out his window.

Cam had perched on the arm of a chair, patiently waiting.

Damon turned to face his brother, having another mouthful before placing his cup on the table. "To be honest. Nothing is going on between us. It's all above board."

Cam chuckled. "Oh, please brother, there is nothing above board the way I see your eyes roam her face, her body. You're different around her. I've never seen you like this before. You treat her almost like she's made of glass."

Damon stared at Cam, then sighed, running his hands through his hair, he walked over and sat down on the couch, placing his hands behind his neck.

Cam watched his brother carefully. "Spill, I know you want to," He chuckled again. "in more ways than one."

Damon raised an eyebrow. "Keep it clean, Cameron."

Cam held up his hands, as he sat opposite his brother, waiting.

"I'm almost twenty-six years old, and I am lusting after an eighteen-year-old. What does that say about me?" He looked disgusted with himself.

"It says you're alive, and that you are human. You would have to be dead not to lust after Lilliana. She is drop dead gorgeous; in the most natural way I've ever seen." Cam reasoned.

"Not to mention intelligent beyond her years. She's a genius the way she writes, and her higher-order thinking skills are unlike anything we've seen in someone so young. She must have close to a photographic memory the way she retains knowledge. Not to mention what a complete sweetheart she is to the new Given. She acts like a professional already, the respect she affords them." Damon leant forward, dropping his elbows onto his knees. He looked at his brother. "Can you imagine her as an adult?" He shook his head. "She is going to be sensational."

"You've fallen hard, brother." Cam said softly.

Damon looked at him, their eyes focused on the others.

"It can never be." Damon replied.

"Why not?" Cam asked, shrugging.

"Are you serious? We are responsible for the care of these children once they enter our door. I will not be like those bastards that take advantage of the young, the innocent."

"Is that how you see her, as a young, innocent child Damon? Come on brother, you are one hundred times any man out there, and do I need to remind you, Lilliana is not an innocent young child any longer."

"All the more reason to be gentle with her, to allow her to concentrate on her career, have fun with a bit of modelling, or relaxing with her friends when she has the chance. Her work will be gruelling once it begins." He shook his head.

"Damon, you need to chill man, take a step back. Look, I've come a long way these past couple of years. I haven't had sex with an employee or a Given for at least eighteen months." He smiled, patting himself on the back. "And that hasn't been such an easy task, that Dr. Clair in Blacks Ops is yummy."

Damon smiled at him, giving him that much credit at least. He knew Cam's condition wasn't easy to live with.

"Yes, I'd have to say, you have come a long way. Would that have anything to do with the way you have been looking at our young friend Josephine?"

Cam met Damon's eyes, unsure at his tone. He shrugged sheepishly. "Probably."

"She is really special to me Cam; I won't have you hurt her. She's like our sister." Damon stated seriously.

"No, she's like your sister. She's never been like a sister to me." Cam stood and walked over to the tea tray, pouring himself a coffee. "I've been watching her grow into such a darling. I like her spunk, her attitude. We'd be good together."

Damon shook his head. "We make a fine pair, you and me. Both wanting someone we shouldn't. Let's just both keep it professional, keep our distance, and play it cool."

"Well, we can only try Brother." Cam grinned, draining his cup.

Damon shook his head. Cam could always see things in a lighter shade. The phone rang, Cam picked it up and tossed it to Damon.

"Damon Night." He answered, going silent, listening to the stressed voice on the other end. His eyes met Cam's across the room.

Cam watched as Damon closed his eyes and pinched the bridge of his nose.

He knew it wasn't good news. What now? he thought.

"Please tell Johnson I'll be there in ten minutes. I will send Cam to the other situation." He punched the dial off, before walking over and dumping it back on its cradle.

He started tugging off his jeans as he headed into the direction of his shower room.

"Cam, we've had a rape behind the stables, I need you to get over there and start dealing with that situation. You've got Bret there waiting for you."

He turned the shower up hot, and got in.

"What have you got Damon?" Cam asked, watching the steam get sucked up the air vats.

"A murder in Black Ops. Not pretty. Johnson's waiting for me. He said we will all rendezvous in two hours' time, my office downstairs. We'll have a meeting, Team Leaders included, plus the training Team Leaders." He turned the shower off and walked under the body drier. He was dried in seconds.

"Well, I'll get on my way then," Cam said, heading out. "see you in a couple."

Damon dressed, trying to imagine the scene in Black Ops.

Apparently, a security guard had his balls cut off and shoved down his throat by a group of three inmates. How they got a hold of him, he had no idea, but Johnson would fill him in. He slipped his feet into his shoes and headed out the door that led to the passageway, entering the Black Ops area, wandering how Cam was getting on with the rape situation. It would be nice to have just one day pass without incident.

***

The situation in Black Ops was contained to that division, so there was no need to cause alarm to the Given in main house.

Johnson and Damon put the right amount of pressure, mental and physical, on a selected few witnesses, who were happy to confess, and throw their fellow inmates under the bus. That situation was easily dealt with and the culprits were punished.

But the rape of young Luke Patterson, was an entirely different story.

The young boy did not see who had snuck up behind him, knocking him half out, and taking advantage of his light frame, raped him cruelly, whilst choking him.

The video feed had been cut, so the culprit got away.

The alarm was sounded, and everyone found themselves in assembly once again.

Lilliana was sitting between Allie and Shelley, as they had been in class together, down in psych, and were sitting right up the front as they were the first to enter the assembly hall. Lilliana was feeling exhausted, and took the opportunity as the hall filled, to close her eyes. Her head slipped onto Allie's shoulder and she was asleep in a second.

Damon, Bret, Billy and Cam entered the stage, calling attention. As the hall fell silent, Damon stepped forward, looking furious.

"Unfortunately, we have a rapist among us, who takes advantage of young, innocent boys." Damon spoke with a hint of disgust. "This, in no uncertain terms will go unpunished. If you are indeed the rapist, sitting among your fellow brothers and sisters, please know, you will be caught sooner or later, and you will be severely punished. All the gentlemen in this room will stay behind. Billy needs your co-operation with some DNA." Damon glanced down, seeing Lilliana asleep on Allie's shoulder. At least in this crime she should be safe, as the perpetrator had a thing for young boys.

"Ladies, you may go to class." Damon headed down the steps towards Allie.

She was sitting still, not wanting to move, as she knew how exhausted Lilliana was.

Damon bent down and scooped Lilliana up in his arms.

As he walked out of the assembly, he caught Natalie watching him, giving him a very peculiar look.

He caught Josephine's eye, and tipped his head up as if to say, 'come here.'

"Yes Sir." She said quietly, not wanting to wake Lilliana.

"Can you come up with me whilst I put her to bed?" He wanted to keep it respectable.

"Sure thing." She nodded as she followed him upstairs and helped him pop Lilliana into bed.

She watched as he carefully removed Lilliana's little ankle boots and slip her feet under the covers.

As he turned to leave, he lifted a piece of long black hair off her face, gently tucking it along her neck.

Josephine almost wanted to say, 'Should I leave you two alone?' But knew better.

She smiled at him as he turned to face her. "She'll be okay, she's just exhausted."

"Yes, I know. Thanks sweetheart, be careful would you, until the dust settles." He squeezed her arm.

"Absolutely." She smiled up at him.

He kissed her head and left the room.

Josephine went to Lilliana's desk, quickly writing a note for when Lilliana woke, and then left to get to her shift in the H.D.

***

Lilliana woke, in the dark, feeling very disoriented. Sitting up, she ran her hands over her face, wondering what time it was, and clapped twice. Light filtered down softly and she saw the note on the desk. Getting out of bed, she walked over to read it.

She smiled at Josephine's smiley face she'd drawn, and her stomach knotted as she read that Damon had carried her to bed.

She felt chilled, like a nice hot bath would warm her bones as her stomach rumbled.

Which to do first. A warm bath. She hurriedly pulled off her clothes and stuffed them into her chute, then grabbed a robe from her closet, slipping it on, she opened her door and looked out. Not a soul was around, and all the lights were set on the softest dim. It was the first time since she'd been here, that she was having a bath at such a strange hour. Whatever that hour was, she couldn't guess. She quietly ran to the bathroom, and slipping in the door, removed her robe and sunk into the always hot bathtub. She turned the jets on softly and lay back in the bubbles. It was so very peaceful; the quietest Lilliana knew it to be. Maybe night shift was the answer?

She thought about Beauty. Was it only yesterday she and Allie had gone for their ride? Yes, of course, then night detention. Dr. Richard, Nasty Natalie. Poor Luke. What a day. How sweet was Cam this morning? She hadn't had a chance to tell Josephine.

And Damon. Always back to Damon. She sighed deeply, then plunged under the water. She spent a good ten minutes swimming around and relaxing in the water, before getting out and going under the body drier. Once her hair was dry, she slipped her robe back on and quickly ran to her room, to put something a little more decent on, for her night romp to the kitchen.

Brushing her hair, she left it to fall softly around her shoulders and down her back.

She slipped on her white nighty with pink butterflies around the lacy hem, matching silk robe then stuffed her feet in cosy white booties. She tiptoed back out of her room and down the stairs. She almost turned back to get one of her girls, but didn't want to interrupt their sleep, but it was almost too much fun not to share.

Reaching the bottom of the stairs, she felt a jolt of joy being totally alone. She walked into the library, all lights downstairs were dimmed, giving the rooms a welcoming feel about them. 'This is my home,' she thought to herself.

She ran her fingers along the Koi pond. It was the first time she thought of this place as hers. She knew she must have felt this way for some time, but to acknowledge it to herself, was like a light bulb had gone on and she felt completely happy in that moment of realisation. She smiled to herself and spun out of the library, in search of the kitchen.

The hallway was darker down this end, and she couldn't quite remember which way to turn once she walked past the last common room. She continued walking, turning down this corridor, then that one. Surely, she didn't walk this far with Mr. Night. Turning down a narrow passage where the light had vanished, she put her hand in front of her as she walked slowly ahead, bumping into a dead-end.

She stumbled back a little, her hand grabbing onto the wall for balance, as her finger caught onto a tiny latch, causing a panel to slide open. There was a small amber light escaping from the cracked panel and Lilliana froze, wishing now she had woken one of her friends. This then, would have seemed a bit more of an adventure.

Okay Lilly, she thought to herself, you have two decisions to make right now: The right one, or the wrong one.

She thought she heard someone shuffling behind her and froze.

She glanced over her shoulder towards the dark, her heart beating a little faster than it should have been. Not another sound or soul in sight. The whole world as she knew it was asleep. What would the harm be, surely? She pushed the panel open and slipped inside, leaving it ajar so she could get back out.

Her memory was pretty good, despite the fact she got lost on the way to the kitchen. She put that down to being totally exhausted that morning.

She kept track of turning left, or right, going up these stairs or along this corridor. She'd been walking for a little while, with signs pointing here and there saying, Laundry, Hospital, Solitaire, Kitchen. Kitchen, she thought, I must remember that one. She stopped, thinking she'd heard a noise behind her again.

What if she wasn't in here alone? Maybe a staff member was making their rounds? Oh no, that would be great. She could pretend she'd been sleepwalking. She chuckled quietly. She was not a very good liar. She continued up the next set of stairs, then across a narrow bridge, that looked over darkness. Stopping in front of an iron gate that read. 'Black Ops. Authorized Personnel Only.' Lilliana's heart was in her mouth. She had heard so much about The Black Ops division, and here she was, standing in front of it.

She now knew, she had gone too far. It was time to turn back.

Only, when she turned around, there on the other side of the bridge, was a looming figure. Her breath caught in her throat, and not in a good way.

"Hello." She called quietly, hoping it was a friendly staff member.

The figure slowly stepped towards her. It did not respond to her friendly greeting.

Lilliana totally panicked and spun around.

She lifted the latch on the old iron gate, pulled it open, and dashed inside the small alcove, reaching the door handle on the other side, she jerked it open.

Which way to run? She thought. Shouldn't there have been a guard posted?

She ran down a corridor that was also dimly lit and felt panicked as the figure was gaining on her. Muffled screams and cursing followed her as she ran past cells, turning left, she quickly risked a glance over her shoulder, and silently cursed.

The figure was almost on her. She put all her might in sprinting down the next corridor, past so many cells, glancing up, she could see there was at least five levels above her, prison like in design. She was running around a pentagon shape.

Down another corridor and turning the corner, she could see, in the distance, the same door in which she entered. If she could just make that door. She heard breathing behind her, coming fast and ragged. He was tiring, even if he was gaining.

She put her everything into reaching that door, and as she grabbed onto the handle, his body slammed into hers from behind.

"*No.*" She groaned not wanting to give up, taking a deep breath, stopping her tears of terror.

His hands reached around her shoulders, turning her around and slamming her hard up against the door, lifting her feet of the ground.

His fingers bit painfully into her arms and she cried out, feeling his nails cut into her soft flesh.

Blake.

"I've got you all alone now you *bitch.*" He snarled, his face close to hers.

"Blake, you don't have to do this," She said softly. "you don't need to do this, please." She pleaded.

He pressed her harder into the door and bending his head, licked her shoulder.

She stiffened, trying not to openly cringe.

He gently placed her feet on the ground, his dangerous eyes, softening. She reminded him so much of his traitor, before she had turned on him, Betrayed him. Maybe this could be a second chance for him, with Lilliana?

Lilliana was barely breathing, terrified she'd make the wrong move. He had issues. Clearly.

His hands eased off her arms, rubbing her soft skin up and down; eyes staring unblinkingly, almost alien like in their paleness.

"Blake, do you want to come to the kitchen, get some food?" She asked quietly, not moving a muscle.

His hands moved up to her throat, his fingers circling around her neck. "So soft," He whispered. "you're going to be mine."

"Okay Blake, I'll be all yours, but, I'm really hungry, so can we get some food please?" She wanted him to feel completely in control. "I make a mean midnight sandwich."

"A sandwich hey?" He nodded. "That sounds good." He sounded normal, almost friendly. It was more frightening then when he seemed out of control.

She nodded, swallowing her tears that threatened. "Shall we go?" She asked softly.

"Yeah, why not." He ran his hand down her arm, linking his large fingers through her small ones.

She turned around, shivering and pushed the door open and moving forward, pushed open the heavy iron gate, clicking it quietly shut behind them they walked across the narrow bridge. As they walked slowly along the passageways, Lilliana kicked herself for her night-time adventure. It had all started off so well. Typical.

"This isn't the right way." Lilliana stopped. "We'll get lost, we should go back that way."

She looked up at him, the light behind him making him look that much bigger.

"Are you trying to trick me?" He asked, becoming angry.

Lilliana slowly shook her head. "Of course not. Let's just go then." Lilliana made to continue the way they had been walking, when he grabbed her long hair and yanked it hard, making her fall back into his chest.

"I think you are playing games with me so the deals off. I'll have you here and now." His eyes looked unpredictable and excited. "What are you going to do, scream? You'll be in just as much trouble. You know these passageways are forbidden."

She stilled, not wanting to excite him in any way, her mouth going dry in fear.

His hands moved up her waist, to cup her firm breasts, his mouth moved along the back of her neck, sucking her ear, removing her robe, he tossed it to the ground.

She rolled her eyes, and squeezed them shut. She knew which way to go, she just had to wait for the right moment. He's not going to win, she whispered to herself, he's not going to win.

She moaned softly, letting him hear what he wanted to hear, that this is what she wanted too. She pushed back against his groin. His moan was exactly what she needed to hear.

His hands left her, and bent over to unbuckle his belt, and unzip his jeans.

She wasted no time and rammed her elbow in hard and fast, smashing it into his sternum, the way Christopher had shown her and all the girls after Sarah's murder.

As Blake bent forward, groaning, she spun around and bought her knee up hard under his chin, then bolted.

As fast as she could, she ran turning down a flight of stairs, then across another section of passageway, then up a flight of stairs, she kept running.

Okay, fear also could make you lose your direction. She swore as she continued.

Blast it, she could hear him catching up. How did he do that? She had hit him hard.

She bolted, and was about to turn around a corner, when he slammed into her, knocking her on the ground.

He sat on her back, and she could hear him tugging off his belt. "You little bitch Lilliana. You liar!"

She felt the sting of the belt across her back before he said another word. Again, and again. She screamed, but it was muffled as he pushed her face into the floor, her teeth cutting into her lip, she tasted blood.

He snarled, hitting her again, "You carry on more than Luke did when I split his ass in half. You tell anyone about this, I'll deny it. Then, I'll find your little friend Jessica, and rip her in half as well." He slammed the belt down again and again. Just when she thought he'd stop; she could feel him licking her wounds. She felt sick at his touch, and a rage brew within her she had not felt in a long time. He was still for a moment, running is fingers softly over her unmarked flesh. She thought, finally, he's had enough. Then she screamed as he bit her, like a deranged animal, again and again. She cried out with all her might, sobbing for him to stop.

He did, finally before he grabbed her ankles and wrists, and hog tied her with his belt. Then, kicked her as hard as he could before running off around the corner.

She lay there, sobbing quietly, trying to get the belt loose, feeling the buckle break her skin. Her ribs were screaming in agony where he had kicked her, her back, stinging and sticky. After an hour, she stopped struggling, and just lay still.

Unfortunately, someone would find her, and when they did, she was in a world of trouble. Just thinking about it set her tears off again.

Her arms and legs tingled with stinging pins and needles, and not too long after, she couldn't feel them at all. She fell into an uncomfortable, tortured sleep, where her tears seemed to flow of their own accord.

CHAPTER 22

Damon was up, showered and dressed early as he had a conference call with a few friends of his that ran some of the other Given Establishments around the globe.

Stepping into his passageway he headed off towards the kitchen, hoping Cook had already got his breakfast going. As he rounded the corner, his heart pounded heavily in his chest.

A figure up ahead, hog tied and what looked like a bloody back faced him.

Long black hair hanging everywhere. He raced towards her, knowing instinctively it was Lilliana, praying to anyone who'd listen, that she was still breathing.

She heard the footsteps, running, waking her from her uncomfortable sleep.

Gentle hands behind her, undoing the belt. Her arms hung uselessly. He gently straightened her legs, pulling her nighty down to cover her bottom.

"Lilliana." He breathed her name, stroking her hair. Her poor back was a mess and he knew it would hurt her, but he had to get her up.

He rolled her over and up, looking at her face for the first time.

Tear tracks ran down her face. She looked devastated, lost, and would not meet his eyes.

He put his arms under her and around her back, lifting her easily.

She gasped in pain as his arm pressed into her wounded flesh.

"Sorry." He murmured, his lips pressed against her hair.

He quickly walked down the corridor, took a left then went down some very deep stairs. She knew he was taking her to the hospital. She was mortified.

She was shivering, and her arms and legs started to sting, as the blood slowly circulated.

Damon pushed a door open, and they entered the hospital from a section Lilliana had never been.

As they walked past a young male nurse, Lilliana pushed her face into Damon's chest, trying to hide. Damon approached the nurse's station after a few minutes.

Billy had just arrived on his shift, and glanced up, ready to smile, until he saw what was in Damon's arms.

"Oh no, Lilliana, darling what has happened?" Billy asked, concerned.

She kept her face pressed to Damon's chest, eyes tightly close with another tear escaping.

"We need a room Billy, I know she's been bitten, and it looks like she's been belted. I don't know what else."

"This way." Billy marched along to an empty room not far from the nurse's station.

Damon walked to the bed and gently placed Lilliana down on her side.

Billy watched as Damon sat in the chair beside the bed, pulling it close to Lilliana. "Are you alright Lilliana?"

She kept her eyes shut, turning her face into the pillow.

He stroked her hair, brushing it off her face. "Lilliana, do you know who this did?"

He watched as another tear escaped her shut eyes.

Damon got up, and said quietly to Billy. "She had her underpants on, but perhaps we need to do a rape kit?"

Billy nodded, scooping up the mass of Lilliana's tangled silken waves, so he could get a better look at her back. He sucked in his breath. "Ouch, Lilliana, I'm going to get you some pain relief, okay?"

She nodded.

Damon was relieved that at least she was acknowledging Billy. He folded his arms as Billy went to leave the room. "Page Johnson would you Billy, and get Rachael."

"Of course, Sir." He said, exiting the room.

Lilliana heard his footsteps come close again, but kept her eyes shut. She was so ashamed that she had broken a house rule and explored in the first place.

She almost felt like she deserved the punishment Blake had inflicted. She was in so much pain, her back was on fire.

"Lilliana, what has happened?" Rachael entered, horrified at the sight of Lilliana's back, with Billy two steps behind her. "Right," She said in her no-nonsense voice. "all males out right now so I can treat Lilliana's back."

Billy nodded and turned back around, leaving the room. He would never mess with one of Rachael's direct orders. Damon was another matter. He stood, facing her, not moving an inch.

Rachael walked over and said to him softly. "I need to remove her pyjama's Damon, I think Lilliana would be more comfortable being naked, if you were not in this room."

Damon flushed and nodded, glancing quickly at Lilliana before walking out, closing the door behind him.

Rachael got busy, placing Lilliana onto her stomach, and cutting the material away. She bathed her back, then sprayed some healing and antiseptic serum over the wounds, clucking her tongue in anger as she completed her task.

Lilliana remained silent, only crying out softly when the antiseptic made contact with the deeper cuts.

Once she was finished, Rachael had her sitting up, holding the sheet to her chest.

"Billy." Rachael called.

He entered, with the pain relief for Lilliana, and handed it to, waiting for her to pop them into her mouth before handing her the cup of water.

She held the sheet to her chest with one hand and said quietly without meeting his eyes. "Thank you, Billy."

"Good girl." He looked at Rachael. "Johnson is outside, wanting to talk to Lilliana."

"He can wait a minute," Rachael touched Lilliana's hand gently. "I'm going to go and get you something for you to wear, okay Lilliana?"

"Wait with her." She told Billy as she slipped from the room.

She walked past Johnson and Damon. "Has she said anything?" Damon asked.

"No, and don't go in there, please Sir," She added to soften her demand.

"Can you bring her to my office when you are done? If she is up to it of course."

"Yes Sir." She replied, hurrying along. A few minutes later she returned to Lilliana with a soft, yellow halter neck dress. "Turn around Billy." She instructed, which he did immediately.

She helped Lilliana step into the dress that floated about her knees, and pulling it up gently, slipped the thin halter material over her neck, allowing her back to be free from any uncomfortable rubbing of material, whilst she was healing. She pulled all of Lilliana's thick long hair over her shoulder, keeping that too, off her back.

She smiled at Lilliana fondly. "Perfect colour on you."

She got a damp face washer and wiped Lilliana's face clean and fresh, removing any dust that she'd collected on the floor that had stuck to her tears, and just as efficiently washed her arms, neck and legs.

"There she is." Rachael said softly.

Nurse Rachael, always so sweet, strong and caring it made fresh tears sting Lilliana's eyes.

"Hey, hey, come on now darling, it's all going to be alright." She rubbed Lilliana's arm gently. "I need to ask you Lilliana, were you raped?"

Lilliana looked Rachael in the eye, and shook her head, replying softly but firmly. "No."

Rachael sighed. "Good, alright then, let's get you along to see Damon. Billy?"

"Yes, Nurse Rachael."

"Can you please take Lilliana to see Damon." She smiled at Lilliana. "We'll see you soon."

Lilliana nodded and taking Billy's arm, walked with him from the room.

Rachael sighed, as she viewed Lilliana's back. She would heal, she was young and healthy, and their healing balms would assist with the scarring.

Billy knocked on Damon's door and walked in with Lilliana once it opened. Johnson was sitting on the couch, Damon was standing near the fish wall.

"Thank you Billy, that will be all." Damon said as Billy helped Lilliana perch on the couch, sitting forward, facing Johnson.

"Buzz me if you need me Sir." Billy said as he left the room.

Damon studied Lilliana. It amazed him how fresh and pretty she appeared, after the state he'd found her, only an hour ago.

She did look pale, and still would not meet his eyes.

"Lilliana, would you like to tell Johnson what happened?" Damon kept his voice calm and gentle.

Her eyes remained on the water jug.

Johnson poured her a glass and pushed it across the table towards her, smiling kindly. "Thirsty work getting your story out."

"Thank you." She said quietly and picked up the glass of water, draining it in five mouthfuls. She placed it on the edge of the table, before whispering. "I'm going to be in big trouble when I tell you."

"Let me be the judge of that, Lilliana." Damon said, equally as quiet before his phone rang. He walked over to his desk and answered it. As his back was turned, Lilliana risked a glance in his direction.

"Damon Night." He turned, listening to his brother, watching Lilliana quickly turn her attention to the fish. "Oh Cam, can you deal with that? If anyone has a problem, tell them to get back to me same time tomorrow." He listened to Cam for another minute before replying. "Yeah, I'm sorting it out now, thanks." He clicked off.

"All good?" Johnson inquired.

"Yes, just another day at the office." He watched Lilliana get up, and walk closer to the fish, looking up as they glided through the water above her.

He felt his blood boil as he looked at her beautiful skin, red welts marring it. Even worse, the large bite marks. That *bastard*. He ran his hand through his hair, and leant his hip against his desk, nodding to Johnson.

"Are you ready Lilliana?"

She nodded her head, keeping her back to them. At least she wouldn't have to see the disappointment on Damon's face when she'd tell him she'd broken one of his important rules.

"I woke up from sleeping after night detention and wasn't aware of the time. I just knew it was either late at night, or very early in the morning, as there wasn't a single soul around. I was so hungry, and my muscles were aching, so I thought I'd have a quick bath and then head off to the kitchen." She paused for a couple of minutes as Damon and Johnson exchanged a glance.

Damon silently fumed, thinking if the bastard had got to her in the bathroom? He had to stop his train of thought, it wouldn't do him or Lilliana any good right in this moment.

"I got lost on my way to the kitchen, as I had only been there once before, and that was the morning Mr. Night took me after all night detention and being exhausted, didn't pay attention to where I was going. I ended up down a small corridor that ended suddenly, and as I lost my balance, my finger caught on a latch and a panel to the passageway opened." She stopped and rubbed the back of her neck.

Damon watched. She was nervous, he knew. And she should be.

"I knew it was wrong, I did. But the house was just so quiet, and I didn't think it would cause any harm."

"Any harm indeed young lady." Johnson couldn't help himself. "You are lucky to be *alive*."

Damon held up his hand to Johnson, calming the other man down before he got himself worked up, although, he knew exactly how he was feeling. Frustrated that they couldn't keep their own safe.

Lilliana had wrapped her arms around herself, her head had dropped.

"Go on, Lilliana." Damon said firmly.

"I'd been walking for a little while," Her voice, quiet. "it sounded like someone was following me, but I thought it may have been a staff member. I came to the Black Ops section, and that's when I knew it was time to get out of there, but when I turned around, a man was blocking my exit, and I had nowhere to run, except into the 'no-go' zone. I ran. So did he. He was faster." She swallowed, shrugging, not liking to remember how terrified she had been.

"Are you going to tell us who it was Lilliana." Johnson asked.

"He said if I do, he'd hurt Jessica." She whispered.

"Lilliana, he can't hurt her if we take him, now can he?" Johnson reassured her, frustrated. He didn't want to tell her that both he and Damon had viewed the security footage in the Black Ops division already, whilst Rachael had taken care of her back.

Damon had been furious, watching her run for her life, and his blood had just about boiled as he watched the way Blake had handled her. Blake was already in a holding cell, whilst he considered what to do with him. It would not be pretty.

"Lilliana," Damon sighed. "tell me."

"It was Blake, Sir."

"Excellent, thank you Lilliana. Johnson, that will be all for now."

Johnson nodded, and left the room.

Damon ran a hand over his face before saying. "Lilliana, please come and sit down."

She turned around and looked at him, was about to say something, but thought better of it, and went and sat down, being careful not to lean back.

Damon walked behind her and gently ran his fingers over her creamy shoulders that had not been marked. He could not speak for a minute and tried to compose himself. His anger towards her, putting herself in such a dangerous position, wouldn't help either of them. But still. "How could you Lilliana?" It was said quietly, with an edge of steel.

She dropped her forehead into her hands as mixed emotions pounded her, from fright, relief, humiliation, pain, anger and shame, which was released in a rush of tears.

"I'm so sorry Mr. Night, I didn't mean to disappoint you."

He dropped his hand, and walked in front of her, sitting on the low table, he took her hands in his.

She looked away not wanting him to see her like this, and still not able to meet his eyes.

"Hey," He said quietly. "you could never disappoint me Lilliana." He reached up, and wiped away her tears, before taking her chin gently, forcing her to meet his eyes.

"I'm not disappointed in you, just this one decision you made. This could have gone in a whole other direction. I could be sitting here, mourning your death. Do you understand how wrong you were?"

Lilliana could not speak due to the complete intensity in his eyes, boring down into hers. She succeeded in a slight nod.

He squeezed her hands before releasing them and stood.

"What am I going to do with you?" He sounded lost and frustrated.

"Solitaire's an option I guess?" So serious.

"Don't think I haven't thought about it Lilliana."

She looked up at him and her heart faltered at how very deadly serious he appeared to be.

"Okay, I'm fine with anything you decide, I guess I deserve it." She looked so guilty.

"I think you've been punished quite enough, don't you?" He sounded tired. "Come on, time for you to recover."

He helped her to her feet and pulled her arm through his, guiding her out the door, and led her up to her friends, food and sleep.

His strong arm and familiar scent gave her a comforting vibe. Amongst other things.

CHAPTER 23

The next few months flew by in a whirlwind and Lilliana loved every moment. Running in the mornings, classes, extra lectures, volunteering at the hospital, stables and fitting in some volunteer work at the H.D, just so she could spend a bit of time with Josephine, she may have been completely exhausted by the end of the night, but also completely satisfied.

She caught up with Allie once a week, when they took their horses out, but had not seen much of Jessica, due to both her and Jessica's routines. So when Jessica suggested a midnight get together in her room for the four of them, Lilliana jumped at the chance.

She had finished a three-hour shift with Allie, had a quick bite at the hospital cafeteria, then together walked upstairs to get changed before going to Jessica's room.

Lilliana stepped into her room, pulling off her all white uniform of long sleeved tee shirt, jeans and ballet slippers.

After tossing them down the chute, she grabbed a green pair of pyjama shorts and matching singlet top from her closet, got dressed quickly, then pulled her hair out of its braid and ran the brush through it, getting excited about the catch up with her friends. Walking past her desk, she smiled at the photo of herself, Jessica and Josephine the first day she'd moved into her room.

Next to it, sat another, recent shot of herself and Allie, sitting proudly on top of their horses. She smiled, remembering that day.

She quickly walked down the deserted hallway, and raised her hand to tap lightly on Jessica's door, and laughed as it opened before she made contact, her wrist grabbed, and she was pulled into the room and given a big hug from Jessica. "Great, we've been waiting for you to get here. Time to spill the beans."

Lilliana smiled at her friends, as she sat on the floor where a nice little spread had been set up, and helped herself to some black olives and cheese.

"Okay, so," Allie started, "guess who Christopher and I caught in the stables going for it early the other morning?"

"I could envision a few people I wouldn't mind catching in the act," Josephine stated, popping a sun dried tomato in her mouth. "and others I cringe to think about."

Allie smiled at her. "I think you may cringe Jose."

"Go for it." Josephine said.

"Rupert and Luke." Allie grabbed a handful of chips.

Lilliana looked at Allie. "How old is Luke?"

"He's about to turn seventeen. Rupert's nineteen." Allie munched on her chips.

"What did they do, did they see you?" Jessica asked.

"Yep, they zipped up fast and ran like rabbits, poor Rupert was beyond bright red. I mean, I don't blame him, if Christopher and I got caught, I would be the same."

"Yes, but Luke's underage, did Christopher report them?" Lilliana asked.

"He was thinking about it, but then, we've been doing the same thing." She trailed off feeling guilty. "Every time we sneak off, I think to myself, 'this will be the last time,' but then when I see Christopher, and look at his sexy body and that sweet, sweet face well, I simply cannot help but want to rip off his clothes and have him at every opportunity I get." She sighed.

"It would be difficult, I mean Christopher's twenty-one, works full time, it's weird when you think about it, asking permission to have sex." Jessica said, grabbing a bottle of water.

"Yeah, well, we all need rules." Josephine said simply.

"I know, but it's not like anything's going to happen, I mean, we were temporarily sterilised when we first arrived at the hospital." Jessica shrugged.

"Speaking of happenings, did anyone hear about Nasty Natalie hitting on Leon at the pool house yesterday?" Allie chuckled.

"Oh no, poor Leon." Lilliana drained her cup and popped another olive into her mouth.

"Oh no, poor Leon handled himself like the champion he is. He was laying down on one of the sun lounges, and Natalie pounced on his chest, her back to his face and full on smashed her teeth into his Jolly-Rodger and tackle." Allie paused as her friends were in fits of laughter.

"Does the girl have any sense of class?" Josephine asked.

"The answer to that is no. Absolutely not. I told you about her masturbating in detention?" Lilliana fell back on the floor, propping her feet up on Jessica's bed, watching her girls upside down.

"I would have loved to have been there for that." Josephine laughed.

"Ah, no, trust me, you wouldn't." Lilliana groaned at the memory.

"So, how did Leon handle himself?" Jessica asked.

"He grabbed her around the waist, got up and dumped her headfirst in the pool. Only when she went down, so did his trunks. Let me tell you ladies. He. Is. Spectacular." Allie held her hands in the prayer position, before slowly stretching them wide apart, cracking up everyone in the room. A pillow hit her head, flung by Jessica.

Allie laughed.

"How are you and Orlando enjoying your Team Leader roles?" Lilliana asked Jessica.

Jessica smiled. "It is the most amazing feeling, being able to guide, support and help with the healing process and assist in settling people into our home. Marcus is just awesome to work with and has been helpful. Tina's cool, although not as patient with the newer Given as Lisa is.

"That's the beauty of Tina, every team needs one leader with balls of steel." Allie nodded.

"Orlando was great the week I joined his running group." Lilliana said. "His skills are perfect for a Team Leader role."

"Does anybody know what Natalie's entering into?" Josephine asked.

"Funnily enough," Allie said. "She has been with Fox's group quite a bit lately, not the H.B.R. but textiles."

"They sure are talented, I mean look what we wear every day." Jessica appreciated that the only uniform she had to wear, was the running one.

"She also went along to the last photo shoot with Fox, which was surprising after their altercation with the scissors in the textile room."

"I heard she's also been assigned to laundry as well." Jessica shrugged, yawning loudly.

"My gosh, it's nearly two am." Josephine looked up from her watch.

Allie yawned, watching Jessica. "I feel it."

"And here I was, thinking about a night bath." Lilliana said.

"Oh, I am in." Josephine jumped up. "Or even better, a stealth mission out to the pool house?"

"Oh no, I don't think so." Jessica said, sounding very 'Team Leader' like, which made the girls chuckle.

"Yeah, actually I think I need to stick to the house rules for the rest of my life after my last incident." Lilliana agreed.

They all shared a quiet laugh, remembering all too well how upset they had been with the 'Blake' incident. After a round of hugs, they bid each other goodnight before heading out, and off to bed.

***

The following morning, Damon and Cam were in one of their weekly meetings with their staff. A representative from each section reported any concerns and shared opinions on how their section was running, talk about their financial loss or gain, if that was relevant. Rachael had the chance to order new equipment and medicines she required, along with recommendations for placements.

"We have a few volunteers and trainees doing extremely well. In fact, some I would recommend for full time positions, even though a few wanting to move into a different career."

Damon sat back in his chair, typing on his tablet. "Send me that list Rachael, I'll look at it."

"Yes Sir." She said.

Cam had already emailed his H.D. report for the last six months. They had some big figures coming in, thanks to their outgoing vegetable, fruit and seedling produce and variety of plants As Cam was in charge of both H.D and Fox's contract, his report looked very positive.

"Fox has another big shoot next week, it's for one of the biggest fragrance agencies and they are paying the big bucks for her services, on a condition, plus flying in six top male models. The ad should only take a couple of hours to shoot, so won't take up much of our time. It's showcasing the old seasons when we used to get four throughout the year."

Damon nodded, glancing over the figures Cam had forwarded him earlier. "Impressive, well done Cam, I see Pier and Tim are on board with this one, excellent. Now, what's the condition?'

"Yes," Cam said. "the client wants Lilliana on board also." He waited as Damon was reading the details of the shoot.

Damon glanced up, and stared at his brother. "No. Next." He looked at Dr. Richard.

"Damon," Cam interrupted. "they want Lilliana too; they won't pay big dollars without her on board."

"Next." Damon kept his eyes on Richard.

Cam sat back and bid his time for the meeting to come to an end and after another hour it did.

Once everyone had left, the door shutting behind them, Cam quickly turned to Damon. The two brothers looked at each other.

"No way." Damon dropped his tablet on the desk and walked over to pour himself a coffee.

"Don't you think you should give Lilliana that option? It's not bloody porn Damon."

"It may as well be." His brother snapped.

"Look, it's a good experience for her, it will be fun, she'll be safe. You can come and supervise with me." Cam added, thinking that would win him over.

Damon sighed, "Ask Lilliana, if she really wants to do it, let me know. I'll be there."

"Brilliant! You won't regret this brother." Cam knocked the top of the desk happily as he turned to go.

"Tell Fox to grab who she wants as a backup, tell Lilliana the same if she decides to do it."

"Okay." Cam saluted as he strolled out.

Lilliana. Damon sighed, sitting down. He hadn't seen a great deal of her since the episode in the passageway.

He was always aware of her whereabouts and knew she had been filling in any free time she had, with work at the hospital, psych ward and classes. He was, as always, impressed with her dedication. He partly wondered if she was keeping her head down and exhaustingly busy, as her own sense of punishment for breaking the house rule. He pulled open his top draw and reached for a black folder.

Opening it, he smiled at the photographs that had been taken with himself, Beast and Lilliana. She was ravishing. He had to admit, looking at the photos, with his hands on her, did things to him. Not respectable things in any way.

He snapped it shut, feeling a stirring in his body, ran his hands through his hair and dropped the album back into the draw, closing it before heading up for a meeting in Black Ops, half hoping that she would say no to the photo shoot.

CHAPTER 24

Lilliana had said yes and was thrilled to have a couple of hours outside in the gorgeous fresh air. The fact that it aligned with her group therapy with Dr. Richard.

Oh, it couldn't have worked out better if she'd planned it herself!

Of course, she had asked Josephine to be her backup, and the two were happy to get whisked away to the shoots location in the jeep.

They arrived not far from the lake, where three large wooden crates had been assembled, 6x6 in width and length. Walking past one box, they had a peek inside.

A glossy black room, minus one wall that was painted white, with a fire place in the centre; fake flames flaring from the logs, the floor covered in black sheets of silk.

The next box was full of white, green, pink and orange flowers and felt very joyful with a white, grand piano sitting in the middle of the room.

The third box was made of mirrored glass, the floor was covered in beautiful large Autumn leaves from a maple tree.

"Ladies, there you are." Cam walked over, smiling. "Let's get you and Fox briefed on the shoot, okay Lilliana?"

"Yes, of course Sir."

Josephine linked her arm through Lilliana's as they followed Cam. He was dressed in blue jeans and a white tee shirt.

"He looks just dashing, doesn't he?" Josephine whispered.

"You should talk." Lilliana nodded her head at her friend.

Josephine wore an off the shoulder white sundress, with strappy sandals. Her long wavy brown curls were left to swing around her pretty face, and she'd popped on a hint of mascara to flare out her big brown eyes.

She grinned cheekily. "Well, I couldn't let Natalie out-do me now could I?"

As they approached a large tent with its door open, Lilliana saw what Josephine was referring to.

Natalie had arrived with Fox, and she was wearing a long black dress, with her hair tied back in a high pony tail. She wore bright red lipstick that matched the poppy in her hair.

Lilliana clamped her mouth shut. She had never seen Natalie look, well, so respectable. Her ass crack and tits were not hanging out.

Josephine jabbed her in the ribs, as if to say, 'told you so'.

Lilliana wondered what Fox's intensions were bringing Natalie along. She had obviously forgiven her for attempting to cut her hair off.

"All right people, you know Fox, this here is our lovely Lilliana, for those of you who have not worked with her before." Cam bought Lilliana under his arm, introducing her to the male models.

"David, Phoenix, Halo, Jeremy, Todd and Michael, this is Lilliana, be kind and gentle with her as it's only her third shoot." The six men nodded and smiled at Lilliana.

Pier and Tim came over quickly and kissed her cheek, saying hello. Lilliana was happy to see Valeria and Nigel amongst the crew.

"Right, can everyone take a seat." Cam called.

Michael could not take his eyes off Josephine, and walked over to her, offering her a seat beside himself. Josephine sat, giving Lilliana the 'Oh my god' look.

Lilliana smiled and sat on the other side of Josephine, Fox sat beside Lilliana and whispered. "Won't this be fun?" As Cam got started.

"We have four sets people, we are shooting a perfume ad. Four sets for the four old seasons. Fox, you've been assigned Summer and Autumn. Lilliana, you have Winter and Spring. Fox, you start with summer, Lilliana, let's do winter. As we need all men in each season, ladies, once you are through with hair and makeup, feel free to watch the others shoot. Let's go, I want this started in twenty minutes." He clapped his hands, and people scattered.

Lilliana moved off as Valerie came to collect her, taking her into a smaller room, she sat for hair and makeup.

Michael smiled at Josephine. "So, what's your name sweet-thing?"

Josephine tried not to cringe, and instantly her awe in him as a supermodel, faded at his attempt to be charming. She never did handle sleazy well. "That's top secret."

He ran a finger along her arm, and her eyes followed his finger, missing the cheeky direction as his head bent to steal a quick kiss.

Josephine flew out of her chair. "Um, I don't think so buddy."

Michael stood, clasping his fingers around her slender wrist, pulling her close.

"Michael." Cam's voice snapped from behind them. "If you want this to be your last shoot, keep it up."

"I apologise Mr. Night; I was simply being polite to the sweet young lady." Michael bowed to Josephine. "Apologies Miss."

Josephine raised an eyebrow, folding her arms as she watched Michael walk off. "Thanks." She looked up at Cam.

He looked down at her, drowning in her gorgeous brown eyes. "Go grab a drink with Natalie."

"Yes Sir." She began walking by him.

He took her arm, holding her still and close.

She glanced up at his face, no grin or smile, just a deep, intense stare. She could smell him, that pure scent that was all Cam. She froze as his head dipped lower, hesitating.

She held her breath, but he wasn't coming closer. She stood on her tiptoes and slid her lips over his, shocking them both.

His hand slid up her arm, to reach her back and press her closer to him, bending lower to deepen the kiss. It was electric.

Then just as suddenly he quickly stepped back, breaking their contact staring at Josephine. "What the hell?" He appeared to be asking himself.

He watched her lips, red and wet. Her breathing was slightly heavy. Her cheeks flushed and her big brown eyes looked like they were ready for the bedroom.

"Right, well I'm off." Josephine spun on her heels, her mind a tornado of thoughts.

Cam shook his head clear and looked around. Thank the stars the tent was empty. Running his hand through his hair, he took off to do the job he was here to do.

Josephine would come later.

Valeria and Lilliana chatted as Nigel straightened Lilliana's hair. Then Valeria applied a very dark make up and bright red lipstick, red fingernails.

A black leather bra, and mini skirt with very tall, black lace boots, that went halfway up her thighs. She looked in the mirror, as Nigel started tugging her skirt this way and that, fixing the bra at the back. Her hair was so much longer when her waves had been taken out.

"Gorgeous my angel." Nigel muttered, taking her by the arm to assist her out of the tent and over to the summertime box, to watch Fox and the models do their shoot.

It was a fun, young theme. Fox, almost gloriously naked in a bright green G-String, tiny bikini, and spiky green high heels.

The perfumes label was stencilled down one long leg and all the male models had hands placed strategically along her body. Flowers covered every inch of the floor and walls looking like a garden festival.

Lilliana couldn't wait to see how that shoot would look.

"Gorgeous." Cam whispered in her ear behind her, breaking her concentration.

She turned, smiling at him, almost meeting his eyes in the ridiculously tall boots.

"I don't know if I'll be able to pull off what you want me to." She shrugged.

"Nonsense." He replied.

"We're done here, next." Tim turned and spotting Lilliana, let out a wolf whistle. "Darling, if ever you want to leave this place, I will make you famous."

"She's already famous." Cam laughed.

"Yes, but in here, she does not feel the fame my friend." He winked at her, then grabbed his gear to take it to the winter set.

Pier smiled at Lilliana. "Let's go have some fun."

She nodded and taking Cam's arm, walked over to the Winter box. A hand reached down to pull her up onto the raised platform.

Damon.

Her heartbeat quickened as she placed her hand in his and he effortlessly pulled her up, close to him.

Lilliana's eyes were almost level to his. Almost. She looked at his lips, then back to his eyes.

If only, he thought. "Hello." He said quietly.

"Hi."

He wanted to tell her she looked stunning. But instead, once he made sure she was not going to fall backwards, stepped back and out of her way so she could see where Pier wanted her.

As she walked past him, he was happy to see her bare back had no scarring at all from her attack by Blake.

"Breathe brother," He heard Cam chuckling behind him. "mouth-watering, wouldn't you say."

"Mm." Was all Damon could reply, before stepping down and out of the way.

He went to stand under the shade of a tree with Josephine to watch.

Natalie and Fox joined them shortly.

Lilliana stood in the middle of the room, the large, blazing fire appeared to be roaring.

"Right Lilliana," Cam began. "you are our Winter Vixen, seductress off the night. Basically, you wear this perfume, you get any man you want. Where is the stencil?" Cam yelled.

Lilliana watched as people fussed about her. Telling her to 'stand here, straighten that leg, bend this one, hold this whip'. She loved it all.

They set up a wind machine, waiting for the go ahead to turn it on, and Lilliana couldn't wait for that moment as she was stinking hot under the lights, wearing the tight leather outfit as the sun heated the box.

A stencil like Fox's, was bought over and handed to Cam, and he jumped up onto the platform and knelt in front of Lilliana. Looking up at her, smiling cheekily he said. "Lilliana, my darling, would you do me the honour of becoming my…" he didn't get to finish, as Fox had thrown the apple she had been munching on, at his back. Lilliana burst out laughing as Cam got to work, gently placing the stencil above Lilliana's belly button.

Damon could feel his gut tighten, watching his brother be so close to her, touching her there.

Cam finished, grabbed the apple and took a big bite out of it, he bent and whispered in Lilliana's ear. "Have fun, make papa proud."

She smiled at him and nodded.

He jumped off the platform, and stood next to Damon.

"She is stunning." Fox said to Cam.

"Yes, isn't she? Let's go people!" He shouted.

The male models were in tight leather boxers, with a dog collar and studs around their necks.

Lilliana was standing, tapping the whip in her hand, looking like she meant business. There was one male, on all fours in front of her, where she placed a boot upon his back. The others were kneeling beside and behind her, their hands wrapped around her tall, black boots. Someone's fingers went too high, and brushed the top of her thigh, very close to her panties. She gasped, momentarily shocked as it tickled so, and jumped at the unexpectedness of it.

"Hey," She called, stepping back slightly. "Watch it please."

Damon stiffened. Cam nudged him and whispered, "Relax brother."

"Michael, watch your Bloody fingers, keep them on the boots!"

Michael apologized, and the shoot resumed.

"Jerk." Josephine muttered.

Cam looked at her, and raised an eyebrow.

"What," She said. "he's a jerk copping a cheap thrill."

Damon smiled whispered to her. "You are the best friend anyone could have my dear girl."

She smiled up at him.

Sitting on David's back, Lilliana posed any which way Pier and Tim directed her.

In her mind, she was wearing more than she would at the pool and felt comfortable enough. But the fact that Damon was down in the small crowd, watching her every move, had a million butterflies attack her stomach, and she was finding it difficult to concentrate.

She was standing, all the men laying around her, in a flower pattern.

The wind machine had been turned on, her long silky hair was flying around and behind her. She looked like a she-devil.

"Done!" Tim called out.

The models got up and headed off to the next shoot.

Lilliana passed the whip to one of the props guys and stretched her arms. Walking over the edge of the box, she contemplated jumping off.

Fox called out. "Don't even think about it, you'll break your leg."

Damon walked over as Cam urged Fox onto her next shoot, hurrying after her with Natalie and Josephine in tow.

Damon stood in front of her, looking up at her. She, down at him.

"Having fun?" He asked, reaching his arms up.

She leant down, offering him her arms. He reached past her arms, grabbing her around the waist and tugged her towards him. As she fell, her body slammed into his, and she waited for them to fall back.

He didn't budge. Her hands were on his shoulders, one hand moving on its own accord to wrap around a black, soft lock of hair near his collar.

"Lilliana." He whispered her name, dropping his forehead against hers, closing his eyes.

"Damon." A voice called, breaking their moment. Thankfully he thought, gently releasing her. Before he did anything stupid.

He made sure she was steady, before turning to face Cam.

Cam was staring at him, a grin on his face. "I'm sorry, was I interrupting something?"

"Yes, thankfully," Damon said quietly as they walked off together. "before I did something I may regret."

"Well, that would make one of us today." Cam chuckled.

Josephine found Lilliana a short while after, getting into a beautiful gown, that sat off her shoulders and hung down to her ankles like a silver waterfall, looking very elegant.

Her hair was held up with many pins and had ringlets drooping prettily here and there. Tiny silver pearls were threaded throughout, giving her a fairy princess look.

"Wow, I think you need to keep this gown." Josephine said.

"And where would I wear it?" Lilliana laughed. "Maybe my rounds in the psych ward?"

Josephine laughed at the thought. "You should see what Fox is wearing for her Autumn shoot."

"Can't wait." And they headed over to the Autumn box.

Fox was naked and laying on the autumn leaves, her glorious red hair fanned out in every direction. Covering her breasts and groin area, were large leaves.

Her skin looked like it had a dusting of bronze shimmer all over it. She looked like a goddess.

"Gorgeous Fox, we are done." Tim walked over to Lilliana.

"The photo shop will be breathtaking," He said. "It will appear as if hands are reaching through the leaves, offering the perfume bottle, it is a gorgeous shape."

"Are they different shapes for each season?" Josephine asked.

"They sure are." He answered her, then looking at Lilliana he said. "You should see what we're going to do with your winter shot" He nodded. "Spectacular."

"Fox, that's a wrap for you." Cam called, after Pier gave him the okay.

Lilliana watched, as the glass room became empty of every single leaf, male and prop hand, before becoming one giant mirrored room.

"Ready Lilliana?" Cam approached her.

She nodded. As they turned to walk up to the set, Damon had jumped up on the platform, and once again, reached his hand down to Lilliana.

Her heartbeat quickened and she swore she heard Josephine mutter something about blue balls, and flushed bright red, hoping no one else heard it.

Turning around, she could see by the way Cam was staring at Josephine, he had.

"What," Josephine shrugged. "I'm just saying." She said it quietly, for only his ears.

He couldn't help his chuckle but turned his attention to Damon.

Damon pulled Lilliana up safely, then quickly stepped back.

"Right darling, you are all alone in this one." Cam jumped up on the stage, positioning her in the centre, adjusting a ringlet here and there, placing a necklace with the perfume symbol around her throat. "Are you afraid of birds Lilliana?" He wiped her cheek.

"Not at all." She answered.

"Good. now, I want you smiling, looking like the prettiest girl in the world, I need you to look at that light, and hold your arms just so."

She nodded. Easy enough.

He jumped off the platform and called out, "Let's do this."

Lilliana was ready. Three prop guys arrived holding a large cage each. They opened the doors, and fifty silver doves were released in the mirrored room with Lilliana. The sight was breathtaking.

Lilliana looked like an angel, a hundred angels as the mirrors sent her image around the room many times over, and into the camera lens. The birds flew gently up and around her, their silver wings reflecting her silver dress.

She found it so easy to smile naturally, the birds gave her a sense of joy.

One landed on her hand, then another, until she had six birds along her arms.

She laughed and looked out to find Josephine, her friend was laughing too. Cam grabbed Josephine by the waist and put her up on the stage beside her friend.

"Do it for me will you Tim." He asked the photographer. Tim was more than happy to oblige Cameron.

The birds left Lilliana and settled on Josephine.

Josephine looked at Lilliana and whispered. "If this bird craps on me?"

Lilliana burst out laughing, as the bird let out a small dropping in Josephine's palm.

She looked out to see if Cam had noticed, and her laughing green eyes met Damon's.

He was standing, arms folded, a smile on his face as he appreciated their happiness.

She looked away and said to Josephine. "That is considered good luck."

"I've had some luck today already." She wore a happy grin.

"That is a wrap!" Tim called as everybody clapped, celebrating a shoot well done.

With a helping hand from Cam, the two girls' left the settled birds, as the handlers had thrown down a box of seed.

"Do tell." Lilliana said quietly as they went to remove her wardrobe and make up.

"All in good time." Josephine nodded as Natalie was in the room with Fox.

Lilliana squeezed her friend's arm gently, and let Nigel and Valeria remove her costume. She had a story to share herself. She looked at her friend in the mirror.

They both wore the same telling expression.

***

Two nights later, after their glorious photo shoot, both Josephine and Lilliana found themselves in Dr. Richard's night detention.

Lilliana had disagreed with Dr. Richard during a class. She had argued with his assessment and the treatment of a patient, and when trying to get her opinion

across, he lost it, saying how disrespectful she was. Of course he was highly offended and no doubt embarrassed, took her out of the classroom and told her if she couldn't be respectful, she would get detention.

She had then asked him what the point of class was, or practical, if she couldn't put her opinion forward, without upsetting him, which resulted in two night's detention.

And on this night, she was selfishly happy that she had a very unexpected companion;

Josephine, who had been caught after hours in the stables

She claimed she was looking for one of her dogs that had been missing all day, but as it was after two am, Thomas had to report Josephine's actions to Damon.

Damon would have let her get away with it, but unfortunately for Josephine, when Thomas went to report her breaking curfew, Damon had had a room full of staff.

So, he immediately buzzed Josephine's Team Leader, to tell her to inform Josephine that she would receive two nights detention also.

There were eleven people in detention, Eric, Trevor, Darren, Owen and Wyatt had a week detention. Skipping class and trying to break into the secret passageways at one am. Rupert and Luke had been caught giving sexual favours to each other and had been reported. They had detention for a month, and no leisure activities for a week.

And of course Natalie, who could never seem to keep her hands to herself, was there.

She didn't seem to care how much detention she received. It was company. Better than hanging out in her room alone.

Naomi was in also. She couldn't stop herself from being such a nasty bitch. Had slapped Dr. Hillary in group, then pounced on young Miranda, tearing out a handful of the girl's blonde curls.

Damon had to drag her off and she was placed in solitaire for a day, followed by therapy to discuss her issues and try to get her on the right track.

There weren't any real security threats in this group, but Damon had issued a Watcher, George, to be present as he knew Eric and Lilliana were not usually a good combination. At least in the past anyway, things had been quiet between them for a long time.

Josephine and Lilliana were sitting close together on a couch, tablets on their laps, pretending to be very interested in what the other was studying.

Lilliana was nodding, looking thoughtful as if trying to help Josephine out on a problem, whilst Josephine was whispering about the moment before she kissed Cam.

"He was just there, grabbing my arm all manly and strong like, oh my god, I just wanted to do a Natalie and pounce on him." Josephine's voice was rising in her excitement to share her story with her friend as they hadn't had an opportunity to talk the past two days.

Lilliana shushed her quietly, trying to look serious, but could feel her laughter rise up as Josephine's voice was getting animated by the minute.

"I was this close, and I thought to myself, I am no longer going to let an opportunity to slap my lips up against his bloody sexy ones, pass me by, and then," She sighed, leaning back into the chair she whispered. "my mouth had an orgasm."

Lilliana's laughter burst out of her, before she had a chance to gather herself.

Josephine too, could not stop once her friend had started.

"Detention these days looks like far too much fun." A voice from the doorway called, before Dr. Richard had a chance to say boo.

Lilliana and Josephine stopped laughing, just, but couldn't keep the smiles off their faces.

Damon stood, leaning against the doorway. Those dark blue, intense eyes stared at Lilliana, as he tapped the rolled-up paper against his thigh.

The longer Lilliana looked at him, her smile disappeared, her mouth went dry. How could he be so devastatingly handsome all the time?

She dropped her eyes to her tablet, sitting still, as Josephine called out. "Sorry Mr. Night."

Lilliana could hear his sigh, before he added, "Richard, I'll be in my office for a few hours. Conference call. If you need me, send someone."

"Yes, of course Sir, but I have it all under control." Richard said drily.

Lilliana looked over at the doctor she could not stomach, then across at Damon, as he looked at her once more before heading out. "I'm sure you do." He said quietly, leaving.

Both Josephine and Lilliana did not move a muscle for the next five minutes, just eyes on their work, fingers typing quickly, for fear the doctor would separate them.

"George, I'm just going to the latrine." Dr. Richard said to the Watcher.

"No problem Sir." George looked around the room as the doctor left, then got back to his reading, as all was quiet.

"Latrine?" Josephine rolled her eyes.

Lillian suppressed a giggle. "Stop, please, I don't want to think off him anywhere near a toilet, and what he might do in one." Lilliana shuddered.

Josephine cracked up.

"Ladies." George said sternly, shaking his head.

"Sorry." They apologized quietly, getting back to their work.

Trevor got up to go to a section of the library that George could not see from where he was sitting. After a few minutes, Naomi got up to follow him. Whispering could be heard in the background; a zipper was quietly drawn.

Lilliana and Josephine looked at each other. There was sucking sounds coming from that part of the library, followed by a long moan.

George moved to stand, but Trevor quickly walked around the corner, holding up his hand. "Jammed it in the shelf, Sir." He said shaking it as if that was the cause for his moan.

A minute later, Naomi walked around the corner with a book in her hand. Sitting in her chair, she wiped the side of her mouth on her sleeve.

Josephine's eyes were round and wide, and she looked at Lilliana. "Really? Did that just happen?" She whispered.

Lilliana raised her eyebrow, nodding.

"Sheesh," Josephine shook her head. "if only Cam was in detention too?"

Lilliana laughed, shaking her head.

"Ladies." George looked stern.

"Never mind George, Lilliana, come sit by me please." Dr. Richard had walked back into the room.

"No, I'm really sorry Sir, it won't happen again." Lilliana kept her eyes down, typing away at a question, hoping if she looked really dedicated, he would leave her alone.

"*Now.*" He snapped, clicking a finger.

Lilliana sighed, and uncrossing her legs from under her, stood and walked over to the couch where Dr. Richard had been seated.

She walked past him, sitting as close to the arm as possible, hoping to leave a huge space between them.

It had been such a hot day and now she regretted her choice of her short blue sundress with thin straps. She pulled her dress as far across her lap as she could, then placed her tablet over any exposed skin.

Her eyes met Josephine's across the room. Her friend smiled apologetically. Lilliana gave her head a small, quick shake, as if to say - not your fault.

She typed away, as Dr. Richard sat beside her and got on with his own work.

She quickly wrote Josephine an email stating that Dr. Spock hated her, sent it, then got back to an essay.

A few minutes later, Josephine cleared her throat, indicating that Lilliana check her emails. It read, -Dr. Spock hates you, because he wants you, and knows that he'll never have you."

Lilliana quickly hit delete, glancing sideways at the doctor and felt a flush as she found him staring at her. She quickly dropped her eyes and got on with her work.

"Excuse me Sir," Wyatt said quietly. "I'm hungry."

"Really, well, you will have to wait till the trolley comes in, if it does tonight."

"He missed out on dinner," His friend, Darren said. "he has low blood sugar, and needs to eat."

"Well, let's hope the trolley comes in soon then, shall we." Dr. Richard said, keeping his head down and continued with his reading.

Josephine cleared her throat again. Lilliana was almost too afraid to open the email, in case the doctor saw. But she crossed her leg, placing it higher, unfortunately revealing a nice piece of leg for the doctor to view, as her dress rode up, but at least she could hide the tablets screen from his eyes.

-Wanker. Josephine had written.

-Have you got a sweet in your pocket?

-No, but there is a bowl of candy on Damon's desk. Josephine responded.

Lilliana looked across at Josephine, as if to say, will you get it?

Josephine pointed a finger to Lilliana, as if to say, you.

Lilliana nodded. "Sir, I'm just going to the ladies." She got up and walked past them all, over to the Koi pond, then looking over her shoulder checked that Dr. Richard wasn't watching, meeting Eric's eyes. He looked back down at his work, and she quickly walked straight past the toilet, and out the wide doors, heading to Damon's office.

She knocked quietly. The door slid open. Damon was on the phone, and held a finger to his lips.

She nodded, and pointed to the candy bowl.

He raised an eyebrow, but nodded, watching as she walked over, the blue dress striking with her black hair and those sea green eyes.

He was wondering what she was up to, when a voice snapped from behind her.

"Have you lost your direction Miss Lilliana?"

She froze, embarrassed to be caught out by Dr. Richard. Her eyes met Damon's.

"Alfred, Russell, I'm afraid I'll have to call you back. Can you give me five minutes? Yes, I know, I'm sorry but it can't be helped. Fabulous, speak to you then."

Damon clicked off the phone.

He leaned forward, placing his elbows on his desk, and arching his fingers together, held them against his lips briefly. He glanced

Richard, noting the man's unhappy, pinched features, before looking back at Lilliana.

Her creamy cheeks, flushed red, she folded her arms across her chest, eyes dropping down.

Damon dropped his hands on the desk, sighing. "What seems to be the problem now Richard?"

"Miss liar here, said she needed to go to the lady's room, clearly she is lost. Sorry Sir." Richard turned to Lilliana. "Lilliana, come."

"Lilliana, back to detention please." Damon said softly.

"Yes, I'm sorry Sir." Lilliana turned around, and seeing Dr. Richard glare at her, made her falter. She knew she was in trouble anyway, so quickly turned back to Damon, who was reaching for the phone.

"I am sorry Mr. Night, but I actually came to get some candy for Wyatt. He missed dinner and has low blood sugar. I just wanted to get him something sweet until the trolley came around." She glanced at him under her long lashes.

He dropped the phone back down and stood.

Walking over, he picked up the candy bowl and held it out for her to take.

"Thank you for considering the health of one of your brothers, Lilliana, maybe next time, just be honest with Dr. Richard."

Sure, she thought, taking the bowl she responded quietly. "Yes Sir, thank you."

He nodded to Richard, who stood waiting for Lilliana to walk out, before following her into the library. Lilliana popped the bowl of candy on the table in front of Wyatt.

Darren smiled at her. "Thanks Lilliana."

She smiled back, gave Josephine a look that said, 'I am in some deep shit' as she sat in her seat.

After a moment's hesitation, Dr. Richard sat beside her, picked up his tablet and got back to work.

She did not bat an eyelash out of place for the next two hours.

Lilliana checked her email as the trolley came round, and nervously opened the one that Dr. Richard had sent.

It read – 'You will not move, speak, eat. Sit and get on with the work I have just emailed you. When detention ends in two hours, you will stay behind.'

Lilliana glanced over at the doctor, wanting to email back if she were permitted to breathe? He was chatting to Owen about a disorder, as he poured a lemon tea.

She was seething. Don't move or eat. She looked up as Josephine reached out her hand to pull her up. She shook her head and whispered. "I'm not permitted to move an inch."

"Pig." Josephine whispered, and guiltily went to get herself some cake and tea, feeling pissed off for her friend.

Lilliana shrugged off the heavy feeling that almost settled on her shoulders, and started on the questions Dr. Richard had set up.

The others were having a twenty minute break, chatting quietly, walking around the library.

A pale hand put a tea cup on the table beside her.

She looked up at the doctor, who was eating a sandwich slowly, whilst he looked down at her. "Thank you." She said and continued with her work. She would rather dehydrate than drink anything he gave her. Immature, she knew, but that was just the way she felt.

Once break was over, the room settled back down again and everyone went back to work.

Rupert had sat down beside Josephine, so they could work on some new ideas on irrigation, and a new seedling he was working on.

Natalie took this as a sign, to go and sit beside Luke.

He edged away from her, uncomfortable.

"Don't be like that Lukey." Natalie cooed quietly. "I bet I can take it up the ass better than carrot top over there."

Luke looked panicked and glanced over at Rupert. Both he and Josephine were watching.

"No thanks." He muttered, embarrassed.

Natalie grabbed her tee shirt, and pulled it up, revealing her very large pale breasts, she yelled out. "Do you want a lick Doc? Go on, I know you want to!"

Naomi, Trevor, Owen and Darren could not help themselves. They were in stitches of laughter, as Natalie stood, and hands on her hips, tee shirt tucked under her chin, strolled over to Dr. Richard.

Rupert, Josephine, and Lilliana were so unimpressed. Not one of them was shocked at her usual display. Even Eric was uncharacteristically, unamused. He and Lilliana made eye contact, and she was surprised and impressed that, instead of one of his past rude gestures to her, he simply raised one eyebrow and shook his head.

Dr. Richard stood and tugged Natalie's shirt down fast.

As Lilliana sat so close, she could see the back of his hairy, pale knuckles, graze Natalie's nipple as he pulled her top down.

She shuddered, and looked back at her work.

"Quiet everyone, get on with your work, or you'll be back for a week. Natalie. Sit, or solitaire."

Natalie held up her hands as she took a step back. "No problem Doc, I'll just leave you to sit back and poke your fingers up Lilliana's sweet ass hole."

Lilliana sat still for a split second as the girl's words sunk in. Unfortunately, fury took over. "Jesus Christ Natalie!" She screamed, and before she knew what she was doing, she threw her tablet at the other girl. It hit Natalie solidly in the face, before bouncing off and smashing to the ground.

Lilliana fled to the toilets, rushing into a stall and slamming the door shut behind her. She was beyond furious, and hearing Natalie go into a screaming frenzy, didn't help. Mental bitch! She thought. It took a few seconds to take that thought back. She knew Natalie had issues, but seriously, living with her the past few years, hadn't endeared the girl to her. She walked over to the sink and splashed cold water on her face, her hands shaking.

The door opened and Josephine stepped in. "Are you okay?"

"Yes, just peachy. She just drives me bloody crazy." Lilliana shook her head.

"Well, at least you're getting trained in the right field, you can sort yourself out." Josephine winked.

Lilliana laughed.

"He wants you out there now." Josephine sounded concerned for her friend

"Just great." Lilliana nodded.

Together, they walked out of the toilet and into the library. Natalie was hunched in a ball, on the ground, sobbing.

Damon was standing above her, with Dr. Richard kneeling beside the inconsolable girl. In Damon's hand, the smashed tablet.

"Alright everyone," Damon looked around the room. "detention is over for tonight excluding Lilliana and Natalie. Goodnight, and we'll see most of you back here tomorrow night."

Rupert smiled at Lilliana as he walked past, as did Owen, Trevor and Darren.

Eric squeezed her shoulder, shocking her somewhat, but said nothing. Josephine gave her a hug. As everyone left, Lilliana walked past the lump that was Natalie, sat in a chair, crossed her legs and placed her hands in her lap.

Damon almost chuckled. She looked like a therapist, ready for a session with a patient.

Natalie had stopped sobbing and raised her head to glare at Lilliana. There was a red welt on the side of her face where the edge of the tablet had whacked her.

Lilliana bit her lip, feeling bad about physically hurting Natalie. She'd wanted to slap her plenty of times, but always resisted the urge.

"I'm sorry about throwing the tablet at you Natalie." She sincerely apologised.

Dr. Richard stood and helped Natalie to her feet.

"How about I take Natalie up to her room," Damon offered. "I'll be back down soon Richard."

"Thank you." Dr. Richard nodded.

Once Damon left the room with Natalie, Dr. Richard sat opposite Lilliana. He crossed a long, thin leg over the other and clicked his fingers together.

"Alright Lilliana, as you can't show me your answers, due to recklessly throwing your tablet, you'll have to tell me. Explain to me about Paraphilia."

Lilliana nodded, "Paraphilia, also known as Sexual deviation, is a type of mental disorder characterized by a preference for, or obsession with unusual sexual practices."

Dr. Richard nodded. "Can you give three examples?"

Lilliana sighed quietly. "Paedophilia, Exhibitionism and Sadomasochism."

"Explain Paedophilia to me." The doctor typed away.

"It is a sexual desire in an adult for a child." Lilliana answered.

"And what would your treatment be for this type of person?" He looked at Lilliana over his glasses.

"A bullet." She responded simply.

"Interesting." He added something to his list.

"Sadomasochism?" He asked.

"Interaction, especially sexual activity, in which one person enjoys inflicting physical or mental suffering on another person, who can also derive pleasure from experiencing pain."

"Last one, Exhibitionism." He watched her.

"It is a disorder characterized by a compulsion to exhibit the genitals in public.

A tendency to behave in such a way to attract attention, such as, flashing, exposing oneself, immodesty."

"Do you know anyone here who fits that category Miss?" He queried.

"Natalie." She answered quietly.

"That's right. Natalie." He stood and walked over to the mantel of the fireplace and said. "Come over here please."

Lilliana nervously stood and walked over to the doctor, his back to her.

"Hold out your palm." He said quietly.

Lilliana swallowed. For real? She looked over her shoulder, thinking she could make a run for it, but he was one of her superiors. He would one day be a work colleague.

He'd turned around, and was watching her look for an escape. "Don't bother. You are going to receive five slaps with this cane, Miss Lilliana. Because you have shown me great disrespect."

She looked up at him, trying to imagine him younger. But she couldn't, she imagined he had always looked this old, pale, dissatisfied and bored his entire life.

She stepped forward and slowly extended her palm, keeping her eyes directly on his.

She didn't expect it to sting so savagely, and could not help the gasp that escaped her lips. She withdrew her hand, holding it to her chest.

His eyes remained unmoved. "Again." He said softly.

She had a few mental disorders running through her brain for him, as she extended her hand again. Of course, the second time hurt more than the first, as did the third, fourth and fifth.

Her palm was bleeding. She had tears, but swallowed them, she would not allow one to fall in front of him.

He moved away from her, picking up his tablet and papers. Standing behind her, he said. "You are one of the most intelligent students we have had for many years. Your mind is phenomenal. But you need to watch your manner. Understood?"

She kept her back to him, but nodded and remained very still until she heard his footsteps leave the library.

When she was sure he'd gone, she sank down in a chair, tucked her legs under her and stared at her bleeding palm. She allowed her tears of humiliation and pain to escape, now that she was alone. What a Bastard. She thought, or was he? Did he have a point? Her frayed emotions had her questioning her usual steady self.

She felt him, before she heard him. Damon.

He stood at the door for a second, feeling her mixed emotions pour from her. He walked over slowly and stood in front of her, seeing her hold her bleeding palm, with tears silently cascading down her smooth pretty cheeks, pulled at his protective heart. My poor baby, he thought.

She took a few seconds to look up at him and brushed her tears away, wondering if she would receive a lecture from him also after physically injuring her Given sister.

"Come with me, Lilliana." He said gently, stepping back and walking from the room.

She stood and followed him out of the library, expecting him to take her to his office, but instead they made their way to the kitchen. As they entered, Damon clapped once and a soft light flickered on.

He took her elbow and guided her to the sink and turning the cold water on gently, he placed her palm under it. "Hold there for a moment." He said and walked to a cupboard by the fridges.

The cool water was a relief and she was grateful to feel the burn lessen. She turned her head to watch him, as he reached inside the cupboard and pulled out a slim, clear plastic container, filled with first aid goodies.

His eyes connected with hers as he walked back to her. Be professional. He told himself firmly. Be professional.

Being 1am, there wasn't another soul around. They were totally alone, and they could both feel it.

What to say? Lilliana felt her heart quickened as he stepped close to her. "Sorry for interrupting your call earlier."

"It wasn't a problem." He reached across her, his arm close to her breasts, as he turned off the tap.

She reminded herself to breathe, as his scent washed over her and her heart hammered away, she was sure he would be able to hear it. Don't get dizzy! She inwardly kicked herself.

Damon dropped the container onto the bench behind her, then gently, ever so slowly, put his hands on her waist, and with no effort, lifted her up placing her bottom on the countertop.

"There we go." He sounded so calm as his hands slid off her waist and opened the first aid container.

Her breathing hitched, she couldn't help herself, whenever he was this close, or handled her, she couldn't focus. At all. She just wanted to grab him by the head, run her fingers through that thick, black hair and bring his mouth to hers. Hussy! She hissed to herself, but even thinking about kissing him as he stood so close, had her mind and body sliding into overdrive.

He took her hand in his, opening her fingers gently so he could inspect the wound.

"No horse riding for a week I'd imagine." He looked at her, they were completely on the same eye level with her sitting on the tall bench.

She forced a swallow. "It feels that way too." She couldn't move or take her eyes off his, before hers dropped to his lips. *Oh my god.* She inwardly cried.

"Right well, this will help." He looked away, as he reached for a tube of cream. Squeezing out a small portion, he rubbed it slowly into her cuts.

He loved the feel of her soft skin, her small hand. It angered him once again, that her beautiful skin had been torn. Bloody Richard.

He could hear her uneven breathing and see her breasts rise and fall through her thin dress. She must be nervous, he thought. Poor baby just do your job and get out of here. God, she smelt divine.

He dropped the cream back into the container, before picking up a small healing spray serum, spraying a cool film over the broken welts, then dropped that too, into the container and snapped the lid shut. He picked up her wrist, and spreading her fingers back a little, blew gently on her palm, as the serum did its work knitting the skin slowly together.

He was driving her crazy. Lilliana forced herself not to move, as every breath of his on her skin, was melting her insides.

He gently placed her hand back on her thigh and placed his hands on the countertop either side of her bottom.

Standing so close, they could both feel the others body heat.

"Thank you Sir." She said softly.

"You are welcome Lilliana." He slowly reached out and hooked a silken wave, pulling it between his fingers, rubbing it, marvelling at the silkiness of it. Right, that's *enough*. He reprimanded himself but was unable to step away from her. Her heat, her scent, her goodness. Pure Lilliana.

She reached out and slowly touched his neck where his shirt was open. She'd been wanting to do that forever. What are you doing? She whispered to herself. This is Mr. Night! Her body ignored her mind and did what it desired.

His skin was hot, firm and soft, her fingers wandered towards his throat, where she wanted to kiss him. She could hear his breath pause, waiting. She slowly drew forward, breathing him in.

His hands ran down her back, and grasping her backside pulled her forward into his groin, wrapping her legs around his hips.

Her lips found the spot she'd been seeking, and she kissed his soft skin, breathing him in.

He heard her moan. That sound, deep in her throat, drove him crazy.

His hands flew up to her head, grabbing a handful of thick, black waves and tugged her head back. His eyes met hers, before dropping to her parted lips, her breathing heavy, he tried to restrain himself, but what was the point? He moved slowly and slid his lips over hers, for a gentle kiss, and devoured her.

She couldn't think, could barely breathe. This was really happening, and she didn't want it to end. Ever.

His lips glided, sucked, brushed and treated hers like she was the most delicious morsel on earth.

The taste of him, his wetness was utterly driving Lilliana insane, and she nibbled and sighed against his devouring lips, finding pleasure unlike anything she had experienced.

He pushed his tongue into her sweet, soft mouth and did to her with his tongue, what he couldn't do just now, with the rest of his body.

Her hands fisted in his hair, holding him close, keeping him there so her mouth could enjoy his. She pressed her breasts hard up against him and wrapped her legs tighter around his hips, sliding her even closer.

He could feel the heat of her, on his sex. It was sweet torture.

She could feel the bulge of him, on hers. She was throbbing. "I've been wanting to do this to you forever." She whispered as he kissed her throat.

"Lilliana." He breathed her name, before kissing her deeply again.

"Mr. Night." She whispered, deepening the kiss they were both relishing.

He stilled in her arms, slamming down harshly, back to reality with her calling him, by his titled name. The name the Given addressed him as their leader, mentor and protector.

He closed his eyes, leaning his forehead against hers. His hands that had been fisted in her dress near her hips, loosened.

They were both breathing heavily. Lilliana gently ran her hands along his shoulders, down his arms.

He was at breaking point and the touch of her could have him falling apart at any second. He had to pull himself together, for the sake of this gifted, tender, beautiful girl.

"I'm so sorry Lilliana." He shook his head, meeting her eyes. "This is wrong of me."

His hands ran up her sides, either side of her breasts.

Her head tipped back, and she couldn't suppress the moan that escaped her lips. His touch was everything she had ever wanted. Her eyes closed softly, as she moaned and moved closer to him, her fingers gripping his biceps.

He couldn't help himself, it was pure animal lust. His lips sought her throat, gliding up and over her chin, claiming her lips once more. It was deep and pulled at every muscle in her stomach.

His too. It was insanity, him taking her like this. His hands framed her face, and after deepening the kiss to a dangerous level, that had his body thrumming in pain, with the intensity to want to take her, here and now, he forced them apart with great difficulty.

Her green eyes sparkled brightly, filling his soul. Her lips, rosy, wet and parted wanting more, waiting. Her breathing, like his was once again, out of control.

He quickly stepped away from her, turning his back to her, trying to regain some sort of composure and sought control over his lust. He ran his hands through his hair, where he could still feel her hands there.

He heard her slide off the countertop, before he felt her hands slip around his waist, to finally come up to his chest, holding his back against her chest.

His hands came down to rest on top of hers.

She kissed his back, through his shirt. The smell of him, she didn't think she would ever get enough.

"We can't do this Lilliana. I can't do this to you." He removed her hands, turning around to face her.

She stepped back to lean on the counter for support, wiping the side of her swollen lips with a finger, meeting his gaze full on. "What if I want you to do this to me?" She raised an eyebrow.

He almost laughed. Almost. If she was this ballsy with Richard, no wonder he had a problem with her.

"Oh I want to do things to you Lilliana." He surprised them both with his honesty.

"Things you couldn't dream about." He said softly, gaging her reaction.

She flushed and averted her eyes. But only for a second. She pushed her hair back. And folded her arms.

"I am eight years your senior." He sighed. "Not to mention your protector."

"My father was twelve years older than my Mother." She reasoned.

"Lilliana please, don't." He shook his head, folding his arms. "I have done the wrong thing tonight. God knows I've resisted you before. I will have to do it again. I'm so sorry. Can you forgive me?"

She looked up into his deep blue eyes. This beautiful caring man, who did so much for so many.

She stepped closer to him.

He stiffened, forcing himself not to move.

She held up her palms, as she would to a shy horse, then another step, keeping her hands off him, she tiptoed up and planted a soft, sweet kiss under his jaw.

She stayed for just one more moment, breathing in his scent before stepping back. She forced a smile and whispered. "Goodnight."

He smiled and nodded, not daring to speak or say her name again. He watched her turn and walk out of the kitchen. Her tight bottom that was in his hands only minutes earlier, swayed, that silken mass of hair, waved to him as it fell down her back.

Once she was out of sight, he sagged against the countertop, dropping his forehead against it, calling himself all the perverted names under the sun.

He was in big trouble.

CHAPTER 25

A week later, Cam had been summoned to Damon's rooms, and when he arrived, he found his brother pacing, looking tired and stressed out.

"What's up brother? You don't look so good." Cam plonked down on the couch after he poured himself a coffee.

"I've been considering what you said a while ago, about me taking some time away. Johnson has a connection with an Official that is linked to an organization, connected to the Underworld. It's a group that abducts young women, gets them pregnant, and flushes their system with a lethal combination drug that attaches itself to the baby's D.N.A pattern, bonding with it, which apparently forms the most potent narcotic on the market to date. As these babies grow, their blood gets richer and their value increases, until they reach eighteen apparently. Before they reach that age, they are highly protected and valuable to their owners, as a never-ending drug supply."

"What happens when they turn eighteen?"

"Their blood becomes defective and then they are slaughtered."

"What the hell?" Cam said in disgust. "So basically, this Underground filth has designed a blood-drug? I mean, what do we call their users, blood-suckers?"

"Parasites. The users are referred to as parasites. They take the blood in varies ways. The more I hear about it, the more disturbed I become."

Damon shook his head. "The organization went under the radar about a year ago, but there's a whiff of a trail. I'll have to go undercover."

"Are you in that much trouble with Lilliana?" Cam asked seriously.

Damon looked at his brother and simply nodded. He felt exhausted, like he hadn't slept for a week. He hadn't

"If I don't leave soon, I will not be able to help myself. I nearly took her on the kitchen bench last week!" He shook his head, trying to block out the memory of her. Her smell, taste, touch. He blew out his breath. "I have to go."

"Well by all means, go brother. I'll hold down the fort, whilst you go play Hero. Just don't get yourself killed; I don't want to be boss forever."

Damon smiled tightly. "Sure thing."

"If you need me to apply any pressure from Black Ops for information, let me know."

Damon nodded. "Johnson and I have been to Black Ops almost every day this week.

We had to apply some serious pressure to Samuel to get information from his last contacts before he arrived here six months ago."

"Well, leads can vanish quickly, even in a shorter amount of time out there."

"Yeah well, whether they pan out, Samuel's name was on the Officials list, and used to deal with this organisation, so it's the closest lead we've got."

They had a small lead on a family name that could help them. Reid.

With the right amount of bribery, or torture, whichever Damon and Johnson saw fit, they could gain a lot of useful information from the prisoners in Black Ops, to help put some of the evil bastards of the world, away.

Cam drained his coffee. "It's good to have leads brother, hopefully they will get you where you need to go, to sort it out, so you can return to us quickly."

Damon nodded. "I've already spoken to the board, I have everybody's support on this, and of course, you'll have all the help you'll need. You know the ropes anyway Cam. It will all work out fine." Damon rubbed the back of his neck.

"What are you going to do about Lilliana?" Cam stood. "I mean, I know what you'd like to do with her." He chuckled.

Damon gave him a stony look "You are not helping Cameron."

Cam shrugged, grinning. "Sorry."

"I've called for an assembly tomorrow morning; I'll be leaving in the afternoon."

"So soon?" He wasn't sure if he felt uncomfortable with the thought of his brother leaving him so soon or leaving him in charge.

"It's better this way. I'll be useful where I'm going." Away from her, he thought. Where temptation will be out of reach.

Cam walked over to his brother. The man that was always in control. Always ready to take responsibility and action against wrong doers. Even at the difficult age of nineteen when their father died, Damon had the task, to step into that role, and run things. Even be a parent to Cam.

It hadn't been an easy task and, Cam knew he hadn't made his brother's life easy. He regretted his actions, sleeping with those he shouldn't have, and acting out in his younger years. He placed his hand on Damon's shoulder, looking him squarely in the eyes. "You do what you have to do. Just be kind to yourself for a change. Okay?"

Damon placed his hand on top of Cam's and squeezed in a brotherly manner.

"Thanks Cameron." He said softly.

"I promise, I'll do everything I can to make things flow smoothly."

"I know you will Cameron. Can I ask, that you'll keep an eye out for Lilliana. Make sure she's happy?"

Cam smiled. "I'll do everything in my power to make her so."

Damon hugged his brother before releasing him. "Thank you."

"Okay brother, I'll leave you to it. Call me if you need me, anytime."

Damon nodded, and watched his brother leave the room, before he got to packing a small suitcase.

***

Before a three hour shift in psych, Lilliana and Allie had decided on an early horse ride, which they enjoyed with a group of riders and then broke away on their own for an hour. Feeling exhilarated and relaxed, they walked Raven and Beauty into the stables, laughing about Josephine's missing dog.

It had been taken by a new Given, Ted, who had sadly been missing his own dog since being with them. He had snuck the dog from the stables and had kept him his room for a week, feeding it scraps from the kitchen, allowing it sleep on the bed, chew up shoes, blankets, anything at all. If the dog seemed happy, Ted didn't care what it chewed. As the dog had nowhere but Ted's room to drop his waste, the stench started to seep under the door, alarming those that walked by, that something was very wrong, and reported it.

Damon and Neo had inspected the room, and both were relieved to see the dog happy and unharmed, as was Josephine.

She had taken Ted, to the stables and told him, that he could spend as much time with the dogs, whenever he had free time. He'd been so happy, and very apologetic for worrying Josephine.

"The stench made Neo's eyes water so bad, he said it was worse than peeling a barrow full of onions for Cook on Christmas day."

Lilliana shook her head, laughing.

Damon had not seen her, since she had been deliciously pressed against him.

Sitting in Thomas's office, he'd been talking about the care of Beast and the other horses, instructing one of the recently qualified vets, about his animals' requirements.

He heard her before he saw her, that rich, velvety laugh, and there she was walking by with Allie to return their horses.

Her boots flanked her calves, black jodhpurs shaped her strong legs and firm behind, like a sculpture.

His chest tightened as he watched her shapely bottom. Her riding jacket, buttoned firmly across her breasts, clung to every curve. Her midnight hair, hanging down her back in a long braid, a few waves had escaped here and there from her ride.

She took Beauty to her stall, and removed the saddle, halter and reins.

Allie was prattling on about petitioning for a double room for her and Christopher.

Lilliana agreed it was time they did, as she started running the brush over Beauty's warm back, down her rear leg, and bent to lift her foot to check her hoof.

Damon found her in that position, as he leaned against the stalls door very much enjoying the view.

Lilliana placed Beauty's foot back down and straightened, resuming brushing her.

As her back was still to Damon, it gave him a few minutes to watch her without her knowledge, as she ran the brush rhythmically over Beauty's back, her other hand following the brush with so much love.

He folded his arms, clenching his fists, as his heart beat quickened. The sensation of knowing he was about to walk away for her, almost devastated him.

She walked around Beauty's other side and spotted Damon watching her.

Her hand stilled, she wanted to smile but the expression on his face made her freeze.

She had not been alone with him since the night he helped dress her hand in the kitchen, and they had ravished each other.

"Hello." His eyes bore across into hers.

"Hi." She swallowed, her throat suddenly very dry.

"Okay Lilly, I'm done so I'll be off, oh, hi Mr. Night." Allie smiled.

"Hello Allie, when are you going to start calling me Damon?" He smiled at her.

"Probably when hell freezers over Sir." She smiled back.

"Well, it won't be too long then, will it." He walked over and stroked Beauty's neck.

Allie met Lilliana's gaze, wanted to say something cheeky, but thought better of it, as Lilliana looked like she was having trouble breathing. "Lilly, I'll see you down in psych."

Lilliana nodded as her friend walked off, then finished brushing Beauty, all too aware of Damon watching her as he stroked the horse on the other side.

As Lilliana placed the brush along Beauty's neck, Damon reached out and grasped her wrist.

She froze, as her eyes drifted to his. Her heart beat quickened, her lips parted.

He couldn't take his eyes off those lips as his fingers stroked over hers. *Stop it now.* He ordered himself.

He removed his hand, placing both his in his pockets, and took he took a few steps back, as she finished brushing Beauty.

She walked over and popped the brush in a bucket, before wiping her hands on her pants facing him.

"I need to talk to you Lilliana, do you mind coming up to the loft where we won't be disturbed?" He had already told Thomas that he needed to talk to Lilliana, and not to allow anyone else up in the stables loft.

"Yes, of course." She was willing to go anywhere with him, if it meant the chance to be alone for even a handful of minutes, and followed him out of the stall.

They walked silently down the aisle and reaching the steps to the loft above, Damon held his hand out for Lilliana to go up first.

She stepped in front of him, her arm brushing his.

He inwardly sighed at the smell of her; horse, sweat and that sweet perfume of her essence.

Walking right behind her, he wanted to reach out and place his hands on her hips, feel them sway beneath his fingers. *Get a solid grip.* He told himself.

Lilliana walked over towards the window, removing her riding jacket as she went, dropping it on a hay bale, revealing a white singlet top. She leaned against the window seat, facing him.

He stood in the middle of the room, placing his hands in his pockets to prevent him from putting them on her. "How have you been Lilliana? Apart from very busy." He smiled.

I can't stop thinking about kissing you, I imagine your hands on me. I want them on me now. She thought, but replied instead, "I've been well, thank you."

She reached behind her, pulling the band from her braid, running her fingers through her silky mass. Popping the band on her wrist, she smiled at him, curious what he wanted to discuss.

With the sun filtering through the clouds behind her, she looked like a sultry angel.

Her eyes stared directly into his. Unblinking. Almost daring him to come closer. He wanted to.

The need on his face mirrored her own. She had to touch him, just briefly, surely it couldn't hurt. She walked towards him, slowly, to give him a chance to stop her.

He didn't.

She stopped with just a hair breath between them. "I sense something isn't quite right."

He looked down at her ever-beautiful face, her sea-green eyes beckoning to him.

He ran a finger along her soft cheek, under her chin, along her throat to circle behind her neck, pulling her towards him, until his forehead found hers. Eyes closed, he breathed her in.

Her hands reached behind him, clasping her fingers together behind his back, feeling his strong muscles through his shirt, she tiptoed up, to push her face into his throat.

His other hand joined behind her neck, and he ran his hands down her back, grasping her hips, pulling her close. He couldn't help himself.

His cheek, grazing the soft, top of her hair, as she nuzzled his neck, turning her lips into an open kiss along his jaw.

It was the spark that set the fire alight in him. His hands reached up, into her hair, pulling her head back so his lips could devour hers.

The kiss was deep, wet and hard, his lips sliding over hers, his hands crushing her hair, holding her head in place so he could take advantage of the angle and deepen the kiss.

She moaned, her hands clinging to his shoulders, pulling him towards her, as close as possible.

God how he wanted her.

His hands, deep in her hair, pulled her lips away from his. They were both panting.

Her eyes, half closed, her fingers tangled in his soft hair near his collar.

His eyes locked on hers, as he bent down towards her parted lips and gently, slowly slid his lips over hers, then, leaning back again to look at her. "You are so beautiful." He whispered.

"So are you." She stroked his face, as her other hand ran along his chest, to reach behind his neck, and pulled him closer to her waiting mouth. Slowly, eyes locked, they sank into a deep, slow kiss.

He moaned this time, as her eyes fluttered closed.

The kiss became hard and fast within seconds, hands clutching the others body wantonly. Her fingers ran under his shirt, to span his firm abs, and she groaned into his mouth, as her fingers brushed just below the belt.

It was nearly his undoing.

What the hell was he doing? He thought. *Fool.* He hissed to himself. He gently, but firmly held her away from him. When she was steady and her eyes fully open and on him, he stepped away from her holding his hands up.

It hurt to do so.

She ran her hands through her hair, then wiped her lips, looking at his, pouting a little that he'd stepped away from her, as she tried to steady her breathing.

"Don't look at me like that Lilliana, or I will take you here and now." He also ran a hand through his hair.

"I want you to." She whispered, stepping towards him.

He quickly stepped back, shaking his head firmly. "Baby, don't!"

She sighed and turning her back to him, walked to stand near the window. She sat on the window seat and crossed her legs.

"I'm sorry Lilliana, I can't seem to keep my hands off you. It is wrong of me." He did in fact look a little guilty.

"Oh please, stop apologizing, I like your hands on me, more than like if we're honest about it."

He smiled at her. "Well, that makes two of us." He sighed. "Lilliana, I came to see you this morning, because I needed to tell you something in person, and I didn't want you hearing about it at assembly. I'm leaving this afternoon for an outside mission."

"Oh, what sort of mission?" She was interested.

"Well, I can't go into details, but I'll be going undercover, to assist in putting an end to a blood-drug trade." That's as detailed as he could give her.

Lilliana nodded. "Well, whoever you will be working for will be blessed to have you with them. How long are you going for?"

He waited a beat before answering. "It could be a year, maybe two." He didn't want to say it could be longer. He watched her become very still.

She stopped breathing and felt ill. "Two years? So long." She whispered, feeling tears threaten. *Don't cry.* She begged herself.

"Undercover work is deep Lilliana, it takes time." He said softly.

Her head had dropped; she was looking at her boots. Possibly two years, without seeing him? The man she knew she had been in love with, since the beginning of time. Her safety, her rock, her centre of thoughts, her anchor in this world, in this place, her home. Home without him. She glanced up, a tear fell from her eyes, so green and misty as another fell.

"Lilliana." He whispered, shocked and frustrated he had made her cry. He quickly walked over, and knelt in front of her, placing his hands either side of her on the seat, but not daring to touch her.

"Sweet girl, please, don't cry. Lilliana?" He didn't know how to console her.

Her eyes did not stray but stared into his. She wiped her tears away and took a deep breath. "I love you." She admitted. Watching his reaction.

He nodded. Knowing that to be true.

"And my feelings for you are deeper than they should be. Have always been deeper than they should've been. Since day one."

He stood, pulling her up into his arms to simply hold her close. For the last time in a long time. He placed his chin on top of her silken hair, enjoying the feel of her soft body pressed into his.

Her arms slowly wrapped around his waist, her face pressed into his chest.

"The assembly this afternoon, was to inform all Given of my departure. Cam will be in charge, if you need anything at all Lilliana, anything. Call Cam."

He felt her head nod, felt her hot tears through his shirt.

"You'll be fine baby, you have your friends and your career will take off in another six months." He swallowed, feeling dreadful. Who was he trying to convince she'd be fine, himself or her? He wished he had more time to comfort her, but he had to go, he had so much to organize before the jet came for him.

He lifted his chin off her head. "I have to go." He said softly.

She looked up at him. "Just kiss me once. Please?"

Like he needed to be asked twice. His lips slowly, gently, brushed against hers, back and forth in a sweet goodbye.

Her lips parted, and he lost himself in her once again. He quickly pulled away as he felt his body heat dangerously and looked down at her.

She smiled through her tears. "Thank you."

He stroked her cheek. "Goodbye, Lilliana." He stepped away from her, and she sank back down onto the seat.

Before going downstairs, he glanced over his shoulder for one final look.

"Goodbye Mr. Night, be safe." She whispered, as he walked down and away.

She sat silently and still, unable to move an inch, as she stared at the last spot, she had seen him, imagining him there still. Se touched her lips, before wrapping her arms around herself, and felt the rush of silent tears consume her.

She reached for her jacket, and curling into a ball on the seat, pulled it over her, and slept the day away. The day Damon had walked away. The day she would be without him for who knew how long.

Cam found her many hours later, sitting, staring into space with tear tracks on her pretty face. He had a tough gig on his hands and felt the urge to protect her.

"There you are." Cam offered her a smile as he walked towards her

She wiped her tears away. "I am so sorry; I have missed all my work today Mr. Night, I was feeling sick and fell asleep. I really am very sorry."

She felt guilty for lying but, what else could she do? Admit to being in love with his brother, and crying from a broken heart? Hardly. She'd heard the jet in her dreams, taking the man she loved away. And when she woke, she realized how very deeply she did love Damon, and felt such deep loss and devastation,

"It's completely understandable, Lilliana." He said quietly. "He'll miss you too."

She looked directly into his eyes, to see his honest blue ones, looking directly at her. So like his brothers, it was comforting.

"Thanks Sir." She whispered.

"Right, well, I told Damon I'd look after you until he returns so, how about dinner and some time with your friends before the day ends?"

"That sounds good." She stood, stretching out her numb body.

Cam watched her as she grabbed her jacket. No bloody wonder his brother was head over heels for this attractive young lady. And no wonder he left, like the hounds from hell were after him. Ah, responsibility and obligation to do the right thing, was so Damon.

Walking together they chatted, as they went down the loft's steps, out of the stables, and into a home where the one person they both loved, was missing.

About the author

MICKEY MARTIN feels blessed to live in beautiful Australia and has lived in both its country and city areas of Victoria, from Woolsthorpe to Warrnambool, to the gorgeous Glenormiston South where she attended High school from year 7 to year 12 at Terang College, frolicked in Bendigo, Coburg, and finally settled in the pretty town by the sea, Frankston where she resides with her handsome hubby and their treasured sons.

Mickey is a lover of animals and nature and believes in the healing power they bring to our souls. An avid gardener, she relishes time spent in her garden with her birds and cats whilst conjuring up worlds full of colourful characters who have travelled and battled the darker paths, hopefully, to lighter days ahead.

Her writing is raw, emotional, compelling and can at times be confronting. She writes passionately about love and the world we live in today, because of it and to escape.

Wanting to put her beloved area, the Mornington Peninsula, on the map, Mickey is in the process of conjuring up a twisted paranormal romance series that will also highlight her favourite towns: Glenormiston South and Inglewood. Mickey is a member of Peninsula Writers Club (PWC) and loves the camaraderie and support of fellow writers.

Next on the agenda, Mickey will be launching Book Two of The Given Trilogy, Dark Angel, and will be finishing The Guardian, Book Three of The Given Trilogy, at the spectacular Historical, Crom Castle, in atmospheric Northern Ireland.

Mickey Martin also writes Non-Fiction under her married name, Michelle Weitering. Michelle writes to make a difference. Through her writing, she becomes a voice for those living and dealing with issues such as anxiety, bullying, school refusal, and discrimination and invites the reader to question what more they can do to make our world a better place.

Her recently published family memoir, *Thirteen and Underwater*, exposes the struggle of anxiety through her family's journey with this increasingly prevalent disorder that wreaks havoc on millions of individuals worldwide. Told with brutal honesty and a good dose of humour *Thirteen and Underwater* is being well received by many.

Michelle has been featured in publications such as *YMAG* and *MORNINGTON PENINSULA MAGAZINE.*

Connect with Michelle on

Email: mickeyslba@hotmail.com

Instagram: www.instagram.com/mickeymartinbooks
Website: www.mickeymartinauthor

Ingram Content Group UK Ltd.
Milton Keynes UK
UKHW040759240323
419106UK00001B/35